D1715750

REDEMPTIVE GUILT

William Earl McBride

Creekwood Publishing

Amarillo, Texas

Redemptive Guilt

Published by Creekwood Publishing

203 West 8th Suite 309 LB 14013

Amarillo, Texas 79101

806-674-0282

Creekwoodpublishing.com

Printed in the United States of America

ISBN-978-0-9849079-0-8

Acknowledgements

I would like to express a heartfelt thanks to these very special people who have been instrumental in the many different facets of an endeavor such as writing one's first Novel:

My special friend and prayer warrior, Connie Carney

My editor and writing coach, Sara Oswald

Scott Reinhard, Kati Jacobs, S. SuSann Harrell

My entire Family,

And also

Tom and Lee Blakeney of Creekwood Publishing

Thank You

Will M

This book is dedicated

to my

College English teacher

Janese Vines

One of the most wonderful people I have ever known,

If she were alive today I know she would be smiling at something only she could have envisioned...

CHAPTER ONE

Sixty-eight Hundred Dollar Jonny Vavas Designer Sunglasses

In a light and carefree mood with her normally overactive mind relaxed, Alexia Klien slides on a pair of black sixty-eight hundred dollar diamond-studded Jonny Vavas designer sunglasses just handed to her by a beautiful young French girl. It is a lovely November morning in Paris, France, and Alexia is spending a few hours shopping on the Avenue des Champs-Élysées.

The CCN Network News broadcast journalist has worked her way to being one of America's top international correspondents by the age of thirty-six. Alexia now has a few hours all to herself before the career that has been her greatest passion again takes center stage in her life. She is in Paris just days prior to the U.S. elections to interview a number of European dignitaries to get their responses to the results of what is shaping up to be an extremely close battle for the Presidency of the United States.

The interviews Alexia is going to perform in the next week will be seen all over the world. Her boss has implied that the success of this assignment could lead to an anchorwoman position at the network. Her mind will have to be fresh and sharp to be on top of her game. Spending a few hours on this Saturday before the election on the beautiful streets of Paris should put her in the right frame of mind for her interviews.

Looking into a full length mirror with absolutely no intentions of buying the ridiculously expensive sunglasses, the American media celebrity suddenly spins around to get a view of another shopper in the very eccentric little fashion boutique, La Boutique de la Renommée, just off the Avenue.

Staring directly at the woman she has just seen pass behind her in the mirror. "What the...?" Alexia says under her breath.

The young French girl opens her mouth, but Alexia quickly puts her right index finger up to her lips expressing a quiet, "Shh," as her eyes follow the woman she has just seen and thinks she recognizes.

Alexia is shocked at who she just caught a very brief glimpse of when she realizes she is staring. Afraid the woman might recognize her, Alexia quickly turns and directs her suddenly intense focus back to the shop girl. Looking into the mirror, the American broadcast journalist continues to watch the woman behind her. As the woman stops to point out a necklace she wants to look at, two women and a thin Frenchman attending her hurry to accommodate her wish.

Through the lenses of the expensive sunglasses, Alexia recognizes the strikingly beautiful woman as someone she had seen two years earlier one December evening at a black-tie dinner affair in Washington D.C. It was a Democratic Christmas party being held in one of the fabulous ballrooms of the extravagant Renaissance Park Hotel in downtown Washington D.C., an event for powerful law makers and their guests. Most of the top news people at CCN were also in attendance.

Then later that very same night, around two A.M. in a hallway on the 18th floor of the hotel, Alexia saw this woman again, hanging all over a United States Senator from California. Both the Senator and the woman were way past drunk. Alexia watched them stumble past her and then enter a private suite about four doors down from the room in which she had been attending a private party.

This Democratic Senator, Walter Franson, is very wealthy and very powerful. Now, two years after seeing him in the hallway of the Renaissance Park Hotel with a woman that was not his wife, he is the leading candidate in the upcoming U.S. Presidential race. In this election year, with the incumbent President having decided not to run for reelection because of undisclosed circumstances, Senator Franson is a full five to eight points ahead of his closest opponent in the contest to win the White House.

The woman Alexia is watching through the Jonny Vavas designer sunglasses is someone who, when she had first seen her two years earlier, Alexia thought was just a highclass Washington D.C. call girl. Now, seeing her in Paris in one of the most expensive fashion boutiques in all of Europe, wearing a black Chanel sheath and Louboutin heels, the reporter's suspicions are raised.

This mysterious woman, who looks to be in her late thirties or early forties, is tall and quite slender, with a long refined face and the most unique dark red hair Alexia has ever seen, hair that hangs nearly to her waist. Alexia marvels at the stranger, thinking she is one of the most beautiful women she has ever seen.

The woman's Eastern European look is what Alexia remembers from when she first saw her in the nation's capital. What Alexia remembers from the Christmas party two years ago is that everyone just sat and stared at this woman. People could not take their eyes off of her. She was a woman who dominated the attention of the entire room as soon as she entered it. Alexia is very familiar with this type of attention, experiencing it herself on many occasions.

Alexia is a very striking and beautiful woman in her own right. She is widely considered one of the most attractive women on television. With her long, coal black hair, dark blue eyes, classic facial features and tall, slender, shapely body, she has been told she is almost too beautiful to be reporting the news. Many think she should have pursued a career in modeling or acting which is something she had considered in college, but those paths did not seem to have the substance that she desired deep down inside. Alexia wanted her life to really make a difference in the world. Studying political science and journalism at the University of Georgia prepared her to do just that. At least that is what she had thought. But her career has seemed to evolve to a place where there are not many possibilities to make a difference. She wonders if maybe stumbling into the mysterious woman today in Paris will give her an opportunity to really do something, to uncover and discover the news instead of just report it.

Who is this woman, and why was she in Washington D.C. two years ago? Alexia thought she knew very well why the woman was in the hallway of the hotel that night. It would have been purely for the pleasure of a U.S. Senator. Now, she doesn't know. Could there be more to it? At this moment, Alexia feels there is some sort of untold story staring her right in the face, something beyond a Senator having a tryst with a call girl, and in just a second of time, the story could vanish. Never to be revealed.

Inconspicuously keeping her focus on the exotic woman as she shops, Alexia continues her exchange with the young French girl over the designer eyewear. The woman has not noticed Alexia in any way. The opportunity to strike up a conversation does not present itself before the woman in question tells those waiting on her to ship the large quantity of items she has picked out. Alexia attempts to eavesdrop on the conversation hoping to hear where the woman's purchases are being sent, but to no avail. She is then shocked as the mysterious woman simply walks out of the store without any form of payment for the items. No ticket is signed, no credit card scanned or cash exchanged.

Free of any responsibilities for the next few hours, Alexia Klien decides to play detective as well as reporter. Quickly she hands the diamond-studded sunglasses back to the young French girl, letting her know she is not going to purchase them today, and sets out to follow the woman.

Trying to stay at least forty feet behind her, Alexia tails the woman out the front door of La Boutique de la Renommée. Walking a block south to the Avenue des Champs-Élysées, the woman turns to the west and walks three blocks at a quick pace. Turning onto a narrow cobblestone street lined with shop windows and busy with foot traffic, she continues four blocks north. The woman shows the confidence of someone very familiar with Paris, not distracted by any of the beautiful historic surroundings.

Staying a safe distance behind the tall and slender redhead to avoid being noticed, and yet following close enough not to lose sight of her, is a challenge Alexia has never faced. *This sure looks a lot easier in the movies,* the CCN reporter-turned-detective thinks to herself as she hurries through the narrow streets of the romantic city.

Having crossed the intersection of Rue d'Artois and Rue de Berri, the woman Alexia is trailing stops and looks down at her watch. She then reaches into her purse and takes out her cell phone and makes a very short call as she slowly looks around as though she is expecting to meet someone here. From the opposite corner of the intersection

Alexia stands with her heart racing as hard as it ever has. And not because of the brisk walk. Alexia freezes as she wonders if the woman is instinctively looking behind her to see if someone is following.

Continuing to look around, the woman makes a second call. Quickly, Alexia turns to face a store window that is angled where she can very clearly see the activity taking place less than a hundred feet away and behind her. Apparently no one answers the second call made by the woman, and she puts her phone back into her purse. Looking into the make-shift mirror, Alexia sees the woman reach back into her purse and pull out her cell phone and answer it. Not on the phone very long, the woman ends her call and begins to walk at a fast and decided pace to the west on Rue d'Artois.

She walks two and a half blocks in that direction without once looking back. The refined woman reaches the edge of the outside seating area of a quaint little French café where an older man in his sixties waits. He is tall, at least six foot three, and has a full head of gray hair that is cut and trimmed to perfection. Not a hair is out of place. The man stands up and greets the woman with a kiss on each cheek.

A table for two next to a large stone wall awaits them. While the two sit to enjoy a bottle of wine the man had ordered for them, Alexia stares from across the street. She wonders what her next move should be. The man has a look of power and wealth. Serious wealth.

A waiter comes to the table to take their order. Alexia turns and enters a small café to the south across the narrow street. Inside the café, she orders a Coke and takes a seat beside a window in the front where she has a direct view across the way. From this vantage point only fifty feet away there is really very little the curious journalist can tell about either person as she watches them dine. Alexia wishes she could hear their conversation. She knows getting any closer could compromise her anonymity.

Alexia is able to take a few pictures with her cell phone of the two people as they eat. The woman is dining on a light salad and the very distinguished well dressed gentleman is having some sort of fish cuisine.

Alexia feels a short hunger pang herself. Surprised that she even has an appetite at this moment, she remembers she has yet to eat anything today. She motions for the young man who had brought her a Coke and asks him in French if he could quickly get her a turkey sandwich on baguette. He assures her it will be right out.

What she can tell in the forty minutes or so she spends watching the man and the woman dine, is that they seem to be very comfortable with each other. Not like lovers, but more like close friends. The woman seems to be more relaxed and at ease sitting with this gray haired gentleman than she did earlier at the clothing boutique, and especially more so than what Alexia could remember from watching her at the black tie dinner affair in Washington D.C.

Totally captivated, Alexia sends a couple of the pictures she has taken on her cell phone to an old flame of hers, Severo Baptiste, to see if he can shed some light on the identity of the mysterious and beautiful woman. Baptiste is a Frenchman and a freelance journalist who lives on the Mediterranean in the south of France. Severo is a handsome, tenacious and tough man in his forties who has traveled the world over writing stories on everything from international sporting events and politics, to terrorism in the Middle East and guerrilla warfare in the deepest parts of Africa.

With a military background and a stint as an officer in the French Foreign Legion, Baptiste has been almost everywhere, and seen and done almost everything one can in life. He is a little rough around the edges, but most who meet him take an immediate liking to him. Severo has the kind of connections to find the identity of pretty much anyone. If this woman is someone as important and connected as she looks like she could be, Severo should be able to find it out. And the more "important" she is, the quicker he can find the answer.

Alexia met Severo Armand Casimiro Baptiste while covering the 2002 Winter Olympics in Salt Lake City. They fell madly in love, and throughout their four and a half year relationship, he had desired to marry her. Alexia broke off the relationship with the Frenchman. The reason she gave him for the break-up was her career and her strong desire to climb as high as she could in broadcast journalism. But her fear of love and commitment played a much larger role in her decision to end the relationship she had with Baptiste.

The woman and the gentleman leave the little Parisian café,

taking a taxi. Immediately, Alexia grabs the next taxi, telling the driver to follow them. As they reach the exit to the Charles de Gaulle International Airport, Alexia receives a text message from Baptiste: "Keep your distance from the woman, very serious."

This message is then followed immediately by another text from Severo saying, "We need to meet, I will call you in an hour or so. How about Monday for lunch?"

Alexia then sends a text message back to Baptiste telling him, "I see your game! Maybe Monday?"

Severo replies back in one final text, "No game here! She may be very dangerous. Be very, very careful! My phone is going dead. I will call you later."

CHAPTER TWO

A Nasty Catch Twenty-Two Situation

In an attempt to change her appearance, Alexia puts on a burgundy and gray knit beret and a pair of big dark Bvlgari sunglasses she always keeps with her to hide behind. She also takes off the black jacket she has been wearing and puts it in her handbag, leaving her in a long-sleeved white shirt, very tight jeans and burgundy thigh-high boots.

As their taxi stops at the curb in front of the entrance to the International airport, the older gentleman and the tall beautiful redhead proceed into the terminal. Neither has luggage. Alexia exits her taxi five cars back.

As she walks towards the front doors watching the mysterious pair, Alexia is a little puzzled by the text messages she has received from Severo. She knew very well he would want to see her while she was in Europe. Even though she had not let him know she was coming to Paris, she knew he would hear she was there. Somehow he always knows everything.

It has been three years since they accidentally ran into each other at an airport in South Africa. They were able to spend thirty or forty minutes reminiscing over a few drinks in a dark little lounge in a busy airport on the outskirts of Johannesburg before Severo had to catch a flight to the South Pacific Islands. "Why don't you come with me?" Severo had asked.

Alexia still can't believe she didn't just leave everything behind that day and go with him. Every part of her wanted to, and every part of her wishes she had.

She thinks back to the few emails and two or three phone calls they have exchanged since then. But Alexia believes her focus now needs to be on her career. Last week she thought of contacting him before she left the States on this assignment, but either fear or good judgment stopped her.

Now, Alexia does not know whether to take Severo's warnings about this woman seriously, or if he is just using this as a ploy to come to Paris and try to rekindle a flame they both know very well has not gone out.

One of the things Alexia always admired about Severo Baptiste was that he had never been the type of man to play games and manipulate people, something she sees all the time in the circles she runs in. But who knows now; it has been a long time since the two of them have spent any real time together, and people change. *Oh, how people change,* she thinks, *especially when they have been hurt.*

Running these emotions through her head and her heart, she tries to keep her eyes on the two people she is trailing through the busy international airport. Alexia knows she will have to devise a scheme to get herself through the metal detectors and ticket terminals and into the concourse area if she is to find out where the beautiful mystery woman is flying off to today.

Alexia has an overwhelming feeling deep down inside that this is not just some wild goose chase she decided to set out on a couple of hours earlier in that high fashion boutique. It is not quite one P.M. yet in Paris, which leaves her with only about two hours to continue her unexpected detective work. By four P.M., she has to be showered, dressed and at the CCN Paris studio ready for five or six hours of the real work Alexia Klien has been sent to Europe to perform.

Alexia knows she needs to devise a scheme fast to get onto the concourse. If this were the U.S., she knows she could just flash her CCN press badge, flick her long black hair and let her dark blue eyes mesmerize some unsuspecting guard as she talks her way past security. But this isn't the U.S., and she isn't as well known in Europe. She will have to use her CCN corporate credit card to purchase a ticket to go any further into the Paris airport.

Alexia heads straight to the closest ticket counter and whips out the plastic to buy her way onto the concourse. As she does, her mind is suddenly flooded with memories from this very same ticket counter. Years before in a hurried frenzy to catch a seat on a last minute flight to Egypt, Alexia bought a ticket to steal a weekend between Christmas and New Years with Severo. Now standing at the same ticket counter she has to fight away a tear. It was there in Cairo that Severo Baptiste first asked her to marry him.

Very late at night in the brightness of a full moon, the two of them stood on a steep bank at the edge of the Nile River. There Severo took Alexia by the hand and asked her to be his wife and to spend the rest of her life with him. With nothing else in her life even comparable, it was the most romantic, wonderful moment she has ever experienced. A memory so perfect and pristine she often wonders if she had only dreamed it. If only she had been able to accept his offer. Cairo had been to Alexia and Severo what Paris had been to Ingrid Bergman and Humphrey Bogart in *Casablanca*.

The man behind the ticket counter breaks the spell Alexia has fallen under when he asks her, "Where do you want to go?"

Still thinking about Egypt, but not wanting to say Cairo, Alexia looks away to see if she can still get a glimpse of the woman she is trailing. "Oh? London. That's it, I want to go to London."

From behind the counter with a raised eyebrow under his wire rimmed glasses, the short bald man comments, "Last minute decision, I take it?"

"Yeah. Can you hurry? I need the next available flight," Alexia replies.

He processes the ticket and Alexia thanks him. She turns quickly and heads off to the security lines leading to the concourse. She sees the two people she is pursuing make it through their line and head onto the concourse, and she worries that she may lose them.

Noticing that the line on the far left is being manned by two men, Alexia walks straight to the front of the line where people have been waiting to go through security. She takes off her sunglasses and turns to the people who have been waiting. She frantically says, "My sister is having a baby in London right now. She's having complications. I need to try to catch a flight that is just about to leave."

The two security guards motion her forward through the metal detector and she places her bag on the conveyor belt leading to the x-ray machine. Alexia hopes cutting in line will get her back the time she has lost buying a ticket.

Standing in her jeans and socks, waiting for her handbag to come through the scanner, she is asked by one of the men to spread her arms and be scanned by hand. Alexia thinks this is because of the erratic manner in which she had moved to the front of the line. But, by the way the other guard is staring at her it makes her wonder if this extra scanning is actually because of her physical assets.

Alexia's arms and legs are very long. Standing there in the airport with her arms raised out to her sides, in her long-sleeved white shirt and tight blue jeans, she looks almost as though she could take off and fly herself to wherever she wants to go.

She turns her head while being scanned. Over her right shoulder Alexia is able to see the older gentleman standing out in front of a women's restroom less than a hundred feet from where Alexia is going through security. He is apparently waiting for the woman. He glances at his watch and then immediately takes out his cell phone and makes a call. At that moment the woman exits the restroom. The two of them stand there while he talks on his phone.

While she slips her thigh-high boots back on, the French security guard scanning her asks Alexia if she is trying to catch up with her older sister, the tall good-looking redhead who has just gone through the line right next to them. Alexia replies with a smile, "No, but I do thank you for the compliment."

"You're welcome," he replies.

"You're rather handsome yourself," she says to stroke the young man's ego. Alexia is an expert at making a man feel good and she loves to flirt. She had picked the line being guarded by the two men because she knew they would be the easiest to slip past. Her flirtatious nature is something most men she has dated in the past could not handle.

Baptiste is the only man she has ever been involved with that it never bothered. He is the most confident person she has ever known. Alexia had met many men of significant political power and wealth working in New York and Washington D.C. and all over the world, but as far as inner strength is concerned, none could compare to Severo Baptiste.

Looking over and seeing the man still on his cell phone, the woman beside him, both standing in plain sight of the security guards and the long line of people she has just cut in front of, Alexia realizes she can't just stand around outside the security gates. She needs to look like she is hurrying to catch a flight to London. She wonders what she will do if the two individuals she is following stay where they are. Not knowing which way to go from here, Alexia feels caught in a nasty catch twenty-two situation.

The airport is busy, but not the busiest she has ever seen it. Crowds are coming and going, which will work to her advantage if she can get a couple hundred feet or so away from the security gates. In a few minutes most of the people she has cut in front of will be on their way and gone. Alexia decides to walk past the couple she has been watching, hoping they will come her way.

Getting about a hundred feet past the restrooms, Alexia is far enough out of sight from the security gates that she feels safe stopping and milling around in front of a little shop that sells newspapers, magazines, beverages and candy. She glances at the headlines on the U.S. papers for a few minutes, constantly looking out the corner of her eye for any change in the activities of the man and the woman.

The tall gray haired gentleman has finished his phone call and is telling the woman something. It has her complete and total attention. Of the times Alexia has seen and watched this woman, she had never seen her look this intense and uncomfortable. Earlier the woman had a look of ease and elegance. Now she has a look of immensely focused concentration.

CHAPTER THREE

Frickin Cell Phone

Alexia sees a short balding man of Middle Eastern descent wearing a dark gray suit walking towards her. In his right hand he is carrying a black brief case with small silver Islamic symbols, the star and crescent in the lower corners of the case. He has a long black coat in his left hand. She recognizes the man from the long line of people she just cut to the front of at security. He slowly shakes his head back and forth and gives Alexia a serious stare of disapproval as he walks past her. She can feel his black eyes pierce through her. *If looks could kill,* Alexia thinks, *I'd be dead.*

As the Arab man passes by her, Alexia gets mad about his glare. Something inside of her boils over. She fights not to follow him down the concourse and fire some smart remark at him about how she refuses to be disrespected like the women in the Middle East.

Suddenly Alexia wonders why he made her so mad. She questions if she would have reacted the same way if someone of German or English descent would have given her the same look for the same reason—cutting in front of a group of people with a fake emergency. She acknowledges that, no, in that case she would have known she was at fault for her deceptive behavior coming through security.

Alexia realizes her sighting of the Muslim moon and star probably had a subconscious effect on her. She lost three very close friends in the 9/11 attacks on the World Trade Center. One was a childhood friend of hers that her mother had always hoped Alexia would someday grow up to marry. She never told her mother that she had also secretly hoped the same all through her teenage years. He was a gem. Alexia never dated him back then in her adolescent years because he was seven years older than her.

No sooner do these thoughts come and go from her mind than the woman Alexia is in the airport to investigate comes walking straight towards her. Alexia quickly turns away from the little beverage shop so as not to let her prey get a good look at her face. Then Alexia simply walks slowly towards the center of the concourse to a stand selling "I Love Paris" t-shirts and other souvenir items.

Fearing the tall redhead will soon be tapping her on the shoulder and not sure she wants to risk looking back, Alexia intentionally drops her lipstick and steals a quick peek back towards the woman when she bends down to retrieve it.

She had often used her dropping-the-lipstick trick to look back to see if someone was watching her without them knowing. Alexia perfected this amateur spy technique in her teenage years growing up just north of Atlanta, Georgia in the wealthy suburb of Marietta. She met her first real boyfriend this way when she was a junior in high school, a guy from California three years older than her attending the University of Georgia on a football scholarship.

She and some girlfriends had walked past a couple of cute guys at the mall and she wanted to see if they were looking back at her. She quickly pulled out her lipstick and dropped it. Sure enough, the two guys had stopped and were staring at her. The poor kid nearly flunked out of school that first semester they dated. He spent more time in Marietta than in Athens where he was supposed to be attending classes and playing football. His was the first heart she tore to shreds.

This time when Alexia drops the lipstick it bounces off her right boot and spins end over end out into the traffic. After a glance at the redhead, she leans down and drops to one knee to pick up her lipstick. This is a little difficult to accomplish with grace and ease. She steadies herself with one hand on the floor and reaches out to grab the lipstick before someone steps on it or kicks it away.

A tall and attractive gentleman heading towards the security gates quickly stops and seizes the opportunity to help her. Alexia sees him stop right in front of her. Out of the corner of her eye she can still see the man and woman she has been watching as they go into the little beverage shop. Alexia redirects her attention back to the man with sandy blond hair wearing khaki pants and a dark blue shirt as he picks up her lipstick. He reached it just before Alexia. He then takes her hand and helps her up. Handing the lipstick back to her he says in a deep southern drawl, "Aren't you Alexia Klien the CCN reporter? You're from Atlanta. I'm from Savannah."

Alexia takes the lipstick from his hand and gives him a blank look. She then shakes her head "no" before turning away coldly. The man shrugs his shoulders and continues on his way. Alexia takes a few steps in the other direction.

A moment later she stops after her curiosity kicks in, and she turns to watch the Good Samaritan walk away. Alexia wonders if she has just missed an opportunity to meet someone special from her home state. He did seem nice, and he sounded like he could have grown up just down the street from her. But her quest to discover the mysterious redhead's identity kept Alexia from giving this man too much attention. She knows she couldn't risk her current mission by speaking to him and letting him know she is just who he thought she is.

Alexia crosses over to the other side of the walkway and looks out at the planes taking off and landing. Every few seconds she glances over her shoulder to see if the man and woman have left the little beverage shop. After just a couple of minutes the pair comes out and proceeds down the concourse in a bit of a hurry. Alexia lets them get about fifty feet ahead of her before she follows on the opposite side. She makes sure to keep her distance, which is not hard considering the accelerated pace the two are walking.

With the couple in such a hurry, Alexia fears they may board a flight and she will lose them before she hears back from Severo. She opens her cell phone and looks up the last text from him again to see exactly when he had sent it. It was thirty-three minutes ago. Alexia reads the warning again, "No game here! She may be very dangerous. Be very, very careful!" This time his words seem to resonate much deeper into her psyche than they did the first time when she was getting out of a cab to hurry into the airport.

Who is this mysterious woman? Is she the wife of one of the world's wealthiest men? Does she have foreign political ties? How was this woman able to be a guest at an exclusive political dinner party in D.C.? Most importantly, what connection does this tall

European beauty have with one of the most prominent Senators in the United States, a man most likely less than one hundred hours from being elected to the most powerful political position in the world? Is she even from Europe? Maybe she is actually from the States, and if so, why is she in Europe now? Has someone sent her over here to keep her out of the U.S. during the campaign?

Then there is this gray haired gentleman who looks like he could be a very powerful man. Alexia has met and interviewed men from all over the world who wield massive amounts of power, and this guy definitely has that aura about him. What is his role in this little play? He does not appear to be the woman's lover. They seemed to be close friends earlier when they were dining over a bottle of wine, but their actions at the airport have the appearance of business. Serious business.

The more Alexia thinks about it, the more she convinces herself that this woman could be—has to be—involved in some sort of espionage or illegal activity. That's the only reason Baptiste would have warned her as he did. But why hasn't he called back if this woman could be so dangerous? If Severo's warnings about this woman are anything close to the scenarios racing through her thoughts, Alexia fears the detective work she is immersed in might be way over her head.

Ring phone, come on ring! Alexia thinks to herself as she continues to follow the mysterious woman and man through the busy Paris airport. She even mutters under her breath as she passes people in the concourse. "Damn it Severo! I really need to hear from you! Get out your frickin cell phone and call me."

CHAPTER FOUR

Coffee and Donuts

"It's a bitterly cold and breezy seven degrees Fahrenheit in Denver, Colorado this morning. The best the good people on the front range of the Rockies can expect today for a high will be something in the low teens. Omaha, Nebraska is experiencing severe winds out of the north/northwest with a morning temperature of twelve which will likely be their high for the day," a meteorologist for CCN reports on a news broadcast. "The weather today will be the same throughout the Midwest. The cities of Minneapolis and Chicago are both currently experiencing brisk morning temperatures in the low twenties with increasing winds from the north. Temperatures will be dropping all across the central two-thirds of the country today ahead of an early season arctic cold front that is slowly beginning to push its way south out of Canada. This front is expected to be enormous and dump large amounts of snow all along its path in the coming days. It will bring many cities and communities to a virtual standstill."

The view on the CCN broadcast switches to anchorman Allan Thomas as he replies, "Yes, people throughout the Midwest, the Northeast, and down the East Coast of the nation will have to brace themselves for the nastiest election weather the United States has ever seen. There have been discussions by some members of congress and the administration to attempt to have Tuesday's elections either extended to include all of Wednesday, or possibly even postponed to the following week to avoid what some would call a political catastrophe."

"And Allan," Mary, a co-anchor cuts in, "These ideas are of course meeting with strong resistance by conservatives. An early season winter storm sweeping across a large portion of the

Northeastern two-thirds of America will only hurt the turn-out for the Democratic Party, and help the Republicans in their bid to win back the Presidency and possibly one or both houses of Congress. While most of the nation today will be cooling off, things in Washington D.C. are just beginning to heat up."

"What the...! Would someone shut that damn thing off? Why do they have to keep bringing up this crap about a cold front? I'm not running the Weather Channel! This damn arctic front's just about got me to the point of shooting myself in the head! We can't lose this one!" Rigger Watson, head of CCN Network News shouts.

"Hope you don't decide to take us with you, Rig!" a network executive shoots back at him.

"Rig, if you need a gun, I've got a brand new handgun you can use," jokes a program editor on the other side of the conference table.

"You probably do, being from Alabama," Watson fires back.

Shirley Hienz, sitting to the left of Mr. Watson, looks up at him and says, "But Rig, we can't shut it off. It's our network!"

"At least this damn country is smart enough to shut down an airport or postpone a baseball game when something like this happens. Having those idiots from the South and the West decide who runs this nation is pure B.S. This weather better not cost us... cost Bob the election."

Rigger Watson and Democratic Presidential candidate Walter Robert Franson were fraternity brothers in college. Only Franson's closest associates ever call him Bob. Most people refer to the Senator as Walter or Walt. Franson first got into politics when he campaigned for his longtime friend Watson's failed bid for the U.S. Senate, a seat Franson would win twelve years later, and would hold for over twenty years.

Switching away from his tirade and back to business, Watson asks, "Has anyone gotten a hold of Alex to let her know she needs to report in early today to get ready for the Prince Charles interview?"

"Oh Rig," Hienz replies, "I knew I'd forgotten something when I came in here."

Watson shakes his head in disgust and barks back at her, "You better get your butt out there and get Alex on the phone. There's no way of telling where she'll be today in Paris, or what she'll be up to."

Shirley Hienz gets up out of her chair and heads to the door.

As he watches Hienz leave, Rigger continues, "Hell, Alex may be somewhere in Africa or Asia by now if she's run into that damned Baptiste, or John the Baptist, or whatever name he is going by these days."

It seriously aggravates Watson that Severo Baptiste has Alexia's heart. He doesn't like Baptiste. Rigger has met him more than once. What he's seen and heard about him makes Watson tell Alexia over and over that he is someone she should be careful of. Rigger Watson thinks Baptiste is too abstruse. But Alexia feels taking relationship advice from Rigger Watson is akin to having Dr. Kevorkian as your family physician.

Severo Baptiste and Rigger Watson are complete opposites in so many respects. Watson's world is inside tall buildings, where Baptiste is more at home in the rubble of a smoldering battlefield, or hidden deep in the confines of a dense jungle. Baptiste's genuineness has always been something Alexia feels threatens Watson.

Alexia has had Rigger wrapped around her little finger for years. He always tells her, "Girl, if I was twenty years younger, we'd go places." To which Alexia replies, "I guess I'll just have to go without you." If he thought he had a chance, Watson would throw away everything he has to run off with her. They both know this. But he doesn't have a chance, and they both know this too.

"Give Alex my love," Rigger sarcastically adds as Shirley Hienz walks out of the CCN conference room.

Everyone in the room knows that Rigger has been having an affair with Shirley for years. Watson always makes little digs like that towards her, thinking he is impressing those around him. The people who work for him at CCN often discuss Rigger Watson, wondering how he had made it to the position of running the world's largest news organization. But most of them have the answer. He knew the right people and walked all over the wrong people.

Some who have known Rig a long time say he was a much more pleasant person to work with when he was younger and more idealistic. Now they say he is just sarcastic and skeptical, a man who seems to have very little hope. When he married his second wife, who he had first met during his failed bid for a U.S. Senate seat, Watson married into more money and connections than most third world countries have. Those connections are what helped to put him in the position to head the world's largest news organization.

His marriage is held together only for status and financial reasons. Watson has a daughter from his first marriage, an actress who is more famous for her failed relationships and landing in and out of rehab than she is for her acting. She occasionally appears on the covers of supermarket tabloids, mainly because of who her father is.

You can say almost anything you want to about his snobby high society wife and Watson will just slap you on the back and tell you he'll buy you a drink for that little slice of humor. It doesn't matter how foully you speak of her either. But no one dares kid Rigger Watson about his daughter.

Outside the conference room, Shirley Hienz digs in her purse for her Blackberry to call Alexia. Before making the call, she asks a young intern to get her a coffee. As the intern hurries to the coffee pot, she asks in her New Jersey accent, "Ms. Hienz, did you hear about what happened to Senator Franson's campaign manager?"

"No! I haven't heard anything."

"Oh really?"

"Why?" Hienz asks. "What happened? Is he OK?"

"I don't think it's that bad," the girl says, "It's just... ah, he got pulled over. DUI."

"That's nothing!" Hienz scoffs.

"Ah, it might be worse than that," the intern replies, "He had a couple of teenage boys with him. They were also drunk. You know what I'm saying?"

"Oh crap! How do you know this?" demands Hienz.

The intern hesitates, not sure what to tell the older woman she respects and looks up to. Her source is someone Ms. Hienz may not approve of, or at least, may not like.

"Come on, where the hell did you hear that?" Hienz asks. "I need to tell Rig about this, but before I walk in that conference room I need to know why we haven't heard about this yet, and why you have!"

"Not sure you will approve of this, but I..."

Hienz quickly interrupts her, "If I walk through that door with this, how much I approve of you doesn't mean a damn thing! I need to know where this came from and if it has any validity. *Now!*"

"A guy I have been sleeping with that works for FX News just texted it to me and said they were about to run with it. I guess he said it happened in Boston," the young girl admits.

A smile breaks across Shirley's face. "OK girl, now you're learning. You might be a natural at this stuff. No harm done. Follow me in here. Don't worry, I will put some flowers around your story so it doesn't become your grave." Hienz stops, turns, and puts her hand on the girl's shoulder, she asks, "Do you trust this guy?"

"Yes, and I really like him," the girl replies. "I think he was just trying to impress me. He's not a bigwig over there."

"Good, that's all I need to know. I'll take care of you, Honey. Let's go." Hienz says, giving the girl's shoulder a reassuring squeeze.

Hienz opens the door and charges into conference room with the girl right in her wake. Watson asks, "Did you get a hold of Alex yet?"

"No, but Rig you've got to hear this, and only you," Shirley responds.

"What the hell could you and Little Miss Kitten Muff have for me that's more important than Alex interviewing the man who is the heir apparent to the throne of England?" Rigger replies harshly. "Please tell me they've decided to postpone the election."

"No, that's not it!" Hienz snaps back at him.

Watson gets out of his chair and tells executive producer Jim Edwards, "Get a hold of Alex and tell her she needs to get her butt in to work over there to prepare for the Prince Charles interview. It is being moved to tomorrow and it's in Paris instead of Wednesday in London."

As he reaches the door to leave the room Watson stops and looks back at Edwards, "Tell her we didn't send her four thousand miles overseas just to have some damn vacation."

Watson steps outside the conference room with Hienz and her new tag-along friend. "What do you got?" he fires at them.

As she glances towards the young intern and turns her head back to Watson, Hienz explains, "She's got a friend at FX that just sent her a text saying Mike Swenson got picked up in Boston with two teenage boys. Drunk, all of them. Swenson was driving and he's got charges being filed against him, and FX is running with it."

"*Mother...!*" Rigger steps back. "How can this kind of stuff happen now? Franson assured me a year ago he'd cleaned up his act before I'd support him, and now this by his campaign manager just three days before the people hit the polls. If this costs us the election I'll personally kill Swenson, Franson and those two fags in Boston! I told Bob to fire that queer little Swenson three months ago. And this, on top of dropping five points in ten days off a nine point lead!"

"What are we gonna do?" Hienz interrupts.

"We have got to find a way to diffuse this, and fast. Who were the cops?" Watson asks. "That's it, find out about them. Get Brandt and Telleson, put them on this right now."

"OK," Hienz replies.

He turns to head back in the direction of the conference room when Terry Telleson yells from down the hall, "Rig! FX just broke a story about Mike Swenson!"

"Yeah, I need you and Brandt to find out everything you can about the arresting officers," Watson fires back at him. "There's got to be a way to spin this."

As Watson walks back into the conference room shaking his head, he asks under his breath, "How much can this world change in three days?"

CHAPTER FIVE

Hyper-Aviophobic

At that moment Alexia's cell phone vibrates. *Oh, thank God! Severo is finally calling back,* she thinks. She quickly pulls her phone out of her pocket and answers it without looking at the caller ID. "Dang you Casimiro! It's about time you called me back. I'm about to go crazy after those messages you sent!"

"This isn't Casimiro," Jim Edwards answers with a laugh. "That's a car isn't it?"

Alexia is momentarily speechless at her mistake.

When she doesn't respond, Edwards continues, "Alex, this is Jim. I take it you're having fun over there if you're hanging out with someone named after a car. Or was the car named after him?"

"Oh Jim, sorry. I thought it was Baptiste. I use his middle name when I want to rile him. What's up?" Jim and Alexia had had a short relationship in the time period since she had last seen Severo. Alexia tends to treat her exes like brothers or cousins; still family, but not lovers. Except for Baptiste.

"Rigger wants you in early today... something about you getting prepared for the Prince Charles thing. It's being bumped up to tomorrow in Paris instead of London next week," Jim was not really fazed about the Casimiro/Severo thing. He isn't a deep enough person to have ever had his heart truly broken, not by Alexia or anyone else. He is always in it just for the fun.

She doesn't hear anything Jim says past "Rigger wants..." The couple she is following have suddenly stopped and Alexia notices the Middle Eastern man she had seen earlier sitting in a chair staring out over the top of a newspaper in the direction of the attractive woman and distinguished man as they stand about thirty feet in front of him.

Alexia looks back towards the couple just in time to catch a subtle nod of acknowledgment exchanged between the gray haired gentleman and the Middle Eastern man. As the mysterious woman glances in the direction of the Arab, she nods her head once in response to a question the gray haired gentleman asks her. The woman then turns and walks about twenty feet over to a large window and stares out at a Boeing 747 that is waiting for passengers to board. A chill runs down Alexia's spine as she considers the possible implications of what she sees.

Alarmed, Alexia steps inside the open doorway of a busy little airport bar to try to keep herself from being noticed by the Arab. From here, nearly fifty feet away, she is still able to keep the people she is spying on in sight through a window, three people now instead of two.

Bringing her attention back to the phone call Alexia asks, "Can you repeat that Jim? I missed most of what you said."

"I said, Rigger wants you in the studio early today to get ready to interview Prince Charles. It's being moved up to tomorrow in Paris instead of Wednesday in London."

"You tell Rig I'll be in when I need to be and not a minute before. He shouldn't worry. I'll woo the British Royalty tomorrow. Hell I could do it today, Jim, " Alexia fires back, "and you know it too."

"Yeah Alex, I know you could. It's just that Rigger..."

"You tell Rigger Watson if he doesn't think I can handle this thing," Alexia abruptly interrupts Edwards. While keeping the couple and the Muslim man in her sight she continues, "Then he should get his pompous ass over here and he can interview Prince Charles himself."

As he laughs, Edwards replies, "Alex dear, you can be nice to me. I'm just the messenger. Anyhow..."

Again her focus is stolen as she directs her attention to the television inside the bar. A BBC news broadcast is reporting that U.S. Presidential candidate Senator Walter Franson's campaign manager, Mark Swenson, has been picked up with two teenage boys who were drunk and barely clothed. The BBC states impending charges are being filed against Swenson in Boston.

"Jim, what's this about Franson's campaign manager and some teenagers I just heard over here on the BBC?"

"I don't know."

"Let me listen."

"What are they saying?" Jim asks.

Before she can answer, Edwards says, "Alex, Hienz left the conference room and was supposed to call you. Then she came in and jerked Rig out of the meeting and he told me to call you. Maybe that's what Shirley grabbed Rigger for."

With the story on BBC over, Alexia explains, "Well, what I caught was something about a DUI in Boston. He had two drunk kids, boys, with him, and they said there are more charges pending. That was it."

"That doesn't surprise me," Edwards sarcastically replies, "Everyone knows Swenson has been a time bomb waiting to go off. We damn sure don't need this crap right now, not with the drop in the polls, plus the damn snow storm that's coming..."

"He's taking a picture! Hey, I've got to go! Later Jim," and Alexia hangs up.

The man from the Middle East has put down his paper and taken out his cell phone. Alexia watches him as he holds it up in front of his face and points the camera at the mysterious woman who is standing all alone looking out at a large plane. Casually, the Middle Eastern man holds his phone with his right hand and takes a picture of the woman with her back towards him. He then turns his phone horizontally to take a second picture. The woman turns her head slightly as she watches another plane land. The man now holding the camera phone more securely with both hands and closer to his eyes takes longer before clicking another picture. Alexia thinks he must be adjusting the zoom or the focus to get a close up of the woman's profile. The man continues to hold his phone up, poised to take another picture.

The woman turns away from the window and faces the Arab man taking her picture. She pauses for a moment as though she knows exactly what is taking place. Alexia thinks, *He was waiting for her to turn around.* The Middle Eastern man clicks a final picture and lowers his phone. He examines the pictures he has taken and types something into his phone.

After having her picture taken, the woman gracefully walks back over to where the tall, gray haired man is standing. He glances down at his watch as she walks back. After watching him check the time, Alexia looks to see the destination listed at the gate. The Boeing 747 the mysterious woman has been looking at is headed to New York

City. The United States. Alexia is filled with sudden fear. *What should I do?*

Still standing inside the little airport bar, the CCN broadcast journalist pulls her own cell phone out of her pocket and looks to see how long it has been since she received the text message warnings from Severo Baptiste. "I wish you would call. There are so many questions staring me right in the face," Alexia says out loud. Some of the people around her turn and look at her.

Again, the television in the bar broadcasts something about how a severe arctic cold front and an untimely DUI in Boston could affect the Presidential election in the United States. This time, Alexia doesn't pay any attention to the report. She feels the biggest news story in the world today is possibly unfolding right here in front of her.

A young waiter inside the bar approaches Alexia and asks in English with a French accent, "May I get you something? The drink?"

Without taking her eyes off of the three people she is watching, Alexia replies, "No thank you."

"Would you like a place to sit? There's an open spot up at the bar, *ma belle.*"

She turns her head and smiles at the attractive young Frenchman. "No, I'm OK, but thank you very much."

Alexia looks back in the direction of the Muslim man. He is looking at his cell phone as if he is reading an email or text message. He stares intensely at his phone for nearly thirty seconds, and then quickly types out a short message and sends it without looking up. After sending the message he makes a call, but he does not stay on the phone very long. The Arab then puts his cell phone into the inside front pocket of his dark gray suit and picks up his paper again.

When she turns her focus back to the couple she has been trailing for nearly three hours, Alexia sees the tall gentleman looking at his phone reading a message he has just received. With his phone still in his hand, he walks over and looks out the same window the woman had just walked away from only a few minutes ago. While standing there alone and staring at the Boeing 747 headed to New York, he pulls up a number on his phone and makes a call.

As more people arrive waiting to board the flight leaving gate 33A to New York, a tall table for two next to where Alexia is standing becomes available after an Asian couple leaves. She quickly moves over and sits down at the table before anyone else can get it. She puts her handbag on the other chair in an attempt to keep anyone from deciding to join her. The table is perfectly situated for her continued spying. The waiter approaches again and asks her, "Have you changed your mind on something to drink?"

"Yeah sure, get me a Coke with plenty of ice please," Alexia answers without taking her eyes off of the people she is watching. She does not really want anything to drink. She just wants to be left alone.

As she sits spying on the man at the window who is still on his phone, the Middle Eastern man looking quite suspicious behind his paper, and the mysterious, possibly dangerous woman standing between them, Alexia's mind begins to race with the possibilities of what she is witnessing. The scenarios are too many to count and the possible consequences endless and terrifying.

With her own political leanings to the left, Alexia questions if she really should or would expose the mysterious European mistress of Senator Walter Franson just three days before the presidential election. *Is the Senator still even involved with this woman?* Alexia wonders, *Should I do the smart thing? Turn away and run from this and make it into work early like Rigger wants?* She knows where Rigger Watson would stand on exposing the Senator's affair. He wouldn't.

Still deep in thought, Alexia is startled when the well dressed Muslim gentleman suddenly folds up his newspaper and stands to his feet. He reaches back and picks up his coat off of the back of the chair where he was sitting. He then slides the paper under his arm and bends down and picks up his black attaché case. He turns and faces in the direction of the airport bar where Alexia is sitting and begins walking straight towards her. Without warning, Alexia suddenly blurts out, "Oh no! He's..." She shuts her mouth and finishes the thought in her head, *coming right at me!*

The people around her look in her direction with puzzled faces. Alexia looks back at them, not knowing what to say. Out of nowhere she quickly states, "Oh, sorry. I'm just hyper-aviophobic!" She almost starts laughing at herself. *What, humor in the face of death and destruction? I am about to lose my mind after all,* she thinks.

It works though, the small number of people close to her in the little airport bar who have heard what she said look at her like she is crazy and then return to their drinks.

CHAPTER SIX

Now what?

After Alexia hangs up on him, Jim Edwards steps out of his office. The first person he runs into is Brenda Smith, an executive with CCN, who has just left the conference room where Rigger Watson is having a brainstorming session. Watson is working on a way to spin the blame for the situation the Democratic Party has been put in because of Mike Swenson's activities in Boston.

"Jim, have you heard yet?" she asks.

"Are you talking about Swenson?"

"Yeah, you've heard."

"Just did. What do you think?"

"I think it's a shame. I mean, I'm definitely a democrat and a party supporter to the end, but this whole gay, homosexual thing is way out of hand if you ask me. I just don't think God intended for men to be with men or women to be with women."

As he hears those words coming from someone he thought would have been a huge supporter of gay rights, Edwards stands in amazement. He then laughs to break the tension of a touchy subject and says, "I'm not sure if there is or isn't a God. But if there is, I'm sure he didn't want Swenson messing around with teenage boys for sure. I know I have no desire to go there."

"That's good to hear," Brenda says. "I do feel sorry for Swenson though. I think people like that are just messed up inside."

"I feel sorry for the two teenager boys," Edwards states.

"Me too, Jim."

"How does that happen to kids today?"

"If you want my opinion Jim," Brenda ventures, "It's because so many people have gotten away from the God you don't know whether or not to believe in."

"More God talk. You surprise me," he replies to the woman in her early fifties. Edwards then asks, "Has the Christian Right gotten to you? Have they convinced you to change your pro-choice stance on abortion too?"

"No and no, to those two questions Jim," answers Brenda. "A woman should always have the right to do with her own body what she wants."

Jim Edwards, who doesn't care either way about abortion, but always has a smart-ass response to everything, wants to ask her if she also thinks a woman should have the right to sell her body into prostitution if she so chooses, but he knows well enough not to open up the abortion subject anymore or he might have a mad woman on his hands.

"See you later, Jim. I've got to run," she tells Edwards.

"Later, Brenda."

Edwards heads towards the conference room. He sees Shirley Hienz standing by the coffee and donuts talking on her Blackberry. Jim gives her a look and silently mouths, "What's up?"

She doesn't pay any attention to him so he decides to grab a cup of coffee and a donut. As he approaches the coffee stand, he overhears Hienz tell Terry Telleson he needs to dig deeper if he can't find anything on the officers in Boston. Edwards is about to head back to the CCN conference room when Hienz puts her hand over her phone. "Jim! That'll make you fat. Did you get Alex?"

Seizing his chance, he replies, "Yes. Hey what's the stuff with Rigger back there? Did it have anything to do with Swenson?"

"How do you know about that?" Hienz asks. She then removes her hand from her phone and instructs Telleson to just get after it. She then ends that call.

"Alexia just heard it in Paris on a BBC feed."

"Wow! It's already airing in Europe. Can you believe how far behind we were on this?" Hienz asks. "You would think since we are supposed to be helping them, they'd help us help them. Wouldn't you?"

"You'd think so. I don't understand why Franson didn't get rid of Swenson a long time ago. Mike's a genius at what he does, but his personal life has always been out of control."

"Amen to that, brother. Amen to that," Hienz replies fervently. With half a smile on his face, Edwards teases her, "Why Shirley Hienz, have you gone and got religion on us too? Brenda was just talking about God also."

"Boy, hell will freeze over before that happens."

"You better watch out, Honey, the weather channel says that'll be Monday or Tuesday," Jim laughs in response as he turns towards the conference room.

"Hey! Before you go in there, what else did Alex say?" Hienz asks.

"Not much. Typical Alex call. You know, full of fire and then gone."

"Jim, are you explaining your phone call with her or your relationship?"

They both laugh.

With a smile on her face, Hienz grins as she says, "Never mind, that girl will never change... God, I wish I was her."

Jim shakes his head and smiles. "There you go with the God stuff again, Honey. That cold weather is coming."

"Christ, Jim! Would you lay off of it?" Hienz spouts, "No, don't even say it! Yes, I know I just said Christ. I went to Sunday school."

"You did?" Edwards asks teasingly.

"Yes, I did," answers Shirley Hienz with some authority. "Now get your butt back in there and face Rigger. You know he's worried about Alex, and he wants a report. And when you're done in there I could use a little help in Boston. You game? Brandt and Terry are on it here."

Jim spins around with a cat-that-ate-the-canary look and laughs. "Why of course, you know I'm just the guy for any job in Boston!"

Hienz rolls her eyes and says, "I'm sure that New England Patriot's cheerleader you know will be happy to see you, Jim."

Jim grins back at Shirley and gives her a wink. "She will be."

Edwards opens the door to the conference room and with a deep Irish brogue says, "This is Officer Patty O'Brien with the BPD, and I'm a-lookin' for a couple o' drunken young boys."

With a frown on his face, Watson looks up at him. "Guess you've heard?"

"Yeah, from Alex. She heard it on the BBC."

"The BBC!" Watson slams his fist on the table. "Damn, everyone knew about it before we did."

"Seems like it, Rig," Edwards comments as he sits down in a chair.

"Is she gonna get in early?"

"What do think?" Jim asks sarcastically.

"That's not what I want to hear," Rigger fires back. "Why'd I have you call her anyway? You two couldn't communicate even when you were sleeping together."

"We could too! She'd talk and I'd listen. That's communication." Everyone in the room breaks out in laughter.

"Well, what was her status? Did you get one?"

"Alex said she has everything under control," Edwards answers. "Told me if you don't think so, you should get over there and do it yourself. Something like that. You know her."

"Yeah, I know her," Watson states. "She's too damn good at what she does for her own good."

"Yep! Then she hung up on me." Edwards replies with some humor.

"Damn it, Jim! We only have one shot at Prince Charles. It has to be her. She's who he wants to do the interview. Did you get that across to her?"

"Yes, I did!" Jim says. "Oh, and Rig, I also told Alex to make sure she asks the Prince if he is *born again*. I said you wanted to know that."

"You better not have, she just might do it. If you put that idea in Alex's head, it'll be *your* head," Watson fires back. "And let's lay off the God crap around here. One employee gets *born again* and the whole damn staff has to joke about it for weeks. I'm sick of hearing it!"

Over a week prior to this, CCN covered Franklin Graham, Billy Graham's son, in a Crusade in New York City that was held in the new Yankee Stadium. A CCN camera man walked away from his camera, leaving it unmanned, and went forward to accept Jesus Christ as his savior. This made big news with the other networks covering the event, especially the following evening when Franklin Graham spoke of it at the end of his sermon.

"Rigger, you know I didn't really tell her to ask Prince Charles that," Edwards laughs as he pushes his chair away from the conference table and stands up. "We all know Alex is going to do just as she pleases. I'm headed to Boston to make some real news. I'm out of here."

———————

The Middle Eastern man glances down at his watch as he approaches the airport bar. He stops at the entrance of the bar and surveys the area inside. He is standing only a few feet from where Alexia Klien is sitting. She pulls out her cell phone and pretends to type a text message. After a moment, he proceeds across the room and stops on the other side of the bar at a booth where some people are leaving. He stands and waits as they gather up their luggage and coats to leave.

A waitress walks out from behind the counter of the bar and goes to the booth and quickly begins clearing the table before the Muslim man can sit down. With her hands full of empty glasses, she asks him if he would like something to drink. He orders a coffee in French. He lays his long black coat down in the padded bench seat facing Alexia. He sits down in the other seat with his right side and back towards her. He is facing the entrance of the bar that leads out onto the concourse. The area around the booth is nearly hidden from anyone outside the bar. But there is a picture of the Eiffel Tower hanging directly above his booth and to Alexia's surprise, she realizes that with the way the lights inside the bar are shining on the glass over the picture, and the way the top of the picture is hanging at an angle away from the wall a couple of inches, she can see perfectly, as if in a mirror, everything the Muslim man is doing.

Alexia's focus is interrupted when she is handed a tall, slender glass full of ice and Coca-Cola. She turns and gives the young Frenchman five Euros knowing that will more than cover cost of the beverage. Alexia takes a sip of her beverage and looks back out the window to check on the mysterious redhead who is looking at the man she is with. He is making a phone call about thirty feet away by the window.

Alexia looks back in the direction of the Middle Eastern man who begins to open his attaché case. Alexia's view of the reflection is obstructed as four people leaving the bar stop right in front of her and begin hugging each other as though they are about to part ways. Alexia can only see one corner of the Arab man's black briefcase as he opens it. The people in front of her move a little closer to her and block her view completely.

Unable to see across the bar, she quickly glances back to where the woman is still standing just in time to see the gray haired gentleman return from the window with the view of the 747 headed to New York. He is lowering his cell phone from his ear.

The four people who were all hugging and kissing are now just holding hands and talking. They are still standing between Alexia and where the Arab man is sitting. As the two couples slowly walk out of the bar and part ways, Alexia can again see the reflection in the picture of the Parisian landmark. The attaché case is now open. The Muslim man reaches inside the case with his right hand. Alexia cannot see inside the case because it is only opened a few inches. She takes out her cell phone and glances at it to see what time it is.

Seeing it is now a little past two P.M., Alexia knows she will need to head in the direction of the news studio soon. With a feeling of fear combined with heightened curiosity, Alexia wishes he would open the black briefcase all the way so she can see what is in it. She also wishes Severo would call because she knows he knows something about the people she is watching.

As the waitress approaches the Middle Eastern man's booth, he closes his attaché case and reaches into the inside pocket of his dark gray suit coat and pulls out his billfold. The waitress sets down a cup of coffee. He gives her a ten euro note and she gives him his change. He puts the change in his billfold and returns it to his coat pocket saying nothing to her. As the waitress turns and walks away from his table, the Arab man takes a drink of the coffee.

Alexia looks back out on the concourse. As she does, a large group of people walk in front of where she sits looking through the window of the bar. As the people are innocently passing by, Alexia realizes she can no longer see the mysterious couple she has had under surveillance since this morning. They are gone.

Suddenly, a group of young men wearing matching soccer warm-up suits come walking past her. When they do, three of them notice her and stop just outside of the window she is staring through. One of them says in Italian to the other two that he thinks she is staring at him. Alexia raises up on the tall bar chair and looks over the shoulders and around the heads of the three men on the other side of the glass to try to catch sight of where the woman and the man have gone. The three men turn around to look in the direction Alexia is looking. The one who thought she was looking at him then says in Italian, "Guess not."

The three men continue on down the concourse to catch up with their group.

After she quickly scans the area, Alexia sighs a deep breath of relief when she spots the woman's long red hair hanging down the middle of her back. They have moved to a place across the concourse where they can see further inside the bar. The woman is talking to the man as he looks over her shoulder and focuses his eyes on the area of the bar where the Muslim man recently entered.

Alexia turns her attention back across the bar. Through the makeshift mirror above the Muslim, she sees he has taken something out of his brief case. As more people leave the bar passing by her, Alexia can only make out that it is a little black box or container of some sort.

Not wanting to lose sight of the couple again, Alexia turns her head and sees the tall slender woman still talking and the man still focused on the entrance of the bar.

She turns back, and with no one in her way now, she is able to see exactly what the Arab man has taken out of his briefcase. Alexia sees that the small box or container is actually a much smaller version of the bigger attaché case. It is an exact replica. Complete with an identical handle and all the very same Islamic symbols on it. The smaller case is about twelve inches in length, and eight or nine inches in height with a width of only about an inch and a half. It is very narrow and quite sleek. *Actually kind of sexy,* Alexia thinks to herself.

Alexia wonders what he is going to do with the smaller briefcase. As she watches from across the bar, he takes the larger of the two attaché cases and sets it on top of the smaller one. He raises his head and looks around to see if anyone is watching. Alexia freezes right where she is sitting. He doesn't notice her inside the poorly lit bar. Alexia quickly glances back at the woman and the gray haired gentleman. They are simply talking to each other, the man with one eye still on the entrance of the bar.

As Alexia looks back to the Muslim man with the two attaché cases, he is taking a silver ballpoint pen out of his shirt pocket. He then twists the silver pen and a very small key comes out of the top of it. He takes the end of the pen with the key on it and inserts it into one end of the handle on the larger attaché case. As he turns the pen, Alexia stands up and tries to look straight across to where he sits hidden in the booth about halfway towards the back of the bar. She can't see anything directly and looks back up to the reflection coming from the picture of the Eiffel tower.

With the light the way it is, she is barely able to see the bottom of the handle on the larger brief case when it pops open as he turns the ballpoint pen. He then looks around again very quickly, but doesn't notice Alexia across the bar as she quickly turns away and picks up her drink. She brings the glass to her lips and slowly looks back up towards the angled picture above him. Looking down again, he takes a small black USB flash drive out of the bottom of the handle of the larger brief case.

After removing the flash drive, he closes the bottom of the secret compartment in the handle. He pulls the smaller attaché case out from under the larger one and puts it on top. The Arab man then uses the key that came out of the top of the ballpoint pen to open the handle on the smaller case. With the bottom of the handle on the smaller case open, he places the small USB flash drive into the hidden compartment and closes the bottom of the handle on the smaller attaché case. He places the silver pen back into his shirt pocket.

With a very cold and calculating look on his face, the Muslim man in the booth slowly looks around for a third time. As Alexia sees him begin to look her way, she takes a long drink of her ice cold Coke and the Arab man's eyes flow right past her. *What is he going to do now?* She asks herself.

The Muslim man picks up the smaller attaché case and covers it with the newspaper he had been reading. He then takes the silver ballpoint pen out of his shirt pocket and secures it to the newspaper with the pen's clip.

As he carefully slips the concealed case down into the darkness under the table, he again looks around to see if anyone in the immediate area is watching him. No one is paying any attention to him except for the American broadcast journalist who sits all the way across the bar. He does not see her. He sets the newspaper-covered case on the floor against the wall beneath the seat he is sitting in.

He slides out of the booth and reaches for his coat and slings it over his arm. He grabs the handle of the large attaché case and picks it up off of the table with his other hand. Knowing the Muslim man is about to leave, Alexia has a sudden urge to quickly get up and go retrieve the small attaché case with the flash drive in its handle. But she knows she shouldn't. She needs to see what will happen next. Alexia expects the Arab man to begin to walk out of the bar, but he doesn't. He stands there in front of the booth he was in with his coat slung over one arm holding the briefcase with his other, he then turns and casually looks out of the bar. He pauses for a moment as he looks directly to where the tall gentleman and the woman are standing across the concourse. Without walking away from the booth, he then looks up to the television set above the counter of the bar. A commercial for women's shampoo is showing on the TV screen.

Alexia's eyes move back to the couple outside the bar. She sees the man lean over and whisper something in the ear of the woman. The woman then gives him a kiss on his cheek. This is the first real affection Alexia has seen between these two since this morning when the man greeted the woman with a kiss on each of her cheeks in front of the café. Immediately after the kiss, the tall woman with long red hair walks straight towards the entrance of the bar. Alexia looks back over to where the Muslim man is standing and watches him turn his attention away from the shampoo commercial and focus on the woman walking towards the bar. When she reaches the entrance, the Arab begins to walk straight to her. They do not stop when they meet. The two pass within inches, never acknowledging each other. Not even with eye contact. When the man leaves the bar, he turns and walks back in the direction of security.

As the mysterious woman stops right where the Arab man had been sitting, Alexia keeps her attention focused inside the bar. Alexia watches her gracefully bend her knees and slide about halfway into the seat the Muslim man just left. The woman leans to the side and reaches underneath the seat to pull the sleek little attaché case covered in newspaper out from under the table. Alexia's heart rate increases as she wonders if the little black case could be a bomb. *Is this woman going to blow herself out of the sky? Is she Vogue's version of a suicide bomber?*

As the woman sits back up in the seat, Alexia glances back to the tall gray haired gentleman. Something is said over the airport loud speaker in what Alexia thinks is Russian. The man turns and walks off in the same direction the Middle Eastern man just went less than a minute earlier.

Totally perplexed, Alexia continues to watch the woman as she slides the ballpoint pen off of the newspaper. She sets the pen and the miniature attaché case down and neatly folds the paper up. Alexia is surprised when she notices the woman is now wearing a pair of very thin black gloves she did not have on earlier. *So much for fingerprints,* Alexia thinks. After folding the newspaper back up, the red headed woman simply lays it back down on the table, picks up the little black briefcase and the silver pen, and slips out of the padded bench seat.

Mesmerized, Alexia just sits there inside the airport bar with her Coke in hand. Something inside of her says that little black briefcase has to be a bomb. *But why the USB flash drive?* She wonders. *Maybe it's just diamonds or rubies or something,* she tries to tell herself. She knows the Arab man went through security with it, but just how good is security? *It's not perfect.*

The woman walks towards the exit of the bar. Not wanting to be noticed, Alexia turns her face to the side as the woman passes by only a few steps away. Alexia takes one last drink of her beverage before setting the glass down on the table. She hopes that someone's life will not be lost today, especially hers. For some reason all of a sudden, the woman's possible connection to a U.S. Presidential election doesn't seem to be all that important when compared to what could be at stake here. People's lives.

The woman heads in the direction of the security gates. Alexia leans over and reaches for her handbag. She grabs it and then slowly steps out of the bar looking around as though she is trying to decide which way she should go in the busy airport. Alexia knows the direction she needs to go. It's just that she needs to allow the woman time to get a safe distance ahead before she follows.

Standing in the traffic of the concourse watching the woman gain ground, Alexia decides to try to call Severo. She can't believe she hasn't thought of this before now. *Why wait for him to call me?* Had it been any other man she wanted information from, she would have called them ten times over by now. That is what was so different about her relationship with Severo Baptiste. She would find herself waiting on him. He always had control. A part of her, deep down inside, loves this.

Alexia digs into her purse to find her cell phone. *I just had it. Where is it?* Frantic, she says out loud to herself, "Please don't tell me I've just lost another one." After quickly searching through her purse she checks the front pockets of her jeans.

Losing cell phones is something she is so accustomed to that CCN has her carry two phones with her at all times. On average, she loses one phone a month. It is quite the joke with her friends and colleagues. Today though, when Alexia dressed rather sparingly and left her hotel for just a casual morning perusing the fashion boutiques of Paris, she grabbed only one phone leaving the other in a clothes bag in her hotel. Which, truth be known, is where it will stay while she is in Europe.

Her cell phone is not in her purse or the pockets of her jeans. Standing in the middle of the concourse, Alexia glances up to make sure she doesn't lose sight of the woman now a safe distance away. She begins to walk with the flow of the traffic. From the open entrance of the airport bar the young waiter who had brought Alexia a Coke suddenly calls out, "Mademoiselle, is this yours

Nearly twenty feet from where he is standing and holding up a blue cell phone, Alexia stops and turns around. With people passing between them, she calls back, "Yes, it's mine. Oh thank you." She slides past some passers-by and quickly makes it over to him before the woman gets too far ahead of her. He takes a couple of steps towards her. When they meet, she reaches out and he hands her the cell phone. Alexia tells him, "Thank you, you're a real darling."

"My pleasure," the young man replies with a brilliant smile. As she turns and hurries away, he calls after her, "I put my number in it. Call me!"

Alexia laughs and shakes her head. As she looks down the concourse, Alexia catchs a glimpse of the tall, slender woman with long red hair just before a crowd of people walking towards her suddenly obstructs her view. What had been only moments ago a safe distance to trail someone in a crowded airport has now quickly become a safe distance to lose someone in a crowded airport. Alexia picks up her pace, lengthening her strides and breaking into a jog until she sees she has closed the gap between herself and the woman now carrying the small black attaché case.

Walking with her cell phone in her hand, Alexia looks down and pulls up the number for Baptiste. It has been well over a year since she has actually heard his voice, and over three years since she has seen him. She pauses before pushing the button to call him. She can feel her heart begin to beat faster. Now she knows why she didn't call him when she first arrived in Paris yesterday. She knows the sound of his voice will be an incredibly beautiful thing. She so desires to hear it again—and that terrifies her.

The oxygen inside Charles de Gaulle International Airport suddenly seems to vanish as Alexia thinks about what she is doing. She cannot get any air into her lungs. She attempts to take a deep breath. Her hands begin to quiver. Finally she says to herself, "Just push the green button." She does.

Having pushed the button, she waits in fear for Severo's phone to ring. She focuses her eyes on the woman ahead of her as she hears the first ring of the call she has placed to Baptiste. The redhead has stopped and is now looking at what appears to be an airline ticket. Alexia looks for somewhere to stand out of sight as her phone continues to ring. Moving over to a large round pillar along the side of the concourse, Alexia assumes the woman is checking which gate she will be leaving from, or the time of her flight's departure. Gate 20A, the gate the woman is standing in front of, shows that the next flight is headed to Miami, Florida and boarding at 2:48.

If this woman carrying a black attaché case filled with who knows what gets on a plane with American citizens, Alexia thinks, *I am going to have to tell the authorities everything I know.* If it comes down to that, and it surely looks like it will, Alexia knows she may be tied up in the airport for the rest of the day. Her wild goose chase may cost her the shot at the anchor position she has worked so hard for with CCN. Failure to make a broadcast is the one thing Rigger Watson does not tolerate, not even by her. Failure to make a special overseas broadcast is something Rigger Watson would not forgive.

Severo's phone has now rung six or seven times and with each ring the beating of Alexia's heart gets louder. *Is he going to answer?*

Finally his phone quits ringing. A computer-generated voice on the other end of the line says in French, "We are sorry but the call you have placed cannot go through at this time. Thank you and please try again later." Alexia was not prepared for this. Her heart goes from beating rapidly to not beating at all.

Alexia looks at her cell phone. The time is 2:17. She feels she is in way over her head, and yet people's lives may very well depend on the decisions that she will make today. With the flight for Miami leaving in thirty minutes, she continues to watch the woman standing by the gate. Alexia wonders why this woman, who appears to be very wealthy and sophisticated, would possibly want to blow up an airplane. *Is she lost and lonely?* She wonders. Just then, the broadcast journalist from Atlanta, Georgia realizes that her own life may be on a similar path that leads to being very rich and wealthy, yet lonely as well. For a moment she sees herself in the woman she is watching.

People waiting to board the plane headed to America begin to form two lines, one line for first class and another for coach. The woman standing among them does not get into either line. Alexia glances down at her phone and presses the button to call Severo again. This time she doesn't really expect to get him. She puts her phone up to her ear with a veiled hope of hearing his voice. As soon as the phone begins to ring, passengers begin boarding at a gate over two hundred feet down the concourse from where Alexia and the woman are standing.

Hearing over the loud speaker in the airport that gate 17A has begun to board, the woman places her ticket in her purse. She quickly makes her way across the concourse and straight to gate 17A. People already in line there begin to go through the final security checks and into the passenger boarding bridge leading to the aircraft. Alexia is baffled. It is almost as though the woman has been standing in front of the wrong counter intentionally until her flight was ready to take on its passengers.

Walking fifty feet behind the elegant redhead and seeing her approach her flight, Alexia wonders if the woman is walking to her death and planning to take many with her. The thought is nearly more than Alexia can conceive. Oblivious to the call she has just placed to Baptiste, Alexia zeroes in on trying to get close enough to see the destination of the flight she fears may soon be doomed.

CCN's top female broadcast journalist thinks that within moments the biggest piece of the puzzle of today's mystery will be solved. With her cell phone still held up to her ear, Alexia again hears the computer-generated message telling her a connection to Baptiste's phone cannot be made at this time. She quickly slides her cell phone in the right front pocket of her jeans.

The woman carrying the small black attaché case that Alexia has convinced herself contains explosives walks directly to the front of the two lines of people waiting to board the flight at gate 17A. Without stopping, she removes her ticket from her purse and flashes it to those guarding the entrance of the aircraft. She walks straight into the walkway leading to the plane. Right past security, ticket takers, everyone in the lines, first class and coach. Nobody even attempts to stop her. Alexia is both alarmed and amazed at the same time. *Who is this woman? Who could possibly get away with that?* Alexia then says out loud, "I can't frickin believe it. They just let this woman walk right on this airplane to blow it out of the sky."

What authority can I go to now? The authorities just let her on the plane. As she continues to walk towards the gate, Alexia is able to read the destination of the flight. She cannot believe her eyes. Moscow. The flight is to Moscow, Russia? Never, not once in the previous four hours of pursuit did Alexia ever imagine that this woman would blow up a plane headed to Russia. *Why? Now what?* She knows there is something not right to all of this, but what?

CHAPTER SEVEN

Fire!

It's very hot and dry with no breeze, and Sheldon Mitchal wonders how his New York Jets are going to fare in tomorrow's NFL match up with the vaunted San Diego Chargers. The Chargers are on a six game winning streak and have been ripping their way through the competition in the AFC this season. Sheldon pushes his heavy fifty-caliber machine gun mounted on a swivel over to the side and picks up a warm bottle of water.

It is amazingly hot for this time of the year even for Kuwait. The temperature is about to hit triple digits. Normally in the Middle East in the first part of November the highs are in the low eighties or upper seventies. The past seven days though, the heat has been more like what the Arabian Desert experiences in the middle of the summer. It has not rained here since March.

A young soldier, nineteen years of age from Glenrock, Wyoming, Will Tillord wipes the sweat off of his brow with his scarf. When he does, he scratches the skin on his forehead right where his helmet sits. His scarf still has sand in it from the day before when he used it to cover his face in a wind storm.

"Guys, can you believe I'm skipping my workout tonight to go see that hot singer?" says Diaz from San Antonio, Texas as he keeps his eyes scanning the miles and miles of nothing from thirty feet above the surface of the earth. "She should be flying in pretty soon."

Lowering the bottle of water from his lips and glancing at his brand new MTM Titanium military wristwatch he just purchased a week ago at the PX, Mitchal says, "Yeah! Sarge said she should be here in an hour or so. He wants to get back from chow before her plane lands."

"Man, you know Tex ain't comin' back early from chow. Don't matter how hot that chick is," Diaz states. He, Mitchal, and Tillord are standing guard in a tower at an entrance gate above the sands of a baking hot desert on the south end of the U.S. Air Force Base, Ali Al Salem, about thirty miles west of Kuwait City.

"Oh yeah, man, Sarge will be back early this time. He says he knows Angie West's brother," Mitchal asserts about Sergeant Spicer Brent Davis of Abilene, Texas. "Davis said he stayed at their ranch once when he was rodeoing with her brother back when she was just a kid."

Diaz rolls his eyes.

"Sarge said he wants to get a chance to talk to her while she is here."

"Davis? He ain't never met Angie West. Sarge knows her just like he'll be back early from lunch," Diaz blasts back at Mitchal.

The younger and shyer Will Tillord turns his head and shoulders to the right towards Diaz, "No, Sarge probably does know her. My brother and my cousins rope against her brother every summer at a lot of rodeos. Trevor West is a World Champion Steer Roper." Looking through a pair of dark aviator style Ray-Ban sunglasses, Tillord returns his eyes to the barren landscape that is the country of Kuwait. "You're right about Sarge gettin' back late from lunch all the time. Yesterday I didn't even get to eat 'cause Sarge got lost at the PX or something like that, he said."

"That's part of having those stripes, guys. Anyway, I'm going with him when she gets here. She's gotta be the finest thing I've ever seen," Mitchal pauses, "Least for a white girl. No woman's as hot as my Halle Berry."

Private Mitchal takes another drink of his water. Diaz pipes in, "Man, you guys wanna talk about hot chicks! The hottest ones I ever saw! 'Bout five years ago, I was about Will's age. Me and some guys went to Italy on leave. Damn! Those Italian girls!"

"Really?" a smiling Private Tillord asks curiously.

Diaz keeps talking. "Yeah. But the hottest one we saw there wasn't even from Italy. She was this Russian chick, I mean a smokin' hot Russian woman in her thirties with a U.S. Senator who had to be almost sixty. Talk about stripes man, this Senator from California had this chick from Russia that would just knock your eyes out!"

"How'd you know he was a Senator?" Mitchal asks.

"One of the guys with us had met him once in Vegas. We only talked to him a bit. He was in hurry to leave, probably somewhere private as hot as she was," answers Diaz.

"Bet it wasn't his wife!" says Mitchal as they all laugh. "Hey Diaz, give me some of that stuff you're chewing over there."

"Can't see how you guys chew that crap. My dad does, and so do my cousins. It makes me sick," Tillord says about the dip of Copenhagen Mitchal is bumming off of Diaz.

Before he puts the pinch of snuff in his bottom lip, Mitchal asks Diaz, "What was the Senator's name?"

"I don't know. We were all wasted the whole time we were there."

Private Tillord, a tall, lanky, good looking kid about six foot two, steps over to a small air conditioning unit and taps it on the side trying to get it to work better, "Damn, it's hot up here. It's probably in the twenties on the Laramie Range. I'd be deer hunting right now with my brother Ty if I was there."

"But you ain't there, cowboy," Diaz says as he sits down and leans back in a tattered camouflage fold up chair that is much more comfortable than it looks.

Tillord moves to where Diaz was just standing and begins to look out over the ocean of endless sand. He continues, "Instead, I'm over here in the middle of hell listening to Mitchal bitch everyday about his quarterback throwing too many interceptions."

"Yeah! And just a month ago, Mitchal was telling us how the Jet's Sanchez was better than Romo," Diaz adds from just a few feet away.

"Tillord, you're still upset that the Broncos traded Cutler," Sheldon fires back as the soldiers try to take their minds off the hours of monotony.

"Who's Denver playing Monday night, Li'l Till?" Before Tillord can speak, Diaz continues, "Oh! I remember it's da Bears. And who's da Bears quarterback? Oh yeah, it's Jake Cutler. And who did Cutler used to play for? Oh, that would be the Denver Broncos."

Tillord throws a half-empty water bottle at Diaz and says, "Man, I used to kinda like the Cowboys til being around your dumb ass, Diaz!"

Diaz picks the bottle up and throws it back at Tillord from the chair he is sitting in. Tillord ducks, and the trajectory of Diaz's throw carries the bottle out of the tower, where it lands over a hundred feet away and bounces into the side of the guard shack at the entrance gate.

"Hey! Quit screwing around up there guys!" Lieutenant Sam Johnson yells in his Boston accent over a radio at the soldiers who are just trying to get through another long, hot day in the War on Terrorism.

"Yes sir!" Mitchal responds quickly over the radio to the Lieutenant. Johnson is ten years older than any of the three enlisted men. He is also a man they all really like and respect.

Diaz then says for just his two buddies to hear, "Johnson's just mad about Brady breaking his thumb last week against the Steelers!"

"Yeah, bet the Pats wish they still had Matt Cassel," young Tillord throws in.

Mitchal fires back with a grin on his dry and dirty face, "I think it's you, Tillord, that wishes Cassel was still with New England the way he tore up the Broncos last week."

"That's for sure! I just wish Denver had one really good quarterback instead of the three guys they got now," Tillord replies to his friend.

Mitchal arches his back to stretch out a muscle he strained playing basketball last night and says, "Hang in there with Tebow, Tillord. I think he will be the really good quarterback you want. Not only that, but Tebow's a good Christian man."

"What you need, Li'l Till, is a good Mexican quarterback like Romo," Diaz interjects.

Mitchal shakes his head back and forth and says, "Romo's no damn Mexican! Why you keep saying that?"

"His dad's Mexican! Why can't you believe that you spook?" The Hispanic from San Antonio fires back at his African American adversary from New York City. Diaz then asks, "How about the Jets Sanchez? You saying he ain't a Mexican?"

"Yeah, Sanchez is a Mexican. But Tony Romo grew up a cheese headed Bret Favre fan! Who's ever heard of a Mexican from Wisconsin?" Mitchal returns with full knowledge the Dallas Cowboys quarterback is half Mexican.

The wide-eyed kid from Wyoming laughs at his friends and asks,

"How is it you guys can give each other crap about your skin color and I can't?"

"'Cause you're white, ya brokeback cowboy queer," returns Diaz.

"Come on, man!" Mitchal says. "Ain't you seen that picture of Will's girl in Montana, Diaz?"

"Yeah, I have!" answers Diaz, "Shoot, everybody has. Tillord's showing it to guys all the time. She is hot. She looks kinda like Angie West too."

"She does," Mitchal agrees.

"You can't be right in the head to sign up to come over here with that at home," Diaz says as he kicks Tillord standing in front of him in the back of the calf muscle.

"Steph's cute, but she's not as hot as the country music babe that's flying in here today." Will then changes the subject away from the eighteen year old girl from Montana who has just recently broken up with him in an email, "I can't wait to see Angie West sing tonight and tell my cousin Casey. He had a crush on her when they were kids. He used to say he was gonna marry her before she got so famous. But she liked Troy and not him."

Diaz rolls his eyes in disbelief as he looks up at a smiling Private Mitchal who is sitting on a black metal stool in front of the air conditioner that only works part of the time. Both soldiers just let Tillord continue to talk.

"Anyway, back to football. I wouldn't care if Tony Romo was Chinese if he was Denver's quarterback."

Diaz shakes his head. "Cowboy, you got to get over losing Cutler. It's gonna screw up your bull roping worse than a girl can. I'm with you on seeing that singer tonight. But really, man... you don't know Angie West."

"I don't know her, but my cousins do. Troy even went to a movie with her once about ten years ago when they were both in high school," answers Tillord.

"Sure," Diaz says sarcastically as he shakes his head, "Whatever, cowboy."

"He did. Troy went with my granddad to Oklahoma to buy a stud horse from her granddad. He took her to dinner and a movie. Our grandfathers are still good friends. They used to trade horses all the time."

"Yeah? And my cousin used to date Eva Mendes too. You're full of it Tillord—just like Sarge," Diaz blasts back at Tillord. "Must be part of being a bull roper or cowboy or whatever."

Young Tillord turns and looks Diaz straight in the eye, "Anyhow, its steer roping, you stupid Texan! Ain't you ever been to a rodeo in that big ass state of yours? There's lots of rodeos there."

"Angie West is from Oklahoma? I thought she was from Texas," says Mitchal in his slow deep voice. After a few seconds of silence, he reflectively asks, "You guys ever wonder if we hold the record in the Middle East for talking the most about football?"

"Not even close," Diaz laughs. "In Iraq, when I was south of Kirkuk, I was with some big white farm boys from Nebraska. That's all those stupid corn shuckers talked about is their Huskers. Drove me nuts."

"That's just cause Texas got their butts kicked by Nebraska last year in the Rose Bowl!" Tillord says hoping to get even with the cocky Texan.

"Up yours, sheep herder! Why are you a Husker fan anyway? Aren't you from Wyoming?" Diaz fires back, a bit ticked off at the smiling Private Tillord.

Diaz is a good guy, a body builder and the toughest of the three, maybe one of the toughest American soldiers in all of Kuwait. He has a very short fuse though, and it doesn't take much to set him off. He has a serious chip on his shoulder.

The sleepy-eyed Mitchal tries to defuse the situation, "All I know is, we talk a lot about football. But hell, there's nothing else to do. Least in Iraq there was something happening all the time."

"You don't want the kind of action I saw up there! You never left the damn Army base up in country, Mitch. Fighting in those Iraqi cities, that's something you don't want, buddy," says Diaz. He is in his mid-twenties and on his second tour to the Middle East. A part of him likes it.

"I don't know. I think I'd like it. I grew up hunting. I know I can outshoot both of you," Tillord says confidently.

"It ain't like shootin' Bambi, you idiot!" Diaz fires back scornfully, "When you kill a man, I mean, I don't care how tough you think you are. It hurts. Inside. It really hurts, like nothing else. If it wasn't for the fear of getting killed yourself, you couldn't handle it.

Usually by the time it takes to get safe, the sick feeling's gone. I ain't never shot no little deer! I've shot a man, and you don't want any of that shit, Will!"

After a brief moment of silence, Will Tillord replies to the U.S. Army Specialist Diaz, "Deer in Wyoming ain't little like Texas deer!"

"I wasn't talking about killing deer, you stupid rookie! You get up in country and think your killin' deer, and your dumb ass'll be dead!" Diaz fires back.

"He's right, Will," Mitchal says. "You don't want no part of killing a man. I thought I was gonna have to one time on an entrance gate in Baghdad. A military contracting truck with two KBR employees wasn't slowing down as it approached the gate. I thought I was gonna have to kill some stupid American not following Army rules. My sergeant told me to shoot, but a small voice inside me said wait. I hesitated. The truck then stopped just before I pulled the trigger. It scared the hell out of me and it happened so fast. It still haunts me and I never even shot one round. Listen to Diaz, Tillord. It might save your life if you have to go to Iraq or Afghanistan."

Mitchal considers the young man from the West a very good friend and thinks very highly of him. In this desolate land, halfway around the world from where they grew up, Will Tillord a cowboy from nowhere Wyoming, and Sheldon Mitchal a street kid from Queens, are as good of friends as either of them has ever known anywhere.

"Man Till, I thought I saw a lot of stuff growin' up. Gangs and drugs," Diaz says. "But that ain't nothing compared to war. Not this kind of war. You don't know when or where it's gonna come at you. You're scared when you don't need to be. And not scared at all when you should be. It's just crazy, man. First time I liked it, or I thought I did. Still don't know why the hell I came back over here. At least this time I'm not in that Godforsaken Iraq."

"Funny how you put that, Diaz. Where we were in Iraq was where the Bible says the Garden of Eden was," says Mitchal.

"What did I say about Iraq that's got to do with the Garden of Eden?"

"You said 'Godforsaken Iraq.' Like God wasn't in Iraq anymore. But the two big rivers in Iraq, the Tigris and the Euphrates are both in the first book of the Bible, Genesis. That's also where Adam and Eve lived," Mitchal tells Diaz.

"Really?" Tillord asks. "How do you know that stuff, Mitch?"

"When I was a kid my mother used to make me read the Bible before she'd let me watch TV," answers Mitchal.

"You don't believe everything you read, do you black man?" Diaz asks Mitchal sarcastically.

"I do if it's in the Bible. It goes back further than any book ever written," Mitchal proclaims confidently.

Tillord turns his head and takes his eyes off the long narrow roadway leading to the entrance gate. Not completely sure of himself, he says, "I think in high school they said the oldest book was some book from China, or maybe Greece, like four or five thousand years ago or something. I think?"

"Well, the story of the Bible goes back further than five thousand years, Will," Mitchal says with authority. "It goes back six thousand years cause that's when Adam and Eve lived." Mitchal points to the northwest. "Right over there, that's where things all started."

"You think it was only six thousand years ago when Adam and Eve were here?" Tillord asks. "How's that? In school they said the earth was like four billion years old," He pauses, "And man has been here for like a million years or something 'cause of evolution."

"That's not right!" Mitchal states. "In high school they are trying to make you believe in evolution so you won't think there is a God."

"Evolution? Now that's one thing I think is a bunch of BS!" Diaz immediately interjects into the conversation, "There ain't no way I came from a monkey. Mitchal might have, but I didn't," he says with a grin.

"Don't make me kick your spic ass," the easy-going Mitchal responds.

"If you could," Diaz says.

"Hey, greaser! I'll bring some prehistoric ape on you, man," Mitchal laughs.

Diaz laughs with him. "Yeah! You know why there aren't any apes in Mexico, man? We killed 'em all off."

"Hey, I know you guys are just jackin' around. But back at Fort Hood before I came over here we had a Sergeant Rook, that's what everyone called him, he used to give nig... I mean, that's what he... sorry Mitch," Tillord says, half embarrassed.

"That's OK, Brokeback. Go on," Mitchal laughs.

Tillord carefully continues, "Well, back at Fort Hood in Texas before I came over here, this Sergeant Rook would give black, uh, African American guys crap about coming from apes. Nobody bothered him. He was a great big tough SOB. Then he kept on a guy from Alabama, and that guy wasn't that big even. Anyway, this little black guy beat the hell out of Rook. It shut him up for a week or two. The guy from Alabama didn't even get in trouble."

Tillord pauses as he thinks he sees a vehicle approaching, and then goes on, "To Sergeant Rook's credit, he didn't make a big deal out of it. He and the black guy actually got along real good after that. But a week or two later Rook was back to being the loud, aggravating Texan he always was. Funny thing was, everyone liked him. Even the blacks liked him, before and after the fight."

"You got it out for us Texans?" asks Diaz.

"No, in fact we always have a bunch of Texans come stay at our ranch in the summer when they come to rope at Sheridan and Cheyenne," Tillord answers. "This one guy from Amarillo has two of the hottest daughters you have ever seen. Beautiful blondes, both of them."

"Hotter than the girl from Montana?" Mitchal asks.

"Yeah. And a lot richer too," Tillord states, "Oil money."

"Man, he's right Mitch! You ought to see them rich chicks in Texas. Better looking than where you come from," Diaz tells Mitchal.

"Not hardly, Diaz. I'm from New York City. The prettiest women in the world come to New York to model," Sheldon informs him. "Plus we got a lot of those Italian girls you thought were so hot when you went to Italy."

Tillord cuts in and brings the talk back to how old the earth is. "Mitch, how do you know the earth is only six thousand years old? I mean, can't they tell how old rocks and bones and stuff like that are?"

"They think they can, but it is kind of a joke how they do it," Mitchal says.

"How's that?" Diaz asks.

"They figure the age of the rocks by how old the fossils are they find in them. And they tell the age of a fossil by how old the rock is where they found it," Mitch continues, "And they tell how old the rock is where they found it by how old the fossil is."

"What?" Tillord asks. "That just goes around in a circle Mitch."

"Yeah," Diaz asserts. "It sounds like they are just making that stuff up."

"It's just like they made all that crap up about global warming," Mitch states. "They're a bunch of unbelievers and they just want to make unbelievers outta everyone else."

"How do you know the earth is only six thousand years old?" asks Tillord.

"First off, one way to know the earth and sun are not four billion years old is the sun is a big ball of gas. It's like fuel, gas up in the sky burning. And what happens when gas is burning? I mean, what happens to the volume of gas you got after it's burned for a while?" Sheldon directs the question to his buddy. "Huh, Will?"

Will Tillord thinks about it a moment, and answers, "Well, I guess if it's gas burning, after a while it will all burn up." He pauses. "Mitch, are you saying the sun is going to quit burning soon?"

"No! I ain't saying it's going to quit burning soon. But what I am saying is… it hasn't been burning nowhere near as long as the scientists and evolutionists all tell you it has," Mitchal replies.

Diaz breaks in, "I think I see what you're saying, Mitch. There is no way the earth could be that old, like four billion years or whatever. 'Cause you'd have to add all the fuel that's been burning up there for four billion years back to the outside of the sun."

"You got it, Diaz!" Private Mitchal takes over the conversation, "Scientists with telescopes know today that the sun is getting smaller by five or six feet a day. If you put all the gas back on the sun's surface that has been burning for…"

"I get it!" Tillord blurts out, "The sun is getting smaller cause of all the gas the sun is burning up every single day. So, if you added that same five or six feet a day of gas back on the sun's surface, the sun would get bigger by five or six feet a day."

"That's it, cowboy," Mitchal tells his friend. "If you went back only 100,000 years in time, the sun would be so big that the heat from it would burn up the earth and a lot of other planets around it."

"Wow!" replies Tillord, "So I guess there's no way that evolution crap is true."

"No, its not," states Mitchal.

"I always knew it wasn't!" Diaz exclaims. "That's a bunch a BS.

Why don't schools teach kids what you just taught us?"

"I don't know," Mitchal replies. He then takes a drink of water and continues, "And where we are right now is only a couple hundred miles from where everything in the Bible started. That's pretty damn cool, don't you think?"

"Yeah. There's still a lot I don't understand," says Tillord. "But I do know this stuff is a heck of a lot more interesting than just talking about football all the time. I've never really thought about evolution before."

"Yeah guys, and they're trying to make people think there is no God," Mitchal states. "The whole basis for evolution is so stupid. Just think about it like this, someone is trying to make us believe that something came from nothing by nothing. That doesn't make any sense at all scientifically. Think about it guys. It's impossible without God."

"How did you say that?" Tillord asks, "Something out of nothing by nothing? That is impossible. Stupid too."

"It is," replies the man from the Big Apple. "You're always talking about hunting, Tillord. You ever cut open the belly of a dead animal?"

"Yeah, lots of times."

"You think all those organs just somehow accidentally fell in place to work together? That's what evolutionists are trying to say. But it's really poor science to believe there isn't a creator."

Diaz stands up to look out the tower and see if Sergeant Davis is anywhere in the area yet. He doesn't see him and then says, "I can tell you guys this. Whoever said there are no atheists in foxholes sure as hell knew what they were talking about. I was in a building up in Iraq and an IED exploded. Blew the whole damn place to pieces and I was covered in rubble. The air was so thick with smoke and concrete. The dirt and the dust were terrible. I couldn't see anything. All I could hear was these crazy Arabs yelling from everywhere. I mean everywhere, man. There must have been a hundred of 'em."

Mitchal and Tillord hang on every word Diaz says. A little choked up, Diaz continues, "I just knew I was dead. I just knew it. Shit, I grew up Catholic, but never really thought about God. Well, anyway these crazy ass Muslims were all over, shooting and yelling. I was as good as dead and I knew it. Then I said, God I can't die today, I can't die today. And just then some of our guys in a tank showed up and blasted the shit out of all those rag heads. I know there's a God. I know. He saw me that day."

"I ain't never heard anything like that," Tillord says. "I'll bet you were scared to death." Will pauses, "Did it scare the hell out of you?"

The soldier from San Antonio nods his head yes as he lets out a deep breath still a little choked up in his memory.

"See why I told you to pay attention and listen to him? Diaz has been there Tillord, and what he says could save your life," Mitchal tells him. "It may scare the hell out of you Will, but that's a good thing."

About half on edge, Tillord sets a pair of 10X50 military binoculars down and grabs a bottle of water out of the army green cooler. He closes the lid and says, "The most scared I've ever been is grizzly bear hunting in Montana in the Bob Marshall Wilderness. We shot a bear just as it was getting dark and then we couldn't find it. Only a trail of blood into the woods. We were still more than a mile from camp in the dark and we could hear the wounded bear stalking us through the trees. I was scared shitless."

"A grizzly bear was stalking you?" asks Diaz.

"Yeah, but the bear didn't have a gun or speak Arabic," Tillord says.

"Did you really kill a grizzly?" Diaz asks.

"Not really, I didn't," Tillord replies. "My uncles Tim and Marty each did. I did shoot the one Marty killed. But it was after he already shot him."

"Was it dead or alive when you shot it?" Diaz asks.

"Oh, it was alive. But that don't count for me 'cause I didn't shoot first. You gotta make damn sure a grizzly's dead before you ride up on one though."

"You never told me about hunting grizzlies, Will. I knew you hunted, but I thought it was just deer and rabbits and stuff like that," says Mitchal.

Tillord laughs. "Rabbits? Hell, Mitch, I killed my first mountain lion when I was twelve."

"No way!" Mitchal says, "A mountain lion when you were twelve?"

"Don't tell anyone. They'd throw me in jail for life for that. Sell drugs to a kid on the street and they just slap your wrist. Least that's what my Grandpa says. Doesn't make any sense, does it? Kids are more important than a damn mountain lion that's killing our sheep."

"How many mountain lions have you killed?"

The ranch kid takes a drink of warm water and thinks for a moment. "I don't know, maybe five or six cats. Bunches of coyotes though. Those mangy coyotes are always killin' our sheep too." Tillord stops and takes another drink, "If they knew about all the cats our family has killed they'd probably take our ranch and send us all to prison."

"My mother's always talkin' about how things are so upside down in this world today," Mitchal says. "Isn't it funny how groups like PETA don't want people to hunt or kill any kind of animal? But then those same people on the left want to protect the right of a woman to have an abortion."

"I've never thought much about abortion before," Tillord replies. "Or compared it to hunting."

"Yeah Will, a lot of people are more worried about animals and trees than they are about human beings," Mitchal states. "They are humanizing animals and animalizing humans."

Uneasy about the abortion talk, Diaz changes the subject. "I'm hungry. All this talk about hunting, I could eat me a great big deer steak right now and I don't even like deer meat."

Mitchal and Tillord both laugh.

"Man, I wish Sarge would get back," Diaz exclaims. "How long has he been gone?"

Mitchal stands up to stretch his back muscle and looks at his watch, "It's been well over an hour. Tex might not make it back to see Angie West fly in."

"I'll bet he does," says Tillord, "As hot as she is. Especially since he knows her."

"He don't know her!" Diaz fires back as he steps on a spider on the floor of the guard tower.

"I'll bet he makes it back," replies Tillord.

Diaz sits down and leans way back in his chair again and puts his military boots up on a metal stool. "Hey, speaking of hot chicks. You guys seen those young babes that came in with that new group of soldiers from North Carolina?"

"Oh yeah, there's two of 'em went in the guard shack when you went to the can," a wide eyed Will Tillord answers. "One is way hot! A blonde. Reminds me of a girl I know from Rapid City... Tina Cunningham, she really likes me too. I should send her an email."

Mitchal picks up the binoculars and leans out around his fifty caliber machine gun to look at the guard shack, trying to see though its dusty windows. "Lieutenant Johnson is training the new girls to check badges and passes. That way they can flirt with everyone who comes through the gate."

"I'm telling you, man. There's at least eight or ten in that new group from Fort Bragg that are smokin' hot. And not any of 'em over twenty years old," Diaz proclaims.

"You probably aren't even counting the two black girls I've seen," Mitchals states.

"Oh yeah, I am. Like the one with the perfect Jennifer Lopez butt I saw you trying to talk to at the PX the other night," answers Diaz.

"Trying to talk to?" Mitchal asks in retaliation. "She talked to me for over five minutes."

Diaz laughs and says, "Yeah, while the Major she was with was in the restroom."

Mitchal flips him off.

"She is hot though. I'd hit that." Not letting up, a smiling Diaz goes on, "But you ain't going to beat out that Major."

"I know... It ain't fair. At home in real clothes that guy wouldn't have a chance," a dejected Private Mitchal replies.

Diaz laughs again. "Yeah, whatever Mitch. Whatever you gotta tell yourself."

"Mitch is right. His rank is all that Major's got going for him. He's a jerk if you ask me," Tillord says, trying to lift his friend's spirits. "You can beat him out Sheldon. Just be yourself and take a good run at her... Be smooth and cool."

"All I know is, it ain't fair, sending a thousand guys out in the damn desert a million miles from home and away from our girls. And then sprinkle about ten hot chicks like that in with us," Diaz exclaims. "It just ain't right."

"Yeah, I was telling my mom on Facebook a couple nights ago about the girl I met in the PX, and the dumbass Major she was with," Mitchal says. "My mom wondered who in their right mind would put together a fighting force of young men and then send in some real pretty young girls to mess with our minds. She said it sounds like a recipe for disaster to her."

Mitchal sets down the binoculars and turns and hits the top of the air conditioner with a closed fist. Cool air immediately starts flowing out of it. "Dang, I wish that Ryna Corp guy would get this thing fixed."

"What they should do if women really want equality, is send a thousand female soldiers over here for every thousand male soldiers," Private Tillord says. "So we could all have a girl of our own."

Diaz laughs at Tillord's comment and then remarks, "That ain't no shit. Or, how about this guys? A thousand female soldiers for every ten male soldiers. And let me be one of the ten."

"Shoot, the Arabs would all probably run the other way if they saw a thousand mad women coming," Mitchal replies as he smiles. "And I know you, Diaz. You would make all of 'em madder than hell in less than a week."

All three men laugh.

Tillord steps over in front of the air conditioner. "Back in Texas at Fort Hood there was this chick, a Sergeant I think, and she had been in the Army a long time. Anyway she was dating this Captain, like engaged or something. Then she started messing around with a couple guys who had just gotten out of basic. They were all in the same unit. She was a nympho or something, and real hot. Anyhow, she had the whole damn platoon screwed up. The Captain she was dating even hung himself over it. It was ugly. A real bad deal. I don't even think she got in trouble for it."

"I heard about that," says Diaz. "I've got a cousin that was there then."

"My mom says some people would say it's sexist, but she thinks women shouldn't even be in combat. Fighting is for men," Mitchal replies.

Mitchal scrunches up his now empty water bottle, throws it away, and pulls his machine gun around to position. He sees traffic approaching and alerts his buddies, "Hey guys, Ryna Corp is coming."

Ryna Corp is the main military contracting company on the Ali Al Salem U.S. Air Force base. They have vehicles coming and going through the gates routinely all day. Mitchal brings the conversation full circle as he asks, "What do you think Tillord? Can your Broncos or my Jets still make the playoffs?"

"More damn football?" Diaz interrupts, "Hell! I'd rather talk about God. You guys are getting as bad as those damn Nebraskans. Hey, there's Tex. I can get out of here!"

Tillord looks at Mitchal, paying no attention to Diaz and replies, "I think your Jets got a lot better chance the way their defense is playing."

"Where you been, Sarge?" Diaz yells out from the gun tower at the soldier coming to replace him, "Did you eat the whole damn DFAC?" He asks, referring to the military dining facility.

Private Mitchal watches the Ryna Corp vehicles approach. They are about five hundred yards away and coming at a higher rate of speed than normal. "Yeah, if it wasn't for the Jets' D, they'd be way out of it," he tells Tillord, who has just picked up his M4 carbine assault rifle. "Our offense needs to get back to running the football more." Mitchal pauses, watching the two trucks, and says, "These idiots are driving way too fast!"

"Yeah, maybe we'll have to shoot 'em," Tillord jokes, because nothing ever happens in Kuwait. The nineteen year old soldier goes on before his football thought slips his mind. "I don't know. Denver's D used to be good. But now they can't stop anybody. They gave up over four hundred yards passing to Buffalo. Damn Mitch, if the freakin' Bills can..."

Suddenly the stocky, redheaded Sergeant Spicer Davis grabs onto the ladder at the bottom of the tower and begins frantically yelling as he quickly climbs, "What the hell's going on! You guys see it? What's that guy doing? They're coming too damn fast! Diaz you see him?"

Davis reaches the top of the ladder welded to the outside of the stand supporting the gun tower. He busts through the door and stays back behind the other enlisted men to keep out of the way of potential gunfire. The two white Chevy Ryna Corp one-ton work trucks are not slowing down at all as they approach the area. They are actually beginning to pick up speed as they get closer to the back entrance gate to the U.S. Air Force Base, Ali Al Salem, about an hour inside the desert from the water's edge of the Persian Gulf.

In the countries of Iraq and Afghanistan throughout the intensely heated War on Terrorism, it has been common to have occasional suicide bomber attacks. Islamic terrorists will attempt to blast their way through a gate and into a military base. Soldiers in those countries are always on alert for such activities. In Kuwait, an attack of this nature is almost completely unheard of.

Sometimes in the Middle East, a new or careless employee of one of the many military contracting companies either doesn't know, or forgets the very strict rules about approaching a military base. When this happens, even in Kuwait, the soldiers have very stringent guidelines they have to abide by. And those guidelines begin with shoot to kill. In a place as laid back as Kuwait, everyone—those coming and going through the gates and those guarding and watching the gates—have a tendency to get lax, it's just human nature. No danger. No fear.

Today is no different as everyone scrambles in a state of panic in the tower and on the ground around the gate itself and in the guard shack. Curse words begin to fly from everywhere in the air, in the tower and on the ground as soldiers not prepared for battle today in the peaceful country of Kuwait are being taken by surprise.

Sergeant Davis, now back at his post of command begins yelling, "Guys get ready to shoot if they don't stop!"

The normally very calm and quiet Sheldon Mitchal blurts out, "Oh shit, not this again!" Once before in Iraq he had seen the very same thing.

The very young and inexperienced Will Tillord says calmly and in a lower and louder voice than normal, "Sarge, I'm ready! You just say when."

"Damn! Here we go again," yells Diaz as he scrambles to man his position on the other mounted fifty-caliber machine gun.

The guard tower had been built to hold more soldiers than most in the Middle East, built for only one or two men. This tower is facing the open desert on the rear side of the Air Base, a crucial base for the flights of dignitaries, Presidents, Senators and Congressmen, not to mention the often visiting celebrities, such as Angie West.

With both Mitchal and Diaz strategically placed, manning loaded fifty-caliber machine guns mounted on the front corners of the partially enclosed room atop the four legged tower skying over the Arabian Desert, U.S. Army Reservist Sergeant Davis, a veteran of two

Gulf Wars, stands directly behind the taller Private Will Tillord. It is Tillord's job to fire a warning shot in a situation like this, a situation which is rapidly presenting itself to all present and accountable.

The warning shot will be fired when, and only when Sergeant Davis gives the order. At that moment, it will be young Will Tillord's duty and obligation as a soldier in the United States Army to fire one warning shot. Not at, but into the interior of the oncoming vehicle. Not to scare, but to stop the intruder. In this case, where there are two approaching targets Private Tillord will be responsible for shooting into the lead vehicle first and then the second upon instruction.

Diaz is positioned much better to shoot the second white Ryna Corp truck still gaining even more speed and showing no signs of letting up, he yells loudly, "Mitch, I got the second mother...! God, I hope they ain't got bombs!"

"OK Diaz!" yells Mitchal, now more scared than he has ever been in his twenty-one years of life because of what Diaz just said about bombs. He then yells out, "Oh Jesus! Sweet Jesus, please be with us!"

Young Tillord now stands upright between his two older friends and stares sternly down the barrel of the M4 carbine Assault Rifle. He doesn't say anything. He stays completely silent and listens only for the sound of his Sergeant's voice to give the order as he zeroes in on the shining face of the dark-skinned Arab driver of the lead vehicle.

Immediately in this incredibly tense situation in the middle of the Middle East, ten thousand miles away from where he grew up, the young Will Tillord is taken back in time to that cool and clear October morning on a wide open, rocky, cactus covered range in central Wyoming. When, at the age of twelve, looking down the barrel of his Grandfather Bud's open-sighted Winchester Model 94 30-30 lever action rifle, he stared silently at the right front shoulder of a mountain lion only fifty yards away. The young boy, Will Tillord, waited for his father Andrew, who passed away just three years ago because of cancer, to say the word, 'fire.'

Today, above the hot sands of the Arabian Desert, Sergeant Spicer Brent Davis, forty-four years of age, from the West Texas town of Abilene, and a good friend of the entire Tillord family in Wyoming, especially Will Tillord's father Andrew, yells, "Fire!"

CHAPTER EIGHT

A Whole Different World

Shirley Hienz sticks her head into the conference room and asks, "Rig, did you get a hold of Senator Franson yet?"

"No," replies Rigger Watson. "You still going to lunch?"

"Yeah, wouldn't miss that for the world today," answers Hienz.

As she is about to let the door close and go back to her office, Watson yells, "Wait! What's going on with Brandt and Telleson?"

Hienz steps back into the room and motions with her head for him to come over to her. She holds the door for Watson. Both of them step out of the CCN conference room and walk down a corridor leading to an area free from ears. Watson stops and asks, "OK, what?"

"Oh, nothing all that big yet. Terry and Brandt are busy here and Jim is heading to Boston," Hienz informs him.

"What's Edwards going up there for?" As he remembers, Rigger shakes his head in disgust. "Oh, yeah. That Patriot cheerleader. We won't see him til Monday."

"You'd be right there with him, Honey, if I'd let you," Hienz pokes Watson in the ribs with her finger.

"Letting doesn't have anything to do with it," Watson replies.

Shirley shakes her head back and forth at him, and in a much firmer voice says, "Just try it and see how fast and far you fall!"

Rigger then smiles and tells her with a tone of sarcasm, "You know you're my one and only."

"Yeah, right! Who's the woman you live with then?" Hienz replies briskly with a look of anger in her eyes.

"Just be ready to get out of here by eleven," Watson starts to turn a way and stops. "Oh, and tell Brandt I need to see him."

"What about Terry?'" she asks.

"No, just Brandt."

———

Dazed, Alexia stands at gate 17A looking through the large windows at the doomed Airbus A330 headed for Moscow, now with well over two hundred passengers aboard. Completely at a loss about what to do, she cannot fathom how today in an international airport this woman has just walked onto an airplane without any airport personnel even bothering to check her. *It's like she owns the airline,* Alexia thinks.

A vision of the very same woman leaving the Boutique de la Renommée this morning without even a hint of paying for what she had picked out flashes into Alexia's mind.

As Alexia wonders just who this woman could possibly be, a thought enters her head. *Well, at least this plane is going to Russia, and isn't full of American citizens heading back to the U.S.* At first she is relieved of some of the pain and anguish she is feeling, but quickly Alexia becomes sickened as she runs the thought through her head a second time. *How could I have a thought this shallow?* She asks herself.

It is true, though. She was genuinely relieved the moment she realized the plane is not going to the United States, but to Russia. *I guess it's just human nature to be more concerned about those people who are closest to you. First your family, then friends, your neighborhood, city, state, and so on.* Alexia wonders if she is just trying to justify the reality that she is not as deeply concerned for the lives of people who live on the other side of the globe.

A question that she once posed at the beginning of an interview she did while working for station WGAT in Atlanta suddenly surfaces in her memory. Over ten years ago, when she was in her mid-twenties, Alexia received the assignment to interview a married couple, David and Sarah Peters from Macon, Georgia. The Peters were missionaries who had lived most of their lives in Malaysia. After living for forty-two years on a tiny island between the Pacific and Indian Oceans, they were returning to Georgia to retire.

The first question Alexia asked the couple was, "So, is it a whole different world over there?"

David Peters responded gently by saying, "No, it is not a whole different world over there." He smiled kindly, and then said, "It's just the other side of the same world we live on, in need of the same Jesus we need in the United States."

Standing today in the Charles de Gaulle International Airport, Alexia freezes for just a second as David Peters' words hit her. She suddenly realizes for the first time since she heard those words that she had only understood half of his message. Alexia had only thought about how the Malaysian people needed Jesus when she interviewed David and Sarah Peters many years ago, not how everyone, even Americans, need Jesus.

Alexia stands and looks at an airplane she thinks is most likely destined for death and destruction and full of people just like her. For the first time in her thirty-six years of life, she sees herself in the other half of the message she had missed when she interviewed the Malaysian missionaries. Overcome, Alexia just stands and stares at the Airbus full of people bound for Moscow, Russia.

She is startled out of the trance she is in as she feels her cell phone vibrating in her front pocket. *I am supposed to be at the studio already,* Alexia thinks, assuming it is someone calling from CCN. Her jeans being very tight, she has trouble digging the phone out of her front pocket as it continues to vibrate and now also ring. Finally she gets the phone out, "I'm on my way!"

There is a pause.

"I didn't expect that," A deep, rough voice says on the other end of the line. The man pauses again, and then asks, "How you doing?"

Hearing who it is, Alexia cannot say anything. She is caught completely off guard. The entire world seems to disappear for just a few seconds, but it seems like forever. The thoughts of her job, the woman she has been following, the Airbus A330 filled with people, all vanish. As hard as she tries to think of something to say, she can't bring any sound out of her lungs.

After what seems like an eternity to Alexia as she is silent, the voice on the other end of her phone says, "Darling are you there? If you are, I would really love to hear your voice."

Alexia says nothing.

The man pauses, and then says in French, "I love you, Alexia."

As scared as she has been all day, Alexia takes a deep breath to calm herself and replies, "I didn't expect it to be you."

"Are you OK with it being me?" the man asks.

"Yes, I am OK with it," Alexia pauses, "More than you know."

"How long has it been?"

"Too long."

"Yes. It has been too long," the man pauses. Alexia can hear him breathe. He continues, "Well over a year I think."

There is silence for a few seconds that seems like minutes to both of them.

"I guess you didn't expect it to be me," the man says.

"I just answered it. I had trouble getting my phone out of my pocket," Alexia replies, "I didn't check the number, I thought it was work."

"It wouldn't have done you any good. My phone is dead."

There is silence for a moment as neither of them says anything.

"Are you OK?"

"Yes, yes, I guess I'm OK. Better now that I've heard from you," responds Alexia. "Are you OK?"

"I am. It's great to hear your voice. The pictures you sent me... what's up?"

"Yes, the woman. Who is she? What's her name?"

"I am not sure I can tell you," Baptiste replies. "Why?"

"Your text said she is dangerous!"

"That is what my sources say."

"I'm at the Charles de Gaulle airport and she just got on a flight for Moscow. I'm afraid she may have a bomb on the plane," Alexia tells him.

"At the airport? In the pictures you sent, she was at a café downtown."

"I followed her here from the café."

"Are you on a story?"

"No. I was shopping and saw her. I recognized her and thought she was suspicious," Alexia tells him not wanting to say too much. "So, I followed her."

"But you are working over here?"

"Yes."

"I heard you were," Severo admits. "The woman is someone to stay clear of. Why were you suspicious of her?"

"I saw her in D.C. a couple years ago at a party with someone. It's too long of a story right now," Alexia replies. "She has a small black briefcase with her that she got from a Muslim man here at the airport. That's why I think she has a bomb. Actually, he left it rolled up in a newspaper in a chair when he walked away and then she picked it up and took it on the plane."

"Really?"

Before Severo can say anything else, Alexia quickly continues in a more frantic tone, "They never even checked her when she walked past the counter! She walked straight through the door and down the tunnel leading to the plane, right past security and everyone waiting to board. They never even looked at her. I've never seen anything like it!"

"What? Not even a look at her ticket?"

"No, they didn't really check her ticket. She flashed the ticket at the man and he glanced at her as she walked past him and both lines of people. It was like she was invisible to security. It was almost like she owned the plane or something. There must be two hundred people on that plane with her."

"That's odd," comments Baptiste.

"Odd?" Alexia asks, perplexed. "I'm scared. Really scared for the people on that plane. What do you think? What should I do?"

Alexia pauses for a moment, Severo in a slow and calm voice replies, "She is dangerous, very dangerous. That is what I've heard." He pauses for a moment. "But I don't think she'll blow up a plane though. Not one she is on anyway."

"What should I do?" Alexia asks, "The way she walked on the plane, I don't... I can't go to security. If I do, I will be hung up here all day and I need to be leaving soon to get to the CCN news studio for work tonight."

"If you don't feel good about airport security, there's nothing you can do." Baptiste pauses, "Something is going on with her and the Muslim man I'm sure. But I don't think she will blow up a plane."

"How do you know she won't?" Alexia asks. "This scares the hell out of me!"

"A hunch I guess. That plane is the responsibility of airport security anyway, not yours," Severo tells her.

"I know, but..."

"I am curious about the man in the picture you sent me. The older guy she was with at the café downtown. Is he still with her?"

"No! Why? Who is he?" Alexia asks. "Is he dangerous too?"

"Maybe."

"Really? He left her when she picked up the little black attaché case. Oh, shit! He went in the same direction the Muslim guy did. Do you know who he is?"

Alexia knows the connections are endless that Severo Baptiste has made covering conflicts and writing stories throughout the entire world. She has hardly been anywhere with him that he did not know someone of significant power or influence.

To some degree this has always puzzled her, considering Baptiste is just a freelance journalist from the South of France and does not seem to be interested in power or position himself. He is very good at what he does, but Severo always seems more interested in the action than getting a story out. Alexia used to kid him that he should have stayed in the French Foreign Legion, as much as he craves being in the middle of conflict. He would always reply back to her, "There is a good time to be in the middle of something, and a good time to be out of the middle of something. Of this I choose every time."

Severo answers Alexia's question about the man in the pictures, "I've seen him and heard some things about him."

"How dangerous is he?" she asks.

"Maybe more than the woman if he is who I think he is."

"How so?"

"I'm not sure I can tell you."

There is a brief moment of silence on both ends of the phone.

"What about the Muslim man who gave the woman the attaché case?" Baptiste asks, "Did you send me a picture of him after my phone went dead? What does he look like?"

———

Sitting in a plush leather seat looking out the window at the terrain of the Midwest 30,000 feet below the private jumbo jet,

Senator Walter Franson answers his personal cell phone. "Hello Rigger, I'm sure you've heard by now."

"Yeah I have, Bob!" Watson answers with a tone of anger in his voice. "It's not good, not good at all. What now?"

"Well, I don't know. We've got people scrambling to minimize this. I just don't think it'll be that bad. What do you think, Rig?"

"What do I think? You really want to know what I think?" Watson fires back at him.

"Yes Rigger, I do!"

"I think it'll cost you five points Bob. Five points you don't have to give. That means instead of a three point win, it'll be a three point loss. That's what I think this Swenson thing will do! I told you over six months ago to get rid of him," the CCN Network News President states. "And then on top of that, there's the damn weather!"

"Rigger, I don't need my butt chewed out by you!" Senator Franson says, adopting a stern tone with his fraternity brother and long-time friend, "We've got to come up with something. I know it's not your nature, but try to be positive."

"What's there to be positive about? I've been telling you for over a year to get rid of that queer! Just because he can run a campaign for Senate in California doesn't mean a thing in a national election."

"I know, and I wish I'd done it when you told me to," answers Franson. "But now we have to come up with a plan. Maybe there's some way we can make this work for us. If anyone can figure out a way to spin this, you can."

"It won't be easy!"

"But it can be done. You think about it, Rig."

Watson pauses, then replies, "I might be able to turn it around so it doesn't cost you as much."

"Good."

"But Walter, it sure would have been nice to know about this crap last night when it first happened!"

"I just learned about it forty minutes ago," Franson replies.

"Don't feed me that BS!"

"I'm not. They just told me about it before I got on this plane."

"Alex heard about it in Paris this morning on the damned BBC," Watson blasts back at the man running for the Presidency of the

United States. "How do they hear about Swenson over there before I do running the biggest news network in the country?"

"I don't know. I just found out myself. That's the truth."

"How the hell are you going to run this nation Bob, if your people are already hiding things from you?"

"Rig, just try to come up with something. We're at our wits end here, short of killing the sorry little..." Senator Franson stops himself as he finishes the thought in his head.

"I'm good with that!" the CCN Network News chief states, "Just make sure I get the story first."

"I'm not serious about that, Rigger."

"I might be," Watson says as he laughs, "and remember, Walter, you came up with it." Watson pauses, "Where are you scheduled to be today?"

Franson looks down at his Rolex and says, "We're about to land in Columbus. Stopping in Pittsburgh after that, then lunch in Philadelphia with the Mayor there. Atlanta at three, Jacksonville and Miami tonight."

"Why the hell are you stopping in Georgia?" Watson asks abruptly. "There's no way you're going to win that damn redneck state!"

"I'm going to give Jackson some help in his House race. And the way things are looking, Fred Bradley might have a chance to win that Senate seat also. We've got something on McSweeny that we're going to let out today. Fred ought to really have a chance then," Franson replies.

"Fred Bradley's as dead as a duck!" Watson laughs loudly, and states, "I've heard what you think you got on McSweeny and it won't fly! His wife will hang with him to the bitter end. McSweeny drove NASCAR for twenty years! Bradley doesn't stand a chance in Georgia."

"What we have on McSweeny will stick."

"Bob! How damn stupid are you? McSweeny's from the South and a Christian. Don't you remember the story we cooked up when he ran for Governor? His wife will stick by him just like she did when we tried that crap about the college intern. And Jackson doesn't need your white ass down there to help him! Who set all this up anyway?

Swenson? He's the one about to cost you the Presidency."

"We haven't lost anything yet and I'm stopping in Atlanta. We have polls that show Bradley has a chance."

"Sure then, go spend some time in Georgia. For that matter, why not Texas or Wyoming! Shoot Bob, you could even go and try to help some poor SOB in Utah that's down by sixty-seven points. You want polls? I can show you polls that will tell you whatever you want to hear!" Watson rips into the man whose political career he has made.

"I knew I'd get at least one of your rants this weekend. And that's it. No more, my time's worth too much. We haven't lost this election yet. When you come up with something let me know," Franson says.

"I may already have something. And you can bet I'll let you know too. A lot sooner than you did me. And don't forget Walter, that I own your time. All of it. You will be hearing from me!" Watson slams the phone down on his desk. He breaks almost as many phones as Alexia Klien loses.

In his office with no one else listening, Rigger Watson goes into another one of his tirades, this time about the ungrateful U.S. Senator he set up for fame and fortune from the first time the dumb kid walked into the fraternity house a young Rigger Watson ruled over as president.

Now the president of CCN Network News, Watson sits at his desk and thinks. He begins to run through his mind an idea of how to turn the incident in Boston involving Franson's campaign manager and the two young teenage boys around to where it may help the cause. It will not take him long to put all the pieces of his plan into action.

CHAPTER NINE

Georgia Peach Farmer

"Dang it, Severo! I didn't even think to take a picture of the Muslim man," Alexia says in panic. "I should have. How stupid of me! We don't even know who he is."

As he sits, talking on a land line phone, in a comfortable recliner in a ski lodge high in the Austrian Alps, Severo replies, "It'll be alright, A.K."

"Severo Armand Casimiro Baptiste, you are the only person who ever calls me A.K. And I love it. I don't know why, but I love it."

"You do?"

"Yes, I do... It calms me to hear you call me A.K."

Severo sighs deeply before he replies, "Alexia Klien, you affect me like no one else. My life has not been the same since the first moment I saw you that night during the opening ceremonies in Salt Lake City."

"I'm so glad you made your way through all the people between us to talk to me," Alexia says.

"Me too, Babe," Baptiste pauses before remembering the business at hand. "But back to Paris today. What about the Arab man who had the attaché case? Is he still around?"

"No, he left. Just before the other man did."

Baptiste, certain that Alexia is not in any immediate danger settles back into his chair. "So Darling, when do I get to see you while you're on this side of the Atlantic Ocea-"

"Oh no, he's walking right at me! I think he sees me. I cut in front of him getting through security," Alexia says as she turns and walks behind some people who are standing on the edge of the concourse.

"Who?" Severo asks.

"It's the Middle Eastern guy!" Alexia says quietly.

In Austria, Baptiste sits up in the recliner and asks, "What's he doing? I thought you said he left."

Alexia carefully looks over her left shoulder to see if the man is still walking her way. "He's looking right at me now. I've got to do something! What shou-...?"

———

"Dad burn it, Martha Jo! Them Arabs are still chantin' in rooms 125 and 127 just like they been doing for two days now," Sharice tells her coworker as she walks into the laundry room on the bottom floor of a little run-down motel on the edge of a small town about eighty miles northwest of New Orleans.

"I knows what you mean. I been hearin' it too. It scares me, Sharice," Martha Jo says to the younger and slightly darker friend she has been cleaning rooms with for three years.

Sharice Jones picks up a basket full of the dirty towels and sheets she has just taken from the rooms she has cleaned and stuffs them into an old commercial washing machine. "I is tellin' you Martha Jo, them people just ain't right. They just ain't right. I think they chantin' them Islamic jihadist prayers. I really do."

As she stops what she is doing, Martha Jo turns to look right at Sharice. "I tell you what, they ain't chantin' to Jesus. It's pure evil what they is doin'. I gets a terrible feelin' way deep inside me when I have to go near those rooms."

Martha Jo Hall is nearly thirty years older than Sharice, who is thirty-eight. The two women are family. Martha Jo is a great-aunt to Sharice's two oldest children. Their father is Martha Jo's nephew. He and Sharice never married, but Martha Jo still treats Sharice like the daughter she never had.

The two women both work at the Motor Inn #16 on the edge of Denham Springs, Louisiana. The motel is about a mile north of the very busy I-12 and just off State Highway 16. Interstate 12 connects to I-10 on both ends at the Louisiana cities of Slidell and Baton Rouge. It is the shortcut that keeps traffic from having to detour south of Lake Pontchartrain on Interstate 10 and get bogged down on the busy freeway in and around New Orleans. I-10 is the main roadway running the full length of the southern border of the United States, from Florida to California.

"What do you think they's up too?" Sharice asks Martha Jo.

"I tells you, Honey, something tells me it ain't no good!" Martha Jo allows as she begins to load her laundry cart to get ready to clean more rooms.

"It scares me Martha, with the boy's ballgame tonight," Sharice replies.

Sharice Jones moved to the Baton Rouge area three years earlier from Houston, Texas to live close to her two sons who are on scholarship to play college football at Louisiana State University. Her oldest son, Derrick Jones-DuPree is six foot six and 285 pounds. He is a senior and ranked as the top defensive end prospect in next April's NFL draft where he is projected to be a top 5 pick, maybe the number one pick overall. As soon as he is drafted and signs his professional football contract, Derrick will most likely be worth in excess of forty million dollars.

Tonight in Baton Rouge, LSU is playing host to the University of Alabama in what is sure to be a game of National Championship proportions. Both Southeastern Conference powerhouses enter this Saturday night's NCAA match-up as teams ranked very high in the Bowl Championship Series poll. TV sets all across America will be tuned into this national broadcast from Tiger Stadium to watch all the action. Tiger Stadium is only a twenty minute drive from the old dumpy two-story motel, the Motor Inn #16 hidden back in the trees along the state highway it is named after.

———

"What should I do?" Alexia asks Baptiste in a panic as she glances back over her shoulder to see the Muslim man still watching her. "The plane the woman is on hasn't left yet. I want to stay and see if she gets off it."

"What's the Arab man doing now?"

"He's just standing there, looking right at me," she glances over her shoulder. "Severo, what should I do? Should I just leave?"

In a very deep, slow, calming voice Severo says, "Do not act like anything is wrong, Darling. Turn and walk towards him. This will show the wolf you are are not scared of him. Do not look him in the eyes. Act like you don't know he is there. Walk past him about thirty feet and stop and turn back arou-"

Alexia's cell phone goes dead. In her panic she did not notice the quiet beeps warning her that the battery was low. But she does not lose her cool. She turns and heads straight for the Arab man just as Baptiste told her to. But Alexia puts a twist of her own in Severo's plan. She keeps her phone held up to her ear and she continues to talk the whole time she walks towards him. As she approaches the Muslim man, she cannot help but do just the thing Severo told her not to do. She looks the man directly in the eyes for just a second and then refocuses her attention to where she is going. She continues walking past him with her cell phone still held up to her ear. He turns his head slightly as she passes.

Alexia walks into a little convenience shop on the opposite side of the airport concourse about fifty feet away from where the Muslim man is standing. There she buys a package of cinnamon flavored chewing gum. She carefully tears off the wrapper and asks the girl behind the counter to throw it away for her before putting a piece of the gum in her mouth. Alexia sees a magazine someone had misplaced on the newspaper rack.

She picks it up and opens it to the celebrity photo section in the middle. Looking at a picture of her good friend Angie West and some guy all the tabloids claim Angie is dating, Alexia laughs to herself. Three years earlier when Angie first broke onto the country music scene in spectacular fashion with four number-one hits in a row, Alexia was sent to Oklahoma to do a special for CCN on the beautiful new face of country music.

Alexia and Angie really hit it off during the three-day interview. Both of them had grown up around horses. Angie was raised competing in rodeos as a barrel racer, and Alexia Klien had ridden jumpers and shown dressage, the most difficult and advanced discipline of all the equine industry. Angie and Alexia have continued a close friendship, getting together a number of times to ride Angie's horses or just hide from the overwhelming pressures of being worldwide celebrities.

Knowing Angie as well as she does, Alexia couldn't help but

laugh when she read in the popular magazine that the country music singer was dating some British rock star. A rumor started just because Angie and Flash Freeman were both seen in the same restaurant in London two weeks earlier. It made no difference to the paparazzi that West and Freeman did not arrive or leave together, or even eat together. Some pictures were snapped when the two were introduced by a common friend in the music industry, and scandalous news was made.

Alexia remembers how she had just talked to her friend a few days ago about Angie's upcoming trip to the Middle East to entertain the troops. Funny thing is they had both joked about how maybe Angie would find the American man of her dreams on the sands of the Arabian Desert, all dressed from head to toe in camouflage. Alexia knew there was no way Angie would be interested in some skinny, stoned, druggy singer from Liverpool, England who sings in a band called Ax-Handle.

After entertaining herself in the face of grave danger, Alexia puts the trashy tabloid magazine back on the rack. She thanks the girl behind the counter and looks to see if the Muslim man is still focused on her. He stands with his back towards Alexia while he watches the door of the walkway leading to the plane headed to Moscow.

Alexia wonders, *Is he waiting to make sure the woman with the little black attaché case stays on the plane? Or could he be waiting for her to come back off, leaving the black case in the plane filled with people?* Knowing she needs to report to work soon, Alexia asks herself very quietly under her breath, "Why am I even still here?"

She sees on a clock behind the counter where she purchased the gum that she still has a little time before she absolutely must leave the airport. Alexia decides to continue her detective work a little while longer. She walks over and sits down in an empty chair in front of gate 18A. From here she has a good view of the doorway leading to and from the Airbus A330.

A minute later, the Middle Eastern man turns from where he has been standing and walks directly to the very same counter in the snack shop where Alexia had just bought her gum. The man stops and asks the pretty little French girl behind the counter a question. He then walks out of the shop and takes his cell phone from the inside pocket of his suit coat and makes a call. He continues his conversation as he walks across the concourse and into the men's restroom.

Puzzled by his actions, Alexia tries to keep one eye on the doorway to the plane and one on the entrance to the restroom. As she sits scanning back and forth between the restroom and gate 17A, Alexia finds herself thinking about the photos of her good friend Angie West the singer. Alexia is amused over how the American magazine in no way showed the truly sweet and kind nature Angie truly possesses. It has painted the now famous singer Angie West, as some sort of fame and fortune chasing celebrity. Alexia thinks that if America only knew how close her friend is to never stepping back on another stage to sing another song, it would absolutely shock the country music world.

Alexia knows Angie has been putting together a string of good young horses as barrel racing prospects. When she was eighteen years old, Angie West had qualified for the National Finals Rodeo in Las Vegas, Nevada riding a horse her mother had raised and trained. This was long before she had even begun to sing in public. A number of times, Angie has told Alexia that her greatest dream in life is to win a PRCA Barrel Racing World Championship on a horse that she herself has trained. Alexia knows Angie would trade all her gold and platinum records just to win that World Championship.

With her attention divided between the door to the walkway leading to the Airbus A330 filled with passengers going to Russia and the opening to the restroom the Muslim man has gone into, Alexia sits and thinks about how Angie and she have dueled throughout the previous year over who should be elected as the next President of the United States. Angie would very seriously proclaim that Senator Walter Franson was the anti-Christian candidate. This always has gotten under Alexia's skin, and she doesn't really know why.

The famous country music singer is a staunch conservative. Alexia is a supporter of Senator Franson, even though she doesn't really care for the man as a person. The Senator has tried to hit on Alexia a number of times over the years with no success. Once he had even sent Alexia some text messages that were a little risqué. But Franson stands on the same sides of the main social issues Alexia feels are so important in America today—a woman's right to make her own choice as far as abortion is concerned, and an individual's rights to marry whoever they wish, man or woman.

Alexia has friends who are gay, and she feels they should have the right to live their lives the way they want. Alexia and her father often argue feverishly at family functions over these issues, as well as his insistence that America suffers from over taxation and too much government spending by Washington D.C.

No one ever really wins the arguments between Alexia and her father. Normally her mother will step in and make them stop and change the subject for the sanity of all listening before anyone's feelings get hurt. One thing Alexia has not admitted to her father is that he has made some serious headway with her on the topic of too much government spending and taxes being too high. The older Alexia gets, the more she realizes that government is not going to solve everyone's problems. She has even come to realize her dad is right when he says government intervention actually makes most problems worse.

Sitting in France's busiest airport with time working against her, Alexia makes the decision to give up her quest to uncover the mystery of the day. Maybe even the mystery of the year. She takes one last look in the direction of the men's restroom where she last saw the Muslim man. She grabs her handbag at her feet and glances back towards the doorway of the tunnel leading to the plane bound for Moscow as she begins to rise. From her seat across the concourse, Alexia sees the enormous white Airbus A330 slowly begin to back away from the gate.

Alexia sits back down. She is filled with fear for the people aboard the plane. As she sits there wishing there was something she could do, the door of the long corridor that leads to the airplane opens. Alexia watches as an olive-skinned female flight attendant who looks to be of Arabian descent appears through the door. Alexia sits motionless as the young woman clears the doorway. To her surprise, Alexia sees the young flight attendant is carrying something black. It is the very same small attaché case with Islamic symbols the mysterious woman with long, dark red hair had just taken onto the plane. Alexia sits perplexed by this new development.

The young flight attendant is of medium height. She is slender, with a long narrow face and an equally long narrow nose. She looks a lot like Sarah Jessica Parker, only with slightly darker skin, dark brown eyes and hair as black as the Arabian night. After exiting the door leading to the passenger boarding bridge, the young flight attendant looks around as though she is expecting to see someone. Alexia presumes she is looking for the Middle Eastern man who had gone into the restroom a few minutes ago and has not yet come back out.

When the flight attendant doesn't see who she is looking for, she walks over to the ticket counter at gate 17A and says something to the man standing behind the counter. Carrying the small attaché case in her right hand and pulling her suitcase with her left, the flight attendant then walks to the women's restroom and enters it.

Just after she enters the restroom, the Muslim man comes out of the men's restroom. He is still holding the large black attaché case. Alexia watches him walk back to the little convenience shop he had just been in before entering the men's room. The Arab man stops at a small rack of paperback books, sets down the briefcase and picks up a book and begins to page through it.

As Alexia turns her attention back in the direction of the women's restroom, she catches a glimpse of the distinguished gray haired gentleman standing nearly two hundred feet down the concourse. Alexia had forgotten about him, thinking he was gone. He stands alone between gates 15A and 14A looking out the large windows at the white Airbus as it taxis towards the runway. As he watches the airplane leave with the mysterious and beautiful woman on board that he had shared a bottle of wine with earlier in the day at the little French Café, Alexia wishes she could know the man's thoughts.

Still focused a couple hundred feet down the concourse, Alexia sees out of the corner of her eye two women leave the opening to the women's restroom. She turns her head and sees the young Arab flight attendant leaving the restroom behind these women. Only now the black haired Sarah Jessica Parker look-a-like has changed her clothes. She is wearing a dark blue Armani pant suit and black Gucci heels. Expecting her to walk in the direction of the Middle Eastern man, Alexia looks back towards the snack shop and sees that the Muslim man is facing away from the center of the concourse, still paging through a paperback book.

Alexia looks back to the young Arab woman. She is walking down the center of the concourse in the direction of the tall gray haired gentleman. When the young flight attendant is about fifty feet from him, he turns and begins to walk directly towards her. *What is going on?* As she watches the young flight attendant walk, getting closer to the man with every step, Alexia wonders, *Why did she go into the restroom to change clothes if she is a flight attendant?* She then thinks, *Maybe she isn't a flight attendant.*

In the middle of the concourse walkway, between gates 16A and 15A the two meet, the young Arab woman and the well dressed gentleman whose appearance gives off the impression of power and wealth, and in this setting, international intrigue. When they meet, the young woman in the expensive dark blue business suit stops and hands the miniature black attaché case to the man. Reaching out with his left hand, he takes it from her. He then hands her a large brown envelope with red letters on it. No words are exchanged, no thank you, no hellos or goodbyes, nothing said, just the exchange of the items. The object that has been causing Alexia Klien so much grief has just switched hands for the third time in less than an hour. The young woman walks away with the brown envelope. Alexia cannot make out what any of the letters say.

As she sits there in the busy international airport, it seems to Alexia that everything she has experienced up to this point in her thirty-six years of life does not compare with what she has witnessed today. And yet, she still has no idea of exactly what it is that she has witnessed in the few short hours since she tried on the pair of sixty-eight hundred dollar designer sunglasses that even she wouldn't buy if she had all the money in the world.

What kind of shell game am I watching here today? Alexia asks herself. She has spent ample time in Monte Carlo with Severo and been to Vegas on numerous occasions, the last time about a year ago in December during the National Finals Rodeo to hang out with Angie for a week and meet a cowboy or two. She has been to Rio, Dubai and Atlantic City over and over. And yet, she is quite sure she has never seen any kind of shell game like the one she has witnessed today, and in of all places, Charles de Gaulle International Airport. *Are the stakes of this shell game higher than I have ever seen wagered before?* A feeling inside of her knows all of this has to have something to do with the upcoming U.S. Presidential election only three days away, but what?

After receiving the little black attaché case from the young Arab woman, the tall gray haired man now carries the small briefcase tightly in his right hand as he proceeds directly down the concourse at a fast pace.

Watching the man walk away in the busy airport, Alexia suddenly giggles to herself, a personal sign she may be about to lose it as she thinks, *OK, I'm in Paris, France and I am watching... whatever it is I'm watching. At any moment now Peter Sellers is going to walk out from behind some wall or through a door or something as Inspector Clouseau.*

As Alexia laughs, she remembers how the old *Pink Panther* movies from the 1960's and 70's are her father's favorite movies of all time. She has seen them over and over with him. He is a prominent Atlanta, Georgia insurance attorney representing some of the largest insurance companies in the South. To know Alexia's father, a person would think his favorite movie character would be out of a movie starring John Wayne, whom he emulates in almost every area of his life. But no, Alexander Jonathon Klien's favorite movie character is Inspector Clouseau, the famous bumbling French detective. Her father loves France. As a family, the Kliens vacationed there numerous times. Alexia always thought that this may have had a lot to do with why her father approved of Severo Baptiste when she was in a serious relationship with the Frenchman.

Her father also loves John Wayne, *Big Jake* being his favorite of The Duke's movies. Growing up, Alexia watched many of these movies with her dad. She remembers her father's favorite scene from the movie *Big Jake* is the one with the dog at the beginning of the film where the sheep herder is about to be hung from a tree by some cattlemen. When threatened by the cattlemen, John Wayne, playing Jacob McCandles says, "Just who do you think I am?" Her father, who goes by John Klien, will from time to time, use those same words in the courtroom for a little humor and sarcasm. As she thinks about it, Severo Baptiste has some of the same John Wayne qualities her father has.

As much as John Klien is like John Wayne—a little rough around the edges—he still insists Peter Sellers playing Inspector Clouseau is his favorite character because Clouseau always makes him laugh. Alexia's father claims that if he watches too much John Wayne or Clint Eastwood, he might just up and hit some poor unsuspecting Ivy League lawyer right square in the nose in the middle of a trial, and be sent straight to the Augusta National Golf Club and permanent retirement from practicing law. But then as John Klien would say, "That really wouldn't be a bad way to go, if you have to."

Alexia dismisses the thoughts of her father and Inspector Clouseau as she becomes intensely curious about the contents of the little black attaché case the tall gray haired gentleman is now carrying at a very brisk walk towards the center of the airport. Alexia feels that if she does not get up right now and follow him, it will be the last she sees of the attaché case. She grabs her handbag, stands up from where she has been sitting in front of gate 18A, and follows him. While she walks down the right side of the concourse, she keeps the man in her sights as she pulls out the pair of big dark sunglasses she has with her and puts them on. She is nearly curious enough to be tempted to run up behind the man and jerk the case out of his hand to find out what's inside. *That would be the John Wayne, or maybe the John Klien coming out in me,* she thinks.

To Alexia's surprise, the man who seems to be in such a hurry suddenly stops and answers his phone. The call does not last long, only a few seconds. After the call, he walks at a slower pace down the concourse, looking at each of the gate numbers. As he reaches gate 13A, he stops, finds an open seat in an area where no one else is, and he sits down.

Alexia stops in front of gate 16A. She can see the gentleman reach into the inside pocket of his suit coat. He pulls out a small case about the size of a large cigar. It is his reading glasses, which he then takes out of the case and puts on.

Standing near the middle of a long line of people waiting to board a flight leaving from gate 16A, Alexia turns her attention back to the Muslim man she last saw looking at a paperback book in the little convenience shop. She sees he is still in the shop standing in front of an open-air cooler full of bottled drinks. He has his back to her as he reaches out to get a beverage. Alexia scans the area to see if she can find the young Arab woman. She does not see her anywhere.

With her dark sunglasses still on, Alexia looks back to the gray haired man just in time to see him open the little black attaché case. She is not close enough to see what is inside of it. The man does not take anything out of the case. Instead, he leaves it setting on his lap. He seems to be pushing buttons in it. Alexia is taken completely by surprise as she realizes the miniature black attaché case is a small laptop computer. *Why didn't I think of this earlier?* She wonders, *Probably because it is disguised to look just like an attaché case.*

The man now staring intently down through his reading glasses at the computerized contents of the little black briefcase reaches into his suit coat and pulls out another cell phone, a completely different one than he had just used a moment ago. On this phone he makes one very short call only speaking a few words without taking his eyes off the screen in front of him. He then hangs up and returns his hand to type something on the keyboard of the mini-computer.

As she watches this, a myriad of possibilities that all pertain to the highly sensitive and top secret information that could be on this computer, race through Alexia's mind. She remembers the serious damage done to the relations between so many nations, especially the United States, by Julian Assange and his dumping of thousands of pages of highly secretive information over his WikiLeaks website. *Could this mysterious man I am looking at be someone like Assange? Or even worse, could what looks like a mini laptop computer be a dirty bomb, or even the operating system for a nuclear missile?* The American broadcast journalist wonders.

As Alexia stands between where the tall gray haired gentleman sits looking at the small laptop computer and the man from the Middle East in the airport snack shop, an image comes back into her mind. A very vivid image of the mysterious woman with the most unique long dark red hair that hung all the way to her waist, walking arm and arm with Senator Walter Franson down a hallway on the 18th floor of the Renaissance Park Hotel in Washington D.C. in the middle of the night, each of them holding the other up as they stumbled their way to a private suite. Alexia has no doubt in her mind this woman was involved in a sexual affair with the man about to be the next leader of the free world.

With the vision still very clear in her head, Alexia suddenly thinks for the first time, *Maybe Angie's right! Maybe Senator Franson is the anti-Christian candidate.* Alexia cannot believe she has just had this thought. She has never agreed with her friend Angie West when it comes to politics. Alexia knows right from wrong and she also knows the actions she witnessed two years ago by her preferred Presidential candidate were very wrong. But Alexia had never seen them as this wrong before today.

The CCN Network News broadcast journalist has always given Franson a pass because of where he stands on the issues important to her. She also knows what she has seen today, if made public, would do nothing but harm to the Presidential hopes of Walter Franson and the whole Democrat Party. Today Alexia feels that she finally sees the Senator as he really is—a narcissistic, egotistical man with great verbal skills, a soft and kind public persona and a very charismatic personality, but phony and shallow to the core. He is the opposite of her own father whom she loves and adores dearly.

Suddenly Alexia remembers some very wise words her grandfather gave her right before she went off to college: "Just because a man's speech is smooth and refined, doesn't mean he is genuine!" He wrote these words down in his rough and shaky handwriting on a piece of scratch paper the morning Alexia left home to attend the University of Georgia. He gave them to her at the breakfast table and she didn't even take the little piece of paper with her to college. Somewhere over the years it was either lost or thrown away. The words he gave her had been forgotten until today.

Her grandfather was an old man who had spent his life raising peaches in South Georgia. He never got rich growing peaches, and never ventured far from home in the South, but he did give his eighteen year old granddaughter some very valuable and insightful words of advice as she went off to college to study political science and broadcast journalism. As a teenage girl leaving home to live on her own for the first time, she had thought her grandfather was giving her dating advice, which she didn't really think she needed. Now that she is older and has seen much more of the world and of life, Alexia recalls these words again, but in a different light. She now sees her grandfather was talking about all men, all people, and especially those in important positions when he wrote down the words, "Just because a man's speech is smooth and refined, doesn't mean he is genuine!" She knows that Senator Walter Franson is a perfect example of a powerful man whose speech and delivery is smooth and refined, but he himself is not at all genuine.

The line of people Alexia stands among at gate 16A is getting shorter as a man in front of her turns around and attempts to strike up a conversation. She has to snub him. While she is stopping the unwanted advance from the complete stranger, something Alexia is very good at, she sees the Muslim man walk up to the counter of the snack shop to pay for the beverage he has in his hand. He sets a bottle of lemon flavored Perrier on the counter and pays for it. He then starts to walk away. After only a step, he stops and turns around and says something to the young French girl behind the counter. As she answers him, he checks his watch and glances quickly over in the direction of Alexia. Before leaving the counter he looks back to the young girl and asks her another question. She replies by nodding her head up and down. He thanks her and begins to walk away.

Nervous, Alexia turns her head away from the snack shop and back down the concourse where she sees the gray haired gentleman still sitting with the miniature laptop computer open in front of him.

With her eyes hidden behind the lenses of her sunglasses, Alexia looks back to the Muslim man. He is walking away from the counter of the airport snack shop when suddenly he stops and turns around and walks back to the newspaper rack he just passed. Holding the Perrier in one hand, he reaches out and takes the very same magazine off the rack that Alexia had been looking at just minutes ago, the one with the pictures of her friend Angie West in it. He steps up to the counter and buys the magazine.

Suddenly Alexia feels fear shoot through her. Immediately every muscle in her arms and shoulders tense up all at once, seizing her in panic and despair. *My finger prints are all over that magazine.*

CHAPTER TEN

Goodbye and Pray For Us

On the back side of a U.S. Air Force Base in Kuwait in the middle of the Middle East, Private Will Tillord has his weapon sighted in on the face of the driver of the first of two white Ryna Corp work trucks rapidly approaching the entrance gate with no sign of stopping. He hears the word "Fire!" and gently squeezes the trigger on his M4 Carbine Assault Rifle.

The 5.56mm round immediately pierces the windshield of the oncoming truck and tears through the top of the white turban on the head of the driver. It rips a portion of his skull away. The white work truck in the lead does not slow down or change direction.

"Fire again!" Sergeant Spicer Davis yells. "Everyone fire at both trucks! Open up and let 'em have it!"

Suddenly the still, quiet afternoon in the normally mundane and monotonous Kuwait has become absolute chaos. Private Tillord takes aim and fires his M4 carbine a little lower towards the body of the driver in the first vehicle. Sheldon Mitchal opens up with his fifty-caliber machine gun scattering rounds all through the front of the lead truck, and Diaz blasts away at the second Ryna Corp truck on his own fifty-cal machine gun. The noise is almost unbearable.

It seems as though it goes on for minutes to the young Will Tillord who started the onslaught with the first shot. Yet only seconds pass as rounds of ammunition are fired directly into the two intruding vehicles. The first white truck proceeds straight for the gate at a very high rate of speed as though no shots have even been fired. Then, at the last moment before ramming into and through the eight inch steel pipe used to control traffic through the entrance gate, the white work truck in the lead swerves directly to the left and into the guard shack at the entrance gate.

The white Ryna Corp work truck explodes upon impact, rocking the ground and the air and everything in the vicinity. It blows the entrance gate wide open, ripping the twenty-five foot long steel pipe that blocks the roadway off its pivot point and sending it fifty feet into the air. The huge block of concrete it had been attached to is left in pieces beside the burning guard shack.

The four men in the tower are rocked back on their heels, their faces blasted with sand, dirt and dust as the guard shack about a hundred feet away with fellow soldiers and friends inside is blown apart. The air, which only seconds ago one could see for miles in any direction across the sands of the Arabian Desert, is now filled with smoke and fire and screaming.

With both hands firmly holding his 50 caliber machine gun, Specialist Diaz sees through the thickened air the second white Ryna Corp work truck coming through where the entrance gate had just been. The speeding truck is only about fifty feet from the tower where he and his three friends sit.

"Oh, shit!" Diaz yells, "They're going to hit us!"

———

"Oh dear Lord, Sharice! We needs to be prayin' to Jesus that nothin' happens tonight at the boys ballgame," Martha Jo proclaims.

The two African American women close the door to the laundry room they are in so they can have some privacy. Then they get down on their knees and Martha Jo prays a very genuine and heartfelt prayer for the safety of their family members and all the communities in the area where they live.

"Should we go and tell Mr. Zahrani about them Muslims in rooms 125 and 127? Or do you think we'd get fired?" Sharice asks as she gets up off the floor.

"No way do we want to tell him!" Martha Jo says, "Jesus will take care of your boys. We prayed, Sharice. Jesus will answer all our prayers. He loves your boys a lot."

Sharice's two oldest sons, Derrick and Darrin Jones-DuPree are good boys well on their way to being very good young men. Sharice and her three sons had moved out of New Orleans to Houston in 2005 when the gulf coast city was struck by Hurricane Katrina. Her two oldest sons finished high school in Texas. The athletically gifted boys had offers to play college football wherever they wanted, from California to Florida. Both boys choose LSU because they had grown up in Louisiana and had always dreamed of playing for the Tigers.

Her oldest son, Derrick is a three-time All-American, and Darrin was the National College Freshman Football Player of the Year just one year ago. Now a sophomore, Darrin is an outside linebacker on the same side of LSU's defense as his older brother, making that side of the Tiger defense nearly impenetrable. Darrin is expected to turn pro next year after his junior season and be one of the first players drafted into the NFL. Darrin is big, six foot four and 235 pounds. He's very smart and very fast, running a 4.36 forty yard dash, almost unheard of for someone his size.

Sharice Jones has the two sons in college and a younger one, Donnie who still lives with her. He is a star wide receiver and defensive back on his Baton Rouge high school football team. Donnie Jones is even faster than his older brothers, having won gold medals in the 100 and 200 meter sprints at the Louisiana State Track Championships the proceeding spring as a junior. Donnie talks like he is going to break the family tradition though and play his college football back in Texas for the Longhorns. This does not sit well with his LSU Tiger brothers. It is a good thing for Donnie he is faster than they are. Maybe that's why he is—self-developed survival skills. But his mother believes that when it comes right down to it, Donnie will follow in his brothers' footsteps and play for LSU. That's what she hopes for anyway.

An hour after they prayed, Martha Jo is cleaning the rooms of the guests she knows have checked out. This does not include rooms 125 and 127. She is across the hall from those two rooms in room 128 and is busy cleaning a filthy toilet left by the previous night's occupants. Martha Jo is not in as good a mood as normal when her phone begins to ring. She recognizes by the ring tone that it is her sister-in-law from Atlanta, Georgia and she decides not to take the call because she is up to her arms in a nasty mess.

She decides she will call her back in a couple of hours on her break. The previous week at the motel the owner and manager, Shahid al-Zahrani, caught Sharice on her cell phone in a room she was cleaning. She was on the phone with one of her sons. Zahrani went into a rage and almost fired Sharice on the spot. Normally he is a moderately pleasant man to be around. He and his family own a number of older run down motels and convenience stores in the area north New Orleans. But something in him snapped that day.

Martha Jo continues to clean room 128. She can hear the noise of the Islamic chants coming from the rooms across the hall. The radical chanting that scared Sharice so much earlier this morning seems to be getting louder. As she thinks about it, the day Mr. Zahrani had lost his temper with Sharice was the same day that six or seven Muslim men had showed up at the motel.

Martha Jo begins to have an uneasy feeling as she is making the beds and straightening the pillows. She again bows her head and prays a prayer asking God what she should do. Before she finishes up in the room and moves her cart down the hall, she has a very strong impression to call her sister-in-law in Georgia back. Martha Jo decides to lock her cart in the room she has just finished cleaning and walk across the street and make the phone call.

There is not any traffic on the little-used side street between the Motor Inn #16 and an old fashioned gas station, the kind that still fixes tires and does a little mechanic work. The station has a small office and a lobby, restrooms, and two garages attached to it that have large roll-up doors that are usually open. Parked beside the old building there are a handful of broken-down vehicles, including an old school bus, and there are stacks of used tires all around out back.

Entering the old filling station, Martha Jo goes straight into the women's bathroom first. Zahrani forbids the two cleaning women from using the toilets at his motel. They have to go to the gas station across the street. It is owned by an old black man, Sims Wilson who is tall and skinny and smokes all the time, even sometimes when he is putting gas in someone's car. It probably costs him some business. He doesn't care though. Whenever anyone asks him about it, he always says, "Ever since I was a little boy I wanted to go up to heaven in a blaze of glory. So why not I just help it happen."

Sharice always kids Martha Jo, who has only been married once and never did have any children of her own, that she is always going over there to flirt with Ol' Sims Wilson. Martha Jo denies it, but part of the time she is. In the five years Martha Jo Hall has worked for the Saudi Arabian Zahrani, Martha Jo and Ol' Sims have gone to the picture show together about once or twice every month.

Working for Shahid al-Zahrani has its drawbacks, but he pays well, which is sort of an oddity considering the condition and clientele of the dumpy little roadside motel built in the 1950's. Working for Zahrani, Sharice and Martha Jo make twice as much money as they would in the big fancy hotels and motels in New Orleans. The two women never could figure out why he pays so well. They just keep their mouths shut and take the money he pays them for the dirty work they do. All they could figure was that Zahrani is either a really good businessman, or he has money coming from somewhere else. He has two sons who live a very high and fast lifestyle that's not common among the rest of the immigrants who live in the Denham Springs, Louisiana area.

Done using the restroom, Martha Jo closes its door and asks, "Sims sweetie, can I use your office to make a quick call on my cell phone?"

"You know you can, Honey," Ol' Sims says, "If you go and get some ice cream with me when you gets off work."

"Thanks, Sweetie," Martha Jo replies as she smiles from ear to ear, a little embarrassed. "Will you let me have a scoop of chocolate and a scoop of vanilla?"

"Whatever you want, Honey."

As she takes her phone out of her pocket, Martha Jo steps into the office to make a call where she will be out of sight of the motel and Zahrani. Martha Jo and Sharice do this occasionally, Sharice more often as she is constantly trying to keep up with her three boys.

In Ol' Sims Wilson's office, Martha Jo pushes the buttons on her cell phone to call her sister-in-law Clarice. Clarice Hall is married to Martha Jo's brother Gene who is retired Military. Gene and Clarice live in Atlanta. Martha Jo hopes that one of Sharice's sons will be drafted in the future by the Atlanta Falcons, giving both Martha Jo and Sharice an excuse to move to Atlanta so Martha Jo can be closer to her brother and Clarice, whom she usually talks to three or four times a day.

It has been forty minutes since Clarice tried to call when Martha Jo was elbows deep in a toilet in room 128. As her cell phone rings five or six times in her ear, Martha Jo thinks she is going to have to leave her sister-in-law a message, which she does not want to do. Martha Jo feels for some reason she needs to talk directly with Clarice. Right before the answering service clicks on Clarice answers, "Hello, Sis. What you been doin'? It's been nearly twenty minutes since I called you."

"I was cleanin' a real dirty bathroom when you called and I wasn't in a very good mood then," Martha Jo replies.

"When y'all comin' to see us?" Clarice asks, "We is makin' plans for y'all to be here for the SEC Championship Game."

"We will come next week if them boys of Sharice's beat Alabama tonight."

"You know they will, Martha Jo."

"I hope so. If not, then probably not till after Christmas."

"We sure will be pullin' for the Tigers tonight so we get to see you soon."

"Clarice, I was thinkin' God was wantin' me to call you," Martha Jo says. "What's been happenin'?"

"Oh, just your brother Gene went and bought him one of them new little foreign trucks to haul grass and shrubs around. A Toyota."

"Really? He didn't buy American?"

"Well, they say this truck is made here in the States by Americans," Clarice replies. "Oh, is he ever proud of it. You should see him. He's just like a little boy with a new toy."

"I bet he is."

"Oh yes, Martha Jo," Clarice pauses, and then continues. "I got to tell you somethin' I forgot. I got an email from my boy Turner P. this morning. He said they had them an attack over there in Kuwait today at the airbase he is on."

Martha Jo interrupts, "Is he OK?"

"Turner P.'s fine."

"Oh, that's good!" Martha Jo says, "Thank God for that."

"He says attacks never happen in Kuwait, but they did today. They was some Saudi Arabians just like you and Sharice work for at that motel," says Clarice. "Them Arabs stole two of the trucks Turner

P.'s company has and they drove them trucks right in to a guard tower and a gate or something."

"Oh no, did anyone get killed?"

"Don't know if anybody died or not."

Gene and Clarice Hall's son, Turner P. Hall works for Ryna Corp, a military contracting company in Kuwait. Turner P. has worked overseas on military contracting jobs ever since he graduated from Florida State University. As well as being a communications major, he was also a starting free safety on FSU's 1993 National Championship football team. College football runs deep in their family as Turner P.'s father Gene had been a tailback for Grambling University, a primarily black college in Grambling, Louisiana.

The people who saw Gene Hall play in the early sixties said he could have been a star in the NFL if it would have been ten years later. In the 1970's more outstanding black players were given chances to make professional football team rosters. After three and a half years of college, Gene Hall joined the U.S. Army and spent thirty-four years serving his country until he retired with honors in 1998.

"Oh, Clarice! You needs to pray for Sharice and her boys. We gots a bunch of crazy chantin' Muslims like that stayin' here at the motel," Martha Jo says in a panic after she thinks about what happened in Kuwait. "I got to find somebody to tell..."

"What about the motel Martha?"

"They has been chantin' for two days now. Sharice is so scared for the LSU ballgame tonight. I got to think of someone to call, a cop or somebody. I got to get off the phone. Goodbye Clarice and pray for us."

"I will, Martha Jo. Tell Sharice I love her and I'll talk to Gene about what to do about the Muslims at the motel. Love you, Sis."

"Oh please do that, Clarice. I know my brother will know someone to call. Love you sister, bye," Martha Jo gets off the phone.

CHAPTER ELEVEN

Kicking a Field Goal

"Chief, it's your turn to drive. I'm getting tired," states FBI agent Rance Patton as he wakes his fellow agent, Chace Wikett, up from a deep sleep. Wikett is the Chief Investigative Detective for the FBI Terrorism Division SW out of Dallas, Texas.

Wikett yawns, "Where we at?" Still quite groggy and not wanting to open his eyes, he asks, "Is it light yet?"

"Not yet," Rance replies. "We're just west of Phoenix somewhere, maybe Wickenburg."

"What time is it?" a bit puzzled, Chace Wikett now tries to get his bearings and wake up completely. "You didn't drive very far." He runs his hand over his face and through his hair and then questions his partner, "What's taken so long? Did they stop or something?"

"No Chief, we're in California already," says Rance as he laughs. "It's a little after five. Actually we went past Blythe a little ways back. You've been out like a light since Tucson. I don't think I've ever seen anyone sleep that hard going down the road."

Now awake and starting to gather his wits, Wikett looks out the side window of the dark blue Cadillac Escalade at the arid desert terrain of southern California. It is still dark, but with the light of the moon shining through a scattering of clouds it is not completely dark. He allows, "No, I haven't slept like that in a vehicle since about twenty years ago. I helped a crazy cousin of mine from Sallisaw, Oklahoma drive from Oklahoma City to Pendleton, Oregon. We only stopped to sleep once and that was after we had gotten most of the way there. We ended up in Kuna, Idaho at the F-Bar Arena, an indoor rodeo arena and a bar. What a place. I'll never forget it."

"Oh, really? A lot of fun, huh?"

"Yeah, it was," states Wikett, "Still don't know how he talked me into that trip."

Agent Patton brings the conversation back to the present, "These guys aren't taking any extra time."

"How about Craddick and Gasperson?" Chief Wikett inquires about two of the other FBI agents engaged in this pursuit.

"They're ahead of 'em now," Rance replies, "Swanson and Garcia are behind us."

"Damn, I wish we knew more about where these guys are going. I don't like getting this close to the second largest population center in the U.S. and not having complete control of the situation," Agent Wikett expresses with deep concern as he looks out the window into the darkness of the desert again. A mile later he asks, "How far out of L.A. are we?"

"Oh, I'd say a little over a hundred miles still. Let's see..." Patton fiddles with the GPS. "Further than I thought, a hundred and seventy-three miles."

"Just over two hours then."

"What exactly did you go from Oklahoma to Oregon with your cousin for?" Patton asks. "Was that before you went overseas?"

"Yes, it was right out of college. We went up there because he was riding bulls in the Pendleton Roundup. He's a hoot, my cousin, lots a fun, everybody loves him. He talked me into the trip as one last thing we could do together before we had to start our real lives. I'm still not sure he has started his yet though," says Wikett with a smirk on his face.

"All the way from Oklahoma to Oregon for a rodeo. Was it fun?"

Wikett laughs and says, "One of the best times I've ever had. 'Cept my cousin J.P. is a big Oklahoma Sooner fan so we argued football all the way up there. I just wish I could have found his off button. He talks nonstop."

"Sounds fun."

"Yeah, it was," Wikett continues, "J.P. wouldn't even root for A&M when I was playing there, except when we played Texas. The one thing we did agree on was our hatred of the Longhorns."

"That'll be enough of that," Rance Patton, the University of Texas grad returns. He then asks, "Did you ever think about trying to kick in the NFL back then? I remember that year you beat us with a fifty-two yarder with seven seconds left. I was in high school and the girl I was dating, she was an Aggie fan and we had a bet. I lost."

"No, that kicking really got to my nerves," Wikett replies.

"Got to your nerves? You're kidding me," says Patton. "And now you're following a guy in an eighteen-wheeler from El Paso to L.A. that may have enough explosives in it to kill over a million people."

"Yeah! At least now I ain't got that million people yelling and hollering and screaming at me. Cheering and calling me a hero when I make a winning kick," Wikett replies, "or, that same million people yelling and screaming at me, calling me a zero when I miss that kick and lose the game. A kick of a stupid little brown ball with white strips that you can buy at any Wal-Mart for twenty bucks, and in a game that isn't anything more than just entertainment."

"Dang Chief, you sound a little sour there."

"No Rance, not at all. I just got things put into perspective the five years I was overseas. You go live and work in third world countries and see how those people live, and our little Saturday and Sunday afternoon football games don't mean much."

"I guess I can see what you mean, Chace. It still surprises me that your nerves got to you the way you kicked in college," Patton ponders, "Especially in the game against us."

"Rance, in college I had a special team's coach who would run up and quote FDR to me right before every big kick," Wikett replies. "He would always say, 'The only thing we have to fear is fear itself.' Well, that worked playing football. But you know when I was overseas, it didn't work then."

Patton thinks for a moment as he absorbs what Wikett has just told him. "I guess I can see what you mean. I guess that had to be a lot more nerve wracking than being a field goal kicker."

"Yeah, when you miss a kick you don't end up in a body bag, or some shallow grave where your family doesn't know where you are," Wikett replies seriously.

"I don't know how you did the stuff you did over there."

"It wasn't any different than what we're doing here, except right now we don't have the ball."

"I think that's the part that's different. We're playing defense now.

You were playing offense overseas," Patton says.

"No, Rance. We, the United States were playing defense over there, just in an offensive way. A way we need to get back to so we don't have to do the kind of crap we're doing right now. If that guy the people voted into the White House would get serious and quit worrying about trying to please everyone with every belief on the globe, you and I would find it a lot easier to do our jobs," Wikett pauses, "And now it looks like we're going to get another one in the White House just like him."

"Yeah, it does," Patton returns as he looks down to check the fuel gage to see how much gas they have in the tank of the Escalade.

"Hey, did you vote before we left Dallas?"

"Yes!" Patton answers, "I always try to send in an absentee ballot early just in case something like this happens. I know who I'm going to vote for these days, as clear cut as the choices are. In fact, the way I see it, those people who don't know who they're voting for up until the last minute in today's political environment, they have no business voting anyway. Sometimes I wonder if we don't need another 9/11 just to straighten half this nation out again."

Agent Wikett raises his eyebrows and looks over at Patton. "Excuse me?"

"I know, that's not too smart for me to say, is it? Not with who we are following. But you know what I mean."

"Rance, you know we don't need another 9/11," Wikett says as he feels his cell phone vibrate. "I do agree that a lot of people sure were quick to forget the last one though."

The two men continue traveling down I-10 in silence for a couple miles as Chace Wikett checks a text message he has just received from his daughter and sends one back to her.

"Did you vote before we left?" Patton asks.

"I didn't get a chance the way we were called out yesterday. This will be the first time I haven't voted since turning eighteen," Wikett replies. "Not unless there is some sort of a miracle and we get home by Tuesday."

"Really? I'm surprised you didn't vote absentee."

"I should have," Wikett breaths a big sigh as he thinks about what he is missing this weekend at home in the Metroplex. "In fact I usually do. This year with my daughter's sixteenth birthday and all, I had no intentions of being gone."

As the two men travel westward on Interstate 10 in the early hours of the morning, with the presence of night less than an hour away from giving way to light and to another day, Chace Wikett pictures in his mind for a few moments what he is going to miss on this day in Texas. His daughter's birthday party is this afternoon in the family's forty-two hundred square foot house in Arlington. Chace and his wife have bought their daughter a little red Ford Mustang with only twenty-one thousand miles on it and he had hoped to be able to surprise her with it this afternoon. Instead he will just have to watch the video when he gets home. It saddens him as he reminisces about how he watched her first birthday on video also. That time because he was in Somalia. *A lot of good that did,* he thinks.

Looking in the rear view mirror to see if he can spot Swanson and Garcia, Wikett's mind goes to how he had also planned on taking his two sons to watch Dallas play Washington this weekend. He has three tickets to the Cowboys game on Sunday afternoon that Jerry Jones personally gave him. *Those are big sacrifices even if you are out trying to save the nation,* the FBI Chief Investigative Detective thinks.

As Agent Wikett is still in deep thought, Patton breaks the silence, "'The only thing we have to fear is fear itself.' I kinda like that, Chief. I had heard it before, but never really ran it through my mind much until now. It does have a good ring to it. Very true also."

"No it's not, Rance! It's not true at all," Wikett replies seriously, "I would say it might be one of the enemy's greatest lies ever. No, it is the enemy's greatest lie. Think about it!"

"OK," Patton replies curiously knowing his boss often looks at things in a completely different light than most. "Where are you going with this?"

"It sounds so good you just think it has to be true. Yet nothing could be further from the truth. And the man who made that statement famous, Franklin Delano Roosevelt, was obviously not familiar with what is written in the Word of God, the Bible. If he was, he didn't understand it. In Proverbs it says the fear of the Lord is the beginning of knowledge."

"Ok, I think I see where you are going with this. Makes sense."

"Rance, I learned this best overseas when I was faced with truly difficult circumstances that most people never face," Wikett states. He then asks, "Who are the most dangerous people we ever have to face in what we do as FBI agents for this country?"

Keeping his eyes focused on the highway he is driving on, Patton pauses to really think about Wikett's question. Rance then says, "Right now in this day and age of terrorism, the most dangerous criminals we face would be the ones who have no fear of dying." Patton pauses again for a moment, "I'd say like the Islamic terrorists we are following."

"That's right Rance, fear can be a good thing."

"Well Chief, you really tore up my view of that quote."

"Yeah," says Wikett, "I know I sorta went on a bit of a tangent there. But what my kicking coach used to tell me is something I like to call one of those, 'Nine parts truth' statements. That is, the best lies are nine parts truth. We as humans are so afraid and fearful of so many things we shouldn't be afraid of. And we know it. So then, when someone comes along and tells us we should not be fearful of anything, we buy it. Fear is a very good thing Rance, especially when the consequences are life and death."

"I see what you mean. I agree," Rance replies. "Fear of the Lord is the beginning of knowledge. I remember that from church."

"After you fear the Lord and truly come to know Him, then that is when you have nothing to fear," says Wikett.

Wikett, Patton and four other men who all work for the FBI have been tracking an eighteen-wheeler ever since they caught up with it on the north side of El Paso, Texas. There, the truck pulled off of I-10 into a large abandoned warehouse behind a truck stop. After only five minutes inside the warehouse, the truck then pulled out of the warehouse and to the truck stop where the federal agents were able to watch the eighteen-wheeler take on two Arab passengers who had entered the U.S. through a tunnel just west of El Paso. The tunnel runs underneath the Rio Grande River, and it was dug by Mexican drug lords to smuggle drugs and illegal immigrants into the United States.

A covert federal agency that is not publicly known, a shirtsleeve operation of the CIA, had tracked the two Arab men for the past three weeks since they left Yemen and entered Mexico through Guatemala. Chace Wikett spent five years of his life working for that covert agency overseas. It is not known if the two terrorist suspects and the driver are the only ones in the truck. Federal agents do not have an explanation for why the truck went through the warehouse behind the truck stop. A complete search of the old building was done by the FBI and the owners of the building after the eighteen-wheeler left the truck stop, and no evidence was found of anything inside the warehouse being disturbed. The floor inside was very dusty with no footprints of any kind, only the tracks of the truck driving through.

The eighteen-wheeler originated in Leesburg, Louisiana and is being driven by Roddy Dale Eddison, a man the FBI has had on a watch list for the last couple of years. The last three months there has been no periodic surveillance of Eddison because of federal budgetary cutbacks that have spread the FBI terrorism division too thin. Authorities were tipped off to pick up Eddison's trail only because he side swiped a road sign, knocking it completely down and running over it as he pulled out of an Allsup's convenience store leaving Sonora, Texas, one hundred and fifty miles west of San Antonio.

A little old Mexican woman working the night shift at Allsup's called the local police with the license plate number and truck description. The local police then ran a check on the plates and contacted the Texas State Highway Patrol, who in turn contacted the FBI.

The State Patrol kept a close trail on the truck's journey from Sonora to El Paso where the FBI could take over. Roddy Dale Eddison has been a fixture in a Louisiana chapter of the KKK for years. But in the previous six to eight months, he had been behaving even more radically in his hatred for one minority group in particular, the Jews. On his own, Eddison has gone outside of the KKK to form new connections with a number of Muslims living in and around the New Orleans area. It is very odd to have someone with KKK connections consorting with those in the Arab and Islamic communities, but Roddy Dale Eddison is a very odd man.

From what the various Federal agencies, the FBI, ATF and DHS can make of the situation, Eddison is playing the role of a pawn. Roddy Dale is not a stable person, mentally or emotionally. The report on him reads that when he gets an idea into his psyche he does not care what the consequences of his actions are to himself or to others; he just acts on it. Many who know Eddison feel it is very possible that he is not just a rebel and potential criminal, but someone possessed. Either way, he stands out as someone who is a serious danger to the people around him, including the terrorist suspects from Yemen.

Being the first time they had ever seen the KKK man from Louisiana, the two Muslim extremists have no idea what kind of a loose cannon they are riding with. Whereas they may be potential suicide bombers, Eddison is simply a ticking time bomb waiting to go off. This makes the three of them very strange and dangerous bedfellows.

After being tipped off that Eddison had left his home area and was driving westward across the Lone Star state, the federal law enforcement community led by agent Wikett began to piece together bits and pieces of incomplete information they already had. The information was gathered from individuals the FBI has embedded in the KKK and in numerous Islamic terrorist sleeper cells worldwide. Putting this information together with a lead the FBI already had from a covert arm of the CIA, Wikett was able to come to the conclusion that Eddison was heading to the El Paso area to pick up the two Arabs coming in from Yemen through Old Mexico. Wikett and five other FBI agents took a plane to El Paso to catch up with Eddison's trail.

A decision not to apprehend Eddison and the pair of Islamic terrorist suspects in El Paso was made based on additional slivers of information by those in the Bureau way above FBI agent Chace Wikett and his team. This decision did not sit well with Wikett who feels it is not wise to let known combatants run loose and free within the borders of the United States.

Information gathered by a number of Federal agencies from a number of sources points to a probability that the two men from Yemen are headed to California to help coordinate and carry out an attack at a very heavily attended event. With the massive number of people who live on the West coast of the United States, any number of events—ranging from sporting events, to concerts or political rallies, or even a large Christian church service—could be the intended terror

Wikett believes he knows better ways of handling situations like this. If there is information that will lead to the discovery of other Islamic terrorist cells within our own borders, Agent Wikett knows techniques to extract that information. Techniques the current administration, known to be soft and weak on terror, does not have the intestinal fortitude to carry out. Chace thinks the powers that be have a pie-in-the-sky approach to stopping a potential terrorist attack. He feels it is utterly ridiculous to rely on following three men of very questionable character in the hopes that they will lead to a bigger jackpot many miles down the road, especially when time is quickly running out. Wikett's methods are seen as too aggressive by the current resident of the White House, who prefers a kinder and gentler approach which will be seen in a better light by other nations around the world.

With the eighteen-wheeler rapidly closing in on the second largest population center in America, Wikett knows a decision needs to be made very quickly whether to continue tracking the suspicious individuals in an attempt to be led to other Islamic terrorists, or to pull the truck over, apprehend the three men and begin an interrogation session. Either way the consequences could be catastrophic. *The ifs and buts in the business of fighting terrorism far outnumber the sure things,* Wikett thinks to himself. *Kicking a field goal to win an NFL game might not really have been all that bad after all.* In issues such as potential terrorist attacks and dealing with this kind of danger, individuals who fight terrorism sometimes have to go with their hunches and rely on half truths. It is not a fun game, especially when someone guesses wrong and someone else pays the price.

"Tell me again, Chace why we've followed these guys all the way across Arizona and this far into California without any help?" FBI agent Patton asks with a touch of sarcasm in his voice.

Wikett laughs briefly. "I'd like to think it is because the guy running the show in California knows we can handle it. But my guess is he's spread too thin because of the budget cuts to send his own people to help."

"I'd have thought they would've at least been at the California border to meet us."

"I'm sure Kennedy doesn't consider that it's actually California until you get to where the population starts," Wikett says. "You know... where the voters are."

"That makes sense," Patton replies. "Well not to me, but to them, I suppose."

"Rance, this whole operation is like playing Russian roulette with two different guns loaded by someone else," Wikett states. "With one gun being completely empty and the other gun fully loaded. We're in a life or death situation and we have to depend on someone with a very sketchy and suspicious character."

"I think they're slowing down," Patton observes

Wikett quickly calls the members of his FBI team in pursuit with him to discuss the options they may face if the truck they are following does exit. They are still over forty miles from where they are to join forces with federal officials from the west coast in this high stakes game of cat and mouse. Something inside of Agent Wikett tells him not to let this eighteen-wheeler and its occupants get any closer to the City of Angels. Two reasons come to his mind. The immediate danger posed by the truck and its occupants, and the fact that in less than an hour a very different man than himself will be calling the shots, a politically correct liberal from California. The final decisions on what actions the federal government will take to stop the threat our country currently faces are going to be in the hands of a man Chace knows has been handpicked by the current U.S. President, a President known to be sympathetic to Muslim extremists.

After he discusses the options with his team, Wikett decides that if an opportunity presents itself to take control of the tractor-trailer without endangering any innocent bystanders, they will do just that. From there the six Texas men will find a location to begin an interrogation that Wikett knows will work if there is any valuable information to be retrieved from Roddy Dale Eddison and the two men from Yemen.

The techniques Wikett will use may not be the type approved of by the politically appointed man only a short distance up the road. These techniques are not for the faint of heart, but they are techniques agent Wikett knows will work in a hurry. In this case, time is not on the side of the people of California. *How ironic,* Chace thinks to himself, *we are in one of the most liberal states in the U.S., very near the liberal mecca of Hollywood, and the supposed torture techniques the rich and famous celebrities of Southern California so hate and despise, may be the very actions that save them and their city.*

Not really wanting to, Wikett pulls up the number for Bart Kennedy on his phone and pushes the send button. Informing Kennedy, the FBI lead investigator on the West Coast is something he has to do, but something Chace is not comfortable with. Wikett and Kennedy have completely different philosophies on most everything. Wikett earned his way to where he is in the Bureau, whereas Kennedy has been given his position.

Wikett's phone rings a number of times with no answer. Chace informs the five agents listening over the radio system, "Well guys, this one is riding on me. We're doing it Texas style. I just wish we'd have done it back in El Paso."

"Yeah," replies Agent Garcia, one of Wikett's closest friends. "It sure would have saved us a lot of windshield time."

"There they go," Patton informs Wikett. "They just hit their right blinker. They're heading for the off ramp. Billy Joe just went past the exit, better tell Trey."

"Trey, they're exiting," Wikett tells Craddick over the radio. "You guys just went past the ramp. We're doing it here and we're doing it my way."

"Good," Craddick replies.

"I ain't handing the ball over to a guy who's just going to kneel on it with the score tied," says Wikett. "Not when we still have time left on the clock."

"That's how we like it, Chief," returns the short African American FBI agent Daniel Trey Craddick, who grew up in the L.A. area. "Guess we won't have time to run by my grandmother's for some cherry pie, will we?"

Wikett ignores Craddick's cherry pie offer as the eighteen-wheeler brakes and slowly veers to the right towards the exit ramp. The two FBI vehicles following a few hundred yards back pick up speed to catch up.

"I'll live or die with this decision," Wikett states, "If I have to."

Continuing west on I-10 in a new burgundy Lexus, Billy Joe

Gasperson shakes his head and laughs at little Craddick and his grandmother's cherry pie comment as the two of them look for a place to make a u-turn through the median so they can return to where the action is most likely to take place.

"Guys we're going have to play this by ear. Let's just see where they go. I don't think we're going to be able to get to 'em on the ramp," Wikett says over an FBI radio system the agents now all have turned on. "I don't want any of 'em dead. I can't make a dead man talk."

"You can't?" says one of the agents listening over the encrypted FBI radio.

"No, I've tried it," returns Wikett. "It doesn't work."

There is nervous laughter heard over the FBI radio system.

"Be careful, we're not gonna have much time once Kennedy's guys figure this out. Let's make it count."

"I bet they're heading to that store. This might be easier than we thought," Agent Patton allows as he watches the truck now a few vehicles ahead of him with its right rear blinker flashing.

"Don't ever think it's going to be easy Rance, never! That's when accidents happen. Even if we do have them out numbered two to one," Wikett informs the younger and less experienced federal agent. "Plus, I don't like the store—too many people. I don't want any innocent bystanders killed this morning."

Rolling up the exit ramp off of I-10, Wikett looks down at his cell phone that has just started vibrating. It's Bart Kennedy calling him back. Chace answers the call, "Hello."

"This is Kennedy. How are things, Wikett?"

"The truck is exiting here at exit 146. I think we should take it now. We're getting way too close to L.A. for comfort."

"Absolutely not! You're in California now. You follow it until it stops somewhere. I'm headed your way. Those are orders from Washington, Wikett."

"OK," Wikett says as he gets off the phone. He continues over the FBI radio, "You guys get that? We are back to following these guys."

The other agents listening over the radio acknowledge they have heard him.

"Letting known terrorists run all over this nation of ours is bullshit," Wikett says with a tone of anger in his voice, "It's a joke just following them around like Andy Griffith and Barney Fife. Hoping they make a mistake before we do is dangerous as hell. We'll be lucky if someone doesn't get killed doing things this way. I don't know if this country can survive four more years of weak liberal policies like this."

Driving the Cadillac Escalade, Patton smiles and in unison Agents Swanson and Craddick proclaim, "Chace Wikett for President!" A little of the tension of this dangerous situation is lifted as the early morning sun is now just starting to peek out over the edge of the horizon to the east above the Sonoran Desert.

As the trailing FBI agents are trapped at a stop sign, the semi pulls past the little convenience store. Patton says, "Chace! I think they're headed over to that motel."

"Dang it guys! Something tells me we may not have them outnumbered after all," Wikett says over the FBI radio system. "I have a feeling this ain't gonna be fun."

CHAPTER TWELVE

Scampering squirrels

Panicked that her fingerprints are all over the magazine just purchased by the Middle Eastern man, Alexia knows she must come up with a way to get the magazine out of his hands, and fast. But as she watches him turn away from the counter of the airport snack shop, her mind is blank. She cannot think of anything.

The Islamic man begins to walk in Alexia's direction. He looks straight at her. Remembering the advice Severo had given her earlier about confronting the wolf head on, she gets up and walks right up to him. She has no idea how dangerous he may be.

Fear has always been something Alexia is capable of conquering. Something she even finds herself drawn towards. It has been awhile since she has faced anything really frightening, and never before has she been exposed to what she has come across today. Alexia feels that whatever she is up against, it seems to be bringing out the best in her.

As she walks towards him, Alexia looks directly at the dark skinned, dark eyed man holding the magazine that has her fingerprints all over it. To Alexia's surprise, he looks for a moment as if he wants to turn and run. He doesn't though. Alexia walks to within a couple feet of him, almost into his personal space.

She stares straight into his eyes and says in French, "That's my magazine. I left it there. Give it to me or I will call security."

The Muslim man smiles and asks in very rough French, "Who are you?"

Without blinking, Alexia glares right into his eyes. She tells him in English, "Give me my magazine!"

He moves back away from her a step. "You are very beautiful. Who are you?" He replies in English with an Arabic accent, "I could buy you everything, make you very rich. You could be mine."

Instantly now furious, Alexia completely forgets she might be in a very dangerous situation and gives this man a look she hopes will pierce his very soul, something she actually doubts even exists. Six months ago CCN aired a special on child kidnapping and how many of the victims are young girls who end up as female sex slaves in the oil-rich Middle East. What this man has just said sickens her.

Alexia steps toward him and reaches out and grabs the magazine. She forcefully tells him in English, "You people have no respect for women. You are a pig. Now let me have my magazine!" She begins to pull the folded magazine out of the Muslim man's hand.

This does not sit well with him. He glares back into the beautiful American woman's blue eyes. Before he lets go of the magazine he says very angrily in Arabic, "You western women are all whores. You are only good for one thing!" He then shoves the magazine into Alexia's hand before turning and walking away in anger.

Relieved, Alexia is quite sure he was simply interested in her for her body and not because he was suspicious of her. Alexia knows the pig comment served to freeze his desire. *A personal crisis has been diverted for the moment*, she thinks as her arms now begin to tremble with fear of what she has just encountered. Walking straight into the face of danger has worked, and she now has the fingerprint-covered magazine in her possession.

Alexia watches as the Islamic man walks away carrying the larger of the two black attaché cases. He is headed down the concourse toward the tall gray haired man, who is sitting with the small laptop still open. He appears to be waiting to board a flight, but with what has been going on, Alexia has no idea if this man is really going to get on a plane or not. He seems to have all his attention focused on the open laptop.

Walking at a fast pace, the man from the Middle East quickly approaches him. Just as he is about to walk past him, the gray haired gentleman looks up from the small laptop computer. He stares directly at the Arab. The Muslim man never breaks stride. He does turn his head slightly in the other man's direction as he walks past him. The CCN broadcast journalist knows she has to be witnessing some sort of high-stakes game of espionage. After passing where the gray haired gentleman sits in front of gate 13A, the Muslim man continues to walk until he is in front of gate 10A where he stops, looks back and then walks over to the window and stands staring out over the tarmac.

With her mind completely focused on what she is watching, Alexia is suddenly startled when she is tapped on the shoulder. Just as she feels the gentle touch, Alexia sees out of the corner of her eye a girl that has approached her from the side. Alexia's first thought is that it must be the young Middle Eastern flight attendant who is still very much on the forefront of her mind. To her surprise, it is not.

As she turns her head, Alexia sees it is a very beautiful young woman about twenty years old.

Alexia is completely stunned for a moment as she thinks she is looking at a younger version of herself. The girl who has boldly walked right up to Alexia Klien is tall, young, and very attractive with long dark black hair. Alexia has never seen her before, unless it was fifteen years ago looking into a mirror. The striking resemblance of the girl to herself has Alexia Klein momentarily stunned.

———

As Clarice Hall gets off the phone with her sister-in-law Martha Jo, she says a short prayer for Sharice and her sons. As she thinks about what she has just heard from Martha Jo about the Muslims who are chanting Islamic prayers in the motel and the email she received this morning from her son Turner P. in Kuwait, Clarice heads outside to find her husband Gene and fill him in on what seems to be an unusual and scary coincidence.

A veteran of over three decades of U.S. Military service, but now retired, Gene Hall still sees protecting and defending his country as one of his main duties in life. He is an African American man in his late sixties, and if the government would let him, he would climb right back into a Humvee and head straight into the middle of any war zone where the U.S. is engaged in battle. Gene has been known to take action whenever he sees something happen in the States that does not line up with what he deems as right and wrong. Most people would call him crazy for intervening in bad situations in Atlanta as an old man. Gene has personally broken up fights, and even stopped a couple of robberies in the years since the military determined him too old to serve.

On this Saturday morning, Gene has been up since daybreak

working around the outside of his house getting ready for the severe drop in temperatures that is forecast to hit the Atlanta area in the next two days. He hopes to finish before noon everything he didn't get done last weekend to winterize the Hall family home. Gene has plans to settle down and watch a little—actually a lot—of college football this afternoon with a couple of old friends and maybe a grandson or two on his new 72-inch high-definition television in the sports room that takes up most of the walkout basement of the very well kept two-story brick home. It's a nice sized brick house built into the side of a small hill on an extra-large lot in a beautiful wooded area on the south edge of Atlanta.

Clarice walks out the back door and onto the redwood deck built directly over the French doors that open to Gene's sports room in the basement. She hopes to hear her husband rustling around somewhere at the back of the house, but hears nothing. With a stronger than normal breeze coming out of the northwest, Clarice thinks that the cold front might get here sooner than the weather channel said. She looks around and doesn't see anything of her husband. She does see some squirrels scampering around through the leaves on the ground by the back fence, and then as they see Clarice on the deck they climb quickly up the side of a big oak tree frightening a flock of brown thrashers and some bluebirds into flight.

"Gene! Are you out here workin'?" Clarice hollers.

"Yeah, Honey," Gene answers back from a lawn chair he is sitting in directly underneath the deck where Clarice is standing. "I'm just sittin' down here taking a little break. Been watchin' all the wild life we have livin' in our back yard. It's really quite wonderful seeing God's little creatures scurrying all around."

Clarice walks to the edge of the deck and leans out over the railing. In a nervous and anxious voice, she tells her husband of almost fifty years, "Gene, you need to get up here right now. Martha Jo and Sharice might be in some kind of trouble."

"What kind of trouble can they be in over there in Louisiana, Miss Clarice?" Gene asks without moving from his favorite old outdoor chair. The wooden recliner doesn't match anything else in their back yard, but every time Clarice threatens to get rid of it, Gene says, "If that chair goes, I go."

"Honey, they got 'em some Muslims there in that motel that been chantin' and chantin' them Islamic Jihadist prayers for two days now," She yells down to him. "Sharice is scarred they might try and blow up a bomb at the boys game tonight."

"Oh dog-gone-it, Honey!" Gene yells as he tries to get his worn out body up and out of his worn out chair. "I better get a hold of George Thompson."

"That would be good. What's he doing now?" Clarice asks from atop of the deck, "Is he still in the CIA?"

"I think he's out of it now. But his sons are still in, I think," Gene says. "I ain't talked to him in a year or so. But he'll know what to do."

Out of his chair, Gene finds a new surge of energy and runs up the flight of wooden stairs leading to the redwood deck as though he's in his teens again, skipping every other step. From the edge of the deck, his sweet wife stares out into the trees at the scampering squirrels and the birds now starting to return to the oak tree.

"Where are George and Margret living now?" Clarice asks.

"I think they're back in upstate New York."

"That's good."

"Where are my reading glasses?" Gene asks Clarice as he passes by her and heads into the house to look up George Thompson's phone number in the little green address book he purchased almost a half a century ago at a PX in Germany when he was just a Private. It contains the addresses and phone numbers of many of the men he served with during his years in the United States Military.

———

After Martha Jo gets off the phone with Clarice, she hurries her way out of Ol' Sims Wilson's gas station without even saying thanks or goodbye. He is at the cash register making change for a little boy whose bicycle tire he just fixed. Quite often if Ol' Sims likes a kid, he will give them all their money back in different bills than they gave him. Sometimes even more money if the kid is real little. Ol' Sims Wilson's heart is bigger than Texas.

"Remember our date tonight," he calls out as Martha Jo heads through the open glass door of his service station. Ol' Sims laughs and shakes his head as he says to himself, "I just love that woman."

With her heart racing, partly because this is the fastest and the farthest she has run in years, and partly because of the fear she feels from Clarice's news of the Islamic attack in Kuwait, Martha Jo makes it across the street and back to the motel faster than she ever has.

Sharice is cleaning rooms on the second floor of the little old rundown motor inn. When Martha Jo reaches the stairwell leading up to the second level, she cannot go any further. She has to stop and turn around to sit down on the bottom step. She has a terrible pain in her chest like she has never felt before. She feels like she can't get any air in her lungs. Martha Jo fears she might be having a heart attack. She bows her head while sitting slumped on the first step of the stairwell and says a quick prayer for her own health and for the safety of Sharice's boys.

Within a few seconds of sitting and relaxing on the exterior stairs of the dilapidated Motor Inn #16, Martha Jo is able to make it up to the second floor where Sharice is cleaning the bathtub in room number 212. Martha steps into the little bathroom, which is hardly big enough for the two of them. She tells Sharice what her sister-in-law Clarice has told her about what happened in Kuwait earlier in the day. Sharice gets up off her knees and throws her wet soapy sponge into the water-stained sink.

"I been thinkin' about it," Sharice says. "I should call that guy I know who's a policeman from up there in Shreveport."

"You better get over there to Ol' Sims and do that right now," Martha Jo tells her, "And don't let Mr. Zahrani know what you're doin'."

"OK," returns Sharice.

"You get goin', girl. I got this room. Get now."

Without wasting any time, Sharice does just as Martha Jo tells her.

When she bursts through the front door of the Ol' Sims gas station, he asks, "What's going on? Why's you in such a hurry, Sharice?"

Sharice quickly fills Ol' Sims in on what is happening as she looks through the contact list in her cell phone for the number of the guy from Shreveport that she had gone out on a few dates with in the past two years. She steps into the rear of Ol' Sims's gas station and hits the green send button on her phone to call Edward Jefferson, a police officer from Shreveport, Louisiana.

The phone rings in her ear six or seven times and then quits ringing. There is a moment of silence before a recorded message says, "You have reached Officer Edward Jefferson's personal cell phone. Please leave your name number and a message. If you have an emergency, please call 911."

Sharice very nervously speaks into her phone, "Eddie, this is Sharice Jones down here in Baton Rouge. And, ah, I think we might have some real bad men here in the motel. They's some of them Muslim Islamic terrorists, I think. I am scared for my boys' ballgame tonight. I didn't know who to call. Please call me back, Eddie."

Off her phone, Sharice thanks Ol' Sims for the use of his back room. He picks up a Snickers candy bar and offers it to her as she passes by headed to the door. Sharice shakes her head no and says back to him with some spice in her voice, "Sims, you know I'm on a diet, you are a bad man sometimes."

Ol' Sims just smiles and then tells her as she is leaving, "Oh Sharice, you is just perfect the way you is... and so is Miss Martha Jo."

As she waits out in front of the gas station to make her way back across the street to the motel, there is traffic coming from both directions. Suddenly Sharice's phone rings. She stops on the edge of the roadway to dig her cell phone out of the front pocket of her wellworn blue jeans to see if it is Edward Jefferson calling her back already. As she stands there, with vehicles approaching from each direction, she sees that the second car turning onto this suddenly busy side street off of Highway 16 is her boss's car.

Shahid al-Zahrani pulls his black Mercedes Benz right up to where Sharice stands. He then stops. She goes ahead and opens her cell phone to see if it is Eddie's number on the caller ID. It is. Her Saudi Arabian boss glares at her through the darkly tinted windows of his ninety-five thousand dollar car. Looking right at him, Sharice Jones answers her phone.

CHAPTER THIRTEEN

The Oil-Rich Middle East

It is barely the first light of day. Chace Wikett rolls down his window to get a little fresh air as the Cadillac Escalade he and Rance Patton are driving slows down for a stop sign at the end of an exit ramp. The air is cool with a touch of moisture and very welcomed. Over an hour east of L.A. the only people out this time of the morning are either those who have been up way too late, or the early birds on their way to work.

Waiting at the stop sign directly behind Agents Wikett and Patton are John Swanson and Tony Garcia. These two very competent and experienced bureau men are in a tan Ford Excursion. The eighteen-wheeler they have been following on I-10 for fifteen hours through three states proceeds past the small convenience store and heads towards an old abandoned three-story motel. The motel is dirty white, with faded yellow and brown trim along its gutters and the railings.

Patton looks over to Wikett and jokingly asks, "Do you think they're gonna get a room?"

"I'm afraid they may already have one," returns Wikett. "Or, all of them."

In the dark shadows on the north side of the motel, the unstable KKK clansman Roddy Dale Eddison brings his blue Freightliner to a stop. For the first time since the Leesburg, Louisiana man left a warehouse just outside of El Paso, the truck with the two Islamic terrorists aboard is out of the sight of the Texas FBI agents.

Now nearly two miles west of exit 146, Agents Gasperson and Craddick come to a paved spot in the middle of I-10 where they can make a u-turn through the muddy median and loop back around into the eastbound traffic. Hoping to get back to where the action will take place before it is too late, Craddick says over the FBI radio, "We're headed back your way, Chace."

Wikett worries that Gasperson and Craddick are going to be a minute or two late to the party if something breaks loose immediately. He is already shorthanded in this operation due to cutbacks in the funding of national security by the current administration.

"I don't like this," Wikett states. "I don't like any part of it."

"It's sure going to be dark back there," Patton adds.

The FBI agents are trapped at a red light about a block and a half away from the entrance to the old motel. In front of Wikett and Patton at the light is a big black Dodge pickup truck with very dark tinted windows and a customized California license plate that reads, LTSBRN1.

Rance starts to say what he thinks the letters stand for when Wikett cuts him off. "Lets burn one."

"How'd you get that so fast?"

"See the sticker of the marijuana leaf in the back window?"

The time Wikett has to wait for the light to turn green is about to kill him. He has a strong suspicion something is not right about this situation. He just cannot put his finger on exactly what it is.

Agent Wikett's biggest fear is that this old run down abandoned motel could possibly be filled with Islamic terrorists. *Why would a viable piece of property in California in this prime location just be sitting here vacant?* He wonders.

The motel sets right alongside I-10 which makes it very improbable it would be someplace used by Islamic terrorists to live and plan their works of evil and hate. If that is the case though, it would mean this location would have slipped past the eyes of the Department of Homeland Security, the FBI, and other federal agencies, as well as local and state police. But sometimes the best place to hide is in plain sight.

The traffic light turns green and the silence of the morning is interrupted with the roar of the engine of the Dodge pickup in front of Wikett and Patton. Laying down two black strips of rubber on the street, the truck speeds away. It leaves a heavy haze of blue smoke smelling like rubber in the middle of the intersection. The smoke drifts slowly towards the little convenience store as the noise of the

Cummins diesel engine disappears with the black truck.

"Chace, do you want to run that guy down and give him a ticket for noise and air pollution?" Patton says as he begins to pull through the smoke still lingering in the air.

"It'd be safer than what we're about to do I'm afraid," Wikett answers.

"But not as rewarding," adds Patton.

"It sure looks like it could start raining anytime now," Garcia says over the radio as he and Swanson drive through the green light right behind Patton and Wikett.

"Yeah Gratcio, the clouds are getting heavier too," Wikett uses the nickname he gave Garcia in college.

With Eddison's eighteen-wheeler out of sight for more than a minute now, Wikett turns and looks back trying to catch a glimpse of Agents Craddick and Gasperson. He asks over the radio, "Trey, you guys make it off I-10 yet?"

"Yeah, we're on the exit ramp. But there's three trucks in front of us."

"He's pulled in behind an old motel right off the westbound exit," Wikett says. "We can't see 'em right now. They're on the northwest side of the building where it's still dark."

"And getting darker," states Swanson.

As Patton turns the dark blue Cadillac Escalade into the virtually vacant motel parking lot, he and Wikett notice a large real estate sign that reads, *For Sale by James Brothers Commercial Properties.* Underneath the name is bolted a smaller sign that reads, *Sold.* Only a couple of old rundown vehicles sit out in front of the old motel. One is a big black Lincoln Continental that's at least twenty-five years old, and the other is a gray work van. Both are parked about halfway between the partially boarded-up motel office and the empty swimming pool, which sets right in the bend of the L shaped building.

Slowly and very carefully, Agents Patton and Wikett follow the same path the semi-truck just took around to the northwest side of the large spread-out building. Swanson and Garcia drive at an equally cautious pace around to the southwest side of the old motel.

The federal law enforcement officers all keep in coordinated contact on their radios as they circle around the ends of the motel. As

Patton and Wikett round the northeast corner they can see through the early morning darkness the locked doors on the back end of the big white reefer trailer. Patton brings the Escalade to a stop. Eddison's Freightliner truck has been out of the FBI's sight now for over three minutes.

In the early morning shade on the west side of the abandoned motel, Swanson and Garcia drive very slowly. When they are able to see the front of the hood of blue semi-truck tractor the crazy Cajun has driven halfway across the United States, they stop.

"Tony, can you or Swanny see anything up there?" Wikett asks.

"No, just the front of the truck. Dark as it is, this whole thing is quite ghostly if you ask me," returns Garcia.

"Dang, I don't like this," says Wikett. "Trey, you guys make it over here yet? We really need your eyes on the other side of this building."

Raw tension is at its peak as the FBI agents do not know for sure what is to come next. The truck and trailer look like something out of a nightmare in the darkness of the early morning shadows behind the large abandoned motel. Not knowing where Eddison and the two Muslim men are seriously worries Agent Wikett.

———

Rigger Watson sits in his office alone. He has a plan he must put into action. Once it is started, it cannot be stopped. When his plan is completed, Watson knows he will be able to turn the tide of public opinion surrounding the predicament that the gay campaign manager, Mike Swenson has thrust upon the man he works for. Rigger knows it will take something drastic to spin the news of the careless homosexual's lifestyle in a way that will help Senator Walter Franson and the entire Democratic Party.

Knowing how fickle so much of America's population is, Rigger laughs to himself and says, "It helped Michael Jackson's popularity. It should help us."

Watson's plan is one that only the most ruthless would ever even consider using, something that must be handled by someone with absolutely no connections to either Senator Franson or to Watson himself. A plan completely against the laws of state and nation, and against the unwritten laws of man.

Watson calls Shirley Hienz over his private intercom system. "I need to have you get a hold of Brandt and send him in here. I need to talk to him."

"Do you want me to get Terry also?" Hienz asks her boss and lover.

"Did I say I wanted to talk to Telleson?" Watson fires back at her.

"OK, I'll get Brandt immediately."

Rigger then reaches down and unlocks the bottom left-hand drawer of his mahogany desk. He reaches in and finds a cell phone he keeps locked in that drawer. He then buzzes his personal secretary Ms. Murphy, whose office sets directly in front of the entrance to his office. He tells her that no one is to be allowed into his office until he notifies her otherwise.

With the rather plain-looking black cell phone he has just taken out of the locked drawer, Rigger Watson, President and CEO of CCN, a man who has complete oversight of the programming and editorial tone of the largest and most influential news network in the United States, maybe the entire world, places a call to a man in New York City. The cell phone is untraceable.

———

"Hi! You're Alexia Klien!" the very excited American girl says as Alexia stands there in a slightly stunned state, "I just love you. You may not believe this, but I have always known I would someday meet you."

Alexia stands speechless.

"My name is Amaya Dawn Blazi. I did my senior paper on you last spring for English. I'm from New Mexico, from Roswell, New Mexico... Wow, I never thought I'd see you here in Paris today."

Before replying, Alexia cautiously examines the girl who has startled her by boldly approaching her and tapping her on the shoulder. "It's nice to meet you... Amaya? Did I say that right?"

"Yes, yes you did," says the tall, dark haired beauty from New Mexico. Still quite giddy, Amaya continues, "This is so incredible. I cannot believe this. God is so wonderful. It's amazing to get to meet the woman I have so admired and looked up to all through high school."

Amaya pauses and Alexia doesn't say anything. The young girl continues, "This is so fantastic. Wow, you are so fabulous in person, even more so than on TV. Everyone has always told me how much I look like you. Now I get to meet you."

"It is quite fascinating, to say the least," Alexia says as she is quite taken back by this girl's jubilation. For some reason, the CCN broadcast journalist feels she has to give this girl some of her time.

Alexia has experienced encounters with fans similar to this on numerous occasions. But never anything exactly like this, and never outside of the U.S. while in the middle of such a mysterious and sensitive situation. And this girl seems to be so genuine and excited to have met someone she has obviously looked up to for some time. Alexia is also quite surprised at just how much this girl from Roswell, New Mexico does look almost exactly like a younger version of herself. Same height, same build, same hair color, same eye color, almost the exact same facial features, and even the same voice and emotional expressions. To see them standing there together, a person would obviously think they were sisters separated by only a few years of age. Alexia still looks to be in her late twenties and Amaya Blazi could easily pass for twenty-one or twenty-two.

"I can't wait to call my mom and tell her I've met you."

Alexia is speechless again as she reflects back on her own life and realizes for the first time that she really is a role model for the young women of America. *It is almost spooky how much she does look just like me,* Alexia thinks to herself as she wonders for a second just how this fits into the whole scheme of things today.

The silence is broken as Amaya asks, "Am I holding you up from going somewhere?"

"No, you're not, Amaya. I've got a little time," Alexia says with a smile and a bit of a laugh. "Wow, we do look an awful lot alike."

"We do... that's what everyone has always told me."

"Amaya Dawn? That is such a beautiful name."

"Oh thank you, Miss Klien."

"Oh, please call me Alexia. And your last name, Blazi? Is that right?"

"Yes it is, Miss Klien. I mean Alexia."

"Are you a model?" Alexia asks, now more enthused and open as she takes off her sunglasses. "You've got to be a model. Is that why you are in Paris?"

"Oh, thank you. But no, I'm not a model. Maybe someday," Amaya replies, a little embarrassed. She smiles a sweet and happy smile and with her eyes glistening she responds, "I'm in Paris to meet some distant relatives from Northern Spain. They are part of the Blazi family. I've never met them."

"Really, that sounds interesting," Alexia says as she glances away to see what is going on with the two men she has been watching.

"It should be. My brother is flying in to go with me. He's never met them either."

Alexia returns her attention to her new friend, "How old are you Amaya? I just love that name."

"I'm nineteen."

"Have you ever done any modeling?"

"Not really. Except at the county fair in 4-H in a dress I made myself. It was fun. I think I'd like it."

Keeping eye contact with Amaya, Alexia steps to her right and turns her body so she can see in the direction she had just glanced. The American broadcast journalist then tells Amaya, "I can make some phone calls for you. Maybe open some doors right here in Paris. I know some of the top people in the modeling world. It would be no problem."

Alexia then looks down the concourse at the two men again.

"Oh, that is so nice of you, Miss Klien. I mean Alexia. But I only have three days here in France. My brother is flying in from Kuwait. He's in the Air Force. We are going to meet our family from Spain and try to see all the sights in Paris in just three days."

"You will be busy if you want to see everything in just three days," Alexia says with only half of her attention fixed on what Amaya is saying.

"But I might be interested in meeting some modeling people next year, like in May or June if you could help me then."

Seeing that the two men have not moved at all, Alexia brings her attention back to the tall, slender, gorgeous teenager. "Amaya darling, as beautiful as you are, by June you could be on the cover of Vogue making more money than you ever dreamed of."

"Oh thank you, Miss Klien," Amaya returns, "But.."

"Why would you want to wait six months to meet someone in the modeling industry?"

"Well..." the bright blue-eyed young girl grins and says, "I am in the middle of a one year missionary commitment to Africa. I flew out of Lubbock, Texas just a few weeks after I graduated from High School. This trip to Paris is the first time in six months I have been out of Zimbabwe."

Alexia's eyes widen.

"When I got on that airplane in Lubbock to start my trip to Africa, it was the first time I had ever flown anywhere," Amaya adds.

Alexia stands there absolutely stunned and amazed at what she has just heard come from the lips of this girl she has just met; a beautiful young girl Alexia thought was patterning her life after her own. Not in a thousand years would Alexia Klien have thought that this girl, who looks like she could have everything in the world she wants with her looks, would be giving up an entire year of her life in the deepest and darkest parts of the darkest continent on the face of the earth to be a Christian missionary.

Staring back at Amaya Blazi in absolute astonishment and not knowing what to say next, Alexia wonders to herself why this young girl's answer to her question has affected her so much. Normally only with Severo Baptiste does Alexia ever find herself speechless.

The extended moment of silence lasts long enough that it becomes a little awkward for Amaya, who is waiting for her new friend to say something. Alexia is not affected by the awkwardness. She is in a slight daze with everything she has seen today suddenly racing through her thoughts. The woman at the expensive boutique, Severo's text messages, the Muslim man, the story on the BBC about the scandal with Senator Franson's gay campaign manager, the phone conversation with Severo Baptiste, a plane full of people on their way to Russia, and now this girl who looks like the very mirror image of herself, doing something so unselfish and so un-Alexia-like, being a missionary in Africa. All of this combined with the memory of her grandfather's wise words, and the comment made ten years ago by a Malaysian missionary of how the people in the United States need

Jesus... It is all adding up to more than even Alexia Klien can begin to comprehend.

"Are you OK?" Amaya asks as she can see that Alexia seems to suddenly be a million miles away.

Alexia takes a deep breath and quickly shakes her head back and forth. "Oh, there is so much going on in my life today. I can't even believe it. It's like no other day I've ever experienced."

"Really?" Amaya asks.

"Yes, it's been a mess," Alexia replies. Then without knowing why, she says, "Meeting you though may go down as one of the most incredible things I have ever experienced."

Amaya is quite taken aback by this. She is not sure what to say. She drops down to one knee and reaches into her bag and pulls out a CD. While still kneeling, she gets a purple marker out of her backpack and writes her name and email address on the outside of the CD case. Amaya then stands up and hands the CD to Alexia.

Alexia looks down at the CD after having glanced back over to where the two men she has under surveillance are. Looking up from the CD and the email address, Alexia asks, "Is this a CD of you singing?"

"Yes, some of it," answers Amaya. "Our church made it. I'm singing in like five or six of the songs at the beginning. And then the last two songs on the CD I wrote and sang myself. I put those on the CD myself, too. I hope you like it."

"I'm sure I will."

"I hope they might help you with whatever you're going through today," Amaya says. "I'd love it if you could email me and let me know what you think of the last two songs that I wrote."

Alexia looks back down at the CD. "I will do that. I promise."

"If I don't respond it's because I'll only be able to check my email about once a month. Most of the time for the next six months I will be in the jungle."

Alexia is so impressed with this young woman. Alexia sees something genuine and real in Amaya. Something that gives Alexia hope in a day that only minutes before seemed hopeless.

After looking down at the CD again Alexia looks up and says, "Thank you very much. I will be sure and listen to it as soon as I can.

I am sure I will like it."

As she looks down at her watch, the beautiful young girl, in a bit of a frenzy says, "Oh, I almost forgot. I've got to go meet my brother's flight. It comes in in just five minutes. Then we have to meet up with Mr. James in front of the airport so he can take us to our hotel." Amaya pauses, "Oh Alexia, you should meet Matt James, you'd really like him. I know he already likes you 'cause he said so. He's from Georgia too, just like you. I think Savannah or something like that. He's gorgeous too, just like you."

Looking down the concourse to where the tall gray haired gentleman and the Muslim man still are, Alexia laughs about a good looking man from Savannah, Georgia. She then opens her purse and digs around in it for a pen and something to write on. She pulls out a small tablet, but can't find anything to write with.

Amaya quickly drops to her knee again and opens a side pocket on her pink backpack and pulls out the purple marker that writes in purple ink. She stands back up and hands it to Alexia. "Here is a pen, and you can keep it too. I've got three more just like it. Purple's my favorite color."

"Thanks for the pen. I will keep it with the CD you gave me and cherish them both." Alexia begins to write her email address and cell phone number down on a little slip of paper for Amaya. As she does, she says, "I have really enjoyed meeting you, Amaya."

"Oh, me to... I still can't believe I met you today."

"Meeting you has been a very special thing for me and I don't really know why yet," Alexia says as she continues to write on the slip of paper. "I just know you are a very special person, and I think I should be looking up to you instead of you looking up to me."

"Thank you, Miss Klien."

"Amaya, it makes me very proud to know that such a fine young woman as you has looked up to me as you have grown."

Alexia hands the slip of paper she has just written her personal information on to Amaya. As she takes it, Amaya says, "You really should come with me and meet my brother, and especially Mr. James." As she tells Alexia about Matt James again, Amaya gets a big mischievous smile on her face.

"Oh, I really wish I could," Alexia replies as she smiles just as big. "I am tied up here for just a little while longer and then I've got to get to our studio here in Paris to do some interviews tonight." A mischievous look of her own comes over Alexia's face as she goes on to disclose, "But, you can tell your Mr. Matt James, who I'm quite sure I met earlier today, hello from me."

"Really? I'll have to ask him about that," Amaya says, "I gotta run, it's been great meeting you."

"Get over here girl and give me a hug. We are going to be friends," Alexia tells Amaya. "We are friends. But we're going to be really good friends in the future."

"I hope so," says Amaya as they give each other a big hug like they have known one another forever.

Amaya turns to leave and Alexia stops her, and in a very serious voice Alexia asks, "Wait. Have you seen the movie *Taken*, with Liam Neeson and Maggie Grace?"

"Yes, I have. My dad made me watch it before I left home."

"Good. You be very careful, and we will talk again soon."

They both say goodbye. To her surprise, Alexia fights back tears as the tall, slender girl hurries off through a crowd of people who are disembarking off a flight that has just landed from London.

Trying to get her bearings back after having what she feels for some reason may have been a life-changing experience, Alexia refocuses her attention to the two mysterious men. She cannot see them now because of the large crowd of people coming off the plane. She knows there is no way she will make it to the studio early as Watson wants her to. *He is going to be so pissed. It's a good thing there's an ocean between us,* Alexia thinks. *He is such a jerk when he's mad.* She then says outloud to herself, "Actually, he is a jerk most of the time."

Alexia begins to walk slowly with the flow of the people in the direction of the center of the airport. In just a moment she knows she will be passing by where the gray haired man was sitting when she last saw him using the small laptop. The seat is empty. Alexia stops by a round concrete pillar and waits for the traffic to thin.

As most of the passengers from the London flight pass by her on their way to baggage, Alexia sees the Muslim man with the large black attaché case. He is sitting in a chair in front of gate 10A opening the large briefcase in front of him. Beside him sets the small black laptop. He reaches over and picks up the computer and puts it back into the case. Alexia looks around the concourse. There is no sign of the tall gray haired man anywhere.

With the large briefcase now closed, the man of Middle Eastern descent gets up and walks over to the counter in front of gate 11A. Alexia looks up and sees the flight leaving from that gate is bound for Dubai. After he says something to the man behind the counter, he stands there for a moment and pulls his phone out of the inside pocket of his suit coat. He looks at it like he is reading something, a text or an email Alexia figures. He then walks over and steps to the front of the first class line waiting for gate 11A to open. There are only a few people in the line and no one seems to mind that he has cut ahead of them. It is the practice of many Muslim men to walk to the front of lines and cut ahead of everyone waiting.

Before the door is opened for people to actually board the plane headed to the Middle East, a blond woman about fifty years old approaches the Muslim man. She is carrying the large brown envelope with red letters on it Alexia last saw in the hands of the Arab flight attendant. The Muslim man takes the envelope, opens his black attaché case, and slides the envelope in it next to the small laptop.

With all she has seen today, Alexia wonders if they are even going to check him. He's a Muslim man carrying a briefcase with Islamic symbols all over it, so surely they will pull him out of the line and check him extensively. Gate 11A opens and the people in first class begin to walk forward. The Arab man with the large black attaché case is waved right on into the passenger boarding bridge leading to the airplane.

Questioning what she should do with all she has witnessed today, Alexia turns and begins walking down the concourse to leave the airport. With her mind full of so many thoughts, she steps up her speed from a walk to a jog. As she quickly jogs past a men's restroom, she catches the slightest glimpse of a gray haired man coming out of it. She slows back to a brisk walk but continues in the direction she was going. While walking, she turns her head and looks over her shoulder. Alexia immediately recognizes the gray haired man as the one she has been following. Seeing that he is headed in the opposite direction she is, Alexia stops on the side of the walkway to watch him.

The man walks straight up to the front of gate 8A. He bypasses both lines of people waiting to board a flight, pulls a ticket out of his coat pocket, and quickly shows it to the ticket takers. The security guard steps over in front of him and opens the door leading into the passenger boarding bridge to the plane. Alexia checks the gate information and sees that the plane is bound for Washington D.C.

"You have got to be kidding me," Alexia says to herself as she shakes her head and shrugs her shoulders. She turns and heads back in the direction of the airport exit. *Why should this even surprise me today?* Alexia thinks as she picks up the pace of her walk.

As she breaks into a jog, the CCN broadcast journalist marvels about all she has seen in the airport today. The Muslim man is on a flight heading to Dubai, the financial capital of the oil-rich Middle East, a place Alexia has heard her friend Angie West refer to as the twenty-first century version of Babylon. The other man is on a flight headed to Washington D.C., arguably the power capital of the world, and where she first saw the mysterious woman with Senator Walter Franson. A woman Alexia had first thought was just a high-dollar call girl hired to entertain a man of questionable morals. *Why is the gray haired gentleman who was with the woman this morning now on his way to Washington D.C.?* Alexia wonders as she quickly walks to the airport exit.

CHAPTER FOURTEEN

Renault Citroen C4

Everything is calm and ghostly quiet. There is very little morning light behind the abandoned three-story motel. It is tough to imagine this scene is just a quarter mile off a very busy interstate highway that runs from the Atlantic Ocean to the Pacific.

"We goin' get out?" Patton asks.

"No, let's set for a moment," Wikett replies. He then asks over the radio, "Craddick, Gasperson! You guys over here yet?"

"No. We did get around the trucks," Craddick answers from the Lexus, "But now we're at a red light on the south side of the overpass. I think it's about to turn green."

"Get over here as soon as you can," Wikett says. "I don't like how this is looking."

Chace Wikett has seen and done things bordering on unthinkable overseas. As part of a little-known covert anti-terrorism agency the United States government used extensively over a decade ago, Wikett and fellow FBI agent Tony Garcia were exposed to the most dangerous assignments a federal law enforcement officer can be. That was under an administration that was much more aggressive at battling the forces of evil.

"We're stopped about forty feet from the truck," Garcia lets the other agents know.

"What can you see over there, Tony?" Wikett asks.

"I think I see a light on in the sleeper of the truck," Garcia calls out over the radio.

Patton turns and looks to his boss. "You think we could be so lucky to catch 'em just pulling back here to get some sleep?"

"God, I hope so, Rance," Wikett replies. "That would be a real stroke of luck. But we can't count on it."

"John and Tony, stay where you are. I'm going to go up the off side of the truck. Rance is going up the driver's side," Wikett tells his men as he plots to take the truck and its passengers. "We're gettin' out. Everyone get your weapons ready."

As they slowly and quietly open the doors of the Cadillac Escalade, the California air sweeps in. It is wet and damp, and much darker than Wikett likes. There is no noise at all on the back side of the empty motel.

In the middle of slowly and carefully closing his door, Wikett stops. In a whisper, he asks agent Patton who has already closed his door, "Hey, you hear that?"

Patton stops in his tracks and listens. He then looks over to Chace and quietly says, "Sounds like a car just started."

"Yeah, it's on the other side of the building," Wikett points to a walkway running through the bottom floor of the motel. "Go see what it is."

With his FBI-issued Glock 23 handgun gripped firmly in his right hand, the lanky, athletic Patton quickly and carefully makes his way into the opening that leads to the front of the closed down motel. He can see through the concrete walkway the motel swimming pool with weeds growing up around its four foot high chainlink fence. As Rance reaches the opening to the south of the sixty foot long rectangular tunnel, he slowly looks out past an old pop machine through some cement covered stairs. He can now hear the running car more clearly.

Patton can see gray fumes coming from a car's exhaust two hundred feet to the southwest of where he is standing. His view of the car is obstructed by an old rugged gray van parked between him and the car.

Patton holds his left hand up to cover his mouth and muffle the sounds of his voice, "Chace, there is a black car running. But it's not moving yet."

"Gratcio, get out and see if you can get a better look at the car from your side," Wikett tells Garcia. "See if you can tell who's in it."

Very quickly Garcia slips out of the Ford Excursion he and Swanson have been sitting in. He sprints about fifty feet back to a walkway running through the southwest wing of the L-shaped motel.

He hustles to the east end of the walkway and comes out just behind the motel office. He can now see the black car, "It's an 80's model Lincoln Continental. Chace, it's moving. I can't see the driver. Looks like two people in it though. It's got to be the Arabs."

Patton runs out to the chainlink fence that encircles the swimming pool where he can see the car in full view. "I can see the driver. He's got to be one of the guys from Yemen."

"The guy in the passenger side has black hair," yells Garcia, "He's got to be the other one. You want us to shoot? They're leaving."

"You see a bald guy anywhere?" Wikett asks wondering if Roddy Dale Eddison is also in the big black Lincoln.

"No! No bald guy in sight!" Patton calls out, "The car's leaving. It's heading to the highway!"

Agent Garcia runs about twenty feet out from the entrance of the walkway. He pulls up his handgun and aims it directly at the back tire of the black car now speeding away. "I've got target, Chace! You want me to shoot?"

"Craddick and Gasperson are coming over the overpass!" yells Patton into the radio.

"No! Don't shoot, Tony!" Wikett quickly says in a loud whisper. "Can you see the black Lincoln leaving the motel Billy, Trey?"

"Yeah, we do," Agents Craddick and Gasperson say in unison as they top the crest of the I-10 interstate overpass and are able to see everything they have been listening to through their FBI earpieces.

"Don't let that car out of your sight," Wikett commands.

With one set of lights and a stop sign to navigate and a half a dozen cars coming and going, Craddick and Gasperson see that they will not be able to block the exit of the motel parking lot before the black Lincoln with the suspected Muslim terrorists aboard escapes.

"Chace, we're not going to make the motel exit in time to cut 'em off!" Gasperson states.

"Just don't let 'em get back on I-10!"

———

In an attempt to get to the Paris CCN News studio on time, Alexia hurries out of the Charles de Gaulle International Airport exit into the blinding sunlight. She tries to wave down a taxi as it races on past her.

Standing on the curb looking for another taxi, she is startled when she hears a man's voice from a distance calling her name. Alexia quickly spins around to see who it is.

"Alexia! Alexia Klien," the man says as he walks towards her. "I knew it was you when I saw you on the concourse. You didn't fool me."

Unusually embarrassed, Alexia stands there wishing the taxi she had attempted to flag down would have stopped and she could have avoided this very awkward situation. She knows there is no way out now. She turns and looks back to the traffic passing by her outside of the busy airport. *This is a first,* she thinks. *Not a taxi in sight in front of CDG.*

Alexia then tells herself to be nice to this man who Amaya Blazi has told her is a fine individual.

Making herself do it, Alexia turns and puts on a smile. She knows she doesn't have any extra time to chitchat regardless of how nice this fine looking gentleman from Savannah, Georgia is. As she looks back his way, she sees he is jogging towards her now. In his khaki colored pants and dark blue shirt, he looks like he could be doing a commercial for Calvin Klein, she thinks. It makes her laugh.

"You look to be quite athletic!" Alexia yells to the approaching Mr. Matthew James. Just as he slows down to a walk about ten feet from her, Alexia says, "Amaya told me you were quite charming. But she didn't say you were a runner."

Matt laughs and replies, "Oh yeah, Amaya told me she had met you. She said you were absolutely delicious."

"Are you sure she didn't mean delirious?" Alexia asks with a smile on her face, recalling the way the tall, handsome southerner had earlier picked up her lipstick when she had intentionally dropped it in the middle of the concourse.

"It looks like you're needing a taxi."

"Yes. And in a hurry."

"I've got to get back to the car so they don't tow it," Matt says. "Amaya and her brother should be out in a minute or so. They went back into the airport to attempt to change his departure time. We can take you whereever you want to go, Miss Klien. It would be our pleasure."

Alexia weighs her options. "The way all this has worked out today, I believe I will take you up on your offer."

"Great!"

"I'm in a hurry though. I've got to get to CCN. You know, late for work."

"We will do our best to get you there."

"I'll race you to the car," she says playfully. "Which one is it?"

Alexia takes off running in the direction Matt James has just come from even before he is able to answer her question of which car is his. He stands there half amazed at what he has just heard before he takes off after her. The two of them are running as fast as they can like teenagers in front of the busy airport.

Just at that moment, Amaya and her brother walk out the front doors of the airport and see Matt James running about ten feet behind Alexia and not really gaining any ground on her.

"Oh, my gosh!" Astonished, Amaya says in amazement to her brother Jeffrey, "Matt is chasing Alexia Klien!"

"This is the guy you have spent the last six months with in the jungles of Zimbabwe?" Jeff Blazi asks his sister as he laughs loudly at what he sees. "He's lost it, been too long without a mate. You're not going back down there with him."

Matt stops by a small green rental car parked along the curb in front of the airport. He yells to the very athletic and swift Alexia Klien, "Hey, you just ran past the car!"

At least twenty feet past the car, Alexia stops and turns around. After she catches her breath she says. "I see. A conservative Christian, I presume. But even you have gone green." Alexia says in reference to the little French car that is a very bright and pretty color of green.

"Yeah, it gets great mileage," Matt James replies as he laughs. "And if you have to, you can pick it up and carry it around with you! You like it?"

"Oh, yeah. But where am I going to ride, on top of it?"

"You have obviously spent too much time being chauffeured around in those CCN owned limos," Matt fires back sarcastically. "But, if we all hold our breath when we get in, we should be able to get the doors closed. Then it'll just be a matter of getting to know each other."

For some reason Alexia feels she can trust Matthew James. Generally she can spot a player immediately, and her radar has not gone off to warn her about this very good-looking man from Savannah, even though he has everything he needs to be a player, personality and looks. She can tell he is just having fun with her and does not have alternative motives in his flirting. To some degree this puzzles her. *Is he a sheep in wolf's clothing?* She wonders.

He might actually be exactly what Amaya said he is, a really nice guy. In the circles Alexia travels in, she does not run into very many men like that, and definitely none as attractive. Twenty-four hours earlier, before hearing Severo Baptiste's voice for the first time in over a year, Alexia would have possibly been the player here. But as nice and as handsome as Matthew James is, he is not Severo Baptiste. Alexia knows her new friendship with this tall, sandy haired man from southern Georgia is going to be just that—a friendship.

Amaya and her brother arrive at the car where the footrace has just finished. Jeff Blazi says to the older and taller Mr. James, "She was outrunning you, Matt."

"Yeah Matt, and you weren't going to catch her either," Amaya adds. "You can really run, Miss Klien. I mean Alexia."

"Thanks. You can call me Miss Klien if you really want."

"I'm sorry. I guess it's just the way I was brought up," Amaya pauses and says, "I guess you two have met. Alexia this is my brother Jeffery. He's an Air Force pilot stationed in Kuwait."

"Where's your luggage?" Matt asks Alexia.

"Oh, I flew in yesterday," Alexia answers. "I was at the airport on a wild goose chase that didn't go anywhere."

"Oh, some of that investigative reporter stuff I presume," Matt returns.

"Something like that," she replies.

As the four of them squeeze into the little green Renault Citroen C4, Alexia says to Amaya's brother, "One of my best friends is flying into Kuwait today to entertain the troops."

"Really?" asks Jeff, "Who's that?"

"Angie West, the country music singer."

"Everyone in?" asks Matt in his slow southern drawl.

A series of "yes's" and "I think so's" follow.

"I really wanted to stay and hear Angie West sing," replies the U.S. Air Force Major. "I'm in love with her and her music. It's so wholesome and pure compared to most everything else the music industry puts out these days."

"Yeah, I agree," Matt says.

Jeff then pulls his sister closer to him with the arm he has around her in the tiny back seat of the French car. "But seeing Sis here in Paris is tops."

From the front seat of the Citroen, Alexia turns and tells Amaya and her brother Jeff, "If Amaya and I stay in contact, I can get both of you backstage at one of Angie's concerts. Or, we could all just go see her in Oklahoma sometime. Hang out with her. Angie would love that."

As the four Americans, stuffed like sardines in the little French car no bigger than a peanut, leave the airport and enter the Paris traffic, Alexia thinks about how safe and secure she suddenly feels with her new friends. There is something about these three people that has given her a calm in what has been one of the most nerve-wracking and stressful days she has ever experienced.

Alexia cannot put a finger on what it is about them or what they have that makes them different. It is obvious to Alexia that these three people have a peace about them she is not familiar with. Something inside of her wants to keep in contact with them in the future.

"You are going to have to tell me where you want to go," Matt tells Alexia. "I'm somewhat familiar with Paris."

"I can do that."

Now on the A1 Autoroute, also known as l'autoroute du Nord, the main roadway back into Paris, Alexia and Matt sit quietly in the two front seats of the cute little French sports car while Jeff and Amaya catch up on things from home. Matt does not seem to be interested in idle chitchat at the moment as he focuses on his driving on the very busy foreign roadway. This gives Alexia a little time to reflect on all she has seen since earlier this morning in the Boutique de la Renommée when she ran across the suspicious woman she had once seen in Washington D.C.

While on this open stretch of freeway north of Paris, Alexia begins to think about the possible political and personal ramifications that would occur if the story she has stumbled onto today in Europe were made known in America. It had entered her mind, but now she realizes that the very story she has been bird dogging, a term her father would use, would only serve to defeat Senator Franson, the Presidential candidate who holds to most of the same political positions as she does. All morning she looked past this. It was as though she could not see the forest for the trees. Sómething in her was seeking the truth.

All she could think of while watching the people she was trailing was the story, the facts. For the last few hours her opinions and viewpoints had not meant anything. Alexia had been in journalism mode—real journalism mode—seeking only the story, not trying to make a story the way she or somebody else wanted it to be made.

Alexia now sees that anything she could find out that hurts CCN's handpicked Presidential candidate will only serve to hurt her in the end. If she were to take this story to Rigger Watson, he would blow his stack. The end results of anything she went public with from today would cost her the job she has worked so hard to attain.

What do I really know? Alexia asks herself. *Not really anything.* Her self preservation instinct kicks in. Alexia lets herself become like the monkeys who see no evil, hear no evil, and speak no evil, all the while covering their eyes and ears with their hands so they do not perceive the evil right in front of them.

The CCN broadcast journalist wonders what the three people she is traveling with in this car would think if they knew everything she has seen and experienced today. Alexia knows she cannot share any of it with them, especially how it might tie directly to the liberal progressive candidate for the Presidency of the United States. Yet, something inside of her wants to share it with them. This baffles her. What is it? But she can't.

As she stares out the window of the little green Citroen at the passing country side of France, into her thoughts a memory appears. It is of a time when she and Severo stopped at a small café only a few kilometers off of the exit they are about to go by. It was the last time she saw him in Paris. After a late breakfast that day over five years ago, Baptiste took her to the airport where Alexia got on a plane to fly back to the United States. It was while eating with Severo that morning that the two of them decided they needed to go in different directions in their lives. Alexia has to fight back tears as they drive past the exit.

On the busy French freeway at a high rate of speed because Matt James knows his passenger is in a hurry to get to her hotel and then to the CCN broadcast studio, Severo Baptiste is suddenly all that is on Alexia's mind.

From the squished confines of the back seat, Amaya smiles and tells Alexia and Matt, "You two sure look like a cute couple up there."

All the occupants of the car laugh as the four Americans reach the outskirts of Paris on an incredibly gorgeous fall day.

CHAPTER FIFTEEN

Eight Dollar Eyeglasses

"Hello, is that you, Eddie?" Sharice Jones answers her cell phone as her Saudi Arabian boss Mr. Shahid al-Zahrani glares at her through the darkly tinted windows of his shiny black Mercedes Benz he has parked in the very middle of the street.

"Yeah, it's me," Police Officer Edward Jefferson says as Sharice continues to stand along the roadway between Ol' Sims Wilson's gas station and the run-down motel. Zahrani stays parked in front of her. He is stopping traffic from both directions.

"Wait a second, Eddie," Sharice says.

Zahrani reaches for the window controls in his car. He lowers the driver side window and tells Sharice, "I do not pay you to talk on the phone. If you want to keep your job you better get back to work. Your boys are not millionaires yet."

He then speeds away throwing loose gravel off the asphalt street. Zahrani turns into the back entrance of the motel without using the brakes of his car. It is as though Sharice Jones was stealing the Saudi Arabian man's very last dollar from him by walking across the street to use the restroom and answering a phone call on her way back to work.

Still very fresh in her memory is how the Muslim man had blown up at her just a week earlier for talking to one of her sons on the phone, and Sharice is quite sure she will probably get fired for this. Part of her would be happy if that happens, yet she so enjoys working with Martha Jo and both of them still need the paychecks.

There are many people who have offered to help Sharice out financially because of the football talents of her sons. But any kind of an infraction of the very strict rules of the college athletics oversight committee, the NCAA, could cost her sons and LSU dearly. For this reason Sharice Jones does not take any favors from anyone. She feels it would be best for everyone involved to just work like a slave until one of her athletically gifted sons gets that big NFL payday they all know is coming.

"OK, I can talk now," Sharice says as she walks back to the motel. "You there?"

"Yeah, Big Momma, this is Eddie Jefferson at your service. How can I help you, Honey Bear?"

Edward Jefferson is a great big man. He had played one year of college football at the smaller, and less prestigious Louisiana Tech University in Rustin, Louisiana. A severe knee injury ended his playing career at the start of his sophomore season and sent him in a completely different direction in life. Jefferson is a very funloving guy with a big heart. He really likes Sharice, and if it were not for the miles between them, the two of them would probably see much more of each other.

"Eddie, did you hear my message?" Sharice asks.

"Why no, Honey. I saw you called, so I just called you back."

"Eddie, I'm thinkin' we might have some real bad guys staying here in the motel. They's some of them Islamic Muslim terrorists I think. I's scared for my boys. You know they play Alabama tonight here in Baton Rouge. I didn't know who to call, so I called you, Eddie."

"Sharice Darlin', you just stay right there and act like nothing's wrong. I'm goin' call our Police Chief. He'll know somebody to get a hold of in some federal agency to deal with this. Love you, Honey, and give my love to Martha Jo and the boys. I'll be callin' back in a bit," Jefferson tells the worried mother.

———

On the south edge of Atlanta in a nice quiet neighborhood with many more trees than houses, the winds well ahead of a cold front are slowly beginning to pick up. The radiant colors of the leaves that are moving back and forth make the trees look nearly alive. It is as though they are waving goodbye to fall and preparing to embrace an early winter.

Having just come inside from his backyard, Gene Hall rummages through an oak desk in his den looking for a pair of his reading glasses. He only has about a dozen pairs of the cheap, narrow-lens reading glasses lying around everywhere from his workshop in the garage to the counter top in his favorite upstairs bathroom. But it never seems to fail, Gene never can find a pair of those elusive glasses when he needs one.

His sweet wife Clarice has followed her husband into the house and while he is searching through his den making more noise than a bull in a China closet, she quickly and quietly retrieves a pair of his reading glasses from atop the refrigerator where she always puts them when she finds a pair laying where Gene had carelessly left them. Clarice hurries into the den before Gene tears it up anymore and hands him a pair of the eight dollar eye glasses she keeps buying for her husband at Wal-Mart.

Mr. Hall thanks his wife before sitting down and pulling open the second drawer down on the right side of his old antique red oak office desk. The desk takes up a good portion of his well-organized den, which is full of keepsakes from all over the world that Staff Sergeant Gene Hall collected in his many years of service to his country. The walls of the cozy little den are covered with pictures of him with many of the great men from all over the United States that he was so blessed to know and to serve with all over the world. Hall's den is a small shrine to one of the many things that he believes have made this nation so great—its dedicated military men.

Hall reaches into the back of the drawer and pulls out one of his most prized possessions, a torn and worn Army green address book he purchased at a PX over forty years ago in Germany, the first country he was stationed in outside of the United States.

In this little book are the names, addresses, and telephone numbers of hundreds of men Gene Hall was privileged to know and to serve within his years in the U.S. Military. It had been his wonderful wife Clarice who first suggested in a love letter written from the States that he go down and buy something to start a log of the individuals he would meet in his travels around the world with the Army. One of many suggestions he is happy she has made over their many years together.

Hall opens his little book up to the T's and looks for retired Lieutenant Colonel George Thompson's home telephone number. Thompson's name is right there at the start of the T's. It was one of the first entries he ever made in this book, back when the pages of it were new and crisp, not faded and frail as they are now. Hall served with Thompson over forty years ago in Germany when George was only a Second Lieutenant fresh out of the Academy, and they were fortunate enough to serve with each other many other times throughout their military careers.

When Thompson eventually left the Army, which was about ten years before Hall did, he was recruited by the CIA to do certain work for them which his specific military skills had qualified him for. He spent fifteen years with the CIA full time, and still works with them as a consultant. Thompson also has two sons that have been with the CIA since they graduated with honors from Ivy League schools.

With his eight dollar Wal-Mart reading glasses resting on the tip of his nose, Hall sits down in his comfortable office chair. He knows a talk with his good friend from New York State might take a while. Gene picks up the phone on his red oak desk and dials the number to the former spy.

———

As the dirt and the dust, the sand and the smoke, and the noise begins to settle, Private Tillord reaches up to grab part of the metal frame inside the guard tower and pull himself to his feet. He is slightly dazed and shaken up, but his senses are quickly coming to him. In all the years he has hunted everything from mountain lions to bears, Tillord has never felt anything close to what he just did. Not only the impact of the vehicle crashing into the guard tower, but the feeling he felt when he did what he was trained to do.

When Private Will Tillord pulled the trigger of his M4 carbine assault rifle, the rush he felt was unlike anything he has ever experienced before. He has pulled the triggers of numerous guns in his life, killing everything from a small bird with a BB gun as a little boy, to a Montana grizzly bear with a .338 Winchester Magnum. As his eyes clear and he tries to locate his fellow soldiers, he is not sure how he feels about what just happened. Part of him hates that he had to shoot another human being, but part of him likes the rush.

The guard tower has just been rocked by the force of a one ton dually work truck. The truck, loaded with a heavey tool box, was traveling at over seventy miles per hour when it hit the legs of the tower.

To the surprise of the three soldiers still conscious, the truck that hit the guard tower did not explode on impact as the first white Ryna Corp work truck did just seconds before when it hit the entrance gate and guard shack about a hundred feet away. The guard shack and entrance gate on the back side of the Ali Al Salem Air Force Base are completely leveled.

Above the Arabian Desert, the 7x7 army green cubicle made out of half-inch-thick steel had been perfectly level atop the sturdy thirty-foot tower. It is now tipped almost forty degrees off kilter and barely standing. Tillord and Specialist Diaz managed to somehow stay inside the tower.

Sergeant Spicer Brent Davis and the soft-spoken Private Sheldon Mitchal have been thrown completely out of the guard tower from the impact of the speeding truck.

Even though the dirt and the dust are beginning to settle and the smoke is starting to rise, chaos still rules the moment on the back side of the airbase. The screams of immediate terror have ceased. Now there are the sounds of pain. They're not as loud, but just as real and disturbing. *At least someone has survived this attack,* Tillord thinks to himself.

As he and Diaz get their bearings, they have to try to keep from falling out of the tilting, damaged guard tower of bent steel and busted welds. Quickly, they are able to locate their two comrades below. Mitchal is conscious and trying to crawl away from the wreckage, not able to put any weight on his twisted and lame left leg that drags behind him.

Sergeant Davis's condition does not look to be nearly as good as that of Mitchal. Davis lays unconscious across the hood, roof and windshield of the white Ryna Corp truck that has just rammed into the guard tower.

"Sarge is out like a light," yells Diaz. "If he's even alive!"

Tillord leans out over one of the mounted fifty-caliber machine guns and yells, "Mitch! Are you all right?"

Mitchal stops crawling, with all the force he can muster, he yells back up to the top of the tower, "Yeah, don't worry about me. It's just my knee. Get Sarge off that truck before it explodes."

"Oh, mother... ," Diaz yells out in a fit of panic and rage. "We got to get out of here!" He jumps down out of the guard tower, hitting the ground and rolling like a Hollywood stuntman jumping from a moving train.

As Tillord begins to climb down out of the steel tower, he feels something like a knife sticking him in the ribs. It is the most excruciating pain he has ever felt, and he suddenly cannot catch his breath. Pain grips every bit of his body instantly as his arms and legs go weak. *What is wrong with me?* Tillord wonders. *Just a few moments ago I thought I had survived this unscathed.*

After having rolled a couple of times in the desert sand at the end of his jump, Diaz gets up. Part of him wants to just run as fast as he can in case the white work truck does have a delayed explosive set in it. But he knows his first responsibility is to his unconscious Sergeant.

Diaz looks up to where Private Tillord has now stopped about half way down the broken and twisted tower ladder. He yells, "Will, are you OK, man? You don't look so good up there."

It takes all the young man has to get the words out of his mouth, "I'm OK... Get Sarge."

Diaz hurries over to where Sergeant Spicer Davis is laid out flat across the top of the white one-ton Islamic terrorist weapon on wheels. Diaz, not even thinking about his Sergeant's possible injuries, grabs Davis's arm and begins to pull him down off the windshield of the totaled truck. As Diaz does, he sees the dead Muslim man behind the steering wheel of the wrecked work truck is almost unrecognizable as a human being. The Arab, who had just driven the white Ryna Corp truck into the guard tower, is shot up so badly it looks like all that is left of him is bloody rags and bloody flesh. It was U.S. Army Specialist Carlos Diaz himself who had just fired multiple rounds of hot ammunition from the 50 caliber machine gun he was on into this man.

After freezing for just a moment while looking at the damage he has caused to the terrorist, Diaz goes ahead and drags his completely unconscious, one hundred and eighty-five pound friend, Spicer Davis off the truck. He puts the Sergeant over his shoulder and carries him away from the smoldering wreckage.

Will Tillord has made it down off the side of the torn-up tower. He is able to get a little more breath into his lungs now that he is standing on the ground and not hanging off the side of a leaning ladder by his arms.

Carrying Davis, Diaz goes past Tillord and asks, "You OK, man?"

"I think it's my ribs," Tillord responds as he grimaces. "My dad got bucked off a colt once and he acted just like I feel. I'll be alright. How's Sarge?"

"He made a grunt when I drug him off the truck, so I think he's still alive. Man, this one arm of his is screwed up!" Diaz replies.

The two men catch up with Mitchal, who has been able to get himself to safety by crawling a ways on his hands and knees in the hot desert sand, and then getting up and limping on his one good leg. They look over to where the guard shack and back entrance gate to Ali Al Salem had once been. All that is left of it is a pile of rubble covered by flames and smoke. There are numerous military vehicles, U.S. Army and Air Force personnel racing to where the disaster has just taken place.

Diaz, after surveying the results of the first Ryna Corp truck explosion, looks over to Tillord and says, "Man, Till, do you think anyone was able to survive that? Damn, we were lucky. We were real lucky."

Just then the young man from Wyoming drops down to his knees and grasps his rib cage. Keeling over onto his left side, he coughs up blood.

CHAPTER SIXTEEN

It's the one that gets you

Everyone in the little green French car laughs at Amaya's comment about Alexia and Matt James being a cute looking couple. No one took it seriously, least of all Matt.

"Oh, Little Blazi, that would be all right with me," Matt responds as everyone's laughter fades, "But I don't think CCN's Alexia Klien wants to spend the next twenty years of her life traipsing through the jungles of Africa."

This comment brings more laughter. Matthew James often refers to Amaya as Little Blazi because she is the youngest of seven children, four boys and three girls. Amaya's oldest brother and one of her sisters have also spent time in Africa as missionaries with Matt, but not until after they had finished college.

Amaya's desire to go to Africa and give a year of her life to the mission field was so strong, she wanted to do it before she went off to college. She and her parents thought it was a good idea and they all felt a peace about the decision. They figured it would also give her a whole different perspective and appreciation for an expensive college education. The fact that two of her older siblings had spent a year in Africa under the watchful eye of Matthew James made it much easier for her family to let Amaya go on such a dangerous and daunting experience at the tender age of eighteen. Amaya recently celebrated her nineteenth birthday on November first in Africa only a few days before her and Matt flew to Paris.

After Matt exclaims he didn't think Alexia would want to spend the next twenty years of her life in Africa, Amaya's brother Jeff pipes up and asks, "Twenty more years down there, Matt? Haven't you already been there that long?"

Matt laughs. "Not quite, Jeff."

"It had to be at least ten years ago when you and Pete were there," Jeff says, "And five years ago, Shelia was in Africa with you."

Alexia turns her head towards Matt and asks, "How long have you been in Zimbabwe?"

"Well, let's see," Matt replies. "It's been over eleven years since I first went to Africa on a hunting safari."

"A hunting safari?" Alexia asks a bit surprised. "You first went to Africa on a hunting safari?" She has a tough time envisioning the guy sitting beside her as a rough, rugged African hunter type.

The nice, decent, clean-cut Matthew James answers, "Yeah, I was thirty-two years old then and a couple of years out of grad school with an MBA in business from Duke. I was living life in the fast lane. I had just closed a big real estate deal in North Carolina that personally netted me a little over a million dollars. I had hunted Alaska and all over Canada and had always wanted to hunt Africa. I had the money so I went on a forty-five day safari through Zimbabwe and Zambia. To my surprise, my heart went out like I never would have guessed to the poor and impoverished people down there."

Matt looks at Alexia to see if she is listening. She is. "The week before I flew out of Atlanta, I had gone home to Savannah to spend some quality time with my parents. On the Sunday before I left for Johannesburg, I went to church with my mother and my father. It had been the first time in well over ten years, I guess since my senior year in high school that I had even been in a church. I'd sort of rebelled, you might say."

He pauses and looks at Alexia again and then continues, "But my mother was worried for my safety—actually for my life—with me going on such a dangerous trip, and she insisted that I attend their little Baptist church with her and dad one last time before I flew off to the rugged plains and jungles of Africa."

When Matt stops talking to check the mirrors of the French sports car before he switches into the left lane, Alexia comments, "Wow, I now have a whole new picture of you, Matt! I would never have guessed any of that a few miles back."

Jeff Blazi laughs as he interrupts Alexia, telling her, "You ought to hear the stories my brother Peter tells of the year he spent with the younger and wilder version of Mr. Matthew James ten years ago. You would have thought the two of them were in Africa hunting for Tarzan instead of there doing God's work. What was it, Matt? You guys got lost or separated from the group for what, a month or something once? Oh yeah, and everyone thought you were dead, that cannibals or something got you."

Everyone laughs, and Matt says, "It was only three weeks that we were lost."

"Then, there is Matt James the Army Ranger in the first gulf war too," Jeff adds. "Pete said those are really good stories too. Just not for the faint of heart."

Matt laughs lightly and says, "Yeah I thought your brother and I were going to meet our end a time or two in those weeks when we were out there on our own. We were never lost though, no matter what Pete says. We were just taking the Gospel to the ends of the earth. Now that Gulf War stuff is no laughing matter, and you know it, Jeffery. War is very serious business and everyone in it needs to take it that way. Our very existence as free people depends on it. Do you agree, Miss World Wide Reporter?"

"You may be surprised, Mr. Conservative," answers Alexia, "But the truth is, I do agree with you on the War on Terrorism. It is about the only political issue my dad, the ultra conservative insurance company lawyer and I agree on."

"Really?" Matt says. "That does surprise me."

"But Matt, I want to know what it was that made you decide to leave life in the fast lane," the curious and clever broadcast journalist asks, "When it sounds like you were doing so well in it. I mean, a million dollars in one deal at the age of, what, thirty-two?"

Matthew James thinks for just a moment and then says, "It was kind of funny. No, it was kind of odd. Just out of high school I enlisted in the Army and shortly thereafter they decided I had what it took to be an Army Ranger. As a Ranger in the first Gulf War, I saw an awful lot of terror and torment. I saw things a young kid should never have to see. Yet even what I saw then didn't take me back to the Christian roots I was brought up with. I was hard and I was cocky. And I pretty much thought I knew damn near everything. Excuse the language. But it must have been something I heard in that Baptist church service right before I went to Zimbabwe that triggered the reopening of my heart. That, combined with the prayers of my parents, especially the prayers of my mother."

"So you are a Baptist then, Matt?" Alexia asks of her new friend just wanting him to continue telling his story.

"No Alexia, I wouldn't say that. I am simply a Christian. And that is the real story. I was a Baptist, or I thought I was one growing up. Then in Zimbabwe on my hunting safari, the words from the Book of John in the New Testament of the Bible kept coming into my mind. Words I had known and heard since childhood. Words from John chapter three, verse three that say that no man may see or know the Kingdom of God unless he is born again. I didn't fully understand what that meant at the age of thirty-two, but I knew I was not born again. So late one night, after almost everyone else in the hunting party had gone to bed, I snuck out into the wild of the African night and prayed to a God I only vaguely knew. It was the first time I had prayed since I was probably twelve or so, and I asked Him to make me 'born again', whatever that meant. And God did the rest."

The air in the little green French sports car becomes thick when Matt finishes the story of his personal testimony. Amaya and Jeffery are both Christians who are very serious about their faith. They are completely silent, knowing very well that the Holy Spirit is at work inside the car they are traveling in at well over a hundred kilometers an hour.

Matt knows the same and stays quiet also to let what he has just been allowed to say sink into the mind, and even more importantly, into the heart of Alexia Klien. What Matt, Amaya and Jeff do not know is that Alexia is very familiar with John 3:3, the verse Matt has just spoken of. As a child, Alexia had to learn that verse for an Easter Pageant she was in at the age of nine.

A short period of time and silence passes. Alexia knows this trip and conversation has entered into a realm she has tried very hard and successfully—up until now—to avoid. She knows it is her turn to speak. She also knows enough about human nature to realize the three very intelligent and kind people with her are not going to let her off the hook by speaking first.

Only a few weeks earlier, her best friend Angie West had tried to explain to Alexia that there is a big difference between faith and religion. Not wanting to have any kind of conversation with her friend about anything to do with God or Jesus, Alexia just tried to play the devil's advocate, and it worked. She put an end to their talk on the subject. Alexia does know that what her good friend Angie was trying to tell her about faith being completely different than religion is right. But something inside of her didn't want to admit it.

With everyone in the car remaining silent, all Alexia can think to ask as she tries to absorb all she has just heard is, "So Matt, you say you are not a Baptist, but just a Christian. Does that mean Baptists are not Christians?"

Alexia knows her question is a little weak with the substance of things that have just been said. But having grown up with a Baptist mother and a Methodist father, Alexia is interested in hearing how he will answer her question.

Still driving on the A1 Autoroute on the outskirts of Paris, Matt glances at Alexia and smiles. In a soft and gentle voice he replies, "Oh, definitely they are! Some, if not most, Baptists are Christians. What I am saying is that it is not the type of building a person enters that makes them a Christian. It's the One who enters into our heart that makes us a Christian. It's accepting Jesus as our Savior that makes a person a Christian."

He pauses and looks in his rear-view mirror and then changes lanes to get around a truck traveling too slow in the left lane. Matt goes on in his slow deep southern drawl, "I know this is awfully heavy stuff for us, I mean for me, to throw on you in this short little trip today, Miss Klien. I will share this with you though. This little trip with me and the Blazi brats might turn out to be the most important trip you have ever taken in Paris in a cute little green sports car." Everyone laughs a little and the heavy atmosphere inside of the speeding vehicle is lightened a bit. Yet, the seriousness of what has just been discussed still hangs in the air.

For the next couple of kilometers while Matt and Jeff talk about how things are going in the Middle East, Alexia ponders everything she has experienced today. She even asks herself why she is so much more comfortable hearing this serious Christianity stuff, this Jesus stuff, from complete strangers as opposed to her best friend Angie

West. Or for that matter, even family members on her mother's side that have attempted numerous times to witness to her in different ways in the past.

She wonders why it is that she, a very intelligent and outgoing person, doesn't even want those people closest to her to talk to her of what deep down inside she knows is probably the most important subject there is—life and death. Yet she feels like she could sit and listen to Amaya Blazi and Matthew James talk about their faith for hours. Alexia can tell that her new friends care for her and like her, but she knows they cannot care as much as her dearest friends and family do.

After a short distance of no one saying anything as the traffic they are traveling in gets heavier, Jeff interrupts the silence and asks, "Matt, you still hunt some, right?"

"Oh yeah, every chance I get."

"I have always wondered," Jeff asks, "What is the most dangerous animal in Africa?"

Matt laughs and then replies, "I once hunted with a man from West Texas for almost three weeks on a safari in Tanzania. Dudley Koleman. He was a wealthy oilman who had hunted all over the world. Well anyway, a reporter we ran into when we were close to the border of the Democratic Republic of the Congo asked Dudley the same question you just asked me, Jeff."

"Hurry up and answer the question Matt," an impatient Amaya blurts out. "You always drag things like this out, suspending the suspense. What is the most dangerous animal in Africa?"

A grinning Matt waits just a little longer and then says, "Well, Amaya... as Dudley Koleman said," Matt stops and looks at the younger Blazi in the mirror holding her in suspense a little longer. "It's the one that gets you."

Everyone in the car laughs except Amaya. She just sits in the back seat with a blank look on her face and then says, "I don't get it."

Her brother elbows her in the ribs and says, "It's the one that gets you. What does it matter which is the most dangerous animal in Africa when there are so many there that can kill you?"

"Oh," Amaya replies with a worried look on her face, "I don't think that's very funny."

"Matt, how do you fund your hunting and missionary work?" Alexia asks, "Do you do it all off of donations from other people?"

"No. There are some churches that help support us, but I funnel that money to help the people in Africa we are witnessing to," Matt James replies. "I still trade some real estate back in the states. I've still got my license in North Carolina, and then I have a little brother in L.A. who I partner with on things out there. We buy and sell a lot of foreclosed properties. That's how I support myself. It's just that I don't desire to be the next Donald Trump anymore."

"There's a lot about you that surprises me, Mr. James," Alexia says. "I thought you were just some guy that was hiding from the real world as a missionary in some land far away from life's troubles."

Matt laughs for a moment and then says, "It's a funny notion so many people have about Christian missionaries. People think we are hiding from life, and maybe some do, but most of the missionaries I have met don't. Most of them are more into life than anyone in Hollywood or on Wall Street could ever dream of being."

"Way to put it, Matt," Jeff says.

"Thanks, Jeff," Matt replies. "I'll tell you something else I think everyone in Christianity needs to realize and come to terms with. We need more rough, rugged, and tough Christian men. Men willing take a stand for what they believe in. Men willing to stand up for what is right and stand up against what is wrong."

Matt looks over and sees Alexia is looking at him and listening to his every word. He continues, "Just think about what the very first disciples were, what they did before they were called to be disciples. They were fishermen, commercial fishermen of that day. They worked long hours with ropes and nets and knives, wooden boats and fish. Today, being a commercial fisherman is considered one of the most dangerous occupations that there is, and it would be my assumption that commercial fisherman today are very rough, tough and rugged men. I do not see why it would have been any different in the time when Jesus called his first disciples out of that very same industry."

"Wow," Alexia says, "I've never thought of it that way."

"I fully agree with you, Matt," Jeff adds.

Alexia thinks about her friend Angie West, a Christian and a cowgirl. Even though the world only sees Angie as a singer, Alexia knows her best friend the cowgirl is actually quite rough and tough when it comes right down to it, working her horses as she does. Thinking about her friend, Alexia realizes it is Angie's Christian faith that is one of the things she so admires and envies about her. Yet every time Angie brings it up, something inside of Alexia tries to hide from the topic. It is a vicious cycle, Alexia concludes. Again, she is reminded of when she interviewed the Malaysian missionary couple, David and Sarah Peters. Once more her mind recalls when David said, "It is just the other side of the same world we live on, in need of the same Jesus we need here in the United States."

What a coincidence, Alexia thinks as it dawns on her that when she had left that interview, now well over ten years ago, she had the very same feelings of comfort and ease she now has with these people she is riding with in the little green Renault Citroen. A feeling of complete calm and peace, even though she just went through so much mental distress while spying on the dangerous trio in the airport.

About to reach the main loop encircling Paris, the Boulevard Périphérique, Alexia tells Matt which direction they need to go on the loop to get to her hotel. As they exit the A1 Autoroute, a thought enters into Alexia's head and even her heart, *I am as Matt James was before he went to Africa on his first hunting safari. I do not really know what it means to be born again.* Something deep down inside of her tells her this is something she needs to know.

CHAPTER SEVENTEEN

U.S. Navy SEAL

Tail lights brighten as the vehicles in front of them prepare to stop at a yellow light that is about to turn red. FBI agents Billy Joe Gasperson and Danny Trey Craddick can see the big black Lincoln Continental pull out onto the highway as it leaves the abandoned three-story motel. The car is heading straight to where the agents are about to be trapped at the red light. In front of the red Lexus, Gasperson is driving in the right lane, a work truck with *Kelton Construction* painted on it has already stopped. A small green car with a tail light out and cardboard duct taped in the back window is slowing down in the left lane where a white Chevy Tahoe waits at the red light. To the Tahoe's left there is a left-hand turn lane that is open.

With their eyes fixed on the black car leaving the motel, neither Craddick nor Gasperson see the school bus coming up behind them in the left turn lane. The black Lincoln now traveling on Dillon road runs the stop sign at the intersection beside the small convenience store and is speeding towards the on-ramp that leads to I-10.

Gasperson grips the steering wheel tight and starts to turn to the left. He tells his partner, "If the light stays red we can cut through the intersection and keep 'em from making it to the interstate,".

"Go for it!" Craddick shouts as he still has his focus on the black car. "Oh sh... do you see the..." Craddick throws his hands up over his head and prepares for a collision.

With the sound of screeching metal and squealing tires, then the shrieking of a horn from the school bus, Gasperson quickly looks in his rear view mirror, "Damn it!" He stomps on the accelerator of the Lexus as its rear end is shoved about two feet to the right.

Stepping on the gas as he did, saved the two FBI agents from being spun completely sideways. The big yellow school bus comes to a complete stop as do all the vehicles in the area, except the black Lincoln and red Lexus. Both vehicles continue in the direction of the I-10 on-ramp. Gasperson barely misses rear ending the little green car whose driver had slammed on the brakes as soon as he heard the noise of the collision behind him.

"Dang, that was close," Gasperson says.

"You guys OK?" Wikett asks over the radio.

"Yeah," Craddick says as he and Gasperson drive through the red light. "We're going to beat 'em to the on-ramp."

"Good," Wikett instructs. "Get 'em stopped!"

Seconds before the black car reaches where Dillon Road meets I-10, Gasperson slides the brand new red Lexus to a stop in the middle of the pathway that leads to Interstate 10. Immediately the driver of the 1980 Lincoln Continental Mark IV steps down on the gas pedal, increasing the speed of the two and half ton car.

"Oh damn, this ain't good!" Craddick yells as the black car made of American steel hits the brand new Lexus IS250 that it out weighs by over a ton. The Lincoln Continental rams directly into the right front tire of the shiny new Lexus causing the airbag to go off, pinning the two FBI agents back against their seats. The Lexus spins all the way around to where Craddick and Gasperson are pointing back in the direction they just came from. As the Lexus spins it drags against the full length of the black car.

The big black Lincoln heads straight down the on-ramp to the interstate leading to Los Angeles. The impact of the crash has left the front end of the Lexus inoperable. The right front wheel and hub have been knocked off the car's axle. The fender and the radiator have been torn away leaving a mangled and smashed hood setting above the exposed motor. Steam is hissing violently out of the front end of the car. Craddick and Gasperson sit pointing south in an un-drivable vehicle that had just carried them half way across the United States. The black Lincoln speeds off to the west. Craddick is in great pain.

"The black Caddy!" Garcia says into his radio, "I mean Lincoln! It just hit 'em and they're not moving."

Through their earpieces the four FBI agents at the motel heard the horrendous sound of the crash less than a quarter of a mile away. They fear the fate of their partners is not good. Garcia is the only one who was able to see the wreck.

"Billy Joe? Trey? Are you guys alright?" Wikett asks.

"Trey, are you Ok?" Gasperson asks his partner as he shoves the airbag out away from his face.

"Yeah, I think so, I'm still alive," Craddick answers. "My neck and back hurt like hell though."

"Where's the black car?" Wikett asks.

"I don't know," Gasperson replies.

"It's on the freeway heading west!" Garcia states.

"Damn it!" Wikett yells. "Billy Joe, you call Kennedy and tell him what has happened and they need to be on the lookout for a black Lincoln coming their way?"

"I will, Chace," Gasperson replies.

"You guys are on your own until we find out who all's in Eddison's truck," Wikett tells Craddick and Gasperson.

"We can handle it," returns Craddick as he fights the pain he is feeling. Gasperson is already calling Bart Kennedy.

Knowing the wreck Craddick and Gasperson experienced will have local police, Sheriff Deputies and the California State Highway Patrol headed their way immediately, Garcia pulls out his cell phone and dials 911 to alert the State Patrol and all other Law enforcement agencies to be on the lookout for the runaway black 80's model Lincoln with no plates and two potentially very dangerous Islamic terrorists aboard.

As the call he placed is ringing, Garcia tells Wikett over the FBI radio, "I'm calling 911." When the police dispatcher picks up, Garcia tells them everything. He also states that it is imperative that these two Muslim men be found as soon as possible.

"Chace, there's a light on in the truck," John Swanson says over the FBI radio.

Through his ear piece, Wikett hears Swanson, "Can you see both doors yet, Swanny?"

"No, I'll be able to in a few feet," answers the big man originally from Oklahoma. "They haven't opened a door yet. But the light is coming from the sleeper."

"Don't get any closer, stay where you're at," Wikett says as he again slowly begins to work his way up the passenger side of the eighteen-wheeler.

"Staying right where I'm at, Chief."

"Tony and Rance," Wikett asks Agents Garcia and Patton, "Are you guys headed back over here?"

Both agents reply affirmative.

"I can hear music," Swanson says over the radio. "Yeah, it's Lynyrd Skynyrd. Got to be the redneck."

"Hold your position, Big John," Wikett commands. "We don't know how many there are in there for sure. That may not have been the guys from Yemen in that car. We can't count on anything being like we think it is."

Wikett and Swanson stay where they are as they wait for Agents Garcia and Patton to return to the north and west sides of the old abandoned three-story motel. All the men stay silent. It begins to rain lightly. The forecast for this weekend's weather in Southern California is scattered showers and possible rain storms. With a heavy black cloud cover that came in off of the Pacific Ocean, it is still fairly dark for this time of morning. The meteorologists seem to be right on target.

Lead FBI agent Chace Wikett is crouched down so he can see underneath Eddison's reefer trailer. He watches Patton make his way back through the walkway from the other side of the motel, "Rance, I see you. Just slowly work your way up to the back of the truck and wait."

"Chace, I'm back too," answers Garcia.

"Guys, we're fairly sure Eddison is in the truck," Wikett says. "John, have you been able to see anyone in the cab?"

"No. Whoever's in there has the curtain pulled in front of the sleeper."

"Guys, this close to the Mexican border those could've been a couple of illegals in that black Lincoln that were just running from the law," Wikett warns.

"I saw how hard the black car hit Billy and Trey's Lexus," Garcia states. "Those weren't wetbacks."

"I'm guessing you're right, Gratcio," Wikett says. "John, Tony, just hold down the front and cover us."

Carefully Patton slowly slips up on the driver's side of the eighteen-wheeler, Wikett on the opposite side. Both men have their grayish black FBI issued Glock 23 semi-automatic handguns drawn and ready to use.

"Chace, I can't see anything through its mirrors," says Patton. "I think he's shut the light off."

"Yeah, he's shut off the light," Swanson replies from about forty feet in front of the truck where he and Garcia stand at the corner of the building.

"I can't see anything in the mirror on this side either," Wikett adds. "I hope that crazy-ass Cajun has no idea we're even here."

"Rance, just keep moving up as I am. I'm at the back tires of the tractor." Wikett looks over and sees Patton, both of them stop right behind the sleeper of the truck. Wikett motions with his hand and they both proceed on towards the doors of the truck.

"Chace, I think I hear another vehicle starting," says Garcia. "It could be that gray van."

"Go check."

Quickly Garcia heads back in the direction he just came from. He runs through the walkway with his gun grasped with both hands and stops just behind boarded up office. "It's not the gray van. Someone has pulled in the parking lot in a red Suburban. They're just sitting there revving up their motor for some reason."

"Stay and watch 'em," says Wikett.

"Are you sure, Wik?" asks Garcia. "You might need me over there."

"No, Gratcio," Wikett fires back to the good friend and colleague he has known for over twenty years, "Just stay there by the office and keep watch on the Suburban."

The first time Wikett and Garcia met was at the beginning of the spring semester of Wikett's sophomore year at Texas A&M. In a bar on the last night of winter break, the two of them almost got into a fight over a girl. The very next morning at eight A.M. on the first day of a scuba diving class the instructor paired them up with each other as partners because they looked to be physical equals in both size and athletic ability.

Wikett had enrolled in the class for fun. He also thought it would be interesting and challenging. Garcia had taken the class for a much more serious and specific reason. He planned to become a Navy SEAL after college, a goal he did achieve. He knew it would be to his advantage to attain as much knowledge as he could about diving, and he also felt that it might save his life or someone else's some day.

As it turned out, Garcia ended up marrying the beautiful blonde he and Wikett had nearly fought over. During and after that very difficult and challenging scuba diving class at Texas A&M University, the two young men became almost inseparable.

Chace Wikett even credited Garcia with helping to make him a two-time Southwest All-Conference field goal kicker. Garcia, who played three years of soccer for A&M, helped Chace learn to kick a football farther than he ever had in his first two years of college. Wikett always told everyone he was just glad Gratcio didn't want to be the place kicker for the Aggie football team or he himself would have been the second string kicker.

Garcia never quite had the accuracy though that Wikett did kicking an American football, but that didn't stop the A&M football coaches from trying to talk the Mexican kid from San Antonio into being a kickoff specialist. The future Navy SEAL could kick a football through the end zone nearly every time on a kickoff.

The A&M soccer coaches were totally opposed to having one of their best players running full blast down a football field weighing only 165 pounds while trying to dodge blockers weighing 250 pounds or more, and attempting to tackle a 200 pound ball carrier. The soccer coaches knew with Garcia's aggressive attitude that after a hit or two he would forget he was just a kickoff specialist and think he was a special teams superstar meant to tackle whoever had the ball.

The Texas A&M soccer team could not afford to lose Garcia, a player they did not have to use an athletic scholarship on because of the number of academic scholarships he already had when he decided to walk on the soccer team. With the restrictions on the number of scholarships the men's soccer team could award because of Title Nine legislation, Garcia was a real luxury for them.

When Garcia decided he wanted to get out of the Navy after four tough years of military service abroad, his former college scuba diving partner was quick to get him into the CIA. Wikett then helped open doors for his friend to transition into the FBI when Tony was ready to quit working overseas. Garcia was a man Chace Wikett knew he could count on, and more than once over the years they had saved one another's lives.

Garcia had grown up on the wrong side of the tracks in the south

Texas town of San Antonio and had to fight his way out of the gutter. His intelligence was off the charts. That and his street smarts were what got him through Texas A&M and then into the Navy SEAL program.

"Rance, are you at the door?" Wikett asks in a whisper over the radio.

"I'm here, Chace."

"When I count to three we both open the front doors of this truck at the same time. If it's locked," Wikett instructs, "you knock on the driver's door and announce the FBI is here."

The two men gently pull on the door handles to the front doors of the blue 1999 Freightliner. Both doors are locked.

"Mine's locked."

"Mine, too," Wikett replies. "Let him know we are here."

Patton reaches up to knock on the door of the truck, but before he can rap his knuckles against the hard steel of the door, Eddison kicks it open from inside.

From over a hundred feet away and through the structure of the old three-story motel building, Garcia hears the blasts of a shotgun and then the sound of Swanson yelling loudly. Through the mirror, Roddy Dale Eddison had seen Patton sneaking up the driver's side of his truck after the noise of the wreck. Eddison had unlocked the driver's side door just after Patton had tried to open it. When Roddy Dale kicked open the door from inside, he shoved his black 12 gauge shotgun out the open door and fired.

Chace Wikett immediately shoots out the passenger side window of the crazy Cajun's truck to enter it. He quickly rethinks the situation. He jumps down off the running board of the Freightliner and sprints to the back of the trailer to be able to cover the exit area behind the eighteen-wheeler. Big John Swanson, who saw Patton get shot and blasted backwards through the air off the side of Eddison's truck yells, "Patton's down! He's been shot!"

The blast hit Rance Patton squarely in the middle of his chest from only a couple of feet away. It was so close that Patton's face and ear drums got the worst of it, burning his face with the escaping heat from the gun and completely blowing out both of his ear drums.

The force of the twelve gauge shot hit Agent Patton right in the center of his chest and knocked him back about fifteen feet into the hard, damp concrete of the sidewalk that runs along the north side of the vacated building. Luckily, the back of his head landed in a spot to the south of the sidewalk in a small strip of what had once been grass, but is now a mixture of sand, dirt, stickers and weeds.

His heels had caught the very top edge of the curb tearing off both of his shoes and severely bruising and scraping his heels. He is not dead though. The bullet proof vest Rance Patton is wearing has saved his life.

After shooting the youngest and least experienced FBI agent of the six men who have been following him, Roddy Dale Eddison scrambles out and jumps off of the truck with his Mossberg Model 500A Magnum 12 gauge shotgun in his hands. The gun is pumped and ready to shoot again.

On the southeast side of the L-shaped building, FBI agent Garcia runs down the sidewalk along the south wing of the motel past where the old gray van still sets. He heard the gunfire of a Glock from Wikett shooting out the passenger side window of the truck. Agent Garcia runs towards an opening in the middle of the L where the two wings of the motel meet. He is still over a hundred feet from the opening. The light rain that has been falling gently suddenly breaks into a downpour as a flash of lightning cracks through the dark southern sky.

When Roddy Dale Eddison hits the wet asphalt his truck is parked on, his feet give way and he falls to the ground. At the very moment Eddison falls, John Swanson takes a shot at him with his handgun and misses. The bullet skips off the top of the big round 100 gallon fuel tank that hangs just behind the truck's running boards. Without actually getting to his feet, the very wiry and surprisingly athletic backwoods maniac from Leesburg, Louisiana bear crawls very quickly with his shotgun in one hand to the opening Garcia is headed straight for from the other side of the motel.

With the rain falling as fast and hard as it can, Wikett and Swanson both fire more rounds with their semi-automatic Glocks as Eddison scampers on all fours towards the walkway where an old pop machine and a broken ice maker set.

Swanson and Wikett are both surprised neither of them hit the man. They have been trained to shoot running men, but never had either of them practiced shooting someone escaping like a wild animal in a downpour. Still both of them are excellent shots and given the distance Roddy Dale had to travel to the edge of the motel, and the short range they were firing from, one of them surely should have at least winged him. But they didn't.

"We missed him, Tony! He's coming your way through the center opening." Wikett yells out to his former scuba class diving partner and Best Man at his wedding.

Once inside the shadows of the ten-foot wide walkway that runs under the second floor of the closed motel, the nearly insane man who had just escaped death by only inches stops between the old pop machine and the broken ice maker. He waits for just a second, ready to shoot anyone following him. When no one appears, the left-handed Eddison takes off running south while still looking north.

Having heard all the shots being fired, and knowing none of them were the shotgun he had first heard, Garcia runs towards the opening. Agent Garcia knows that fellow FBI agent Patton has already been hit because of what he heard through his earpiece from Swanson.

As the sound of thunder fills the air following another flash of lightning in the distance, Garcia stops about twenty feet from the walkway. He knows the crazy Cajun will be running through it very quickly. Garcia pulls his Glock 23 semi-automatic FBI issued handgun up and holds it with both hands. He points it directly at the opening where he expects the KKK clansman to come running through. In the matter of only a second or two after Garcia pulled his gun up and pointed it, the Cajun suddenly appears running as fast as he can, very wildly, looking back over his left shoulder.

Without any warning, Garcia pulls the trigger to his handgun and shoots the running man where he is aiming. He hits Eddison in the right shoulder and knocks him to the cool wet pavement. On his way down Eddison is able to turn and twist his body and get off one shot with the gun he is carrying in his left hand. It is a very lucky shot for Eddison, a very unlucky shot for Garcia who is standing only twenty feet away.

Roddy Dale Eddison's wild shot with his black Mossberg Model 500A 12-gauge Magnum shot gun, filled with very heavy shot, hits FBI agent and former U.S. Navy SEAL Tony Garcia in the neck and the left jaw. The blast goes up and through the bottom of his left ear and out the back of Garcia's head. Antonio Ramirez Garcia, a faithful husband and father of three, is dead before his body hits the earth from which it came.

The Leesburg, Louisiana man will now be charged for the murder of the United States Federal Law Enforcement Officer who lies flat on his back on the hard, coarse, deteriorating concrete patio just outside the empty swimming pool of the abandoned California motel. As Eddison falls to his back, he lets out a series of screams and drops the shotgun he has just used to kill the FBI agent.

The last shot Tony Garcia ever fired from his handgun hit the Cajun in his right shoulder. The bullet from Garcia's Glock entered Eddison's body just above his clavicle barely grazing the bone, but ripping through the muscle and flesh that runs from the shoulder to the base of the neck. Garcia's bullet from his Glock then exited Eddison's body and harmlessly hit a concrete pillar holding up the stairwell that runs up to the empty second and third stories of the motel. Screaming in pain, Roddy Dale lies at the opening of the walkway with rain pouring down on him. He is still in much better shape than Garcia, at least physically. The Hispanic Christian, FBI agent Tony Garcia, is now in a much better place.

Over twenty years ago on a warm, humid night in May in College Station, Texas, just after graduation, a very teary-eyed Chace Wikett led an equally emotional twenty-two year old Antonio Ramirez Garcia to accept Jesus as his personal Savior and become born again. Garcia was raised Catholic, but did not have any idea what it meant to be born again. Not until the guy he had almost gotten into a fight with two and a half years earlier explained what being "saved" meant. Wikett explained to Garcia what it meant to be born again and become a Christian. To truly gain eternal life and have all of one's sins forgiven forever. Garcia made his decision to accept Christ right before he entered into one of the toughest parts of his life—the years he spent in the United States Navy as a SEAL. That decision, made over two decades ago, is now worth an eternity to him.

FBI agents Swanson and Wikett immediately come running through the rectangular passageway, only to find their fellow agent and faithful friend lying in a pool of his own blood with half of his head blown off. Neither Swanson nor Wikett is able to say anything. They just stand there for a few seconds not able to believe their eyes.

Wikett, with his Glock 23 still in his hand, spins around and points it directly at the chest of the man who has just killed Agent Tony Garcia. Big John Swanson quickly reaches out with his massive left hand and grabs his friend and boss by the right arm. With a very strong grip, Swanson pulls Wikett's gun hand down towards the ground.

"Get a hold of yourself, Chace," Swanson says as he continues to hold Wikett's arm. "We need him alive to make him talk."

In shock at what has just transpired, Wikett suddenly hears Craddick's voice through his earpiece. Agent Craddick is still at the scene of the wreck at the I-10 on-ramp a few hundred yards away. "Chace, is everything all right?" This does not snap Wikett out of his trance.

"Rance and Tony got shot. Tony is dead and I don't know about Rance," answers Swanson.

"Oh, dear Jesus," says Craddick. "We heard the shots John. Is Chace OK?"

"Yeah."

To Wikett and Swanson's surprise, they hear Patton's voice in their earpieces. In a quiet, slow, raspy voice Patton says, "Help. Help... Somebody help me."

"Rance!" Swanson replies. "We'll be right there."

After a few seconds of silence, Wikett and Swanson hear Patton moaning again. Patton calls out, "Can anyone hear me? Help... I've been shot... I think I'm still alive... Where's everyone at? I can't hear anything. My ears are ringing."

After hearing Patton's pleas for help, Wikett is able to speak. He looks at Swanson and tells him, "We've got to take care of those still alive." Wikett pauses and then says as he looks back at Garcia's body. "Tony is standing in front of Jesus now. God, how sweet that must be."

This catches FBI agent John Swanson off guard, and he freezes for a moment as he thinks about what he has just heard. The other FBI agents listening do not say anything for what seems like minutes, even though it is only a few seconds.

The silence is broken when Swanson lets go of Wikett's arm and says, "I've got this covered. Chace, you go tend to Patton. I'll cuff Eddison."

As Wikett goes to the other side of the motel, Eddison briefly quits screaming and starts into an expletive-filled rage about how he needs to be taken to a hospital immediately.

Swanson kicks Eddison in the face without thinking about how that could set the criminal free in a liberal state like California if caught on video. Big John then tells the Cajun, "Shut the hell up or I'll shoot you in the head just like you did Tony." Eddison lies there and winces in pain as he cusses the big FBI agent under his breath.

Having run back to where the injured Rance Patton is now sitting up on the edge of the sidewalk behind the motel, Wikett stops and gets his breath. Patton looks up and with great difficulty says, "It hurts to breathe... and my chest feels like I've been hit with a ten pound sledge hammer."

"Patton's sitting up and I don't see any blood," Wikett informs the other agents listening.

"I can't hear... my ears are ringing... is everyone OK... did you get him?" Patton asks.

Knowing his partner cannot hear, Wikett just nods his head up and down. He does not tell Patton about the fate FBI agent Garcia has met. Chace does not see that it should be any concern of Rance Patton's at this moment.

During the very brief amount of time it took for the unstable KKK clansman to seriously injure one FBI agent and kill another, an aggravated Billy Joe Gasperson has been on the phone informing California FBI agent Bart Kennedy about what has transpired. Kennedy and four of his West Coast agents had been waiting about thirty minutes further west on I-10 where they were planning to join the Texas agents trailing Eddison and the two Yemeni Islamic terrorists.

Standing outside of the wrecked red Lexus helping to direct the early morning traffic around the collision site, Gasperson, with a rain coat held up over his head to keep his cell phone from getting wet in the pouring rain, has told Kennedy about the speeding black 80's model Lincoln Continental coming his way. He also informed Kennedy about the gun shots as they happened from the old abandoned three-story motel.

The petulant California liberal started to chew on Gasperson's case about how the Texas agents handled the situation. Billy Joe blasted back at Kennedy and told him very bluntly that it was liberal politicians like him and ignorant politically correct decisions that have caused what has just transpired. He also exclaimed that if this matter would have been stopped in El Paso like it should have been, none of this would have happened.

Gasperson then told Kennedy to get his act together and try and find that black car. With a changed attitude, Kennedy informed Gasperson that his men would be right on it. Billy Joe then hung up the phone in anger.

Gasperson is seriously upset that he was not at the old motel to help. Craddick still sits inside the crashed Lexus with great pain in his upper back and lower neck. He is sure he will be alright though. He can still move all of his extremities.

"Chace, I got a hold of Kennedy and told him everything," Gasperson tells Wikett. "He tried to be an ass, but I was a bigger one back at him and his tune changed. They're hunting the black car now."

"Trey, if an ambulance shows up for you up there, send it down here for Rance, too," Wikett says.

"Yeah, I already thought of that, Chief."

Still standing over Eddison, Swanson asks, "What about Eddison's injuries?"

"I'll doctor him myself with a towel and some duct tape," Wikett replies.

Swanson looks over towards the highway where he hears a vehicle approaching, "Hey Chace, that red Suburban is headed this way."

As the driving rain begins to let up for a moment just outside of Indio, California, the heavy black clouds show that more moisture is evident. Death seems to hang in the damp California air.

CHAPTER EIGHTEEN

Ginger or Mary Ann

As the phone rings five or six times in his ear, Gene Hall is afraid he is going to get an answering machine. He does not want to resort to leaving a message and is not really sure exactly what to say if he does have to leave one. The situation he is calling about is serious enough that he knows he needs to leave a message of some type if that's his only option. But he really needs to talk to his friend.

"Hello, is this old Gene Hall from down Georgia way?" George Thompson asks as he answers his phone right before it goes to the answering service. Before Gene can answer, George says, "Old boy, my caller ID says it's you."

"Yeah George, this is Gene. How are things in Western New York? Y'all ready for the big winter storm coming your way?"

"Oh, I guess we're as ready as a couple of old folks can get for two or three feet of snow," the former Colonel in the U.S. Army replies. "Don't know if we'll get that much, but we have a lot of wood cut, and some hot chocolate for the grandkids if we do."

"Three feet of snow?" asks Gene. "What do you do with three feet of snow, George?"

"I'm going to sit in the living room and look at it through the big picture window."

The two men laugh and then Gene asks, "So you won't even leave the house?"

"No, I will," Thompson says. "I'll have to get out there and move it around a bit with my little Japanese-built tractor."

"What? A Japanese tractor?"

"Yep," answers Thompson. "Who would have ever thought that I, of all people, would have a tractor that was built in Japan?"

"One of those orange ones?"

"Yeah, it's a Kubota."

"I got a neighbor down here that has one of those," Gene says. "He says it's ugly, but a real tough little tractor."

"You know with everything they build and sell us, it kind of makes me kinda wonder who really won that Second World War."

"I know what you mean. I just bought a Toyota pickup the other day, but they say it was built here in the U.S. by Americans."

"I hear those are some real good trucks."

"I like it so far," answers Gene Hall. "Hey, you said something about your grandkids, George. Are they there with you?"

"No, but they're supposed to be in here from D.C. sometime this afternoon. I'm afraid if this storm is as bad as they say it'll be, they may not make it back home to Washington till next weekend. But that'll be OK with me. I love having those kids around here. Gene, you get to see those little ones of yours much in Atlanta?"

"Oh, you betcha I do," Gene replies. "Having them all live within an hour of us is a lot of fun. Sometimes even a little work. But it's worth every bit of it."

"I know what you mean there. They wear me out in a hurry anymore," Thompson agrees.

"Last I talked to you, you thought Rodger and his wife were going to move up there by you. I guess that ain't happened yet, huh?" Gene Hall asks of his unlikely friend.

George Thompson had grown up in a very wealthy family in Upstate New York. George's grandfather and great grandfather, and their father before them owned lots of land and a number of businesses though out the Northeast. They were major players in the New York Stock Exchange a hundred years ago, around the turn of the twentieth century. Thompson's father had built a large law firm in New York State after World War II and eventually took over all the families' business holdings. It shocked almost everyone in his politically left-leaning family in 1961 when a young George Thompson opted to attend the United States Military Academy at West Point instead of studying law at Yale or business at Harvard.

Though he grew up a fairly spoiled kid in an upper class white family, when Sergeant Major Paul McDonnell at West Point got a hold of him, George Thompson became a man. McDonnell had been a heavily decorated soldier in World War II and he saw something he liked in Thompson. And a few things he didn't like. Colonel Thompson always said it was Sergeant Major McDonnell that made him what he became.

It also took his wealthy New York family by surprise when they found out that George, the oldest of three boys and two girls, had voted for Barry Goldwater in the 1964 Presidential election. George Thompson was almost written out of the family will over that.

Now after almost fifty years of perseverance, each of Thompson's brothers and his one remaining sister are all strong conservatives because of George's example of what Christian conservatism is really all about. Even a few of his well-to-do cousins and their offspring now support candidates that adhere to the conservative Christian principles that the country Thompson so loves was built on. This is an oddity when so many old-money New Yorkers fall into the trap of voting religiously for candidates that push liberalism and socialism.

Gene Hall, on the other hand, had grown up dirt-poor in a small town in the south. A small football scholarship, plus a lot of odd jobs and hard work had allowed him to go to college at Grambling prior to enlisting in the U.S. Army. He enlisted in the Army because he feared being drafted. He felt if he joined on his own terms with a partial college education, three years worth, he would be able to have a better chance of staying out of the jungles of Vietnam. It didn't work that way.

It was in the jungles of Vietnam that Private Hall and the wealthy kid from Upstate New York, Second Lieutenant Thompson really formed a friendship and a bond that would last them a lifetime. In a fiercely heated battle with the Vietcong on the twenty-third of September, 1965 Private Hall dragged his friend and Second Lieutenant who was unconscious off of a narrow path and into some heavy wet foliage only moments before North Vietnamese soldiers came running through. Thompson's injuries were minimal and he was back in action in a matter of weeks.

After some long talks, the two men had together on the importance of strong and brave men dedicating their lives to the defense of what they felt was the greatest nation on earth, the United States of America, both of them decided to stay in the military well after their initial tours of duty were up.

The two men also shared a strong faith in God. Hall credited his faith to his upbringing by his father and mother in a rural run-down little town in Mississippi; whereas it was a chance meeting of a girl in New York City at a football game that brought George Thompson to what he referred to as a real man's faith. She invited the eighteen-year-old Thompson to a Billy Graham Crusade in Madison Square Garden in October of 1960. The Crusade started the day after the New York Giants vs Philadelphia Eagles football game where he met the girl. She was pretty and very nice so the young Thompson, a senior in high school, skipped a couple of days of school to stay in New York City and chase the girl.

After taking the girl to an early evening dinner, George went to the first night of the Crusade with her and heard Billy Graham preach things he had never heard before. He walked forward during the invitation to accept Jesus as his Savior. He never saw the girl again. She had disappeared into the large crowd of people. Thompson stayed in New York City for two more days attending the Crusade each night, but not to find the girl. He wanted to hear Mr. Graham preach again.

When he got home, his family was deathly afraid that George was going to end up as a preacher or a missionary somewhere. When he did finally decide to attend West Point they all said, "Well, at least he isn't going into the ministry." How wrong they were in the end, and they didn't even know it. George Thompson spent his entire life ministering to everyone he came into contact with. His mission field was first the U.S. Army, and then the deepest and darkest parts of the CIA.

A thousand miles north of Atlanta, Thompson sits down in a large comfortable recliner and leans back as he answers his good friend's question, "No, Rodger and his wife are still living in a small town just outside of Manassas. Not too far from Langley. They still want to get up here, but it just hasn't happened yet. What brings me to your mind Gene, the weather?"

"No George, not the weather," answers Hall. "This may not be anything, but my sister Martha Jo and a gal she works with at a little motel outside of Baton Rouge are scared some Muslims that are staying there might be planning a terrorist attack on the LSU Alabama game tonight. Martha says they've been chantin' and carrying on for the past couple of days in their rooms I guess. They're worried about the big LSU football game 'cause two of Sharice's boys are a playin' in it."

"Oh, those boys of Sharice's," Thompson replies. "I saw that game a couple of weeks ago when that oldest one had three sacks and the younger one, the linebacker I think, forced two fumbles and intercepted a pass for a touchdown. I mean it now Gene, my Giants need those two boys playing for 'em in a couple of years. That youngest one plays just like Lawrence Taylor did, only maybe faster. But about the motel, do you have the information on it Gene?"

Moving the phone away from his face, Hall yells out the door of his little den to his sweet wife, "Hey Clarice, do you remember the name of that motel the girls are workin' at?"

"I'll get this to Rodger as soon as I get off the phone," Thompson tells his friend. "With this election coming up there's no telling what kind of stuff could happen."

Clarice pokes her head into the den and says, "I think it is the Motor Inn 16 or something like that. I know it's off of I-12 and on that little highway that runs into Denham Springs."

George Thompson, able to over hear everything Clarice says, tells Hall, "I got all that. Motor Inn 16 just north of I-12 and Highway 16. I'm looking at the atlas right now, Gene. You going to be available if I need some telephone numbers?"

"Yeah," answers Hall.

"Ah, just go ahead and give them to me now if you have 'em."

"I'm going to give the phone to Clarice. I'll talk to you later George," Gene Hall hands the phone to his wife.

Clarice and George Thompson exchange greetings and Clarice asks George about his wife while he is looking for a pen that works to write the numbers down. When he finds one, George writes down the Louisiana cell phone numbers of Martha Jo Hall and Sharice Jones to give to his son Rodger who is still an active CIA operative.

After writing down the numbers, Clarice asks Thompson, "Do you want me to give the phone back to Gene?"

"No, I'd better call Rodger and get him and some of his men looking into this. Inside the U.S. isn't his area, but Baton Rouge is not too far from one of Rodger's friends in Dallas who's with the FBI. Tell Gene I'll call him back later to talk more football. God Bless you

Clarice."

"God has blessed us, George, and you know that. He has you too. Please give your sweet little Mrs. my love you ol' softy."

"I'll tell Margret you said hi. You take care of that old man of yours."

————

Having traveled about thirty kilometers in the little green Citroen, most of that on l'autoroute du Nord from Charles de Gaulle International Airport and the rest on the main loop encircling Paris, the Boulevard Périphérique, the trip from one side of Paris to the other is almost over. As tight and cramped as things are for the CCN broadcast journalist inside the little car, there is something very comforting about riding with the three Americans she had just met. Alexia feels like she could travel all over France with them and never even think of getting bored. Seldom has she ever been around people who come across as so genuine. With most of the people she is around on a daily basis she gets very bored with them in only a few minutes and she has to move on to something or someone else new. In the past it was only Severo Baptiste who had been able to keep Alexia's attention without losing it.

After she gives Matthew James the final instructions on how to get to her hotel from the busy Boulevard Périphérique, Alexia regrets that she has to say goodbye to her new friends. She hopes she will get to see them again in the future.

"Miss Klien, which lane do I get in?" Matt asks, trying to think ahead.

"Oh, this one here," Alexia says as she points where to go. "There it is! See the one on the corner across the roundabout? Yeah, that's it, The Hotel Gabriel Issy les Moulineax."

As he laughs at the name of the hotel, Matt looks in the very small rearview mirror and changes lanes while commenting about the French Alexia had just spoken, "If you say so, just don't ask me to repeat it."

Amaya leans forward from right behind the driver's seat and touches Alexia on the shoulder, "It was so great to get to meet you, Alexia. I always knew I would. I just didn't know it would be today."

Amaya's brother Jeff laughs and then informs Alexia, "She's not kidding either, Miss Klien. Ever since Middle School when all the boys started telling her she looked like you she has been saying she would meet you someday. They even used to call her Amaya Klien."

Everyone in the car laughs. Alexia is a little embarrassed, but feels very proud inside that such an incredible young woman as Amaya Blazi would look up to and idolize her. She responds, "Amaya Dawn Blazi, you are going to be my new little sister. You and I are going to be the best of friends."

"Really?" Amaya asks.

"Yes, and we are going to do lots of things together in the future. I have never met anyone who impressed me as much as you have today, girl."

"Thank you very much, Miss Klien."

Alexia smiles and continues, "If you want to model when you're done in Africa, I will pull all the strings I can to help you. If you want to do something else and need help, any kind of help, I will do what I can. I make really good money and I would be privileged to help you with school or anything. You don't know this, but in the very short time I have known you, Amaya, I already look up to you more than you ever could have me. Someone did a terrific job of raising you, and after meeting your brother I know it had to be your parents."

They are nearing the hotel and Matt slows down not to miss the entrance. Amaya is almost shell-shocked at the words she has heard come from the beautiful woman she has been watching on TV and reading about in magazines for nearly ten years.

"Miss Klien, that is so nice of you to say about my sister and our parents," Jeff says from directly behind Alexia. "I will be sure to tell them of your compliments on their efforts. I still think they spanked us way too much."

Everyone laughs and Amaya is able to say, "Maybe me, but not you. You picked on me so much, Jeffery, and you never got spanked for that. Then I'd get spanked for getting back at you."

They all laugh, prolonging the moment before they have to say their goodbyes. The entire time Jeff and Amaya were talking and everyone was laughing, Alexia was writing down every single telephone number and address she could think of, from her home in Washington D.C., her cabin in Aspen, and her parent's house outside of Atlanta, Georgia. All on a piece of blank paper she had just torn out of the inside cover of the little car's owner's manual she dug out of the glove box.

As Matt pulls the green Citroen up to the curb in front of the Hotel Gabriel Issy les Moulineax, Alexia turns in her seat as far as she can and leans into the center of the car to get closer to Jeff and Amaya. When she does, she hands Amaya the list of addresses and phone numbers and even a couple of different email addresses with her most private one circled.

As she hands Amaya the paper Alexia tells her, "I am very serious. You write me, call me, and email me all of your contact information and for God's sake get a hold of me as soon as you get out of that jungle down there in Africa. I never had a sister and I always wanted one. So you're going to be it. You are now my little sister."

Alexia turns her head as far as she can to the left to where she can see Jeff and says, "And if you want to be my little brother, that's fine with me, as long as you give me a ride in one of those fighter jets." They all laugh.

"Your little brother?" U.S. Air Force Major and fighter pilot Jeff Blazi replies humorously. "I'll give you a ride in my F-16 if you'll marry me, Miss Klien."

"Wait a minute, Jeff," Matt cuts in, "I want to marry her!"

"I asked first!" Jeff exclaims.

"I saw her first," Matt asserts.

"Oh yeah, and she wouldn't even speak to you when you saw her first," Jeffrey points out as the whole car bursts out in laughter.

With tears of joy and laughter coming out of her dark blue eyes, the young and beautiful Amaya tells Alexia, "You better hurry up and get out of here before you have to change your last name to Blazi or James."

Everyone laughs as Alexia reaches for the door handle of the car. "I thank you all so much for the lift," she says to all of them still scrunched in the little green Citroen. "It was a lift in so many different ways. Y'all will never know how much I enjoyed this ride. Amaya, call me while you're here in Paris and let me know what you're doing. Love y'all. I'd better run, I'm already gonna be late for work tonight."

Alexia gets out of the car in front of her hotel. When she does,

Jeff climbs out from the seat behind her and gives Alexia a hug. Amaya jumps out from the back seat behind Matt and runs around to the other side of the car. As Jeff sits down in the front seat that the American broadcast journalist has just vacated, Amaya throws her arms around Alexia and gives her a great big hug. It is like they have known each other their whole lives.

"This has been so fabulous, Miss Klien," Amaya expresses. "So incredibly fabulous."

"Amaya dear, today has been absolutely fabulous for me too," Alexia declares. "You be safe out in the jungles of Africa. Don't let some lion or tiger get you. Or an elephant trample you."

"I won't," Amaya replies with tears running down her cheeks.

"We're going to have a lot of fun together, little sister. A lot of fun," Alexia says fighting back tears of her own.

"Fantastic! I can't wait," exclaims Amaya as she opens the door her brother Jeff just got out of and crawls back into the little French car.

With his window rolled down, Jeff yells to Alexia as she is walking backwards away from them, "Remember! You're supposed to set me up with Angie West!"

"I will for that ride in your F-16!"

"It's a deal!"

As Matt starts to pull away from the curb to leave the hotel, he comments, "Amaya, it is fascinating just how much you and Alexia Klien do look alike. Anyone would think you two are sisters."

"They do look an awful lot alike, Matt," Jeff says with a smile on his face. "But I think my sister is more of a Mary Ann, whereas Alexia Klien is definitely a Ginger."

"Does that make me the Professor and you Gilligan then?" Matt asks as he laughs.

"No, Matt," Jeff returns, "You'd be the Skipper."

Nineteen year old Amaya sits in the back seat of the car with a blank look on her face. She has never seen *Gilligan's Island*.

As the cute little sports car drives away, Alexia turns and literally runs towards the front door of the four-star hotel CCN put her in for her stay in Paris.

Knowing her cell phone has been dead now for almost an hour, Alexia enters the big beautiful building and hurries up to the front desk and in French asks the clerk behind the counter if there have been any messages left for her while she has been out. She knows very well that Rigger Watson has probably had someone trying to get in touch with her, she just doesn't know which of his henchmen he will have hounding her this time.

The clerk behind the big marble counter says back to her in English, "Oh yes, Mademoiselle. You have only one message. It is from a Mr. Severo Baptiste. He is worried if you are alright and he says he will be here in Paris late on Sunday night."

She is absolutely baffled. It confounds Alexia how Severo knew her hotel, since she had not told him where she was staying. She tells the clerk, "Merci."

Alexia turns and heads to the elevator. *How did he know? How does he always know?* She wonders. He is without exception the most mysterious and interesting person she has ever known. There never seems to be anything that Severo Arman Casimiro Baptiste doesn't know, especially about her.

A string of thoughts enter her mind that do not have anything to do with her being late to the CCN news studio in Paris, or the mysterious woman on a large plane headed for Moscow. The thoughts in her mind have nothing to with the two very suspicious looking men at the airport or the little black attaché case covered with Islamic symbols. Nothing to do with the three really friendly and nice Christians from America she had just caught a ride with to her hotel. Instead all Alexia can think is, *Severo is going to be here tomorrow. How long has it been since I've seen him? Will he still love me? Have I changed any? What will I wear? Will he still think I am the most beautiful woman he has ever seen? Do I really want to see him?*

CHAPTER NINETEEN

The Good, the Bad and the Ugly

"Hello?" a man answers his cell phone.

"Yeah, hello. Is this Chief Carl J. Thomas?" the man who placed the call asks.

"Yes it is, who's this? I don't recognize your number," a gruff and half grouchy Police Chief asks of the man who has just called him on his private personal cell phone.

"Chief, this is Big Eddie Jefferson."

"Not very many people have this number, Big Ed. How'd you get it?"

"I got your number off Joe's phone one day when he gave it to me to show me one of those nasty videos he's always showin' everyone. Anyway, I ain't given your number to anyone," Officer Edward Jefferson tells his boss.

"You damn well better not give this number out," Chief Thomas snaps back at Jefferson, now a little less tense. "You might outweigh me by a hundred pounds, Big Ed, but I'll kick your big black butt if you do."

Shreveport, Louisiana Police Chief Carl J. Thomas is originally from New Orleans. He is also an African American, but his skin is much lighter than Jefferson's. Chief Thomas's mother was a very beautiful black woman from New Orleans, a woman of the oldest known profession—a prostitute. Thomas's mother had a very long-lived and secretive relationship with a well-to-do white man from the small town of Leesville, Louisiana. The secret relationship lasted for nearly two decades throughout the nineteen fifties and sixties.

Mr. Jackson Lee Thomas, Carl J. Thomas's father was a large land owner. He kept a house in New Orleans as well as his home outside the little logging and agriculture community of Leesville, an Army town located just on the edge of the Fort Polk U.S. Army Base. Jack Thomas owned a percentage of interest in most of the businesses in Leesville. About twice a month he would go to New Orleans on business trips. There he would spend most of his time with the woman who lived in his New Orleans house under the guise of a house keeper.

When she became pregnant with a son, Thomas let her give the boy his name, but they kept the whole thing a secret. That is until Jack Thomas attempted to run for the U.S. Senate in the early 1970's. The dirty little secret of his twenty-year relationship with a former prostitute got out and Carl J. Thomas's mother left New Orleans and moved Carl and her two other children fathered by Thomas to Shreveport, Louisiana where her two sisters lived. Thomas then began making business trips to Shreveport instead of New Orleans.

"Chief, we may have a problem that is a little out of our jurisdiction," Big Eddie says in his deep, slow drawl.

"What do you mean—out of our jurisdiction?" the quicker talking Chief Thomas abruptly asks, "How far out?"

"Well... Baton Rouge, Chief."

"What da hell do you mean Baton Rouge?"

"Well Chief, I gots this girl from down there that has two boys playin' for LSU. The DuPree boys."

"Yeah, I know 'em," replies Thomas, a big LSU fan himself. "What? Them boys in trouble?"

"No, no, they ain't in trouble" the big gentle hearted man tells his superior officer. "It's their mom, she's afraid 'cause she thinks there's some Muslim terrorists going to try to bomb the game tonight. I thought we should call someone in the FBI or something and have them check it out. She's real scared for her boys."

"Why does she think that?"

"She cleans rooms at an old motel in Denham Springs owned by a Muslim man and some other Muslims came in a few days ago and have been carrying on chantin' them crazy Islamic prayers that those people chant when they're going into Jihad I guess."

"And how do you know the DuPree boys's mother, Big Ed?"

"I met her a while back and we really do get along good. She is a great woman," Edward Jefferson answers.

"I want to meet those Dupree boys sometime before the season is over and they get out of LSU. We can take a trip down to the capital or something in a couple of weeks."

"Whenever you want, Chief," Big Ed says. "I'll set it up so you can meet 'em."

"But right now I've got to call a guy in Dallas that busted up that East Texas drug ring last month," says Chief Thomas who is already looking up a telephone number. "You met him I think, that Mexican FBI agent Tony Garcia. I can guarantee he can get to the bottom of this thing in Denham Springs if anyone can, and fast."

"Thanks, Chief."

"Hey, what's the name of that motel the DuPree boys' momma works at?" the Shreveport Police Chief asks before he lets Jefferson off the phone.

"You know, I'm not sure. I'll text you Sharice Jones's cell number and you can call her."

"No, you call her back. Get all the information about the motel, the name, the address, who owns it, and who runs it. And Big Ed, give her my private number and tell her to feel free to call me if she needs to. You call her right away. I'm going to try to get a hold of Agent Garcia right now."

———

Seeing the red Suburban slowly approaching the motel, Big John Swanson grabs Roddy Dale Eddison by his left arm and drags him, kicking and screaming back into the walkway. While he cuffs Eddison to a water pipe against the wall between the ice maker and pop machine, Swanson calls Agent Wikett over the radio. "Chace, if you can leave Rance, you might ought to come out here and find out who's in the red Suburban. They're driving in here."

Knowing Patton can sit on the curb in pain and wait for an ambulance without his help, Wikett quickly ducks into the walkway in the middle of the northeast wing of the old motel. As he spots the Suburban, he pulls out his Glock and gets ready for more action. And action is not what he wants.

"How bad is Eddison bleeding?" Wikett asks.

"Not really that bad. It looks like just a flesh wound," Swanson replies. "I'll grab some towels or a T-shirt to bandage him up. I'm heading to get the duct tape right now for his mouth."

"Hurry, John! That Suburban is still coming, but not very fast."

"I'll be right back. I just got the tape. Two passes around his head and mouth and he won't make a sound."

Wikett hides behind a two-foot wide concrete pillar that holds up a set of stairs leading to the second and third floors. The rain has let up some. He can see the red Suburban has Arizona license plates and the driver is a man who looks to be in his sixties. The man is wearing a dark blue ball cap. After the Suburban passes behind the old gray van it comes to a stop and the man driving it can now see the body of agent Tony Garcia laying on the ground. He just sits there in his vehicle looking around at the area. FBI agent Wikett makes a deduction that this is only an innocent bystander who has let his curiosity lead him someplace he really should not be. Wikett decides to approach the man.

"Swanson, you got me covered?"

"Yeah, Chace. I think it's just some old geezer snooping around," says Swanson as he peeks out from the hallway where he has Eddison hidden.

Wikett walks slowly towards the Suburban, carefully keeping the old gray van between himself and the man behind the wheel of the big red SUV. Agent Wikett can see through the window of the van that the man has seen him. The elderly man rolls down the passenger side window of the Suburban. When Wikett reaches the gray van, he stops behind the back end of it for cover.

"What's going on here?" the man in the Suburban yells.

"I'm FBI agent Chace Wikett and you need to get out of here, sir. This is a crime scene."

"Well, Sonny," the man hollers back, "I'm retired Brigadier General Harold R. Bumguardner of the United States Air Force, and I own this property. So don't be telling me to leave!"

"Well sir, if that's the truth, then we could use some help."

"Son, that's damn sure the truth. And if you really are the FBI, I'll need to see some identification and then I'll do whatever you need me to."

Wikett can hear John Swanson in his ear as he slips around the back of the old van to approach the retired Air Force General in the Suburban. Swanson says, "Can you believe this, Chace? Someone has sent the Air Force in to help us."

"Just keep me backed up, Swanny. And stay out of sight."

Agent Wikett walks up to the back of the Suburban and approaches the passenger side window very carefully. He takes out his FBI badge with his left hand while still holding his handgun firmly in his right hand. As he gets about half way up the side of the Suburban the man in the blue ball cap behind the steering wheel says rather loudly, "I can't see your badge yet, Sonny, but you sure are acting like the FBI. Don't worry, I ain't going to shoot you. Your big man over there in the corner has a real sharp bead on me. I'd be dead in a second."

Wikett eases up a little as he gets to the open window of the vehicle. He shows the old man his badge and sees the blue ball cap on his head says *Air Force* across the front.

"I see you got one dead man and another live one I saw your man drag into the walkway. Is the dead one a good guy or a bad guy?" asks Brigadier General Bumguardner.

"The dead guy is Agent Garcia," Wikett replies.

"I'm sorry about that," says Bumguardner. "It always hurts to lose a man."

"You've got good eyesight if you saw Swanson drag that guy in there from where you were in this rain."

"A pilot has to have good eyesight. How can I help?"

"I've got a man on the back side of the building that needs to be taken to a hospital... and maybe one up there by the intersection."

"That's you guys too, huh? What are you going to do with the guy you drug into the hallway?"

"As far as you are concerned, sir, he doesn't exist."

"I understand. Show me to your man back behind."

"Hey, I'm curious," Wikett asks, "Why were you sitting out front revving your motor up when you first pulled in here?"

"Oh, this dang Chevy has something wrong with the computer system in it," Bumguardner says. "You have to rev it up to get it to idle down sometimes. I need to get it into the shop."

"Oh," Wikett allows.

"I'm going to drive around back. I'm guessing you guys got work to do with the guy that doesn't exist."

Wikett turns around to head back to the other side of the motel as retired General Bumguardner puts his Suburban into gear and rolls up the window.

"John, this guy is the real deal. Go ahead and bandage up Eddison and get him to your vehicle. This place will be crawling with locals anytime now," Wikett says into his radio. The sound of sirens can be heard as the Indio City Police and the Riverside County Sheriff's Department both have officers arriving at the scene of Craddick and Gasperson's wreck less than a quarter of a mile away.

On his way back to the north side of the motel, Chace Wikett's cell phone begins to vibrate, and he figures it is California FBI agent Bart Kennedy. He looks down at his phone and sees his caller ID shows the personal number of Rodger G. Thompson, a CIA operative Chace knows from Washington D.C. Wikett immediately answers the phone.

As Swanson reaches down to uncuff Roddy Dale Eddison to drag him back behind the three story motel where he can put him in the Ford Excursion, he hears his dead partner's cell phone go off. It is the theme song to the Clint Eastwood western, *The Good, the Bad and the Ugly.* John Swanson cannot believe Agent Garcia was so careless to not have his cell phone set to vibrate in a situation like they had just experienced.

Big John drops the left arm of Eddison and runs to answer Tony's phone. He fears it will be Garcia's wife or kids. As the big blond-headed man from Oklahoma pulls the ringing cell phone out of his dead partner's front pants pocket it gives him an eerie feeling, like he is robbing the dead. Swanson wishes he could be as sure as Chace is of Garcia's eternal destination, but he just does not know. He himself has never really thought that much about what happens after death.

With his dead partner's Motorola W7 waterproof cell phone in his hand, FBI agent Swanson sees that the number on the caller ID is from the 318 area code. He knows this is a Northern Louisiana number. A little over a month ago, Agents Swanson and Garcia helped the DEA bust a large meth operation in East Texas and Northwest

Louisiana. Swanson figures the call has something to do with that and he almost doesn't answer it.

At the last moment before the call is routed to an answering service, Big John decides he will go ahead and answer it. No one probably knows Tony's pass code anyway, and the message will just get lost in cyber cell phone space somewhere.

"Hello, you have reached FBI agent Tony Garcia's cell phone. This is John Swanson. How may I help you?"

"John, this is Shreveport, Louisiana Police Chief Carl J. Thomas. Is Agent Garcia available?"

"No. I am sorry, Carl, but Agent Garcia is not available right now. Is there anything important that I can help you with?" Swanson asks as he heads back over to the walkway where Eddison is still cuffed to a water pipe fitting in the wall.

"Yes there is, Big John," Chief Thomas replies. "That's right, isn't it? They call you Big John, don't they?"

Somehow in all this, a smile comes across John Swanson's face. It was Garcia who first started calling him Big John to distinguish John Swanson from another FBI agent named John Billingsly who also works out of the Dallas office. "Oh yeah, everyone calls me Big John thanks to Tony. You're going to have to hurry. We're in a situation here. No time for chit-chat."

"I've had some information come to me that there may be some suspicious activities going on at a motel over by Baton Rouge. I've been told there's a group of Muslim men exhibiting suspicious behavior staying at a motel owned by a Muslim. I'm not sure what it's all about. My source is worried about a terrorist attack on the LSU Alabama game tonight. I've just heard about it, and Tony was the first person I called."

"We haven't heard anything like that. We're in California right now chasing something that sounds very similar. What motel in Baton Rouge?" John Swanson asks.

"The motel is in Denham Springs just outside of Baton Rouge. I don't know anything else. Big Eddie's chasing down the lead to learn more right now," Thomas states.

"I'll make some calls. I'll call you back on my phone. Can I reach you on this number?"

"Yeah. What's your number, so I'll have it if I find out more?"

Swanson pulls his phone out of his cell phone holder on his belt, "Here, Chief. I'll call you on it right now so you have the number. Don't answer it. I'll talk to you later."

"Thanks, John."

Swanson knows he needs to get the homegrown KKK terrorist Roddy Dale Eddison stuffed in the back of the tan Excursion immediately. As he uncuffs the criminal from the water pipe, Big John sees that Eddison has been able to rub some of the duct tape away from his mouth on the pipe he has been attached to. Swanson makes a mental note to put three or four wraps around the criminal's head and mouth next time. Eddison, who is still bleeding, says with great difficulty through the loosened duct tape, "I hope you die today."

In a quick fit of anger, Swanson grabs the injured outlaw by the back of his left knee and leg and drags him about fifty feet on his back on the concrete out of the walkway and around the corner of the three story building to the Ford Excursion. Bumguardner is on the north side of the motel now helping Patton get into his Suburban, and when Swanson comes out of the walkway dragging Eddison behind him, the retired Brigadier General watches the mistreatment of the man who just killed FBI agent Garcia. Wikett is just getting off of his phone call with the CIA operative when Bumguardner remarks, "Good thing that guy doesn't exist, or I'd have to turn you guys in to the Justice Department for cruel and unusual punishment of a prisoner."

Not in any mood for humor, Wikett only glances over at the Air Force retiree.

"I'll tell you this, Son, these liberal SOB's we have in Washington D.C. today don't have any idea what torture really is," Harold Bumguardner states. "They need to read up a little on how our boys were treated in those North Vietnam prison camps, or what the Japanese did to American soldiers in World War II. That was torture. This country is getting too damn soft, if you ask me. Too damn soft."

"I agree with you sir," Wikett replies.

"But don't worry about me. I never saw a thing," Bumguardner returns as he sees Agent Swanson jogging towards them.

As Swanson reaches the back of the red Suburban, Wikett tells Bumguardner, "Thanks. Stop up there at the wreck and get Craddick if an ambulance isn't there yet."

"I'll do that, Sonny. You guys take care and do what you got to do. Oh, and if a big crazy blond headed guy named Chance Kelton shows up over here, he's my contractor. Tell him I'll be back. We're gonna remodel this place, but don't worry about him either. He did two tours in Vietnam. He's one of us." The retired Air Force commander then gets into his red Suburban and drives off.

Swanson looks over at Wikett and says, "Chace, I just took a call on Tony's phone from Shreveport about a possible terrorist attack in Louisiana we ain't even heard about yet."

Agent Wikett cuts in on the bigger man, "Yeah John, me too. I got a call from D.C.—a CIA agent telling me about a possible attack in Baton Rouge tonight no one knows anything about. Guess some cleaning ladies at an old motel have sniffed it out. Worried about the LSU Alabama game. Is that what you heard?"

"Almost exactly, 'cept I heard it from that crazy ol' Police Chief over there in Shreveport. The one that took us all to that crawfish feed at the casino that night." Swanson replies.

"We better get someone we can trust over there in Louisiana so it doesn't end up a goddamned nightmare," Wikett says, "Like this shit has."

FBI agent Swanson uses lots of foul language when he loses his temper, but he is surprised to hear the four letter words come out of Chace Wikett's mouth. He knows Chace is a serious and very strong Christian, and he admires him for that. But Big John also knows how close Chace Wikett and Agent Garcia have always been, and how losing Tony today is really tough on all of them.

John Swanson knows no one is perfect, and trying to hold his friend up to a higher standard in a situation like this, well, that would not be fair to Chace, even if that higher standard is just in his own mind. His heart goes out to Wikett, and also to Garcia's family, who he knows will not take this news very well.

Wikett's phone begins to vibrate, and this time it is California FBI agent Bart Kennedy. Chace opens his phone and answers it, "Yeah, Bart, hold on for just a second."

"OK, but hurry. I don't have all day," returns Kennedy

FBI agent Wikett holds his hand over the phone and tells Swanson, "You call Tom Smith and Bill Jones in Houston and get them on that thing in Baton Rouge. They'll know who to call in Louisiana and what to do. And tell them not to let Avery or Johnson in on what they know. You make darn sure they keep Avery and his men out of this. We don't need another mess like the one we're in here."

Swanson hits his speed dial for FBI agent Bill Jones, knowing Agent Tom Smith will most likely be in the middle of a Saturday morning round of golf, whereas Jones' wife always has him doing things around the house on the weekends. When Agent Jones does not answer his phone, Swanson leaves him a quick message to call him back. He then calls the number he has for Tom Smith's personal cell phone. Bill Jones answers it. Big John recognizes FBI agent Jones's voice right away and asks Bill, "Hey, what's up with you answering Tom's phone? But you won't answer your own?"

Jones laughs and says, "We left mine in Tom's clubhouse locker. My wife is gone this weekend to her sister's in Austin and she thinks I'm mowing the lawn. I hired a neighbor kid to do it and I gave him an extra twenty to keep his mouth shut. Actually, Tom is about to tee off here on the third hole. I just hit mine into a sand trap. What's up, Swanny? Things OK in California?"

"No, they're not," a more sober and solemn John Swanson answers. "This is a real screw-up out here."

"Man, I'm glad you guys went on that one."

"You don't know the half of it," Swanson tells the FBI agent based out of Houston. "And now there is something in Baton Rouge Chace wants you and Tom, and only you and Tom to look into. He wants Avery and Johnson kept completely out of the loop on this thing in Louisiana until we have it under wraps. I mean don't even breathe a word of it to 'em."

"Those are instructions I like. You tell Chace he can count on us. I know a guy in New Orleans and another in Baton Rouge to call. Do we need to get over there too?"

"Not sure yet. We're waitin' for more info. It has to do with some Muslims that have gathered at a motel outside of Baton Rouge and maybe the LSU Alabama game tonight also. I'll text you the personal number of the Police Chief from Shreveport. He might know more than I do."

"I know him, got his number right here. Well, I got it back in the clubhouse anyway, in my phone."

"He's the one that called me. A man in the CIA called Wikett on this same situation at the same time Chief Thomas called me. Chace will have to get you the number of the CIA guy. But to be safe, you better put the clubs up and head for a plane," Swanson tells Jones.

"Good, I was already four strokes behind Tom anyway after only two holes. I'll enjoy telling him he's done," Jones says, smiling as he watches Smith slide his nine iron in his bag after hitting his Titleist Pro V1X golf ball to within about four feet of the pin on the very narrow par-three third hole. "Getting a plane past Avery will be tough, but it's a weekend so we can do it. You guys be safe."

"Yeah, it's too late for that," Swanson replies soberly. "You guys be smart and aggressive and if there's something over there, stop it before it starts. Be talking to you."

"You get home safe, Big John," Jones says as he walks over to tell fellow FBI agent Tom Smith that his round of golf is over for the morning.

Back at the Ford Excursion, Swanson grabs a couple of T-shirts out of his own bag. With the roll of duct tape he doctors up Roddy Dale Eddison's wounds, even though by now they have pretty much clotted. *I'd like to just let this sorry, no-account swamp rat die,* Swanson thinks as he works on Eddison. If it were not for the information he and Chace Wikett hope to extract from the injured Leesburg, Louisiana man, Swanson is quite sure the Cajun would already be dead.

"Big John, there's a California State P. that just came off I-10. I'm goin' to have him bring me down there," Gasperson tells Swanson.

"OK, Billy Joe. That trooper doesn't need to see Eddison, so keep him away from the Excursion."

While Agents Gasperson and Swanson are discussing the patrolman, an argument has broken out between Wikett and Bart Kennedy over the phone. The two men from opposite ends of the political spectrum were discussing what had just happened and what needs to be done to locate the two escaped Islamic terrorists from

Yemen.

Bart Kennedy had started to reprimand Wikett for not allowing Eddison and the "terror suspects," as Kennedy referred to them, to drive further towards Los Angeles before chasing them into the old motel. Texas FBI agent Wikett could not believe the stupidity coming out of the mouth of this politically appointed moron from Massachusetts.

Angry and emotionally drained, Wikett interrupts Kennedy and tells him, "You don't understand a damn thing, Kennedy. Eddison picked this place to pull off, and the Lincoln had been left specifically for the Muslims to take. We didn't have a chance to wait for things to happen on our terms. The way you guys work out here this whole motel could have been full of terrorists, and you guys wouldn't have had a clue."

Belligerently, Bart Kennedy takes his turn at cussing Wikett. "You listen here, you ignorant Texas redneck. We don't go for all your cowboy shit out here. We're civilized people on the coasts of this country, and you guys from Farmerville just screw things up more than the Muslims do. Look at that dumb ass President the state of Texas gave us, George W. Bush. Now that guy didn't even try to make peace with the Arab nations, and look at where we are now."

"Still blaming it on Bush? Why should I expect anything less from someone appointed by a President with Islamic roots?" Wikett fires back, "What I do know is Garcia would still be alive if things had been done my way. The right way, instead of the politically correct way. I think you people are either real freakin' stupid, or you want to see this nation fall on its knees to the rest of the world."

"You Texans can just load yourselves up and go back to Hickville for all I care. I call the shots out here," returns Kennedy, who grew up with a silver spoon in his mouth.

"Yeah, you do that, Bart. Send us home. If we were still in Texas, we'd still have the Yemeni terrorists in hand and we would have already gathered the information we need. You better hope and pray that we can get what we need out of Eddison to save lives here in California." Wikett is about to hang up, but he decides to continue, "I've got ways to find out what we need to know. Ways you don't know anything about with your elitist Ivy League education, Bart.

And you don't want to know anything about 'em either. But you damn well better beg me to use 'em for California's sake. Now you stay the hell out of my way and give me all the help I need. I'm here to help, not to hurt the people of California."

"You might ought to remember who you are talking to, Tex," the arrogant California FBI lead fires back.

Wikett decides to play a card the spoiled Kennedy doesn't know the Texan has. "You get in my way and I guarantee you I will let all the major networks know what happened between you and that philosophy professor of yours at Harvard. You know the one. The guy you went to France with during spring break your junior year."

Shocked at what he has just heard, the New England liberal is silent. Bart Kennedy then swallows his pride and eats some crow, "I will call you as soon as we locate the black car with the two terrorists."

CHAPTER TWENTY

Fixing the News

In Washington D.C., CCN President and network boss Rigger Watson is about to place a private call on an untraceable cell phone he has taken from the locked bottom drawer of his mahogany desk.

The call is to a man in New York City. A man Watson has done business with for over two decades. A man he has used in the past in matters that he thought needed to be redirected or terminated, whichever the case called for. Watson is about to make a call that will produce wall-to-wall national and worldwide news coverage of an incident which is already a big story, but not near as big as what it is going to be. Watson pushes the green send button on the phone. He waits as the black cell phone begins to ring.

The man in New York City is a businessman, strictly concerned with the revenue he can generate for himself. He does not care at all about policies, politics, candidates, or even people for that matter, only money. He does most of his business on a very strict cash only basis—small, old, nonsequential bills. When hired by someone, the job will be done just as it has been requested to be done and he will get paid accordingly. This is not the first time Rigger Watson has hired him to fix what the head man at CCN deems to be a problem.

Because of the magnitude of the majority of Rigger's requests and the size of the payments, the man generally waives his cash-only policy for Watson and opts for funds to be exchanged via wire transfer to banks outside the U.S.

———

It is seventy-two degrees and the sun is shining. There is a slight breeze out of the west and a variety of birds can be heard this morning in the tall pine trees that surround the driveway that leads into the Woodlands Golf and Country Club north of Houston. FBI Agents Tom Smith and Bill Jones head to Tom's house to get Bill's car. Bill has the window rolled down on the passenger side of Smith's yellow 1973 Corvette Stingray that Tom only drives on Saturdays to go play golf. Once they've switched to Bill's Ford Taurus, the two men are on their way to the George Bush Intercontinental Airport in Houston to catch a private plane to fly to Baton Rouge, Louisiana.

After putting Tom's golf cart up and before leaving the Woodlands clubhouse, Jones received a phone call from Shreveport, Louisiana Police Chief Carl J. Thomas. It was all the pertinent information about the motel in Denham Springs, Louisiana.

Federal agent Tom Smith has been on two different phone calls, one with a man from Baton Rouge and another with a man from New Orleans—two Louisiana-based FBI agents that Texas Agents Smith and Jones know they can trust. They are seasoned and experienced Cajuns who love their country and their home state of Louisiana, and would risk life and limb to protect the Cajun people and their wild and carefree lifestyles.

Bobby LeBlanc and Patrick Theriot were both raised on crawfish and catfish with a little alligator and lots of extra-hot hotsauce thrown in to spice things up. Tom Smith and Bill Jones jumped at the chance to get on a private federal jet and fly to the New Orleans area from Houston for a chance to work with LeBlanc and Theriot. There will not be anything routine or boring about this mission into the swampy lands of Louisiana.

In the northern part of Baton Rouge, Bobby LeBlanc had just finished helping his wife Silvia straighten up their house when he received the phone call from Tom Smith letting him know of a potentially dangerous situation developing at a motel in Denham Springs. LeBlanc and his wife were preparing for two couples who are coming over later for a mid afternoon pregame party before the big football game between the LSU Tigers and the Alabama Crimson Tide tonight.

After the call from Jones, LeBlanc immediately begins making phone calls. With her cleaning chores complete, Bobby's wife kisses him on the cheek and heads out the door with their nine year old son to a PeeWee football game which is scheduled to start at 11:00 A.M.

Before she leaves in the family minivan, Bobby runs outside and gives his little boy a hug and a high-five. It's the Pee Wee league championship game. Silvia LeBlanc tells her husband, "Don't worry, honey. I'll video tape it."

When Patrick Theriot's iPhone rang, he was at his father's home in Metairie, a community on the west edge of New Orleans. Theriot had just hooked his white half-ton Chevy pickup to a boat trailer carrying his purple and gold 2007 Nitro Z9 fishing boat. Theriot's plans were to do a little fishing on his day off on Lake Pontchartrain. He keeps his boat in his parent's three car garage because there is no place safe and secure to keep it at the condo he and his girlfriend own together.

News of a possible Islamic terror threat in Louisiana on the Saturday before the Presidential election is something neither LeBlanc nor Theriot have heard anything about until the phone calls from Houston. There had been no other signs or leaks of information of a potential threat to the area of any kind from the many sources the federal, state, and local law enforcement agencies have throughout the south. But FBI Agents LeBlanc and Theriot are not going to take this threat lightly, not if there is the slightest chance it could be for real. This is the main reason the Houston based Bureau men Tom Smith and Bill Jones specifically contacted LeBlanc and Theriot directly to alert Louisiana of a possible national disaster rather than going through the normal Washington D.C. based bureaucratic channels.

So often when someone goes through the normal channels of government appointed bureaucracy, the ball gets dropped or delayed somewhere along the way, and the person who drops the ball is normally not the one who gets the blame. It generally lands on those who are seriously trying to do their jobs out in the field.

Time is of the essence. There are less than twelve hours before two of the reigning superpowers in college football are to take the field and square off for the right to go to the SEC Championship Game and then on to the BCS College Football Championship. The people of Baton Rouge, the people of Louisiana, and the people of the United States don't have time for some desk jockey to rubber stamp a plan. Not when there are outsiders here from another land that have it as their only goal to cause death on a large scale in the United States. Fighting Islamic terrorism is never an easy task and it becomes much more difficult when those individuals trying to fight such an evil have to fight the very people above them.

The reason Wikett made it very clear to John Swanson that Smith and Jones are to keep the federally appointed FBI bureaucrats Avery and Johnson completely out of the loop on this Louisiana lead is because the Washington-based men are so politically motivated in everything they do. Wikett has dealt with them stalling on important issues in the past. Stalling until they knew exactly how their decisions would affect their own careers. Avery and Johnson are two men who have risen faster on fewer credentials than almost anyone else in the Bureau, with the possible exception of Bart Kennedy in California.

Family connections are what elevated FBI Agent Kennedy to where he is. Everyone knows this too. There are many tested veterans in the California branch of the Bureau that wish the young Kennedy would spend even more time vacationing in the east than he already does, which is far more than anyone else in the FBI could ever get away with. Some joke that Kennedy vacations nearly as much as the current President.

After he makes several phone calls contacting other law enforcement personnel in the area notifying them of the suspected Islamic terrorist cell in Denham Springs, FBI agent LeBlanc dispatches men to start an immediate surveillance of the old rundown Saudi Arabian owned motel. The men he sends are a combined team of federal agents and S.W.A.T. personnel from different branches of law enforcement, men well-equipped to deal with anything they might encounter.

Agent LeBlanc's next phone call is to U.S. Federal District Court Judge Jerald Kryer to have him issue a search warrant for the Motor Inn #16. Eighteen months earlier that motel had been on a potential watch list the FBI had comprised of locations of suspicious Islamic activities. Federally mandated budget cuts coming down from the current administration known to be weak on the War on Terrorism had caused the Bureau to downsize their list considerably. Bobby LeBlanc and Patrick Theriot were not surprised when they received the calls from the Texas agents that out-of-the-ordinary activities were taking place at a motel owned by the Saudi Arabian businessman Shahid al-Zahrani.

In the city referred to as the Big Easy, FBI agent Patrick Theriot made phone calls of his own, putting together a small team of five Bureau men he trusted from New Orleans. Including the pilot, six men climbed into a Bell UH-1H FBI helicopter and headed northwest out of New Orleans for Denham Springs. They flew directly over Lake Pontchartrain, the very lake where Agent Theriot had planned to spend the entire day fishing for bass, trout and redfish. Flying over the large body of water a hundred feet above the tree tops, they see someone below in a fishing boat. Theriot yells to those riding with him in the chopper, "That'd be me if it weren't for this damn job."

After talking with U.S. Federal District Court Judge Jerald Kryer, LeBlanc calls Smith and Jones who are en route from Houston. He tells them he will pick them up from a private air strip they are landing at after he gets the search warrant from Judge Kryer. According to their calculations, the timing should be almost perfect between the time the Learjet carrying Jones and Smith from Houston lands and when agent LeBlanc is there to pick them up.

Agents LeBlanc, Theriot, Smith and Jones all agree that once they have the federal search warrant in hand they are going to go with a full scale ambush of the motel, storming the two rooms the suspected terrorists are in, rooms 125 and 127. With the attack taking place around noon, there should be a minimum of other guests still there. Precautions will have to be made to make sure the two brave women who are responsible for tipping off authorities of the situation do not come into harm's way. Agent Theriot brings up a good point on a conference call that word needs to be sent to Sharice Jones and Martha Jo Hall to go on about their business as usual until notified to keep from tipping off al-Zahrani about the forthcoming barrage.

If this turns out to be a false alarm, or a wild goose chase the four FBI agents responsible could possibly be faced with severe reprimands for their actions. That is a risk all four serious Bureau men are willing to take. They feel it is much better to err on the side of the American people than on the side of the forces of evil.

———

In the lobby of the fancy French hotel the silver sliding doors of the elevator open and a tall man wearing a black suit steps out first, followed by a mother with three small children. The CCN broadcast journalist moves aside to give them room to walk past. Alexia assumes they are all together when she steps into the elevator and turns around, but as the doors slide shut she sees the man go in the opposite direction of the woman with the children.

Riding the elevator up, Alexia's thoughts are racing. Everything she has experienced in this whirlwind of a day in Paris loops over and over in her mind. As she gets off of the elevator on the floor where her private suite is located, her emotions are going around in circles in her heart just as fast as her thoughts are spinning in her head. She can actually feel her heart beating inside her chest as she thinks about how Severo Baptiste may very well be joining her in her hotel suite in a little over twenty-four hours. Anxiety and anticipation are battling for the top spot in the deepest and dearest parts of her heart.

What else could I experience today? She thinks to herself as she tries to open her hotel room with a keycard that doesn't seem to want to work. Perplexed and now beginning to panic about how late she is going to be arriving for work this evening at the Paris CCN Network studios, Alexia is about to scream when the door she is trying to open suddenly opens from the inside.

When it does, a very tall and handsome man about fifty years old says to her in French, "Hello, go ahead and come on in. I don't know you, but I think I want to."

Alexia is surprised to find this strange man she has never met or seen before in her room. She doesn't have any idea what to do. She stands there scared and startled for just a second and then sees out of the corner of her eye that she is on the wrong floor. She is on the tenth floor and has walked to the room that would be directly under hers.

Quickly, she says to the tall French man who was very willing to let her into his room, "I am sorry, I have the wrong floor. I am on the next floor," she pauses, not wanting to let him know where her room is. She looks down at her keycard then goes on and says, "I am on the ninth floor. I am one floor too high. I'm so sorry."

"Oh, that is too bad," the Frenchman responds in English. "I was hoping maybe we could share this room."

As Alexia turns and heads to the elevator, the man says to her, "If you are free for dinner tonight, I will take you any place you wish."

Out of courtesy and kindness, Alexia stops and turns back to him, "Oh thank you, sir. But I am meeting my fiancé later tonight for drinks and dinner. Thanks anyway."

When she gets on the elevator, Alexia takes it one floor down to the ninth floor. She then gets on a different elevator and takes it to the eleventh floor where her suite really is. This time her keycard works on the first swipe.

As she walks into her business suite that CCN foots all the bills for, she turns on the lights. Suddenly she remembers her cell phone has been dead for well over an hour, so she plugs it into the wall charger and lays it on the nightstand beside the bed.

Alexia quickly slips out of her clothes and heads to the bathroom, where she steps into a very hot and steamy shower. She closes her eyes and wishes that she did not have to report to the studio tonight.

While she has her eyes closed, she wishes she could just stand there. Let the hot soothing water run down off her head and through her hair onto her back and down her body for the rest of the night. Standing there in the hot steamy shower dreaming of letting herself relax the night away, Alexia's mind wanders off to three years ago when she last saw Severo Baptiste in South Africa.

Thinking about South Africa and Severo Baptiste, she dreams of where she might be today had she just abandoned her job and her career and left Johannesburg with him for the South Pacific Islands as he wished she would do. As she thinks of this, her mind jumps even further back in time. A time when the two of them were standing alone on the west bank of the Nile River in Cairo, Egypt very late one night in the moonlight. A time when Severo asked her to marry him.

With the soothing hot water running down over her face and across her closed eyes, she envisions where she might actually be right now had she said yes. It is quite possibly the most beautiful place her mind has ever been. She is lost in her vision when all of a sudden, through the water-covered glass shower door, she hears her cell phone ringing in the other room.

CHAPTER TWENTY-ONE

Found in the Book of Revelation

With the dry, scorching heat beating down on him, the young man from Wyoming grasps his rib cage and lies on his side in pain in the hot desert sand after coughing up some blood. After a moment, he slowly gets back to his feet. There is blood on his chin.

Still carrying Sergeant Davis, Diaz stops after he realizes that Private Tillord is not keeping up with him. He turns and sees Tillord just getting back to his feet beside Sheldon Mitchal, who has rolled over to his back out of pure exhaustion in the sands of the Arabian Desert.

Laying on his back and looking up at his good friend, Mitchal says, "Man, Tillord, you got blood all over your chin. Did you bite your tongue or something?"

"You do, Will. What the... ? It wasn't like that back there a ways," the tough Mexican says.

Sore and now starting to really ache, Tillord replies, "Yeah guys, I just coughed it up. I don't know where it came from. I feel OK except for my ribs hurt like hell. The pain just kind of comes and goes."

The man Diaz has draped over his shoulder starts to move and groan. Diaz drops down to one knee on the desert floor to let Davis get his feet under him. The Sergeant stands on his own while Diaz holds him up and helps him balance.

"What just happened?" Davis asks slowly. "Damn, my head and my arm hurt."

"Sarge, you were thrown out of the tower when that Ryna Corp truck hit us. I think your arm is broke bad," Diaz replies.

"Is everyone OK?" Davis asks in pain.

"We're all still alive," Diaz answers. "Sheldon screwed his knee up and Tillord has some broken ribs and is coughing up blood. I think everyone in the shack is dead though."

Sergeant Davis turns his head in the direction of the guard shack and says, "Damn, that don't look good. There ain't no one alive over there... They were training today too."

"Three of them haven't even been here a week yet. Damn, that's some bad luck," the normally tough and uncaring Diaz replies as he realizes the very young soldiers just out of boot camp did not survive even seven days in their first tour of duty overseas.

"There had to be eight people in that guard shack," Private Mitchal comments, still sitting on the desert floor in the hot, gritty sand with his torn-up knee. "Actually nine if Lieutenant Johnson was still in there."

Davis shakes his head in disgust. "Oh yeah, Sam was in there."

The fine dust hanging in the air slowly starts to settle and drift away as rays of the hot afternoon sun again dominate the atmosphere surrounding the Ali Al Salem Air Force Base. Help is beginning to show up in the form of concerned soldiers for the men who have been on guard since early this morning, but badly needed medical help has not yet arrived.

It looks like body bags are all that will be needed for the military personnel who had been working in the guard shack at the rear entrance gate to the air base. All that is left of the truck that hit the guard shack are the axles, the twisted frame, and the back bumper that was bolted to the now blackened and burnt American-made vehicle.

Curious and concerned soldiers are arriving. They find tools of all kinds and sizes scattered across the floor of the Arabian Desert. The tools had been in the work truck for Ryna Corp employees to use in their assistance of the U.S. Military in the War on Terrorism. Crescent wrenches, vise grips, hammers, screw drivers, pliers, and all kinds and sizes of socket wrenches and sockets are scattered across the hot desert sand.

A really tall, skinny soldier from the Deep South walks over to where the unexploded white Ryna Corp work truck has smashed into the legs of the leaning guard tower and hollers out to all the other soldiers in the area, "Hey y'all ought to come on over here and look at this. Whoever shot this rag-head blowed him to freakin' pieces. He looks like Muslim hamburger or something. Damn! I'll bet Allah won't even know who he is."

Another soldier on his way over to see what the guy from Mississippi is talking about asks, "Does he look like he's enjoying his seventy-two virgins yet?"

"You two guys get the hell away from that truck until a demo squad gets here," a Major in the Air Force who has just arrived on the scene in an open-topped Humvee yells over to the two careless and inexperienced Army Privates. "If that truck is rigged with a bomb, you'll end up being two of that dead Arab's virgins yourselves."

The lanky kid fresh from Mississippi immediately takes off running away from the truck. An older soldier sees some humor in the situation and hollers, "Hey boys! It looks like ol' Mississip doesn't want to be loved on from now til eternity by a dead Muslim!"

In the terrible, tense aftermath of an Islamic terrorist attack here in the hot and dry Kuwaiti desert, this gets a laugh out of some of those present. But not the Hispanic soldier from San Antonio, Texas. Specialist Carlos Diaz cannot get the image of the dead Saudi Arabian man out of his own head. It was he who had killed the driver of the second truck.

Only thirty minutes earlier, Diaz was sitting in the top of the thirty-foot tower and schooling the young Private Tillord on how truly hard it is to have to shoot another human being. He thinks about how he had just told Will that he hoped that the eager young man from Wyoming would never have to feel what it is like to have to pull the trigger of a gun and kill another human being.

Specialist Diaz also remembers telling Mitchal and Tillord that the only thing that keeps the inner pain of killing another person from ripping away at a soldier's soul was the immediate fear of losing one's own life that he felt while in battle. Then, by the time the soldier is finally able to get to real safety, the incredibly empty feeling of having had to shoot another member of the human race has lessened because of the passage of time.

Now, U.S. Army Specialist Carlos Diaz has just shot and killed someone, a human being, and only moments later he is in a completely safe and secure environment with no fear for his own life. He'd had to shoot and kill people before in war. But something is different this time, and it is the time itself that is different. There is none. The time gap between when Diaz shot the crazy Arab terrorist and then being free from danger is so much shorter than he has ever experienced before. The reality of having taken another man's life is really starting to sink into the tough Texan's psyche. Diaz can already tell that this time he may not be able to handle it.

Having just stepped out of the passenger side of a tan Humvee, Air Force Major Scott McQueen walks up to the four men who have miraculously survived the surprise attack and asks, "Are you guys alright?"

Before one of the three soldiers who have suffered serious physical injuries can say anything, a disturbed looking Diaz says, "I need to see a Chaplain. I really need to see a Chaplain."

Seeing that Mitchal, Tillord, and Davis are still alive and do not appear to be in grave danger, the observant and experienced Major McQueen turns his full attention to the man not injured at all. He asks Diaz, "Do you want to see a Catholic Priest?"

"No," answers the visibly shaken soldier. "I want to see a Christian Chaplain, like the guy Sheldon is good friends with."

Major McQueen does not say anything as he glances at the other soldiers.

Diaz looks over at the injured African American from Queens and says, "You know who I am talking about, Mitch. The guy you're always studying the Bible with. The older guy from Florida."

"Oh, Sergeant Glen Davis," replies the twenty-one year old Christian. "Yeah... but he's not a Chaplain. He's a preacher back in Jacksonville, Florida where he's from. But I know he would be more than happy to talk with you, Diaz."

Mitchal looks over to the Air Force Major. "Sergeant Glen Davis is a real good man. If Diaz needs someone to talk to, Davis would be a great choice, sir."

"We need to get you guys some medical attention," the officer from the other branch of the U.S. Military acknowledges. "If Sergeant Glen Davis is who we need, he is who we'll get."

"Sergeant Davis is usually done with his duties by mid afternoon," Mitchal informs McQueen. "I can get his number for you."

"Thanks, I'll get a hold of him as soon as I can," the higher ranked man declares.

"Thank you, Mitch," the tough and gritty Diaz says as he looks over to Private Mitchal. "I never have told you this, but I really respect you because of your faith."

In the hot, dry heat of the Arabian Desert, a number of U.S. Air Force and Army personnel have arrived to secure the area and inspect the extent of the damage from the bomb blast that was heard and seen from many miles away. Suddenly a soldier who is beginning to dig through the rubble of what used to be the guard shack, yells, "Hey! I think somebody might still be alive over here! I just heard someone cry for help!"

————

With the water in her hotel shower turned up as high and as hot as she can get it, Alexia hears her little blue cell phone ringing the special tone she has programmed in for her friend Angie West. She quickly steps out of the shower and runs through her expensive hotel room soaking wet and without a stitch of clothing, getting water everywhere.

"Angie, you there? I was in the shower! I barely heard the phone!" Excited and drenched, Alexia pauses and doesn't hear anything. "You there, girl?"

"Yes! Yes! I'm here," Angie West says after she quits laughing. "Can you hear me, Klien?"

"Yeah Ange, I can hear you. You in Kuwait or still in Iraq?"

"You wouldn't believe it, Klien. We just landed in Kuwait a few minutes ago and they just had a terrorist attack here."

"What... In Kuwait?"

"We could still see the fires burning at one of the gates coming into the air base. It's unbelievable. I hope it wasn't because I was flying in today." Disturbed and concerned, the blonde beauty from Oklahoma asks, "Have you heard anything about this in France yet?"

"No, I haven't," Alexia replies. "But I haven't made it to the studio yet, either. Wow, what a day I've had too. I can't tell you about it right now. I've got to get to work and I'm going to be late. Are you OK, Ange?"

"Oh yeah, I'm OK," the country music singer allows. "I should be OK, anyway. I'll have a hundred thousand U.S. troops guarding me once I get to Camp Arifjan. They're taking me over there on a helicopter after I meet some people here at the air base."

"You're going to be busy. Those trips are always hurry, hurry, hurry."

"I had a blast in Iraq. The troops there were awesome. What a great experience. I think I get more out of this than my fans do."

"Oh, yeah. Those trips are fun. A lot of work, but fun."

"Have you had contact with Severo yet?" Angie pauses and then says, "I'm guessing you have. Am I right?"

"Yes, yes, yes, you're right," Alexia answers still dripping water everywhere. "But there's so much more. I'll call you when I get in a taxi."

"I'll be busy for awhile. Let's talk later tonight or in the morning. You take care, girl. And give that Severo my love if you see him," Angie laughs goodnaturedly at her friend who has been running away from love ever since she has known her and then says, "Bye, girl."

"I will. Love you. Be careful in Kuwait. Talk to you later maybe. Bye." Alexia gets off the call with her closest friend and confidant.

Still standing in her birthday suit in the middle of her hotel room, Alexia is about half dried off now and her hair looks about as wild as she can be at times. She sets her phone down and heads back to the bathroom to finish getting ready to leave and head to the neverending cycle of news story after news story after news story.

Riding the elevator down to the lobby of the Hotel Gabriel Issy les Moulineax, Alexia thinks, *At least when Angie is done with a show she can get away from work. The career I have chosen never ends. It follows me everywhere I go and it's in everything I do.*

Then the door to the elevator opens and Alexia steps out into the lobby of the French hotel.

———

The rain has dissipated and the heavy dark clouds of the morning have given way to sunshine. It has been over three hours since Texas FBI agents Rance Patton and Danny Trey Craddick were taken to John F. Kennedy Memorial Hospital in Indio, California for medical attention. The body of fallen FBI agent Antonio Ramirez Garcia is in the L.A. County Morgue awaiting transfer back to Dallas. Ironically, Dallas is the town where John F. Kennedy was assassinated. Tony's family has yet to be contacted about his death. Chace Wikett plans to do this himself.

The California team of federal law enforcement agents led by Bart Kennedy has had no luck in finding the black 1980 Lincoln Continental or its occupants. Kennedy has helped Agent Wikett in every way he could, giving the Texas agent the freedom he needs to interrogate the only remaining link the U.S. Government has to a suspected terrorist plot on the people of Los Angeles. The man from Massachusetts has bent over backwards to accommodate Wikett ever since the wily and experienced federal lawman from Dallas mentioned the Paris incident. An incident Kennedy didn't think anyone inside the Bureau knew anything about. Something he wanted kept that way. Kennedy even helped Wikett find a safe, secluded, and out-of-the-way place to conduct the interrogation of Eddison. In their talks, Wikett informed Kennedy of his wishes to be the one to take the news of Garcia's death to the Garcia family. An agreeable Bart Kennedy was good with everything the former CIA operative asked.

Agent Wikett and his remaining men, Swanson and Gasperson, have spent two hours straight in an intense interrogation of Eddison, who shows no signs of breaking. With no idea of the targeted location of the suspected Islamic terrorist plot, the three agents who comprise only half of the FBI team that drove across a thousand miles of desert know the lives of thousands, if not millions of people may depend on the information they can coerce from the rogue KKK clansman.

Wikett and Big John Swanson walk out of the small room in a large abandoned warehouse an hour east of L.A. that they are using in their attempt to interrogate the crazy Cajun from Louisiana. The brick warehouse, which was built in the 1950's, is now owned by the U.S. government. Billy Joe Gasperson stays in the room with Eddison, where he continues to grill him with a very bright light shining into Eddison's taped-open eyes.

"Chace, you seem to know for sure that Tony went to Heaven when he died," Swanson says to his friend as they exit the room. "How do you really know he did?"

As he consideres Big John's very serious and heartfelt question, FBI agent Wikett's cell phone begins to vibrate. He says to Swanson, "Hold that thought. I do want to answer you."

After pulling his phone out of the front pocket of his jeans, Wikett sees it is Bart Kennedy. He hopes to hear good news about the location of the two Muslim terrorists from Yemen. "Yeah Bart, this is Wikett."

"Do you have anything yet?" the quick-talking man from Boston asks in his high-pitched voice.

"No Kennedy, I don't. I'll call you as soon as we do. Have you found anything?"

"W-well we did find the black Lincoln about an hour ago," a hesitant and stuttering Kennedy replies. "It was ditched in a salvage yard only about ten miles down the road from where they got away from you."

Agent Wikett tries to keep his cool. "They wouldn't have gotten away from us in El Paso! And we'd have three people to interrogate instead of one." Still grieving deeply over the loss of his best friend's life, Chace Wikett is more sensitive than he normally would be.

"That's not what I meant, Chace," Kennedy recants. "It's just that we don't even know what they are driving now."

"When you find out something solid call me back. Right now, I'm busy." Wikett closes his phone and thinks to himself how much easier it would have been to interrogate three suspects instead of just one. With two suspects it is possible to work one person against the other. With three suspected terrorists he could work two against one and one against two, and he can do it in three different ways.

This would have been so much easier to do the Texas way in Texas, rather than the politically correct way in California, he thinks. In Chace Wikett's vast experience all over the globe he has seen what he calls the Texas way work hundreds and hundreds of times more than he had ever seen the politically correct way work. The only thing he had seen the politically correct way do was cost good people their lives. Being a student of history, he thinks the best example of the failures of political correctness is Britain's Neville Chamberlain in the years leading up to the Second World War. The politically correct ways in which Prime Minister Chamberlain dealt with Adolf Hitler's aggression cost England and many other nations thousands of thousands of lives. Very good, innocent people died because of the bad decisions of people wanting to remain neutral.

Every time Wikett thinks about what is happening to the great country he and his family live in at the hands of people who do not fully understand or even care about the strong Christian roots on which America was built, it makes him furious. The only way he is able to deal with the destruction of the values and morals of the home country that he so dearly loves is to remember that in the very end, good prevails over evil. The end found in the last chapters of the Book of Revelation.

CHAPTER TWENTY-TWO

Cornfields in North Central Iowa

With the sirens of two military ambulances getting louder as they approach, the first U.S. Military personnel to show up begin to dig through the remains of what was once a small building. The guard shack used to regulate the traffic entering and leaving the back side of U.S. Air Force Base Ali Al Salem. To everyone's amazement and joy, they witness the recovery of two very lucky soldiers. Of the nine who had been in the explosion, Lieutenant Sam Johnson from Boston, Massachusetts and Private Melinda Rozi of Carlsbad, California have survived.

Johnson and Rozi are now tied to fellow soldiers Tillord, Mitchal, Diaz and Davis as the six survivors of an attack that killed seven Americans today.

A team of specialists are being flown in by helicopter from Camp Arifjan, the largest U.S. Military facility in Kuwait. Kuwait is a country that sets on the east side of the continent on which the majority of the ancient history of the Bible took place over two thousand years ago. U.S. Air Force base Ali Al Salem is approximately 750 miles east of Jerusalem, the capital of Israel. Israel is at the most inner part of the Mediterranean Sea, and Kuwait, on the same land mass, is located at the most inner part of the Persian Gulf. Arifjan is about thirty miles south and east of the U.S Air Base Ali Al Salem. Mitchal, Diaz, Davis and Tillord live at Camp Arifjan and make the trip to the air base each day to perform their guard duties.

Military commanders from Camp Arifjan have sent a team of demo specialists to locate and defuse any unexploded IED's that might be in the white truck that crashed into the base of the now leaning guard tower. The specialists will soon be arriving to risk their lives to save others.

As sad and angry as those around the area are where this uncalled for Islamic terrorist attack has taken place in the peaceful country of Kuwait, they are even more excited and emotionally uplifted to find Johnson and Rozi alive. Thirty-seven year old Lieutenant Sam Johnson and twenty year old Melinda Rozi will again see their families and loved ones.

———

Wikett stands and thinks to himself for a moment in the warehouse. The large, empty building was once used to store the produce raised on the California farms in the area, but many of the farms have been turned into suburbs and housing developments. Wikett and Swanson are in the big open area outside the room where Gasperson is still drilling Eddison with questions. In this part of the warehouse the ceilings are twenty feet tall, and the two FBI men look rather small standing all alone on 30,000 square feet of concrete.

"John, about that question of yours."

"Yeah, Chace. You seem to believe that Tony went straight to heaven when he died. How do you really know that?" Swanson asks. Before Wikett can answer, Big John continues, "I mean, just how can you be so sure of that? Tony wasn't perfect. He was a good guy, but he sure wasn't perfect."

Very seriously concerned with what he is going to say, Chace Wikett takes a deep breath and thinks for a moment before he speaks. "Antonio Garcia and I are Christians. I was there over twenty years ago when Tony accepted Jesus Christ as his personal Savior." Wikett pauses, "John, the Bible specifically says in many places that nothing, nothing on this earth or anything else can separate us from the love of God after we have accepted his Son Jesus as our Lord and Savior. I know Tony wasn't perfect. None of us are. But I do know that Tony was saved, which makes him a Christian, and he will be with God forever."

"I understand some of that, Chace. I was raised Lutheran," Swanson tells Wikett, whom he has known for nearly ten years. "I was even confirmed into the Lutheran Church when I was about fourteen. But I have never really felt or known for sure if I was a

Christian, or if I would go to heaven if I died."

John Swanson pauses and looks down at the ground. When Chace doesn't say anything, John continues, "Chace, I did a lot of really bad things in high school and in college. I treated girls terribly. I used them. And I've always cussed like a sailor any time anything goes wrong. You know how bad my temper can be. You've seen it on the golf course. I just never have felt I was good enough to be a Christian. I guess I always hoped someday when I got older I would be able to control myself better and actually be good enough to be a Christian."

For a few seconds the two grown men stand in silence in the middle of the wide open area about a hundred feet from where agent Gasperson is trying to break down the crazy hardened man who only a few hours ago killed their friend and partner, Tony Garcia.

As Wikett thinks about everything he wants to say and what he knows that he needs to say, he stands silent formulating his thoughts. Expecting his friend and boss to speak, but not hearing anything, Swanson asks, "What if that had been me out there this morning getting my head shot half off? What if I had been killed instead of Tony?" Swanson pauses and then wonders, "Would I have gone to heaven? I don't think so. I really don't think so."

FBI agent Chace Wikett believes everyone at different times throughout their lives will have moments when they ask very deep and meaningful questions about life and death. In the middle of everything that is going on here today, Wikett can tell that fellow Bureau man John Swanson is at one of those points in his life today.

Wikett knows it is the depth of the person and the seriousness with which they search that sometimes determines whether they find the real answer to those questions, or just substitute answers that divert the individual searching for the truth. This is a moment in the lives of both men that could have eternal consequences, especially for Swanson.

"John, do you know what it means to be *born again*?" Wikett asks.

"No Chace, I don't think I really do. I've heard a few jokes about *born again* people. I've never told any of them to you or to Tony 'cause I knew both of you called yourselves *born again*."

Knowing he needs to be careful how he phrases his next question,

Wikett pasuses and then asks, "OK John, you were raised in a Lutheran Church in Oklahoma, right?"

"Well, I was born in Oklahoma," Swanson says. "But when I was six we moved to Iowa and my dad farmed with my grandfather for about ten years. Then we moved back to Oklahoma after grandpa sold the farm. It was when we lived in Iowa that us kids always went to church with my grandmother. Dad and grandpa always seemed to have farm work to do on Sunday mornings and my mother waited tables at a local restaurant every Sunday. The tips were best then with the church crowds, plus the younger girls that worked at the restaurant never wanted to work early on Sunday mornings after being out late on Saturday nights. But Chace, I don't really remember ever being taught what 'born again' means, not in church or in the Catechism classes my grandma took us to every Wednesday after school."

"You know how there are many different kinds of FBI agents out there, right?" Swanson nods his head and Wikett continues, "Well just as there are different types of agents—some on the mark and some off the mark, some that you trust to get things right and others who you know only go through the motions—there are many different types of Christian churches out there. Some churches avoid the hard, tough subjects of the Bible and just go through the motions only trying to get by. I don't know that much about the Lutheran Church John, but in my opinion if they are not teaching a strong message that a person must to be born again, then I'm afraid they are watering down the real message of the Gospel of Jesus Christ. They are not telling how a person truly becomes a Christian. A huge pet peeve I have is a watered-down version of the Gospel of Jesus Christ. I hope I am not stepping on your toes, Big John."

"Oh, you're not, Chace," declares the man truly worried about where his soul might go when he dies. "I've been wanting to ask you these questions about your Christianity for a long time and haven't. I don't know why I haven't, I just haven't." Swanson's eyes drop to the floor as he says the last part.

"Well we are here now, and we're in the middle of it. Shoot me your questions."

John Swanson raises his head and looks Chace right in the eye and asks, "How do I become born again, Chace? How can I have the same assurance you and Tony have, or in Tony's case, had?"

In this day filled with so much grief and anguish, Chace Wikett is very pleased inside to see that his friend John has the substance to ask the questions that he has. Wikett then goes on to explain the very basic and simple plan of salvation. "Jesus says in the third chapter of the book of John that we must be born again to enter the Kingdom of Heaven. It is really very simple. Salvation is really much simpler than many people make it, Big John. You have probably heard and maybe even know John 3:16, right?"

Very attentive and interested, John Swanson nods his head yes and says, "I looked John 3:16 up one day on the computer after seeing it on a sign hanging in the end zone of a football game."

Wikett smiles, and then goes on with his explanation of how a person truly becomes a Christian, "You remember how just a little while ago you told me you didn't think you are even good enough to be a Christian?"

"Yes," replies Swanson as he nods his head.

"On your own John, you cannot be good enough. None of us can be good enough. There is no way apart from God's Son Jesus to be good enough. Without Jesus Christ in our lives, we are simply doomed to fail when it comes to sin. And it is sin that separates us from God."

"Yeah, that is all the kinds of stuff I sorta remember learning in my Lutheran confirmation classes," Swanson cuts in on his friend. "But what about the born again part?"

"I'm just about to that part," Wikett replies. "See John, your Lutheran upbringing did teach you some of what you need to know. It is my experience from some of the exposure I've had with some of the nonevangelical Churches out there, that they stop short of telling you that every individual must make a conscious decision to accept the free gift of God's deliverance from sin before you actually become a Christian." Wikett pauses and then asks, "Are you following me so far on this? You look a little bit lost."

"Oh yeah," Swanson nods his head and says. "I think I see what you are saying. Go on."

"John, we have to make a conscious decision to accept Jesus

Christ as our Savior. At the exact moment when we do is when we become *born again.* Usually a person has to come to a point in their lives where they recognize they are a sinner, which you have obviously done. I take it that you do believe there is a God, and a heaven and a hell, right?"

"Yeah."

"And you do know who Jesus was?" FBI agent Wikett pauses. "Actually, who Jesus still is. Correct?"

"Yes, Chace. I believe in God and in hell and heaven. And I know who Jesus was," Swanson says nodding his head. "But what do you mean by *who Jesus is?*"

"Yes John, this is a very important point. So many churches today teach about a Jesus that was here 2,000 years ago. They even still have crosses all over in their churches where a dead Jesus is still hanging on the cross."

"Yeah, like a crucifix."

"I am here to tell you that the Jesus of the Bible, the real Jesus who died for the forgiveness of your sins and for the forgiveness of my sins, is alive and well and is not still hanging dead on a cross anymore," Wikett declares.

"OK, I see what you mean," Swanson allows.

"You cannot be good enough on your own to please God. It is only by what Jesus did for us on the cross to take away your sins that you can ever please God. If you admit you are a sinner, which you have done, believe in your heart that God raised Jesus from the dead three days after He died on the cross, and then confess with your mouth that Jesus is your Lord, you will be saved. This is what the Apostle Paul writes in the tenth chapter of the book of Romans in the New Testament."

"I can do that."

"In Romans 10:13, it says that everyone who calls on the name of the Lord will be saved," Wikett says. "Big John, if you call on the name of Jesus to be your savior He will make you a better person. You can't do it without Him."

Gasperson sticks his head out of the little room the FBI agents are using to interrogate Roddy Dale Eddison and yells out, "Hey! I think he's about to give something up!"

After looking over towards Gasperson, Wikett turns his head back to Swanson and asks, "You OK with all of this?"

"No Chace, I am not," answers Swanson. "I want what you have. I want to be the kind of Christian you are, and that Tony was. I have wanted it for a long time and something has kept me from asking you about it until today."

FBI agent Wikett knows he now has two very important things that need his attention. He says, "John, you and I can pray right now if you want to and you can ask Jesus to come into your life forever. It won't take long."

"Yeah, I don't want to wait any longer," Big John asserts. "I know I'll probably never be as good of a Christian as you are, Chace. But I want to start this thing right now. I have always known there was more to Christianity than what I grew up with, but I always thought it was something I needed to do myself to clean my life up. I know I need to do this." FBI agent Swanson has never been more serious about anything in his life.

Wikett turns his head to where Gasperson still has the door to the make-shift interrogation room about halfway open and yells, "Billy Joe! We will be there in just a minute!"

Having heard the last little bit of the conversation between Wikett and Swanson, Gasperson yells back, "I've got this covered, take as long as you need!"

A nervous and anxious John Swanson knows he is about to do something that will change his life forever as he asks, "Chace, what do I need to do?"

"It's really very simple, John," Wikett gives his friend counsel on what he may expect to feel. "Now, you may have a lot of emotions when you do this or you may not have any. Either way it will be just as real if you mean it. And I know you well enough to know you do. All you have to do is believe in your heart the things I've told you earlier about being *born again*, and God will do the rest. He will catch your mind up with your heart's belief. Once you've prayed and ask Jesus to be your personal Savior, He will be your Savior, even if the devil comes along and tells you nothing happened. You just continue to trust in God."

"Alright, I got that," replies Swanson.

"So, all you need to do next is to simply pray to God and confess with your mouth that you believe in Him and in His Son Jesus, and in your own words ask Jesus to be your Savior, and it will be. God is faithful to those who seek Him."

The two grown men stand in the middle of an empty red brick warehouse east of Los Angeles. Both men bow their heads and close their eyes. FBI agent John Swanson folds his hands together just as he used to do as a small child when he would sit with his grandmother on Sunday mornings in a little white Lutheran church that sat between two cornfields in North Central Iowa. Agent Wikett reaches out with his right hand and puts it on his friend's massive left shoulder.

Chace Wikett closes his eyes and starts the prayer. "Lord, I come to you this day to thank you for my friend John's decision to ask you into his heart. I thank you, Lord Jesus, for your incredible faithfulness. It's your turn John. Just in your own words ask Jesus into your heart and into your life to be your Savior."

"Oh God, I am simply doing what my friend Chace Wikett has told me I need to do. Jesus, please come into my life and be my Savior. I believe in you and I want to believe in you more. You know how messed up I am. Please come into my life and make me a Christian and give me the kind of faith you have given my friend Chace and, and..." Tears begin to run down the face of the big man who had been holding back from asking Wikett about God and Christianity for almost two years. "And, ah, God, if Tony is already up there and you see him tell him thanks. It was his death... no. It was his life that brought me to You today."

After a short pause, Wikett prays, "Oh Lord God Almighty, I thank You so much for this day and for all that You have done to bring this friend of mine to You. And I thank You for letting me be a tool to lead my friend John to Jesus. I lift my new brother in Christ up to You and pray that You will guide him and lead him and mold him as You want him. In the holy, precious name of Jesus Christ. Amen."

The two men open their eyes. Swanson has tears still on his cheeks. Wikett's eyes are wet, but no tears have fallen from them.

"You are already as good a Christian as I am, Big John," Chace Wikett assures his new brother in Christ with a big smile on his face. "God sees you through the blood of Jesus now."

"I think I know what you mean. I feel as though I am clean for the first time in my life. And I feel like you and I are equals, too. I can't explain it, Chace, but something did happen. I know I am the same person as I was just a little bit ago, but something happened down deep inside of me. I just know it did," Swanson states.

"I'm so happy for you. So happy. Now, let's go help Gasperson and see if we can save California. Maybe with God's help we can," Agent Wikett says with a touch of humor, but a much bigger touch of faith.

As they approach the room where Gasperson has been interrogating Eddison, Billy Joe walks out and meets them just outside the door. Wikett steps into the room to see if he can make any headway with a couple of questions that have just come to him.

Gasperson reaches out to shake Big John's hand, saying, "I am so glad for you, Swanny. I heard what you two were talking about out there and I heard what you did. I'm really happy for you."

Swanson doesn't know Gasperson as well as he knows some of the other agents. "Are you a Christian too, Billy Joe?"

With a smile on his face, Gasperson nods his head and exclaims, "Yes Big John, I am a Christian. Maybe I'm not as open about it as I should be. Guess God is still working on me in that area, among other areas too. It was actually Tony, Tony Garcia himself that led me to Jesus about five years ago. Kind of like Chace did with you today, except Tony and I were on a golf course of all places in South Carolina. I'm really stoked for you, man. Best decision you will ever make."

With the crazy man from Leesburg, Louisiana duct taped to an old wooden chair with his eyes taped to stay open and a hot, bright light shining directly into his face, FBI agent Chace Wikett decides to change his course of questioning. He begins to ask the tired and unstable Ku Klux Klan member questions pertaining to Christianity, the Bible, and God.

CHAPTER TWENTY-THREE

Could I Be a Lawyer?

Just as she sprays the fingerprinted bedroom mirror above the dresser with a cleaning solution, Sharice Jones' cell phone rings. She sets the cleaner down. With a towel in one hand, she reaches in her pocket and pulls out her phone, looking down she sees it is Big Eddie Jefferson calling her from Shreveport. She knows she will be putting her job in jeopardy by answering the call while still in the middle of cleaning a room at the Saudi Arabian owned motel in Denham Springs, Louisiana, "Hello, wait just a second."

The big black woman goes ahead and steps into the tiny bathroom that is in room 107 and closes the door behind her. She even turns on the sink faucet for noise and then steps into the bathtub and pulls the shower curtain closed to try and hide the sound of her voice from Mr. Shahid al-Zahrani, the owner of the motel. She almost feels like she is playing a part in a James Bond movie. It is a little exciting to her.

Worried and scared about where her boss might be, Sharice answers her phone again in a very quiet voice. "Hello Eddie, I can't talk, but I can listen."

Shreveport, Louisiana Police Officer Edward Jefferson, tells the woman he has casually dated, "Sharice Honey, you and Miss Martha Jo gots to get out of there right now. The FBI has been watchin' that place for a few hours and they're ready to take it in about twenty minutes. They wanted me to call and get you girls out of there so as you won't get hurt."

"Eddie, it's almost noon. Martha and I always go over to Ol' Sims Wilson's gas station to eat our lunches, so that's where we're headed," Sharice tells the man she wishes lived closer to her.

"OK Sharice, I'll call the FBI back and tell them when they see two big beautiful black women walking over to that old man's filling station, then they can do what they came for. You two be sure and get out of there right now," Jefferson relays to Sharice, whom he has ideas of someday making his wife.

"OK Eddie, we'll hurry," replies the nervous and excited mother of three boys.

Half scared and half elated over what she has just heard, Sharice Jones quickly straightens out the bathroom she is still in, shuts off the light in it, wipes off the dresser mirror, and then hurriedly remakes the two already slept-in beds in room 107. Normally, Sharice would never leave the old dirty sheets on a bed in a motel room she has cleaned.

Sharice is very particular about how she does her job, something that was instilled in her by her grandmother when she was very little. But this is a whole new ballgame for her. She has never been part of an FBI caper like she is now, and she doesn't want to get caught in the crossfire between good and evil.

After leaving room 107, Sharice pushes her cleaning and laundry cart towards the laundry room that leads to a small housekeeping room where the cleaning carts are stored. As she is almost there, she sees Mr. Zahrani walking straight towards her with a mean and evil look on his face.

Sharice is scared that Zahrani knows what is going on and that she might even be taken hostage. The thought goes through her head that maybe they have already taken Martha Jo. She thinks back to a show she had just watched a couple of nights ago on television where every room in a fancy French hotel was bugged with cameras and microphones. Sharice is worried that maybe Zahrani has done that to his motel.

Maybe these Muslim terrorists heard everything Eddie and I talked about, she thinks. Sharice is almost ready to push the cart into her Saudi Arabian boss and start running across the street to Ol' Sims Wilson's when Zahrani says, "Don't you ever be on your phone on my time again. Not even in the middle of the street." Zahrani doesn't even break stride as he continues to walk right on past her. To her amazement he actually walks all the way down to room 125 and knocks on the door.

Sharice looks back one more time as she nears the end of the sidewalk by the laundry room. She sees that Zahrani has entered one of the rooms where the Islamic men have been sitting and chanting Islamic prayers to Allah for almost three days straight. Sharice Jones pushes her cleaning cart into the laundry room and asks, "Are you in here Martha Jo?"

From back in the rear of the housekeeping room behind some boxes stacked in a corner, her best friend and motherlike figure says, "Yeah, Honey. I'm in here. Do you remember where we put those new cleaning rags?"

"Martha Jo! We's got to be gettin' out of here right now. We is goin' over to Ol' Sim's. Don't ask any questions, just get your lunch and let's go!" Sharice demands as she digs through some misplaced dirty laundry looking for her little purple and yellow LSU lunch cooler. Someone besides Sharice or Martha Jo had been in the laundry room and moved the dirty sheets and towels.

"Does this have to do with them Muslims?" Martha Jo asks.

"Shhh..." Sharice turns and looks. She nods her head at Martha Jo who is coming through the door between the laundry room and the housekeeping room. She quickly whispers, "Mr. Zahrani might be right outside. Somebody's been in here snooping. We gots to get out of here right now, Martha Jo."

The two large African American women, with their lunches in hand, leave the laundry room and quickly make their way across the street to Ol' Sims Wilson's 1960's style gas station not saying anything to each other as they walk. When they enter the little filling station lobby they see Ol' Sims standing behind the cash register as always. Two tall men wearing gray suits and very dark sunglasses stand over by the candy and pop machines. Sharice and Martha Jo cannot see the men's eyes.

"Looks like we sure is going to have us some excitement today, girls," Ol' Sims says when they walk in.

"Are you Sharice Jones and Martha Jo Hall?" asks the taller of the two men who are dressed much nicer than Ol' Sims' normal clientele.

"Oh yes sir, we is," Martha Jo responds to the gentleman who is now taking off his sunglasses. "Are you the police or something?"

"Yes ma'am. We are with the FBI. I am agent Bill Jones and this is agent Tom Smith. We're from Houston and we are here primarily for your safety."

"Oh, thank you so much for gettin' us out of there," Martha Jo says.

"There are now over fifty law enforcement officers surrounding the motel. Ladies, this will probably be your last day of employment at the Motor Inn #16. But don't worry, we're going to make sure you're taken care of financially."

"But now, we better get you two fine ladies out of here and to safety," Agent Smith cuts in.

"Are y'all fixin' to raid that place with all them Muslims congregatin' to do harm?" Ol' Sims asks with his half-burnt cigarette hanging out the side of his mouth where it looks as if it could fall to the floor any second.

"Yes sir, we are," answers Smith.

"Will there be any shootin'?" Sims asks.

"I sure hope not, sir," Jones replies. "Nothing good ever happens when there's shooting."

Grinning with the half-burnt cigarette still hanging out the side of his mouth, Ol' Sims Wilson laughs and says, "Oh, dang burnit, I was hopin' to see somethin' out there today like we sees on TV."

"Sims, you ol' fool! You knows better than that," Martha Jo scolds him. "He's right and you knows it. Don't do no one no good if somebody gets killed."

With Martha Jo glaring at him, Ol' Sims just stands there smiling behind the cash register. His eyes even have a bit of a sparkle to them.

———

A slight and very welcome breeze moves the dry arid air through the seams of the canvas covered tents. There looks to be thousands of them all lined up perfectly in rows upon rows, upon rows. As the sun leaves the Arabian Desert, the shadows cast by each tent now stretch farther to the east than the tents themselves stand tall. The near-blistering heat that has been the day is about to give way to the night.

This time of evening right before nightfall, a peace comes over this place brought about only by the sheer numbers of its inhabitants, and the miles and miles of concrete walls, chain link fence, and the partially uncoiled barbed wire atop the chain link fence. The place is Camp Arifjan.

"Did you guys hear they found a live IED in the truck that hit our tower?" Sergeant Spicer Davis asks Privates Mitchal and Tillord as he sticks his head into their tent.

"No sir, we did not!" Mitchal fires back as he struggles to sit up with his left leg elevated above his head and pointed perfectly straight. It is in an air cast and covered with ice.

"Relax. Mitchal," Sergeant Davis returns. "This is just a social call."

"Yes, sir."

"Yeah, they say it's a miracle that IED didn't explode on impact," Davis states. "The two guys that disarmed it said they couldn't believe it didn't go off just like the one that hit the guard shack."

"We hadn't heard anything, Sarge," Private Mitchal says. "But we've been asleep for a couple hours since we got back here. Guess til about twenty minutes ago."

"Dang, Spicer, we're real lucky to still be alive then," says Tillord, with very sore and severely bruised and cracked ribs.

The Sergeant from Abilene, Texas, who is a good friend of Private Tillord's family in Wyoming, steps on into the tent. "It sure appears that somebody up there in Heaven wasn't ready quite to take the four of us home to meet our Maker."

"It may be that the four of us were not all ready to meet our maker yet," Mitchal allows, realizing the gravity of what fellow Christian Spicer Davis has just said. After a pause, the Private asks, "You considered that, Sarge?"

"I get what you mean, Mitch," replies Davis. "Either way, I am sure God does have a lot more for all us to do down here on earth."

"One of the things I wanted to do was," a grinning Will Tillord stops and tries hard not to laugh because of the pain of his rib injuries. "Was be there when Angie West landed to find out if you really do know her." He already suspects his Sergeant does know the singer. "Guess we missed that though."

Sergeant Davis laughs with the two men he just survived a near-death experience. "Actually guys, as soon as I got some of those good pain killers in me and I got this arm set and casted, I found a computer and emailed her brother. I told Trevor what happened with the attack and all. He wrote back and said he got a hold of her and she wants to meet you guys."

"You're jerkin' our chain. I wish Diaz was here to listen to this crap," Sheldon Mitchal laughs. "But go on, Sarge. It's funnier than heck."

"No! And that ain't the end of it either," Sergeant Davis continues, "You two make darn sure Diaz is over here tomorrow morning. Angie emailed me. I gave her my number over here and she called me. And guess what?"

"What?" Mitchal asks as he laughs. Tillord refrains from laughing because of the pain in his ribs, but he is smiling from ear to ear.

"She wants to meet all of you guys tomorrow morning before she leaves for Afghanistan," Davis comments. "So just make sure Specialist Carlos Diaz is here at 0900 hours sharp."

"That's crazy, Sarge," Mitchal responds as he starts to believe what his superior officer is telling him. "You're tellin' the truth, aren't you?"

"Yes, Mitchal. I am telling the truth," Davis states with authority.

"I told you guys he probably knows her," Tillord claims as he nods his head while looking over at Mitchal. "I can't wait to tell Diaz."

"You guys get some sleep. I'll see y'all in the morning," Sergeant Davis tells the two soldiers as he stands up to leave their tent.

"We will, sir," Mitchal answers as their Sergeant reaches to open the large canvas flap that serves as a door to the U.S. Army tent.

Sergeant Davis stops before he leaves the confines of the tent. He turns around and says, "Hey, just thought I'd let you guys know we found out the two Arabs in the Ryna Corp trucks today were Saudi Arabian. They weren't Kuwaiti."

"I thought we're supposed to be on good terms with Saudi Arabia?" Private Mitchal asks sarcastically as he shakes his head.

"We are supposed to be," replies Davis, "but radical Islam knows no borders, guys." The older, more seasoned man pauses for a moment as a serious question comes to his mind, "Anyway, just how are you guys doing with what you had to do out there today?"

"We're OK, Sarge," Tillord replies at the same time as Mitchal nods in agreement.

Their Sergeant nods his head back at them.

"See y'all in the morning," Davis says as he leaves their tent and steps out into darkness that has now fallen on the desert they all live in.

A suddenly very serious Sheldon Mitchal looks over to his younger and less experienced friend and asks, "Will, how are you doing with havin' to shoot someone?"

"I'm OK, Mitch. Just did what I was trained to do," Private Tillord tells his friend who grew up in an entirely different environment than he did.

"Really, Will? It ain't got to you that you had to kill someone today?" the somewhat puzzled twenty-one year old asks the nineteen year old ranch kid.

"No."

"Seriously?"

"No Mitch, not yet," the young man who grew up on the edge of the Rockies tells the African American from the East Coast. "Maybe it will. But not yet."

"Yeah, I suppose we shouldn't really be talking about it," Private Mitchal allows thoughtfully. "Or, we may start letting it bother us."

"No Mitch, I think it's good we talk about it," Tillord says. "Here's the way I see it. Those guys in those trucks were going to die anyway. They knew it before we did. They knew they had bombs on board. All we did was speed up the deaths that they wanted by only a few seconds. Plus, we have been trained to do what we did."

With his injured knee starting to hurt, Mitchal sits listening.

"Somebody had to do it and it was us this time. It's just like being back at home, Sheldon," Tillord states. "When work needs to be done. Like workin' cattle or dockin' sheep. Somebody's got to it, or it ain't gonna get done."

"I never thought of it that way, Will. But I guess you're right."

Tillord reflects back on something one of his uncles had shared with him. "I guess it's just pure country logic. Since my dad passed away from cancer three years ago, my uncle Tim had a real long talk with me before I came over here. He told me I might have to do something like we just did today. He also said that our great nation was built on men doing exactly those kinds of things for the safety of others. Anyway, my Uncle Tim's talk really helped me. I think even more so than what they taught us back at Fort Hood in basic training."

"I don't really know what I feel, Will. You know it really tore Diaz up shooting that guy today," Mitchal states.

Tillord nods his head.

"I know we did what we had to do," says Mitchal. "And we were doing it for good and not for evil, but I am not really sure how I feel. I think I'm OK."

In deep thought, Private Tillord relates what they are talking about to what he is most familiar with. "As I've been thinking about it Mitch—good and evil—I guess it's a lot like when I have had to shoot a coyote or even a mountain lion. I never have felt any remorse for doing that. Mountain lions and coyotes have nothing but bad intentions for our sheep. They want to kill 'em and eat 'em. And we're entrusted to keep those sheep safe and alive."

Mitchal moves around some in his bunk to get more comfortable.

After a moment of thought, Tillord asks, "Mitch, doesn't the Bible say a lot about sheep or something? I think there's a plaque on the wall at the Mills Ranch that says something about Jesus and sheep. Maybe a Bible verse is on it too, I think."

Mitchal nods. "Yes Will, the Bible talks a lot about sheep."

Tillord gets up from a chair and grabs a bottle of Gatorade out of a cooler of partially melted ice and cold water. He settles back down and says, "Once I had to shoot a crippled filly that was only about six months old. She got her leg stuck in a crack in some big, rough rocks on our ranch. It broke her left hind leg right below the hock. She couldn't travel with the other horses or even get up to the water. It really hurt me inside to have to shoot that filly. I guess because that little horse had its whole life ahead of it. And she didn't have any evil in her at all like the coyotes and mountain lions do."

"I cannot believe all the things you have had to do in your life, Tillord," Sheldon Mitchal comments. "It is like you still live in the Wild Wild West with the stories you tell."

With a slight grin on his face, the soldier from the wide open state of Wyoming smiles and laughs lightly. "It is sort of the Wild West. Especially compared to where you come from. Our family owns almost 150,000 acres. I think that's maybe even bigger than some of your states back there in the east. I don't know that for sure, though. I know it's bigger than most of the cities in the east, least it seems so. You can see for 40 or 50 miles if you get up on top of some of our biggest hills."

"Man, that's just crazy. I've got to come out and see it. Maybe I can shoot me a grizzly or something. What do you think Tillord, can a black dude shoot a grizzly bear?" Sheldon Mitchal jokes.

"It would be great to have you come out, Mitch," replies Tillord. "I'll tell you this though, when I shot and killed that grizzly, I sort of had a little bit of the same feeling as when I had to shoot the crippled filly out in the pasture."

"Really?" asks the New Yorker. "Why was that?"

"I guess because that bear wasn't a threat to us or to our ranch," says Tillord. "Oh, I'm sure it was to the ranchers in Montana. But also I think I felt that way 'cause we weren't going to eat him I guess, like we do deer and elk." Tillord pauses, "You know Mitch, it doesn't make me feel bad to shoot animals I know we're going to eat either. But, isn't that what God gave us animals for? To eat?"

"Yeah, you're right, Will," Mitchal answers as he nods. "We're supposed to tend to and care for the animals of the earth. And yes, we can eat them too. I've never heard you mention God quite so much as you have today, Will. What's up with that?"

"Yeah, that's been on my mind ever since we had to do what we did," replies Tillord. "Also, just before we were attacked we were talking about all that Bible stuff... creation, evolution, how old the earth was, the Garden of Eden being in Iraq. You remember, the Adam and Eve stuff."

"Yeah, I remember."

"Shoot, Sheldon. Diaz was even talking about what it was like to have to kill someone," Tillord comments. "That's bizarre when you really think about it. We were talking about it and then we had to do it."

"Yeah it really is, isn't it?" says Mitchal. "Then, seeing the guard shack all blown up and all those guys that got killed in it... and that could have been us. That should have been us, Will."

"I know, and I am not anywhere near ready to die yet," the tall, handsome Private Tillord states. "I have so much I want to do in my life. There's a lot of girls I still want to meet."

Do I need to ask Tillord if he knows Jesus as his personal Savior right now? Sheldon Mitchal thinks to himself. As he contemplates asking the very serious question, another soldier sticks his head into the tent.

"Hey, can I come in? How you guys feelin'? Are the pain killers helpin'?" asks a U.S. Army combat medic as he pokes his head through the opening in the tent.

"Yeah, come on in," answers Mitchal as he realizes he will not be able to ask his friend Will Tillord about salvation at this time. "Those new meds you gave us have really helped. I almost feel like playin' a game of one on one."

Corporal Manny Gonzales, a medical specialist who is waiting to be deployed to Iraq laughs and says, "Man, you better wait quite a while before hittin' the court again for some round ball. You're probably going to need to have some sort of reconstructive surgery on that knee."

Mitchal's eyes widen as Tillord looks over at him and says, "At least we're alive, Sheldon."

"That's just my unprofessional opinion, mind you," the medic continues. "I did have a brother that played baseball at Cal Poly and he tore his left knee up real bad sliding into third one time and it ended his baseball career. He's now a lawyer."

"Hear that, Mitch? Maybe the Army will send you to lawyer school," Tillord tells his friend in humor.

"For you to make a funny, your ribs must be feeling better, Cowboy," the medic says. "Earlier you were hurtin' pretty bad."

"Oh, it's got to be those new pain pills you gave us," Tillord says. "What was it you called 'em? I can't remember… so I can tell my grandpa about em."

"They're not on the open market in the U.S. yet," the Medical Specialist from Bakersfield, California replies. "It might be another five years or more before you can get that stuff in the States. You go to Mexico and buy the stuff under the Mexican trade name of Cantreato."

"You're Mexican, right?" Mitchal asks the medic.

"Yeah, I'm Hispanic. Why?" the medic asks.

The tall, slow talking African American tries to sit up a little in his bed. He repositions his pillow under his back and right arm and says, "Well we were just wondering about our buddy Diaz, Specialist Carlos Diaz. The guy that was in the tower with us. You remember, the one who didn't get hurt? Have you heard anything about him? He was really shaken up mentally, I think."

"Oh, sure," replies the twenty-eight year old from the southern part of the San Joaquin Valley. "I know him. I just talked to a guy that works out with Carlos before I came over here. Freddie, I think his name is. He said Diaz was being taken to the SPOD, that Army base down on the Persian Gulf or something. They tell me that's where all the ships loaded with trucks and tanks and stuff come in. Right?"

"Yep, everything that's big and heavy going to or coming back from Iraq goes through the SPOD," Private Mitchal states.

"I heard one of the new girls from Fort Bragg pronounce it as, spa'ed, instead of S—POD at the DEFAC the other day and everyone laughed," Tillord says as he smiles. "Then a guy from Florida said, 'She's a real blond,' and everyone really laughed."

"I spent over a month down there last summer. It is like a spa," proclaims Mitchal. "That's the most humid place in the world when it is 130 degrees and the wind is coming off the Persian Gulf. It's hot, real hot and real humid. Gotta be the most miserable place I've ever been. I bet I sweat off ten pounds a day down there."

"Why they taking Diaz down there?" Tillord asks.

"Freddie said there's some Sergeant down there Diaz wants to talk to," the medic replies. "I guess he's at the SPOD to see his son or something."

"Oh yeah, Sergeant Glen Davis, he told me his oldest boy was going to be through here sometime soon on a ship he's riding military guard on," Mitchal remembers.

"You mean like one of those guys that got to shoot at some high seas pirates the other day?" Tillord asks, "You know, that deal with the Somalian pirates by the Suez canal. It was all over the internet and the news channels for a couple of days about our soldiers firing a few rounds into some little boat that tried to hijack an American cargo ship."

Mitchal and the medic both nod their heads acknowledging that they had seen the same thing on the internet. Mitchal then says, "Yeah, Davis's son is in the Navy and rides the cargo ships. He's even on some commercial freighters sometimes. That's if they're hauling U.S. military equipment. Someone's got to protect them from the pirates. There are getting to be so many of them nowadays."

"I've watched some of that stuff on Somalian pirates on TV. Man, what a messed up world we are living in," proclaims the medic.

"That sounds cool," says Tillord. "I'd like to take a shot or two at some of them."

The medic laughs at Tillord. "I saw a thing on CCN the other day that made us out to be the bad guys in that deal shooting at the Somalian pirates."

"That's great Diaz is going down to talk with Sergeant Davis," Mitchal says thoughtfully. "He's as neat a guy as I have ever met. Talkin' with him will really help Carlos. I just know it will."

"If I don't see you guys again, take care," says Corporal Gonzales. "They're flyin' me to LSA Anaconda tomorrow afternoon, so stay cool and heal up. I just wanted to come by and see how you guys were doin' before I left."

"Thanks," Tillord replies.

With a big smile on his face, the concerned medic then points directly at Private Mitchal and tells him, "You stay the hell off that leg. I mean, don't you play any basketball until it's one hundred percent. You got it?"

"Yes sir!" Mitchal returns loudly with a nod and a smile.

Corporal Gonzales then turns to leave the little area belonging to the most unlikely of best friends, Mitchal and Tillord.

"Sir," Private Tillord quickly asks, "What about the blood I was coughing up. What was that all about?"

Stopping and turning around, the Army Medical Specialist that helped with the treatment of the injured soldiers from the Islamic terrorist attack earlier that afternoon shrugs his shoulders and replies, "Tillord, we are not sure what that was. Dr. Bruning checked you and your x-rays out very thoroughly, and he could not find an explanation for it other than a nervous or stressful side effect from the trauma and the experience you had. That's all we got now. But I'm sure he will keep close tabs on you if it happens again. Other than that, it's a mystery to us."

When the U.S. combat medic from California leaves their tent and steps back out into the now cool blackness of the Arabain night, Mitch looks over to Private Tillord and asks, "Will, what are you going to do when you get out of the Army?"

"I don't know... I just got in the Army. I guess I will go home and ranch, maybe rodeo some too. I don't rope as good as my brother or my cousins. But I've never worked at it like them."

"I always thought about being a cop," Mitchal says.

"Really?" replies Tillord. "That's funny, 'cause Carlos was just sayin' the other day that he wants to become an FBI agent."

"Yeah, I knew that," says Mitchal.

Tillord continues, "Diaz has an uncle in Dallas who is in the FBI and can help get him into it."

"I've heard him mention his uncle before. He talks about him all the time," states Mitchal as he laughs. "Uncle Tony Garcia. That's funny. How many Uncle Tony Garcias do you think there are in Texas?"

"I don't know," Tillord answers as he shrugs his shoulders, not really seeing the humor in what Mitchal is asking.

"I know three Tony Garcias from right where I grew up in New York, all within a half a mile of my house."

"Oh, I get it," replies Tillord. "Is that the uncle Diaz talks about who was also in the CIA?"

"I think so."

"Wow! That guy must be some kind of tough."

"That's what Diaz says. And you know how tough Carlos is. He says his uncle is over forty and could still kick his ass if he wanted to."

"Doesn't Diaz have to have a college degree to be in the FBI?" Tillord asks.

"I think so," Mitchal replies. "He's been taking classes over the internet for a couple of years, I think. His uncle tells him they need all the Hispanic officers they can get on the Mexican border to fight the drug war."

"Diaz would be good at that," Tillord states. "Man, he hates drugs worse than anything."

"Yeah."

"Sheldon, you want a water?" Tillord asks.

"No, I'm good," Mitchal replies. "Will, I've always been pretty good in school. I wonder if I really could become a lawyer."

"I'm sure you could, Mitch," Tillord replies. "It would take a lot of work, but you like to read. Lawyers have to read a lot I think."

An idea has been planted in the kid who grew up in the slums of the Big Apple, a place Sheldon Mitchal used to think was in severe poverty until he saw the rest of the world.

CHAPTER TWENTY-FOUR

Bernie's Joint

She is over three hours into her evening's work schedule and no one in the Paris CCN news studio has said anything about her being nearly thirty minutes late arriving for makeup. One of the things Alexia really likes about an occasional work assignment in Paris is that she is treated by them as an even bigger celebrity than she may actually be in the United States. It doesn't hurt either that one of the men who runs the Paris bureau has a definite personal interest in her, even though Alexia has none for him. She flirts with him on occasion to maintain the little perks she enjoys when she works in France.

The first thing Alexia did when she arrived at the Paris news studio today was ask about what she had learned from her friend Angie West about a terrorist attack on a U.S. Air Force Base in Kuwait. Those pulling all the strings and making the real decisions in the European division of CCN had informed the people in charge of editing the news that it was a back page news story. Alexia was also given strict instruction that she is not to bring up anything regarding this matter in any of her interviews. They told her this had come from CCN Washington. She could sense Rigger Watson's political angle all over this.

She also knows deep down inside that the story, the truth about Senator Franson and whoever the woman is that Alexia had seen with him two years ago, should and needs to be exposed. The CCN broadcast journalist knows too that if she is the one who shines a light on a story seeking the truth about Franson and the mysterious woman he was with in Washington D.C., it would be a political ax that would sever her from the career she has fought and worked so hard to attain for all these years. Her fate would be the same as that of Juan

Williams when he worked for NPR. FX News would be the only place that would hire her.

Keeping all this in mind, the last thing Alexia is going to bring up in the confines of the French CCN Network News studios is the mysterious woman she had followed for most of the day until that woman boarded an airplane bound for Moscow. Alexia is going to keep everything she has seen and experienced in Paris today completely to herself—the mysterious woman, the rich looking man with her, and the Muslim man with the two attaché cases covered in Islamic symbols.

It is nearly seven P.M. in Western Europe and Alexia has completed two scheduled interviews that were taped for future use. In the first interview she garnered the political viewpoints of the world-renowned British soccer star David Beckham and his famous and beautiful wife Victoria who is a former Spice Girl. Though they are from Europe, Beckham and his wife have a home in Beverly Hills, California where they spend a large portion of their time. The other interview she did was a short one with Prince Albert II of Monaco who was in Paris today on business. Prince Albert's mother was the great American screen actress Grace Kelly.

The interview with Beckham and his wife was quite uneventful, it was the typical questioning of a celebrity couple trying to put their best faces forward and portray to the public that everything in their star-studded lives is perfect. Shortly into the interview with Prince Albert II of Monaco, he asked Alexia about having seen her in Salt Lake City, Utah during the 2002 Winter Olympics where he was an actual participant in the bobsled completion. With her memories of meeting Severo Baptiste at those Olympics, she had a tough time keeping herself focused on her job for the rest of the interview. Nothing overwhelming or surprising was uncovered in the remainder of the interview, just the normal save-the-planet, work-towards-world peace, be in unity with all others, focus on humanity, and social justice kind of talk.

With the evening's studio business complete, CCN's plan is to take the beautiful international correspondent out on the streets of Paris to do some on-the-spot interviews with the people of the world. Alexia knows this will not take long. The network doesn't really take this thing very seriously, and neither does Alexia. She is quite sure these street interviews are something the man in the French CCN bureau, who has always had his desires set on her, has put together to get Alexia out of the studio and into a fine French restaurant for a late night dinner. It will be a dinner Alexia will agree to only if the entire CCN night crew is invited to go with her.

She knows that after the dinner, the Frenchman in charge of political coverage and content at the Paris CCN Bureau will probably suggest that she take him back to her hotel room for a nightcap. Alexia already has plans to leave the dinner early to avoid this situation. But, being a team player when it is to her best interests, she will play along for awhile until everything is set for the whole crew to have a good time drinking expensive wine and eating whatever they want in a fine restaurant. All while CCN spends a couple thousand Euros. Alexia knows it is smart to cater to the people behind the scenes of a broadcast effort who never receive the notoriety or the pay the stars do. Tonight, there will be a couple of cameramen and their assistants, a makeup artist, set-up people, a director, and a large handful of helpers and tag-alongs. They are all people who appreciate being entertained, and this is a chance to do it on CCN's dime, while Alexia herself, dines and dashes.

The plan to fly Alexia Klien to Paris and then to London was thrown together at the last minute when Prince Charles expressed interest in speaking to the American people through CCN. He had specifically requested that Alexia Klien would do the sit-down interview with him. Originally the schedule had been set for her to interview the Prince in London on the day after the U.S. Presidential election. But a last-minute change in Prince Charles's schedule dictated that the interview take place on Sunday afternoon, as the Prince would be somewhere in France on Saturday and Sunday and would make a stop in Paris specifically for the interview. He is reportedly on his way to somewhere in the Middle East on undisclosed business.

A news network never knows when, where, or if they will actually get to do an interview that is scheduled with people this far up the food chain. Members of the British Royal Family have time tables and schedules that all others have to bend and break to accommodate. Alexia suspects that Prince Charles intended on being interviewed in Paris from the very start, but he had scheduled a Wednesday interview in London to possibly help conceal his trip to the oil rich Middle East. Either way, the Prince Charles interview is now scheduled for two P.M. Sunday afternoon at an undisclosed location in Paris.

It is this interview that CCN Network boss Rigger Watson is the most concerned with of everything that Alexia is scheduled to do in Europe. Watson feels Prince Charles is the best hope the world has to bring the troubled Middle East to peace. This does not make sense to the American broadcast journalist herself who doesn't see Prince Charles as a very important player in the world today. Nor does most of the world see the Prince as a very powerful person—apparently only Watson does, but he is the boss.

She sits by herself at a long table in an otherwise empty conference room in the Paris CCN studio going over a list of questions Rigger Watson wants her to ask Prince Charles. She is waiting to leave for the street interviews that she really doesn't feel like doing considering the day she has already had. Alexia is somewhat surprised that Rigger himself has not contacted her at all today to make sure she will be ready for tomorrow. He must be preoccupied with something else he has up his sleeve, she figures. As long as it keeps Watson from bugging her, she is good with it. *Probably the Swenson thing,* she thinks.

Sunday evening Alexia is scheduled to have a sit-down interview with the President of France and his controversial wife. This is the interview Alexia herself looks forward to the most. A chance to interview Carla Bruni sounds like a lot more fun than interviewing Prince Charles. There is something about the French President's wife that has intrigued Alexia for quite some time. She has always hoped she would someday get to meet her. To start with, Carla Bruni is a very beautiful woman who everyone knows had posed nude several times in her modeling career. The pictures are everywhere.

Numerous times in Alexia Klien's life she has been approached by different magazines and photographers about doing a nude photo shoot. Each time Alexia has turned them down even though the money gets bigger and bigger with every offer. With no intentions of ever giving into the money and the temptation, Alexia still wonders what it would be like to pose nude.

Alexia actually has a lot of questions for the French President's wife, some in front of the camera and some not in front of the camera. Alexia has an inkling that possibly, long before she had ever met him, Severo Baptiste had known either Carla Bruni-Sarkozy or her sister Valeri Bruni Tedeschi, the Italian actress. There really isn't anything concrete that makes Alexia think this, just a way in which Severo reacted once when the French President's wife's name came up in conversation.

Getting bored with the questions Rigger Watson has sent her to ask Prince Charles, Alexia's mind slips back to the day she just experienced. Sitting in the familiar surroundings of a CCN News studio, it now seems like her day seeing the mysterious woman who left Paris on a plane bound for Moscow, and watching the two suspicious men and the black attaché cases has all been a dream. But she knows it was not.

As bizarre as her day was, the part that is the most surreal in her thoughts is the thirty minute trip with the three American Christians in a little green sports car. As surreal as it seems, something inside of Alexia knows it is the most real thing she experienced today. Hearing Matt James's testimony about his life, and how a hunting safari to Africa changed it, is something she knows she will never forget. This day is something she will never forget. *What will tomorrow bring with two of the most important interviews of my professional life?* She wonders.

Thinking of tomorrow, one thing trumps everything else. She talked to Severo Baptiste for the first time in well over a year today. And tomorrow night after her big interviews she will see him for the first time in three years. Tomorrow will be the day she will never forget.

Tonight is not over yet. There are still the street interviews, and a late-night dinner. Alexia wishes she could just go back to her plush Paris hotel room and curl up in bed with her arms wrapped around a pillow and fall asleep until the moment Severo knocks on her door. But she can't. She has to play the games she has been playing ever since she entered this business.

———

With their hearts beating faster than normal, partly because of their quick walk across the street, but more so because of the anticipation hanging in the air, the two women who spend six days a week cleaning the old run-down Motor Inn #16 climb into the back seat of a black Suburban with heavily tinted windows. It is parked inside the first garage stall of Ol' Sims Wilson's filling station and mechanic shop. Once Sharice and Martha Jo are in, FBI agent Tom Smith opens the driver side door and gets in. Agent Bill Jones is already in the front passenger seat. Smith starts the car and slowly backs out of Ol' Sim's building. He then turns around and pulls out onto Highway 16 and heads south.

"May I call my sons?" Sharice Jones asks Agent Smith.

"No ma'am, not until we get completely away from this area," the Texas agent politely tells her. "Then you can call them."

Both agents Smith and Jones put in their FBI ear pieces so they can stay abreast on the ensuing apprehension of the potential Islamic terrorists at the motel. Martha Jo, attempting to make conversation says, "Sharice, you should tell these men about your boys Derrick and Darrin who will be playin' in tonight's LSU Alabama game."

"Oh no, what if Mr. Zahrani's sons are part of this plot too?" Sharice asks with her mind still working like she is playing a part in a James Bond movie. "I didn't even think of that."

Bill Jones, a tall, easy talking South Texan originally from Del Rio, turns to where Sharice is sitting in the back seat behind agent Smith. "We already thought about that. We've got people in place to nab al-Zahrani's two sons just as soon as we start the raid."

"How did y'all knows to get Shahid's boys if you just heard about this from us?" a curious Martha Jo asks.

"We had Shahid al-Zahrani and his family under surveillance a few months ago," agent Jones replies. "We assume his whole family may be in on something if he is. His one son goes to school at LSU and has said and written some very anti-American things in class that have been reported back to us."

Driving south on Highway 16, agent Tom Smith checks his rear view mirror as he slows down and prepares to turn onto Rushing

Road. He adds, "Some actual students at LSU were the ones who reported al-Zahrani's son to the police, and then we heard about it from them."

"If you've been warned about the Zahrani family," Martha Jo asks, "Why did you quit watching them?'

"They hadn't done anything against the law to start with," Bill Jones says. "And because of fiscal cutbacks combined with the elevated level of political correctness these days," he pauses and then says, "We just couldn't do anything more without some substantial cause."

Martha Jo is a little lost in what Bill Jones has just said, but Sharice understands it perfectly. Sharice looks over at Martha Jo and tells her, "What he is saying is we are real lucky we called somebody about all this."

"Yes, you are," adds Agent Smith. "We're all real lucky you both tried to find out what was really going on back there where you work."

"Yeah, you girls were very thoughtful to call someone you trusted on this," Agent Jones says. "From what we've been able to piece together, the men in rooms 125 and 127 came here from a terrorist training camp in Yemen."

"Where is Yemen?" Martha Jo asks.

"It's over in the Middle East," Sharice tells her friend.

"We were able to find out this morning they were from Yemen after you brave women contacted your friends about the strange things you heard happening in those rooms," Agent Jones says.

"Sharice, what's this that I hear about your sons being the DuPree brothers who play on that nasty defense of LSU's?" Tom Smith asks to change the subject. "Is that right?"

"Yeah, they're my little boys," Sharice replies. "But they ain't so little no more."

"Is it right that you have a younger boy who might come over and play receiver for the Longhorns?" Smith, a curious University of Texas graduate asks the mother of three potential NFL football players.

"Oh, I don't know. Donnie sure wants to go to Texas, but his big brothers would kill him if he does. Well, they won't kill him. You know what I mean," the very proud mother replies.

"That youngest one of yours ought to go out and play in Lubbock for the Red Raiders," says Texas Tech Grad Bill Jones.

Laughing, Smith looks over at his partner and then comments, "No kid from Louisiana wants to go play in the West Texas desert and live in all that wind and dust if they can go to Austin."

Agent Jones laughs and says, "You're probably right."

As they enter the community of Denham Springs, Agent Smith slows down and pulls the black GMC Suburban into a parking lot at a seafood restaurant and stops. As he waits for a member of the local police department to show up, he jokingly asks Sharice, "Do you think your boys could get us a couple of tickets to the LSU Alabama game tonight?"

"I don't know," Sharice says. "I can ask the boys to talk to their coach about some tickets for you."

"He's just kiddin', Sharice," Agent Jones tells her. "We can't stay for it even if we did have tickets and he knows that. Anyway your boys don't need to be thinking about getting us tickets before such a big game. They need to be thinking about beatin' Alabama."

"You know what, Martha," Sharice pauses as she continues her thought. "We shouldn't tell them anything about this today until after they have played tonight. I don't want to upset them."

"You're right, Sharice," answers Martha Jo.

As they sit and wait for the police car they can see coming down the street, FBI agent Smith turns and looks at Sharice and tells her, "If someday, any of your sons ever decide that the NFL isn't exciting enough for them, the FBI can always use a few more big tough smart guys with lots of street smarts. And I'm not joking about this like I was the tickets. I read that article about your boys in Sports Illustrated a couple of months ago. They're the kind of guys we are always looking for."

"What I read about them, Tom," comments Jones "Is they would have to take a big pay cut to be FBI agents with the kind of money they're goin' to make in the NFL."

Smith laughs, "Yeah, that's for sure."

The local Denham Springs police car pulls up in the parking lot adjacent to the black FBI Suburban and a female officer gets out.

Both Sharice and Martha Jo get out of the Suburban after Agents Smith and Jones tell them they are handing them off to the local police so that the two FBI agents can return to the Motor Inn #16.

After saying their goodbyes to the two women, the agents pull out of the parking lot in front of Don's Seafood Hut. Smith and Jones are returning to assist Louisiana FBI agents LeBlanc and Theriot. As Smith turns the Suburban right onto Rushing Road to return to the motel, the two Texas agents hear through their ear pieces that the Louisiana team of local, state, and federal officers led by LeBlanc and Theriot are in place to launch their siege on the small motel that is being used to house Islamic terrorists who have recently arrived in the U.S. from the Middle East.

"Better hurry or we're going to miss the real game," Jones tells Smith.

Shirley Hienz writes down the amount she is going to tip the waitress on the credit card receipt at a little bar and grill called Bernie's Joint. It is just a few blocks east of the Washington D.C. CCN Network News Studios and national business headquarters. Hienz always takes care of the bill at Bernie's with the CCN company credit card on the four or five days a week that she and her boss Rigger Watson come to this little out-of-the way place to eat and have a couple of drinks. Today is no different.

While Shirley pays the bill at the cash register nearly every day, Watson will stand at the end of the bar and watch FX News Network's program, 'Live in America.' He will do this nearly every day to see just what the competition is putting out there for the public to view.

Watson will then rant and rave about what he has just seen broadcast on the FX News channel as the two of them walk back to either the offices of CCN News, or to a secret apartment just a block and a half south of Bernie's Joint. Watson leases the apartment to give them a place where the two of them can steal some forbidden physical pleasures before returning to work.

Watson is the boss. He always decides what's more important each day—the news and work—or the sex. Today, the Saturday afternoon before a pivotal Presidential election, Watson chooses the news and work.

Something is different today though when Hienz walks back to work with her boss and lover. He is not ranting and raving about the dual opinions he has just heard aired on FX News, the fastest growing news network in the nation. He walks along without talking. He is completely silent. Rigger Watson is rarely quiet, and almost never completely silent. It is as though Watson's mind is a million miles away from where they are in Washington D.C.

Worried, Hienz asks, "What's bothering you, Rig darling?"

"Nothing," Watson replies.

"Is it that thing with Michael Swenson?" Shirley pries a little.

"No, that Swenson thing will take care of itself I am sure," Rigger replies about the sticky situation the entire Democrat Party has found itself in because of the gay campaign manager of the Presidential front runner Senator Franson.

Walking alongside him, Hienz knows Watson well enough to know not to ask any more questions. She also knows him well enough to know from the way he answered the Swenson question that he knows something she doesn't. Something she can tell he has his hand in. This scares her.

She knows Watson better than anyone else, and she also knows there are no ends to which he will not go to get what he wants. He wants control of the White House and she knows nothing will stand in his way. As much as Shirley loves him, she also knows he will never truly love her. Rigger Watson's only true love is for power. She loves him, but she doesn't trust him.

She will stand behind Watson and support him though, in whatever he believes he has to do to make things come out the way he wants. To not stand behind him would be a very dangerous decision for Hienz. Rigger says nothing more as the two of them walk back to work along a busy street on a breezy day in the nation's capital.

CHAPTER TWENTY-FIVE

Old Mexico

On the northeast edge of the community of Moreno Valley in a part of Southern California just west of the Mojave Desert, Agents Wikett, Gasperson, and Swanson are still in an old produce warehouse grilling the man they plan to see convicted for the murder of Antonio Ramirez Garcia, a fellow FBI agent and a man they all called their friend.

Inside the federally owned building, the room being used for the interrogation is twelve by twelve, with an eight foot ceiling, only one door and no windows. The walls and the ceilings are all painted a dull brownish green color and the dirty floor is solid gray concrete. There is one square metal table in the middle of the room and two cheap, but sturdy wooden chairs. Roddy Dale Eddison sits duct taped into one of the chairs. A large round clock hangs on the wall directly in front of where Eddison sits.

One 60-watt light bulb hangs from the center of the ceiling. On the black metal table there is a desk lamp with a two and a half foot flexible arm leading to the light fixture. A 120-watt bulb is screwed into the fixture. Eddison's face is only a couple of feet from the light of the lamp shining directly into his beady eyes, which have been taped open for the last three hours. The chair he sits in has a five foot long, two by six wooden board that has been nailed to the back of the chair. The board extends upward well past Eddison's head. He has his ankles secured to the front legs of the chair with gray duct tape. His arms extend straight down along his sides from his shoulders, with his wrists wrapped tightly with the tape and then taped securely to where the back legs and seat of the chair come together. Three full loops of the industrial-strength duct tape wrap around Eddison's bald head, affixing it to the wooden two by six.

With his eyes taped wide open and having had no sleep for well over twenty-four hours, Eddison is in the early stages of sleep deprivation. It is easy for the FBI agents to see he is beginning to seriously weaken physically. He is in some pain from the gunshot wound to his shoulder, but the injury is not anything that is life threatening. It merely tore through muscle.

Eddison has hinted he knows what the agents want him to tell them, but he has not broken yet. There is no way Wikett wants to hand the Cajun over to California FBI lead Bart Kennedy and his men before the Texas agents have made the crazy man from Louisiana talk. Chace Wikett fears he would be risking the possibility that the liberal New Englander would offer Roddy Dale Eddison immunity for the information he has acknowledged he knows, but has not yet relinquished. Time is running out.

Agent Wikett walks out of the room. He has in his hands a King James Bible he carries in his clothes bag. Chace used it to quiz the KKK member about his distorted religious beliefs. This effort was to no avail as it appears any sliver of goodness that had possibly ever been instilled in Eddison is now gone. When Wikett and Gasperson were both in the room with him, Eddison had spit into the pages of the Bible and yelled out that all the Jews must die.

In the past, Agent Wikett has actually been able to turn the direction an interrogation was going by using scripture from God's Word to work on a suspects' psyche. But with what he has just seen from the remorseless man who killed Agent Garcia, Wikett is fairly sure now that Roddy Dale Eddison has gone completely evil. Standing outside of the room with Agent Swanson, Wikett hands Big John his Bible and asks him to hold it for him. Wikett returns to the room. Swanson opens up Wikett's Bible and starts reading Genesis 1:1.

Many methods and techniques of information extraction are still available to Wikett and his team. Methods they would have already used if the three American citizens didn't fear their own politically correct justice system which has in the previous few years ruled these methods illegal. But why should they risk the lives of thousands or possibly millions of people because of the rights of one person who today has already stolen all the rights of Antonio Ramirez Garcia, a husband, a father, and an FBI agent? To the logical mind it doesn't make sense to protect Eddison at the risk of the lives of millions of California citizens.

Being this close to the border, it occurs to Wikett that it would be easy to take the crazy Cajun to Old Mexico and finish the work already started. The big clock hanging on the wall inside the interrogation room says it is 10:14 PST. So far this morning Kennedy and his team of Los Angeles based FBI men have not had any luck tracking down the two Yemeni terrorists who had escaped earlier in an old black Lincoln before ditching it in a salvage yard.

It is only the highly classified information that Wikett has on Bart Kennedy about the secret gay lifestyle he lived during his college years that is keeping Kennedy from trying to take over the interrogation of Eddison. Everyone in the Bureau knows Kennedy has long-term hopes of entering politics. Wikett knows it had to come as quite a surprise to the Massachusetts man to find out that the Texan and maybe others know of the long-held secret of the escapades the college student from a very famous political family had with Dr. R. H. Landley, a professor of Philosophy at Harvard.

Wikett chuckles to himself as he thinks about how Kennedy's mind must be swimming with questions of how something he thought was gone from his past is still alive. Wikett shakes his head in disgust about the fact that in America today in some circles, some parts of the country it might actually help Kennedy in politics to have his secret college love affair with a male professor exposed. Either way though, right now, Wikett is sure that Bart Kennedy does not want to suffer the shame of his sinful lifestyle from the past.

Kennedy's tendency will be to protect himself at all costs. This is not the attitude of FBI agent Wikett or his men. If something doesn't give soon with Roddy Dale Eddison, there are no U.S. laws or jurisdictions that will stop Wikett and his men from doing what they need to do to protect the lives of the people of Southern California. They will get the information they need.

It doesn't matter to the three conservative-minded men from Dallas if the American citizens they save live in California, Texas or Delaware. They will do what they must before this day is over to protect the people they are sworn to protect. If he has to, Wikett will even consider transporting Eddison south of the border, if for no other reason than the psychological effect. In Southern California, Eddison knows he is protected by the liberal laws Wikett, Gasperson, and Swanson are sworn to uphold. In Mexico, maybe Eddison might rethink his stance on his own life and death. As bad as Wikett would like to leave the man who killed his best friend in a dry dusty ditch somewhere dead, he will not do that. But he will make Eddison think he will do it if the occasion calls for him to.

Wikett is about to give up on the soft torture techniques approved by those above him and revert back to the proven methods and skills he learned and perfected over a decade ago working deep undercover overseas in the CIA. The Texas FBI agent is seriously thinking of making that trip to the Mexican border with Eddison tied up and gagged in the back of the Ford Excursion. Once at the southern border of the United States, they would take the man from Louisiana into Old Mexico through a tunnel originally dug by drug smugglers. A pair of FBI agents discovered the tunnel a few years ago and they have kept the location secret, even from most of the people in the higher ranks of the Bureau. Wikett knows about the tunnel because it was a very good friend of his in the California division of the Bureau who had made the drug bust and sealed off the south end of the tunnel and redirected it to a safe house in Mexico. Wikett is quite sure even Kennedy doesn't know anything about the now FBI-controlled route to and from Old Mexico.

Wikett looks down at his watch wondering if he really has the time he needs to take Eddison all the way to the border. He turns around and walks back into the room he just left.

———

"Hello Bobby, this is Tom. We've got about three minutes of driving time before we're back," FBI agent Smith tells LeBlanc over his cell phone.

"I don't think we can wait three minutes, Tom," LeBlanc replies. "Zahrani is still in room 125. I'd like to catch him in there if we can."

"Go with it then if you're ready. It's your call, we'll be right behind you," Agent Smith says. "We're here as observers anyway."

LeBlanc laughs. "We both know better than that. See you when it's over. We're on go."

With a smirk on his face, Texas agent Bill Jones looks over at Smith and says, "Looks like we got drug off the golf course to help transfer two women a couple of miles to the parking lot of a seafood place."

"Well, Bill," Smith smiles, "We did do a good job of it."

"Yeah, we did."

As the black Suburban rounds the long curve on Rushing Road about a quarter of a mile before it meets Highway 16, Agent Jones makes a call on his cell phone to two other FBI agents who are in Baton Rouge, initiating the plan to arrest the sons of motel owner Shahid al-Zahrani. While he does, he listens through his earpiece to the voices of LeBlanc and Theriot as they set off the raid on rooms 125 and 127 at the Saudi Arabian owned and operated motel.

The rundown two story motel is still about two minutes of driving time north of Agents Smith and Jones. If all goes as planned by Bobby LeBlanc and Patrick Theriot, by the time Smith and Jones get back to Ol' Sims Wilson's filling station, the Islamic terrorists will all be in the custody of the federal government. The only thing left to clean up will be making sure that al-Zahrani and his sons will all be tied to the illegal activities of the foreign inhabitants of the two motel rooms being raided today.

As LeBlanc and Theriot proceed with the raid, Smith and Jones both wish they were there. Jones looks over to Smith and says, "I just hope someone at the top in the U.S. Justice Department doesn't turn around and let all these guys go because of some legal loophole some defense attorney comes up with."

"You know they'll try," allows Smith. "Look at the leniency this Justice Department has shown the Islamic terrorists we have had detained at Guantanamo Bay."

With al-Zahrani still in one of the connecting rooms of 125 and 127 and federal agents along with state and local S.W.A.T. teams all in position within a stone's throw away from the rooms, a gray minivan that has seen its better days pulls up and parks in front of room 127. Two elderly couples slowly get out of the 1996 Chrysler Plymouth Grand Voyager. It has a broken headlight and a large dent in the driver's side front fender. The foursome all look to be in their seventies. After getting out of the front seats of the van, the old men both help the two elderly women out of the back seats through the sliding doors on each side of the minivan.

Parked directly in front of where the FBI wants to initiate their raid on the Muslims from the Middle East, the four senior citizens are now all standing outside of their vehicle when they suddenly turn around and reach back in the minivan and pull out weapons that look like shotguns. All four of the elderly people then run like teenagers to the front of rooms 125 and 127 and fire canisters filled with tear gas and black smoke through the windows of the two rooms. The four agents who were disguised as the elderly then immediately climb quickly back into the gray minivan, back out of the parking spot and speed away to safety. The four federal agents who pulled off this stunt had been flown in specifically from Mobile, Alabama at the request of Texas FBI agent Bill Jones. It was this that Smith and Jones wanted to see most of all and they missed it by only a minute.

As the Plymouth Grand Voyager leaves the motel parking lot, over twenty law enforcement personnel, all wearing black gas masks and full body armor, suddenly come running up from three different directions. Out of a S.W.A.T. van painted to look like a Frito Lays potato chip delivery truck, twelve members of a special police force from Baton Rouge race across the street from Ol' Sims' Wilson's gas station where it had looked like someone was just there to deliver bags of potato chips. Ten more S.W.A.T. team members from New Orleans burst out of the sliding side doors of two white vans that have *Joe's Plumbing* painted on the sides of them. The plumbing vans were parked strategically in front of rooms 121 and 129 about fifteen minutes before the agents dressed as the elderly arrived to start the raid.

The S.W.A.T. team members who came out of the potato chip and plumbing vans bust into the two rooms now filled with billows of dark black smoke. The officers forgot to knock, unless you consider the first hits on the doors with the police force's four foot long, forty pound, heavy-walled steel pipe battering rams as knocking. Knocking on doors 125 and 127 was not a prerequisite of the LeBlanc and Theriot raid. It was a no-knock search warrant that U.S. Federal

District Court Judge Jerald Kryer issued today after he heard the details of the situation the people of Louisiana and America faced in Denham Springs.

Once in the rooms the agents took to the ground anyone who wasn't already on the floor because of the smoke. The specialized tear gas and smoke used in this federal law enforcement operation will render anyone who breathes it unconscious in less than five seconds. The effects of the gas will last for about ten to twenty minutes before that person regains consciousness. The smoke is designed to black out a room immediately and then begin to rise and be gone completely in a matter of just a few minutes. There are no serious side effects to the exposure of this very important weapon, other than the memory of the extreme anxiety and horrible feeling that you are going to die from first breathing it.

As the Muslim men inside the two motel rooms are being physically subdued by the two S.W.A.T. teams, more than thirty state, federal and local law enforcement officers, most of them from Louisiana, close in on the area in front of the busted down doors of the rooms the Islamic jihadists inhabited. With the entire area sealed off and under total surveillance, Texas FBI agents Smith and Jones arrive off of Highway 16. Smith turns the black Suburban onto the side street that runs between Ol' Sims Wilson's gas station and the motel. FBI agent LeBlanc, who is leading the large group of officers now approaching the doorways to rooms 125 and 127, sees the black FBI Suburban. He motions with his arm for Smith and Jones to drive right up to the parking spot in front of the two rooms that the old mini-van just drove away from.

Bill Jones's cell phone rings. "Yeah, this is Agent Jones."

"Bill, we were able to get the one son that goes to school at LSU," female FBI agent Susan Pettit tells Jones. "But the older one slipped away. We don't even have a trail to follow."

"Well, one out of two is better than none," Jones says. "Just keep trying to find a trail."

"We already are."

"Take care, Susan."

"I will, sir. Talk to you later."

As he is parking the Suburban, FBI agent Smith turns and looks at Jones. "So it sounds like we may be staying over here a few more days."

"I think so," Jones says with a sour look on his face. Agent Jones's wife is to be back from her sister's in Austin on Sunday afternoon and they have reservations to take Bill's parents out Sunday night to dinner at Michelangelo's Italian Restaurant, one of Houston's finest dining establishments.

Smith and Jones get out of the Suburban. With the blackish gray smoke still drifting upwards out the open doorways and through the broken windows of the two motel rooms, FBI agents are now starting to remove the Arab men out of the rooms. Jones joins LeBlanc and Theriot where they are standing on the sidewalk between the black Suburban and the motel. "I just spoke with Agent Pettit. She said one of Zahrani's sons got away. The oldest one."

"Don't worry about that. I've got a way to get him," Agent Patrick Theriot claims, "I've got a guy on the inside. Zahrani's oldest kid has been dealing some bad meth down in New Orleans. His dad didn't know anything about it. We've had him under tight surveillance for over a month now."

LeBlanc turns and looks at Smith and Jones, "You two will still have to stay until tomorrow. Plus, my wife has a little sister she wants to introduce to Tom."

"Sounds OK to me," the perennial bachelor Tom Smith replies. "Does she have a couple of tickets to the LSU Alabama game tonight?"

The agents all laugh as they stand on the backside of the face of the day's danger. LeBlanc says, "If you really want to go to the game, we can find you a couple of tickets."

"I've seen her, and I know you, Tom," Agent Theriot says as he scrolls through the contacts in his iPhone. "Once you get a look at Silvia's sister, watching a football game will be the last thing on your mind."

The agents all laugh again as Patrick Theriot walks away to make a phone call to track down Shahid al-Zahrani's oldest son.

The days of the Motor Inn #16 as it had been called since it was last remodeled in the mid 1970's are now numbered. The little motel has been doing business on the edge of Denham Springs for nearly six decades now. When it was first opened in the 1950's, it was one of the nicest places to stay on the outskirts of Baton Rouge. It was originally set back into a peaceful wooded area with a little pond filled with bass just a few hundred feet behind it. It was a scenic spot for travelers to spend a couple of days resting and relaxing back then. Now, many of the trees right around the motel are gone or close to dead, and the pond has been filled in with dirt, rocks and debris. Nothing about the area is as pristine as it once was. After this, it will only be a matter of months before it will be torn down and the area will be subdivided into a residential district. This will make Ol' Sims Wilson's property much more valuable.

Ol' Sims began working at the filling station he now owns just a few weeks after he came home from Vietnam in 1969. He started out washing windows and filling people's cars with gas. He then learned from the old Irish man who owned the station to fix just about everything that could be fixed on the old style cars before the new computerized models came out. In the 1980's, the old man who owned the business made Sims Wilson his partner and then about ten years later when the Irishman died, he willed the rest of the business and the property to Ol' Sims. The old man, whose parents had come to America from Ireland around the turn of the century, had a son who had been drafted and sent to Vietnam in 1967 and then never returned. Everyone who knew him said the Irishman felt like Ol' Sims was God's replacement for the son he lost in the pointless war.

After the law enforcement personnel broke down the doors of rooms 125 and 127 where the Islamic terrorists have been residing for the past week, the four FBI agents in charge of this raid were able to go into the rooms and find out what act of evil was being staged. With the air in the rooms mostly free of the debilitating tear gas and smoke used to initiate the raid, plans were found inside rooms 125 and 127 to perpetrate an act of terror on a football game that would be telecast nationally all across the United States. But it was not the Saturday night game between LSU and Alabama that Sharice Jones and Martha Jo Hall had suspected it would be.

The Muslims terrorists, who had recently arrived in America from the Middle East and were being housed and partially financed by Mr. Shahid al-Zahrani, were planning to release a deadly toxin into the air within the Louisiana Superdome. The target of the Islamic jihadists was a game being hosted by the city of New Orleans the following day, a match-up between two of the NFL's powerhouses, the New Orleans Saints and the New England Patriots.

A classic NFL showdown in the making that will pit quarterbacks Drew Breese against Tom Brady, coaches Shawn Peyton against Bill Belichick, two of the top teams in each of their conferences, the Saints and the Patriots, will be played as scheduled. The Sunday night football game broadcast all over the world by NBC with millions and millions of football fans and potential voters watching, a game being played just thirty-six hours before the polls open on a very pivotal Presidential election, will be seen without incident.

The actions of two worried cleaning women at a little rundown out-of-the-way motel in southeastern Louisiana have diverted a national catastrophe. The heavily anticipated Sunday night NFL football matchup between the New Orleans Saints and the New England Patriots held in the Louisiana Superdome will be safe for all to attend.

CHAPTER TWENTY-SIX

Kuwait Towers

As the wind picks up the low hanging clouds begin to drift faster through the sky. The once beautiful fall day in Washington D.C. is giving way to weather that won't be as agreeable and pleasant. Fifty feet before entering a door on the back side of the CCN Network News building, Rigger Watson looks over to Shirley Hienz. They have walked together in silence for many minutes when he speaks. "Shirley, what I used to love about the news industry was that it was like being a painter or a sculptor. I could make and mold the news just as I wanted to, just as I wished, without any interference from anyone."

"Is that what's bothering you, Rig?" Hienz asks. "Was it something you saw on FX News back at Bernie's?"

"Before that damn Murdoch got into this business and before Rush Limbaugh got so popular on the radio," says Watson as he stops at the door. He pauses for a moment as he punches the entrance code on the keypad to open the private backdoor to CCN Network News headquarters. Rigger continues his tirade, "And then all those damned Christian conservatives got computers." He pauses again, "Before the damn internet it was a lot easier to make the people of America believe something. The way it used to be we didn't have to try half this hard to... I just hope Franson hasn't blown this thing because of that damned Mike Swenson. We had this thing won for sure before that pedophile fag in Boston screwed things up."

He opens the door and they enter the CCN building. As Watson and the woman who loves him because of his powerful position walk over to the elevator leading up to the sixth floor where their offices are, neither says anything. Rigger Watson, one of the most powerful

media men in the world for almost thirty years now is in deep thought
about how his power has been slowly slipping away from him over
the past decade. Shirley knows to keep her mouth shut when Watson
is like this. It is something Watson's rich wife never does.

———

This time of the year at around seventeen hundred hours each
afternoon, the sun passes on to the west and disappears from this
windswept land of sand and oil. That time of the day has past and
darkness has fallen. Three hours is all that remains before midnight on
this first Saturday in November.

In the blackness that is night in the Middle East, a very bright half
moon can be seen to the distant east. In the pitch black sky over the
Arabian Desert stars can be seen, but they all seem so far away. A
countless number of stars that have been watched by people for
thousands of years, watched and followed. Along the crest of the
earth's surface to the north are the many bright lights shining from
Kuwait City. All around in the distance are more and more lights that
illuminate the area from connected communities and lit highways that
run up and down the ancient coastline. But the dark, deadly skyline
U.S. Army Specialist Carlos Diaz and Air Force Major Scott
McQueen are looking at leading out over the Persian Gulf is
dominated by flames of fire.

They are leaving the search area at the entrance gate to the place
called SPOD. Both are traveling in a dark gray military-owned Chevy
Tahoe with McQueen behind the wheel as they stare at the flares of
bright orange and yellow flames shooting straight up into the black
sky all around them. Neither man has ever been here in the day or in
the night. This is quite a sight to them. Only a half a mile from the
edge of the Persian Gulf, the U.S. Army base is surrounded by two
huge Arab-owned oil refineries, one on the north and one on the
south. Nearly nonstop, day and night, the oil refineries burn off
unwanted gases into the skies of the Middle East.

Inside the refineries, very tall pipes pointing towards heaven
shoot red hot flames forty, fifty, even sixty feet into the atmosphere.
The height of the flames depends on the amount of excess gases being
disposed of by the refinery. At night in this place, just east of the land

of the Bible, being encircled by fiery flames shooting from the tops of pipes standing well over a hundred feet above the floor of the desert, is quite an experience to see. Feeling the heat from those flames nearly a mile away in the darkness of a Middle Eastern sky, Diaz and McQueen know it is an experience they will never forget.

The military base Camp Spearhead, more commonly known as SPOD, is the Sea Port of Debarkation and Embarkation. Its location is about a half a mile west off of the Shuaiba Port, a Kuwaiti shipping pier used by the U.S. Military. By road, the SPOD is a mile from the port on the Persian Gulf.

Nearly all the military equipment used in Iraq in the War on Terrorism has arrived by ship at the Shuaiba Port. After hitting ground, tanks, trucks, trailers, humvees, MRAPs, heavy construction equipment, and all other types of mobile military vehicles are driven the one mile route up the Kuwaiti streets and roads to the SPOD where they are parked, stored, and inventoried until they are shipped north to Iraq.

Iraq's two main express highways follow the paths of the great Euphrates and Tigris rivers. They are the veins and arteries used to supply the U.S. Military with what they need for battle in the land that was known as Babylon three thousand years ago. The massive quantity of iron and steel formed into the weapons of war that travel to and from Iraq through the SPOD is mind-boggling.

Diaz is troubled inside about what he had to do today, shoot and kill another human being, and he needs to speak with someone about issues that are very deep. After spending the afternoon digging through the hot, dry sands of the desolate desert for clues as to who was responsible for the attack on the U.S. Air Force Base Ali Al Salem, Major Scott McQueen has driven Army Specialist Carlos Diaz down to the humid Persian Gulf.

On the trip to the SPOD, McQueen has attempted a couple of times to see if he can break through the hard shell Diaz seems to have put up around himself. He cannot. A very sharp and intelligent man, McQueen knows that what is bothering Specialist Diaz is not something his U.S. Air Force training has equipped him to deal with. Major McQueen does not consider himself a religious man. When he has tried to pry into what is at the core of the Army Specialist's thoughts and emotions, Diaz has brought the conversation around to Christianity each time, and says he just wants to wait and discuss it with Sergeant Glen Davis.

McQueen knows Sergeant Glen Davis is a preacher back in the states, so after a couple of failed attempts at serious conversation, he decides to let Sergeant Davis open this can of worms. Having seen the death and destruction he has today, where seven American soldiers in a guard shack lost their young lives, Major McQueen is also looking forward to meeting Sergeant Glen Davis from Jacksonville, Florida. Although he's not a religious man, Scott McQueen does have a respect for those who put an emphasis on their faith. Today more so than yesterday.

A ship has come into port this evening that carries Sergeant Davis's son. Major McQueen talked with Davis briefly a few hours ago when the Sergeant was on his way to the Shuaiba Port to see his son and take him to dinner. When McQueen and Diaz arrive at Camp Spearhead, the SPOD, Davis and his son have just returned from eating at a Chili's about a thirty minute drive to the north up the coastline from the SPOD. The Chili's restaurant in Kuwait sets right on the edge of the Persian Gulf and just south of the famous Kuwait Towers. It is thought to be one of the biggest Chili's restaurants in the world and many American's say it's the best place to eat in Kuwait City.

Army Specialist Diaz and the U.S. Air Force Major have passed through the checkpoint to enter the fenced area next to what is known as the Denver Yard on the SPOD. They are now driving towards the pier where Sergeant Davis's son's ship is docked. In the gray Chevy Tahoe traveling east on a four lane street that runs along the south side of the SPOD, Diaz and McQueen can see military equipment, tanks, trucks, and humvees all parked in long lines waiting further transportation to be deployed in the war zone of Iraq.

To the south of where they are driving is one of Kuwaiti National Petroleum's largest oil refineries owned by the Kuwaiti government. With the lights of the SPOD on one side of the Chevy Tahoe and the fiery flames of the numerous KNP gas burn-off flares on the other side, the route down to the pier on the Persian Gulf is as bright as if this street in the Middle East has street lights all along its path, but it does not.

Diaz and McQueen finally arrive at pier seventeen. Piers sixteen, seventeen, and eighteen on the Shuaiba Port are used by the United States Military for the debarkation and embarkation, unloading and loading of ships. There is one more military entrance gate to pass through to get on the actual pier where Sergeant Davis's son's ship is docked. A few hundred yards before they reach this gate, McQueen attempts to call Sergeant Glen Davis for the exact location where they can meet.

With Major McQueen listening to the phone ringing, Diaz sees the entrance gate they are about to approach. He says, "Major, we've got a gate up ahead. We can't be on the phone."

The use of a cell phone is prohibited by the very strict rules that apply to everyone approaching a military entrance point. The gate Diaz and McQueen are approaching has a guard tower set a hundred feet or so behind it with armed soldiers zeroed in on all who advance towards the entrance point. The same rules of engagement apply for the soldiers in this guard tower here tonight as did earlier today for Mitchal, Tillord, and Diaz in the guard tower on the back side of the Ali Al Salem air base.

The ship Sergeant Glen Davis's oldest son has been riding guard on for over thirty days since it left the States is loaded with weapons of war. At 950 feet long, the USNS Mendonca is one of the largest cargo ships in the United States Navy. With U.S. military personnel and a number of different military contracting crews working around the clock, it takes four to five days to unload and reload this ship. That is, if things go smoothly. Davis will be able to spend more time with his son in the coming days.

Earlier in the afternoon, Sergeant Davis heard about the attack on the U.S. Air Force Base by the two Saudi Arabian terrorists driving trucks disguised as Ryna Corp military contract vehicles. The pastor of a nondenominational church in Jacksonville, Florida has an idea why Major Scott McQueen and Specialist Carlos Diaz have driven down from Ali Al Salem. From two separate phone conversations he has had today with McQueen, Davis has put together that Diaz is close to breaking.

Davis does not know Diaz. He has seen him a number of times

around Camp Arifjan where both men live. Once he witnessed Carlos Diaz and another soldier nearly get into a fight in the gym. The incident was broken up quite quickly by the other soldier's friends who knew their friend was no match for the hot tempered Hispanic. When Davis witnessed the near-fight incident a few months ago it left an impression in his mind that somehow, someday he would get the opportunity to share his own experiences with Diaz. Davis didn't know how he knew this, he just knew he would. From that day forward whenever he saw Diaz, Davis would say a short prayer for whatever God had set forth for the future between the two men.

Sergeant Davis, a reservist, is almost twice as old as Specialist Diaz. Davis knows if Carlos Diaz is about to break because of the horrible things life and this war have thrown at him, it will be a blessing to help point the young man in the only direction a person can truly find real peace and eternal hope.

After passing through the final checkpoint before entering pier seventeen on this very dark night, Major McQueen again places a call to Sergeant Davis for directions. Davis answers his phone and quickly tells McQueen at which end of the Mendonca he and his son are still standing and chatting.

Closing his phone, fifty-one year old Sergeant Davis thinks back in time three decades to when someone pointed him, a hopeless and angry kid who had stolen a car in Miami, in the same direction he hopes to point a troubled and disturbed Carlos Diaz. At the age of nineteen, a restless and reckless young man named Glen David Davis was pointed towards Christ by a police officer in the Miami-Dade Police Department. A young felon in south Florida was then transformed into a productive and respected citizen.

The tall, handsome black man, from Jacksonville, Florida still feels he owes his life to that police officer who went above and beyond his call of duty to help straighten out a college dropout and point him in a direction other than crime and prison. Sergeant Glen Davis has made it his lifelong calling to return the favor that was extended to him as many times over as he can.

The unloading of the Mendonca is underway and there are trucks and tanks and military equipment of many types going in all directions. The two men who have driven down from the air base try to navigate their way through unfamiliar territory.

Neither Diaz nor McQueen have ever been on the pier in Kuwait before. At night, it is very dark in most places of the pier, and to an outsider it looks like one wrong turn and a vehicle like a Chevy Tahoe could be run over by a 70 ton M1 Abrams tank. It looks that way because it is that way. There is no war going on in this area where the Mendonca is being unloaded, but it is still a very dangerous place to be, especially if you do not know and see everything going on around you. There are tanks, trucks, forklifts, and people going every which direction—all at the same time. From above, it must look like an ant mound does after someone has drug the toe of their boot through its center—coordinated chaos.

"Damn Diaz, I wish we were in an airplane above all this stuff. This war on the ground could get a person killed," Major McQueen says as their Tahoe barely misses being sandwiched between a truck and trailer going one direction and a big army green pay loader coming from the opposite direction.

"Just please pay attention and be careful," Diaz responds. "I'm not ready to die yet."

"I'm not either. There are three little kids back in Colorado Springs who expect me home for Christmas in a month."

"That's great that you get to go home for Christmas," Diaz says. "Do you get to stay, or do you have to come back over here?"

"Don't know yet," the Major answers back. "Hoping that I can get transferred to Cannon Air Force Base outside of Clovis, New Mexico. That would only be a couple hours from where I grew up in Pampa, Texas."

"Hope it all works out for you."

As they make their way through the traffic on pier seventeen with a series of stops and starts, McQueen is able to drive to the place where Sergeant Davis reported he and his son are waiting at the south end of the very large gray Navy ship.

The Mendonca is a completely different color of gray than the Chevy Tahoe Diaz and McQueen are traveling in. The color of the Tahoe is a deep smoky gray with tiny bits of silver that almost glitter. It is a very rich and beautiful color. The paint on the very large U.S. Navy cargo ship is a flat dull color of gray. It is closer to that of gray primer paint. Both colors are gray though, two different shades of gray, but still gray.

———

The ignorant and arrogant Roddy Dale Eddison is as close as he can get to experiencing pain and anguish very few people ever experience. FBI agent Chace Wikett, a good man by all standards, is prepared to elevate the level of interrogation he is using on Eddison to a point that most people in the U.S. could not fathom experiencing or even witnessing. It is a level he will only go to for the express purpose of protecting the citizens of the United States of America. Wikett's goal is to save innocent people from the kind of pain and anguish they do not deserve to experience.

Knowing time is quickly getting away from them, and having lost the two very dangerous Islamic terrorists from Yemen, the Texas FBI men know any information they can get from the Ku Klux Klansman could be vitally important to the nation they serve. Eddison may be the only link left to discover where a Muslim-led terrorist strike on the West Coast will occur.

Agent Wikett is about to the point of duct taping Roddy Dale's mouth shut and loading him in the back of the Ford Excursion to transport him to the Mexican border where an old drug smuggling tunnel could then be used to sneak Eddison into Mexico. The trip the Texas agents would make south of the border would be for psychological purposes as much as logistical ones. Once in Mexico, Wikett believes it will be much more convincing to Eddison that he and his fellow agents are willing to use any possible torture technique they need for the purposes of interrogation. Right now, Eddison does not believe the three American men who have been questioning him are willing to do things that many would call inhumane. The psychological advantage of being in Mexico occurred to Wikett after he heard Eddison making fun of Texas FBI agent Gasperson for following the rules he is bound to on this side of the border.

In the small room, contemplating whether to head to Mexico or not, Wikett once again turns and heads for the door. The sleep deprived Eddison, already guilty of the cold blooded murder of Antonio Garcia and showing no remorse for his actions, mouths off.

"You stupid assed FBI men. Don't you know it will only help your cause if some Islamic terrorists blow up a bunch of long haired hippie liberals on the West Coast? I'll tell you what you want to know! Yeah, I'll tell you."

Wikett stops in his tracks and turns around. Both he and Gasperson stare silently into the wide open eyes of the crazy man.

Eddison pauses for a moment and grins an evil smile. He then continues, "But not until it's too late for y'all to do anything about it. Right before it happens, or as it's happening, I'll tell you. Then it'll be too late for anyone to stop it. I'll just sit here and watch you dumb asses squirm."

Wikett is taken by surprise. This is the first time the Louisiana native has acknowledged knowing something about the actual Islamic terror target. Before this slip up by Eddison, Wikett was beginning to think that either the Cajun didn't know anything, or it was going to take much greater methods of persuasion to find out what he did know. An idea, a very simple idea comes into FBI agent Wikett's head. Something he has used in the past. Whether it will work this time he does not know, but hearing what Eddison has just said, the Texas lawman is going to give it a try.

"Guys, we're barking up the wrong tree here," Wikett says in a loud voice to Agents Gasperson and Swanson. Big John is standing just outside the door of the interrogation room. "Let's lock this idiot up and leave him. He doesn't know anything anyway. If he did he'd tell us."

Wikett reaches over and rips off the tape that's been holding Eddison's eyes open. He then jerks the lamp's power cord out of the electrical outlet in the wall eliminating the majority of the light in the room. He and Gasperson walk out of the room. Wikett shuts off the light switch as he leaves and Gasperson closes the door. They leave the twelve by twelve room with no windows as dark as they had found it earlier in the day, only now Roddy Dale Eddison sits in it all alone. From outside the small interrogation room, Wikett locks the door and puts the key in his pocket.

CHAPTER TWENTY-SEVEN

A Sin from the Past

"Do you know Sergeant Glen Davis?" U.S. Army Specialist Carlos Diaz asks Air Force Major Scott McQueen.

"No, I don't know him," the Major replies. "Do you?"

"No, I've never met him," answers Diaz. "Just seen him with Mitch. But I don't see anyone down here that looks like him yet."

"Well, we're at the south end of the ship where he said he was," replies McQueen. "After I find a place to park, I'll call him again."

"There's one," Diaz points to a location about fifty yards away.

McQueen pulls the gray Chevy Tahoe over to the parking area by some office buildings and a long row of brown Porta-Potties. Here they will be out of the way of the heavy military equipment still rolling nonstop all over the pier on this dark sultry night under the coal black Arabian sky. The spot where Major McQueen parks the Tahoe is just to the north of a short white picket fence that is part of a large square gazebo structure about twenty-five feet by twenty-five feet. Inside the gazebo are a couple of metal picnic tables on one side and numerous white plastic chairs scattered around with a small round metal table in one corner. The whole thing looks like something you would see in a city park in Ohio or Wisconsin instead of on one of the busiest military ports in the world in the Middle East.

Diaz opens the passenger side door of the Tahoe and gets out. The deafening sound of an M1 Abrams tank's 1500 horsepower Honeywell turbine engine roars past as the tank heads out into the darkness of the pier. Every hundred yards or so there are fifty foot tall metal poles with flood lights mounted on them. Some of the flood lights on the Kuwaiti-owned pier are on, but most are either shut off or burnt out, mostly burnt out. After one Abrams tank has roared past and its sound goes with it, another one comes barreling down the large ramp extending off the back end of the Mendonca. The deafening sound of the diesel engine of the next M1 Abrams tank now fills the air. Those who work on the pier and inside the large ships all wear heavy duty ear protection to save their hearing. Noise is part of war.

As the second Abrams tank passes, Diaz looks back over to the large gray ship as he hears a third tank coming out from the bowels of the floating steel fortress. He shakes his head as he thinks about what these very expensive pieces of equipment were built for. Each time one passes where he stands, there is a rush of wind from the powerful engines that drive these weapons of war and he can feel the ground move under his feet.

The air is filled with the smell of the ocean and of fish as a slight breeze blows out of the east off the warm waters of the Persian Gulf. The hot, heavy humidity of the gulf lands on Diaz and McQueen as soon as they step out of the vehicle. Immediately they both feel like they weigh twice what they did out on the arid sands of Ali Al Salem.

As the two men walk to the front of the Chevy Tahoe, McQueen pulls out his cell phone to call Sergeant Davis. When he looks at his phone, he sees it is already ringing. The Major could not hear the ringing because of the combined noises of the M1 Abrams tanks racing by and a large orange crawler crane that is now slowly making its way to pier seventeen from pier sixteen. The crane is headed to the north end of the Mendonca to move an M88 recovery tank out of the roadway that runs along the pier. The M88 recovery tank has run one of its tracks off while towing an Abrams tank that had died while coming off the ship. The crawler crane weighs in excess of 100 tons.

"This is Major Scott McQueen."

"Yes, this is Sergeant Glen Davis. Is that you who just pulled up in front of the smoking pavilion?"

"Yeah, I guess... If that's what this gazebo we're parked by is used for. We're in a gray Tahoe."

"Yes, that's you guys. I can see you," Sergeant Davis replies. "I'll be right over."

Major McQueen turns to Diaz, "Well, we made it. How are you doing?"

"OK."

"Ready to get a few things off your chest?"

"Yeah, I am," Specialist Diaz answers. "I can't really explain it. There's a lot of things going on inside of me and for some reason I think they're all about to come out."

"Well Carlos, you can talk with Sergeant Davis now," McQueen says to Diaz. "Go ahead and take as long as you need."

The two soldiers, one from the U.S. Army and one from the Air Force, both stand waiting in the busy Kuwaiti port. They can see two African American soldiers approaching from across the pier. Diaz can tell that one of those men is Sergeant Davis and he presumes the other is his son who is in the U.S. Navy. As he watches the father and son both walk his way, Diaz tells McQueen, "If you would like to sit in on my conversation with Sergeant Davis that'd be all right with me."

"I just might. I think that attack today rattled something loose inside of me too," Major McQueen replies. "But first, I need to make a quick trip to the can. Drank too much coffee on the way down here."

As he and his son arrive where Diaz and McQueen are standing in front of the smoky gray Chevy Tahoe under one of the working flood lights, Sergeant Davis sticks his hand out to greet the two men who have driven down from Ali Al Salem. As Major McQueen reaches out to shake the Sergeant's hand, Davis says, "Hello, I'm Sergeant Glen Davis. It's good to meet you."

"You too, Sergeant," McQueen replies. The four men introduce themselves and shake hands and exchange some short conversation about the massive operation taking place around them.

McQueen excuses himself and turns to head off to one of the Porta-Potties only about thirty feet from where they are standing. In the dark area to the west, there are at least twenty of the dirty looking portable plastic outhouses the Air Force Major can choose from. He has taken a few steps in that direction when Sergeant Davis' son speaks loudly, "Sir! If you're needin' a restroom," Davis's son pauses as McQueen stops and looks back. "There's a military latrine just over there behind that office building." He points to the south of the smoking pavilion. "It's a lot cleaner than those trashy Porta-Pots you're heading to."

"Thanks," McQueen returns as he stops and proceeds in the direction of the latrine.

Sergeant Davis's son looks at his father and Specialist Diaz and says, "Those Porta-Pots are mainly used by the TCNs and the Kuwaitis that work down here."

The Navy midshipman then reaches out to shake his father's hand. When he does, Davis grabs his son's hand and jerks him up to him and gives the twenty year old seaman a hug. Sergeant Davis's son then thanks his father for dinner. As Davis's son turns to walk back to the Mendonca, the doors of a couple of the brown Porta-Potties open and two dark skinned TCNs, both wearing turbans, step out of the brown weathered plastic outhouses. One of them is laughing because the other has said something funny in Arabic. They pay no attention to the American military men standing and looking at them.

The two TCNs both work for one of the military contracting companies that assists the U.S. military in the loading and unloading of ships in Kuwait. Still laughing and joking with each other, they walk over and climb up into a 19 ton HEMTT wrecker that is still running and is hooked up to an MRAP. The two TCNs then drive off pulling the MRAP out onto the pier to park it at the end of a line of over forty of the armored fighting vehicles. The initial cost to the American taxpayer for the purchase of a single MRAP is in the neighborhood of a million dollars each. That is, before maintenance and use. Still, this military equipment is cheaper than the lives of the American soldiers who climb into them.

With Sergeant Glen Davis's son headed back to his ship for some sleep and Major McQueen still at the latrine, Sergeant Davis and Specialist Diaz walk over and step across the short little plastic PVC picket fence into the smoking pavilion. Each man grabs a white plastic chair and they sit down across from one another at a small round table in the corner of the open sided building.

Just after sitting down, Davis gets up and walks over to a large green cooler setting on one of the picnic tables on the other side of the courtyard they are in. He reaches in and grabs an ice cold bottle of water out of it and asks Diaz, "Do you want one?"

"Sure! Can't drink too much water over here in the Middle East," Diaz replies as he takes off his ACU patrol cap and lays it on the table in front of him. "Not when it's been as hot as it's been lately."

Both men can still hear the roars of diesel engines as more trucks, tanks, and other military equipment and vehicles are constantly being driven down the very large heavy-duty ramp and off the back end of the enormous military cargo ship. Where Diaz and Davis are sitting is only a couple hundred feet away from where military personnel are scanning every piece of weaponry that rolls or is towed off of the Mendonca. The smell of burnt fuel drifts through the air as the wind off the ancient gulf carries the smoke from the massive machines to the south and the west. Any logical person would wonder why it would even be necessary to have a designated smoking area in this setting.

Just to the south of the smoking pavilion about forty feet away from Diaz and Davis, the open roadway between piers seventeen and sixteen is lit up by a pair of lights on top of a steel pipe protruding out from the side of a mobile generator on wheels. Each time when the loud noises of the weapons of war that roar past die down, the constant humming of the motor coming from the electrical generator powering the lights can be heard. A week from now, when the Bob Hope class navy cargo ship is gone and the pier is empty from all activity, the sounds of the waves of the Persian Gulf slowly splashing up against the rocks that jet eastward away from the port will again be able to be heard by the very few who will be up this late. Now though, the sounds of steel and iron rule the night beneath the Arabian sky.

"So, Carlos," Sergeant Davis says. "Can I call you Carlos?"

"Yes, sir. You can call me Carlos, Sergeant Davis."

"So Carlos, where are you from?"

"I'm from San Antonio, sir... and you're from Florida, aren't you?"

"Yes, from Jacksonville in fact," answers the U.S. Army Reservist. "It won't be until April that I get to go back home. This is my last tour of duty."

"Your son sure seemed to be a nice young man," Diaz states.

"Yeah, I had a little to do with that. But it was his mother who gave him the most spankings," Sergeant Davis says with a smile on his face, "So I guess she gets most of the credit for how he has turned out. I am proud of him though."

There is a pause with neither soldier saying anything. It is broken by the Sergeant asking, "So... how are you doing?"

Diaz glances down and says, "OK, I guess." He looks back up, but then his eyes wander out towards the area where the unloading of the Mendonca is taking place.

"I hear you have had a rough day, Carlos."

As he sits staring past Sergeant Davis and into the blackest of night in the very center of the most dangerous land mass in the world, the Middle East, Specialist Diaz thinks about what he wants to say. In the forefront of his view is iron and steel that has been forged into the tools of today's weapons for today's warriors. Within only a few miles of this place where these two soldiers sit, there is more iron and steel forged into the instruments of war for this age than what would have been used in all of the great wars of centuries ago combined. In this setting, these two men have sat down to talk about real peace. The kind of peace one only seeks way deep down inside of one's own being. The kind of peace only a person's Maker can give.

"It was rough," Diaz finally says. "But I've had worse days, I think."

"They tell me you guys had a close encounter with death," Sergeant Davis pauses and then adds. "Something about an IED that didn't go off. Is that right?"

"Yeah, we were lucky there, I guess. The whole thing was pretty tough. I've been in tougher situations," answers the normally very confident and cocky Hispanic. He then says, "But there's something about it this time. I guess maybe I'm reaching my end. I don't know. It's just that I've done so much stuff in my life that ain't good."

"Well, Carlos, we have all done things in our lives we are not proud of," Sergeant Davis allows. "We have all made mistakes."

"I know you're not a Chaplin over here. I thought you were, but Mitchal, Sheldon Mitchal, says you're not," Diaz says as he looks towards Davis. "He says that you are a preacher back in Florida or something. But I know most preachers ain't done half the stuff in their lives that I've done. Not even close."

The fifty-one year old black man from Jacksonville, Florida looks Diaz straight in the eye and says, "Carlos, you might be right about some, or even most preachers. But not this one. Not this one at all."

Diaz's mind opens up for what he is about to hear. He trusts Sergeant Davis and he really doesn't know why. Intently, the troubled man from San Antonio listens as Davis continues.

"Before I got my life turned around, and I was about your age then, I had gotten into just about every kind of trouble you can get into in South Florida. Drugs, carjacking, gang wars, you name it. I was either in it, or right on the edge of it. I even knifed a guy once in Miami. I've never killed anyone like some, like you have had to do in war. But if that guy I knifed would have died, I'd be guilty of much more than any soldier ever has been."

The wide-eyed, tight-jawed Mexican from Texas sits and stares at Davis as he takes in every word he has just heard. "Now, I guess I know why I felt I needed to come talk to you. You might be able to understand me and where I came from."

"If anyone can, son, it would be me."

"So the church you preach at," Diaz asks, "Is it one of those crazy all black churches where everybody's always yelling and hollering, singing and shouting to Jesus and stuff?"

"No, it's not an all black church," Sergeant Davis says as he smiles and laughs, "It's actually about half and half. Half white, and the other half black, Cuban, Puerto Rican, and a variety of races. We have quite a few Hispanic families who worship with us. We're a smaller church with a few hundred members or so. We have been growing a lot over the last couple of years. The main thing is, we don't fly any other flag above the Jesus flag. Way too many churches in my opinion fly their denominational flag above the Jesus flag."

"I don't know much about denominations or whatever," Diaz replies. "I was raised Catholic. We went a lot when I was little. But then when I got older I quit going. It seems to me that they always flew the Catholic flag above everything else."

"So, what's on your mind?" Sergeant Davis asks as he redirects the conversation back to the basics. "More specifically, what's on your heart, Carlos? Tell me how you are doing with what you experienced today."

Specialist Diaz takes a deep breath and leans forward and puts his elbows and forearms on the table in front of him. When he does, he clasps his hands together and grips his palms tightly and lets out the deep breath he has just taken before he speaks. "I shot a man today. I knew I had to do it. He was going to kill all of us in the tower and for some reason he didn't. For some reason, the bomb he had didn't go off."

Diaz pauses and looks down at his hands. Sergeant Davis says, "Yes, I have heard that from a couple people I have talked to."

After taking another deep breath, Diaz looks up and continues, "I know it was what I had to do today. I had to kill quite a few Iraqis when I was up there the first time I was over here. That was a couple of years ago."

Carlos Diaz stops talking. He begins to choke up a little. Sergeant Davis says, "Go on, I'm listening."

Diaz's attention is caught as he sees U.S. Air Force Major Scott McQueen come walking around the corner of a building about fifty feet away. When McQueen sees Davis and Diaz sitting in the smoking pavilion talking, he stops at the back of a metal sided office building. Specialist Diaz says to Sergeant Davis, "Here's the Major. I want him to hear this too."

Sergeant Davis then motions for McQueen to go ahead and join them in one of the empty chairs. Major McQueen walks over and joins them.

With two higher ranked soldiers listening, who have never experienced what U.S. Army Specialist Diaz has, in having to shoot an enemy combatant, Diaz continues. "Like I just told Sergeant Davis. I've killed lots of Iraqis up north the first time I was over here. That was a few years ago. I asked for Kuwait this time because I didn't think I'd have to shoot anyone over here. Then today, I had to. The thing that bothers me... that I have never told anyone, and I am about to tell both of you is..."

Specialist Diaz pauses again. He takes a deep breath while he runs his hands back over his head with his fingers running through his coal black hair.

Neither Davis nor McQueen say anything. They just wait and listen.

With his hands beginning to tremble, Carlos Diaz braces himself for what he is about to say. "Every time I have had to shoot someone over here it takes me back to when I was sixteen."

Diaz pauses, but Davis and McQueen do not speak.

"When I was sixteen years old, I killed a man that had been raping one of my sisters. I have never told anyone this. I know it was wrong. I knew it was wrong then, but I also knew it had to be done. Someone had to stop him. He was my stepfather. My mother thought it was some drug dealers he owed money to that killed him. He was an evil man. I guess it was because of him I always stayed away from the drugs all my friends got mixed up in."

Sergeant Glen Davis and Major Scott McQueen cannot hardly believe what their ears have just heard. Both stay completely silent as Diaz pauses again to gain his composure.

"When I got old enough," the tough San Antonio native continues, "I joined the Army as soon as I could. How can I ever be forgiven for what all I have done? Every time I kill someone over here I am reminded of what I did. And each time it gets tougher and tougher to deal with."

———

FBI agent Wikett looks down at the wristwatch his wife had given him as a special gift on their twentieth anniversary. The watch is set on Texas Time. It reads 12:27 P.M.

Having been able to get more sleep on the trip to California than either Gasperson or Swanson, Wikett has them stay behind in the warehouse to watch the room where Roddy Dale Eddison is locked up. Before he leaves, the three men push by hand the Ford Excursion right up next to the door of the room they had been grilling Eddison in for the past three hours.

With the Ford Excursion now parked inside the abandoned warehouse, Swanson and Gasperson climb into the two bucket seats of the tan vehicle and lay them back to try to get a little power nap. Over the years, the old abandoned warehouse has been used by law enforcement agencies for a variety of things, but probably not as a place to try to steal a nap after a long trip driving across four states.

Wikett locks the big outer doors of the building when he walks out. He gets in the dark blue Cadillac Escalade and heads to a Home Depot he had seen on his way to the warehouse. It is about ten minutes back towards I-10.

Tired, thirsty and a little hungry, Chace sees a convenience store on his side of the highway about halfway to the Home Depot. Driving a little too fast, he quickly switches lanes before he runs past it and pulls into the store. As Wikett gets out of the Escalade to go in, he sees a police car with its lights on coming from a block away. Something inside of him says, *You're busted. You didn't use your blinker.* He never even thought about what speed he was going.

A brown and white Riverside County Sheriff's car slows down and pulls into the parking lot of the Stop-N-Shop convenience store. It stops right behind the dark blue FBI vehicle. Wikett stands at the back of the Cadillac Escalade as a woman in her mid-twenties slowly and cautiously gets out of the brown and white car that still has its lights on. She is accompanied by an older male officer who gets out of the passenger side of the Sheriff Department vehicle.

While still behind her car door, she stops and says, "Sir, would you please step away from your vehicle."

Oh here we go, they're training someone new today, the Texas FBI agent thinks as he does what the tall blonde asks him to do. The young woman with long blonde hair is wearing very dark sunglasses and looks exactly how Hollywood would portray a female Deputy Sherriff in Southern California. Like someone from *Baywatch.* As he holds his hands and arms out to his sides, Wikett wonders if the officer with her will be David Hasselhoff.

Before Wikett can say anything, the blonde wearing a tightly fitted tan Sheriff's department uniform steps out from behind the driver's door and asks, "Sir, do you know how fast you were going back there?"

Wikett laughs and shakes his head, "No, I don't have any idea. Was I speeding?"

"Yes," she says. "You were going 63 in a 45."

"I was thirsty," Wikett humorously replies as he can't believe what is happening.

"Sir, this isn't funny," the male officer tells Wikett.

The tall man with the trainee is now out from behind the passenger side door where Chace can see him. He is in his fifties and has a badge pinned to his shirt that indicates he is the Sheriff of

Riverside County. The man is also wearing a large, dark brown cowboy hat with a small thin hat band that appears to be made of rattlesnake skin. With his thick mustache, broad shoulders and narrow hips, he looks like he could have ridden up here on a big black horse with a six shooter strapped down low on his leg.

"Sir, I am FBI agent Chace Wikett from Dallas, Texas. I'm sorry about the speeding. If you will let me reach in my pocket I will show you my credentials."

The tall blonde in her twenties looks over to her superior.

The Sheriff pulls his hand gun out and aims it at Wikett. He then nods his head to the Texan and says, "OK, but do it very slowly."

Oh great, I've run across California's version of Wyatt Earp here, Wikett thinks as he slowly and carefully reaches into his pocket to get out his FBI badge.

With Wikett's badge held up for the two California law enforcement officers to see, the Riverside County Sheriff walks up and looks the federal badge over in detail. He then says, "That's good, you can put it away. I'm Sheriff James Rozi. You were speeding back there, but I don't think that really matters now. Are you part of the bunch from Texas that's lookin' for the two Islamic terrorists that are on the loose?"

"Yes sir, I am," Wikett says as he grins and nods his head. "I was afraid my picture was on a wanted poster down at the jailhouse the way you pulled your gun on me."

"I'm sorry about that. Just can't be too careful these days," the Sheriff says.

"No, you can't," Wikett replies as he reaches out to shake the Sheriff's hand.

"This is Officer Amy Meadors," the Sheriff says as he introduces his female trainee.

"Nice to meet you," Wikett says.

"You too, sir," she returns.

"Sorry to hear you lost a man today," says Sheriff Rozi.

"Thank you," Wikett replies. "He was a good man."

"I sure hope we find them. I've got a daughter in Kuwait in the U.S. Army, my youngest, and just earlier today they had an attack over there at a base where she was on guard. Guess it almost killed her, but it didn't."

Knowing he is on a short time table to get back to the abandoned warehouse, Wikett doesn't say anything more that would spark any further conversation with Moreno Valley's Marshall Matt Dillon.

"I'm sorry, sir," the tall blonde says from behind her stylish black Ray-Bans. "We had to be careful. Last night there was a report from Palm Springs of a Cadillac Escalade that same color being stolen."

"I understand," Agent Wikett tells the young officer. "And I was speeding, too. If you will let me, I have to get moving."

"Yes, sir," says Sheriff Rozi. "Is there anything we can help you with?"

"If you could find the two Muslim terrorists from Yemen that I let slip through my hands, that would be great."

"We're lookin' for 'em," states the Sheriff.

"Thanks," says Wikett. "I've got to get something for my men to drink, if you'll excuse me."

"Sure, we'll be on our way," the Sheriff replies as he turns around to walk back to the car that he and the deputy trainee are patrolling in. Wikett turns and walks into the Stop-N-Shop convenience store.

Inside the convenience store, the Texas FBI agent grabs a couple of Snickers bars, a case of Dasani water and a bag of ice. He buys a cheap Styrofoam cooler to put the ice and the water in and sets it in the back of the Cadillac. Before Wikett is out of the parking lot of the Stop-N-Shop, he has one of the Snickers bars eaten and is unwrapping the other.

Wikett arrives at the very busy Home Depot on this Saturday morning at almost a quarter till eleven local time. Wikett pushes the button on the key fob to lock the doors on the nearly new Escalade and heads into the store where it looks like hundreds of ambitious Californians are preparing to do some home improvements over the weekend. The weekend before most Californians hope their U.S. Senator, Walter Franson, will be elected President.

With the rainy weather that opened this day in the land of almonds and nuts and movie stars now burnt off and given way to the sunshine which is more the order of the day in Southern California, it should be a pleasant day for people to work on their homes. FBI agent Wikett is headed to the paint section in the Home Depot to get a few cheap cans of black spray paint. He quickly passes by the part of the store that has spools of rope and wire for sale, nearly any size and any length that the normal shopper might need.

The man who has been fighting terrorism all around the globe since graduating from Texas A&M with a Masters degree in Military Psychology, figures it will take him twenty to thirty minutes to get back to the warehouse. Inside the busy Home Depot on his way to get the spray cans of black paint, Chace Wikett makes a mental note to go back to where he saw the wire and rope. He knows he might need some very thin wire and about thirty to forty feet of three-eighth-inch manila rope later.

Putting the cheapest cans of black spray paint the store has into the basket he picked up when he came through the front door, Wikett's mind wanders back to the rope and the thin wire. *I hope this paint works,* he thinks. Even though Wikett is an expert in the type of interrogation he has seen and personally used a number of years ago overseas in countries never to be named, he didn't like it then and doesn't like the idea of it now.

CHAPTER TWENTY-EIGHT

There's No Gray Area, It's Either Black or White, In or Out

Hearing what Army Specialist Carlos Diaz has just confessed to being guilty of as a sixteen year old kid, Sergeant Glen Davis wastes no time getting to the point in his counseling of the troubled soldier who has come to him for help. "Carlos, are you a Christian?"

"I don't know," says the emotional young man from San Antonio, who has just told Sergeant Davis and Major McQueen something he had never told anyone, something he had held all to himself for over ten years, something he could be sent to prison for life for, shrugs his shoulders and slowly shakes his head back and forth. "I don't know if I'm a Christian."

"Do you think you might be a Christian?"

"I'm Catholic, I guess, or at least I was raised a Catholic," Diaz pauses. "Why do I want to answer your question, 'I'm Catholic'?" He pauses again, "How would I know if I'm a Christian? Is there a difference between being Catholic and being a Christian?"

As Sergeant Davis tries to formulate the best answer he can in response to what Specialist Diaz has just asked him, Diaz continues, "Private Mitchal is always talking like he knows he's going to Heaven, like he has no doubts, like it's a done deal. How is that possible?"

"Sheldon's right," Sergeant Davis says. "It is possible to know you are going to go to heaven."

"But how does he know? Is it that he hasn't done all the bad things I have? You said you knifed a guy once in Miami. How do you know you are forgiven for that?" Without waiting for an answer, Specialist Diaz continues spilling out everything that is inside him before Sergeant Davis can reply to his questions. "I never, I mean I never, wanted to tell a Catholic priest that I killed my stepfather. Most of those priests have done worse than I did. So how the hell can they be the ones forgiving me for what I have done? What I did, I did to a dirty old man. What they do, they do to children, to young, innocent little kids. Ain't none of it makes any sense to me."

Having just heard much more than he ever expected out of the tough soldier from Texas who he has only seen a few times around Camp Arifjan where they are both stationed, Sergeant Davis knows this is more than he can respond to in just one sitting. The African American pastor from Jacksonville, Florida knows he has to get to the root of the problem first, and that is the guilt that is obviously eating at the insides of the young man from the city of the Alamo.

"No one's perfect, Carlos. Not you, not me. The Catholic priests are not perfect, Sheldon Mitchal's not perfect, Major Scott McQueen right here beside us is not perfect. No one who has ever lived on this earth, except for one man named Jesus, has ever been perfect. And that one man, Jesus, still is perfect. I am sure you learned this in your Catholic upbringing."

"Yes, I did learn all that as a child in church," Diaz replies. "Or in Sunday school when my mom took us."

U.S. Air Force Major Scott McQueen, who gave Specialist Diaz a ride down to the edge of the Persian Gulf tonight, watches in total fascination at everything he is hearing from both men. McQueen has lived the first thirty-eight years of his life without ever really thinking much about God or Jesus in any kind of a serious way before, and he now finds himself absolutely captivated by the conversation he is listening to. He thinks to himself, *Maybe all this stuff about Heaven and Hell is for real.*

Sergeant Davis glances at McQueen and then goes on to tell Diaz, "You are not perfect, and I am not perfect. The only way we can ever be made perfect is to let the only person who has ever been perfect be our sacrifice, our substitute to pay for the sins that you and I are both so guilty of. Me for knifing that man in Miami, and you for defending the honor of your sister in San Antonio."

Diaz sits with tears building up in his eyes.

"What we both did was very wrong in the eyes of God," Davis states. "But if we come to God and ask His forgiveness for what we have done and believe on the name of His Son Jesus Christ, we will not be held responsible for our sins. Don't ask me exactly how it works, only God knows that."

Davis pauses for a moment to catch his breath and let what he just said sink in. He then continues, "But, if you ask me *if* it works, I can tell you that I am one hundred percent sure that it does. And believe me, I am every bit as bad a sinner and as bad a person as you are, Diaz. I knifed a man because I was robbing him of his Rolex watch, his rings, and the jewelry he had around his neck so I could buy some drugs. I was eighteen years old. I never got caught either, for knifing that man. A year later, I got busted for stealing a car in Miami and a police officer there had this same talk with me I am having with you."

Air Force Major Scott McQueen sits listening to things he would have never imagined he would hear when he woke up this morning.

Sergeant Glen Davis takes a drink out of his cool bottle of water before adding, "You're right when you think a Catholic Priest can't forgive you of your sins, because they cannot. They are just human, just as you and I are. I believe whole-heartedly that it is wrong for the Catholic Church to be in the business of forgiving sins. That's what God does. He is the only One who can forgive you of your sins. And Carlos, it is God you must turn to for forgiveness. It is only by having faith and believing in his Son, Jesus, that you can know for sure that you are a Christian."

"I kind of understand what you are saying," Diaz replies. "But there are so many other bad things I have done. I can't even think to remember all of 'em. How could I be forgiven for everything I've done wrong? How could I ever get to the point where I know I am going to Heaven like Sheldon does?"

Sergeant Davis knows he is facing a very tough question from a very tough character. He realizes he needs to try to put the entire message of the Gospel in a very simple form. He must come up with a way to express the truth of God's forgiveness in a way that will resonate with someone who has some very deep and complex questions.

As just a man, Glen Davis understands how truly simple the real message is of how God in the form of Jesus came to earth to cover the sins of all who will simply turn to Him and ask for His help and His forgiveness. Davis also knows that through the centuries overly religious bodies of men representing Christianity have added things they made up to the very simple message first preached by Jesus Himself, a message later preached by His twelve disciples. Sergeant Davis knows that some of the things added by men to the original message of Jesus may be holding Carlos Diaz back from understanding just how truly simple becoming a Christian really is.

U.S. Army Sergeant Glen Davis looks Specialist Carlos Diaz in the eyes. He then looks over to Major Scott McQueen who is paying very close attention to everything being said. Knowing he has their attention, Davis points over to the smoky gray Chevy Tahoe that Diaz and McQueen drove to the pier tonight. "See that vehicle parked right there? It is gray. Right?"

Both Diaz and McQueen nod their heads.

"Now look over at that ship," Davis says. "The Mendonca. It is gray also. A much duller and flatter gray, but still gray. Right?"

On this dark night under the same stars and sky in a land only a few hundred miles to the east of where the accounts of the Bible actually took place, Diaz and McQueen both agree with Davis in regards to his very simple question about the colors gray.

"The Tahoe and the ship are both gray," Sergeant Davis continues, "But two completely different shades of gray. God never meant for His message to us to be gray. Or, to be in different shades of gray. He meant for His message for all of mankind to be black and white, yes and no."

The Major in the United States Air Force, Scott McQueen smiles and nods his head up and down signaling he understands.

Davis takes another drink of water. "God meant for us to be able to know if we are right with Him. He never meant it to be some kind of a guessing game. He simply meant for it to be yes God, or no God. Black or white. There is nothing gray about it. You are either a Christian, or you are not a Christian. It is as simple as that. You either trust and believe in Jesus or you do not. It's all in the Bible in a very simple and easy to understand message."

The highest ranked soldier of the three men sitting under the little open sided building a couple hundred feet from the hot dirty waters of the Persian Gulf, thirty-eight year old Scott McQueen, a Major in the

U.S. Air Force, a father and a husband back in the States, a man who up until now has been a silent spectator in this trio, says to Sergeant Glen Davis, "I have never in all of my life heard Christianity explained like that. I always thought it had a lot more to do with how we lived our lives and whether or not we went to church, and just how much money and time we gave to the church. You make it sound like it has nothing to do with whether we go to a church or not. Is that right?"

"That's right. Having faith in Jesus is what counts."

"Is that really what the Bible says?" McQueen asks. "I've never even picked up a Bible. Don't know why, just never have."

"Yes, there are numerous places in God's Word where it is stated just as simple as that. Black or white, in or out, you believe or you don't believe," says Davis.

"I'll have to get a Bible and look that up for myself," Major McQueen states. "It sure seems to make more sense than what I've thought before. Leave it up to man to mess something up that is supposed to be simple."

"All I know is I want the same kind of assurance Sheldon Mitchal has that I am a Christian and going to Heaven if I get killed over here. What do I need to do? Do I need to read the Bible more? What do I need to do to be forgiven of all the horrible stuff I've done in my life?" asks a disturbed Specialist Carlos Diaz, the twenty-six year old whose grandparents had come to Texas from Mexico as children in the 1950's with their parents to work the fields in the Southwest.

"Carlos my friend, we will pray right here and now and you can accept Jesus as your Savior, as your personal Savior, and as soon as you do, you will be a Christian and have that assurance," Sergeant Glen Davis shares in a very gentle and low voice with his new friend.

"It's as easy as that?" Specialist Diaz asks. "All I have to do is pray to Jesus? Or to God, which one?"

"Jesus and God are one and the same," Davis says. "Like I said earlier, with our human minds we cannot understand everything about God. But we must trust Him and believe on what we do know and He will slowly help us to understand more and more as we grow in our Christianity. That is where reading the Bible comes in. It is what helps you grow to be a stronger Christian and a stronger person."

"What about my cussing?" Diaz asks. "I cuss worse than anyone. I say the 'F' word in almost every sentence I say in some way. Do I have to stop that first? Will it keep me out of Heaven?"

"No Diaz, your language will not keep you out of Heaven. When you accept Jesus as your savior, all of your sins will be paid for by Christ. They will be paid for by His blood on the cross," Davis assures the very rough and tough Texan. "Carlos, have you noticed how little you have cussed here tonight?"

Diaz looks right at Davis and thinks about how he hasn't been cussing hardly at all tonight.

"The Holy Spirit has already been working on you and you didn't even know it," Davis states. "And believe me, He will continue to work on you... and in the future you will learn to know it."

Major McQueen looks away from Diaz and back to Davis. He then asks, "Can two people pray at the same time to accept Jesus as their Savior and both become Christians?"

Before Sergeant Davis can answer his question, McQueen continues, "If they can, I would like to pray with Carlos and also become a Christian tonight too. I've never thought of doing this before in all my life, but I don't see any reason to put it off any longer."

"Yes Sir, that is definitely OK. Both you and Carlos can pray to accept Jesus Christ as your personal Savior at the same time," Sergeant Davis says. "Is that all right with you, Carlos?"

"Yes, that would be great," replies Diaz.

"What you two will feel or experience in this may differ," Davis tells Diaz and McQueen. "Both of you have come to this point in your lives from different places and you both are carrying different loads. The changes you will experience tonight will be from within. And the enemy, Satan, the devil, will immediately come and try to tell you that nothing has happened. But trust me, a lot will have happened. You will find that some of your old ways, your language, your habits will be changed, or at least there will be a very quiet, still voice inside of you that will tell you some of your old sinful ways need to change. But don't worry, that voice is just trying to make you a better person. It is not condemning you to hell or anything. That voice is just God wanting to help you live a better life."

Sergeant Davis pauses as a large tank drives by slowly. Its motor is making a loud knocking noise that momentarily steals the three men's attention. Davis continues, "Now, I want each of you to just bow your heads with me and after I start a prayer to God, then I want each of you in your own words to admit you are a sinner and ask God to bring Jesus into your lives to be your personal Savior. It's that easy."

Diaz and McQueen both nod their heads acknowledging that they understand, and then they close their eyes and clasp their hands together to pray.

Sergeant Glen Davis, the black man who grew up in a very tough neighborhood in Miami reaches across the little table and takes a hold of the hands of Specialist Diaz and Major McQueen. He grips their hands tightly with his big, strong fists and prays, "Dear Heavenly Father. I come to You here tonight on the east side of the very continent You once walked on. I come to You with two men who want to ask You to be their Lord and their Savior. Two men that desire to have Jesus in their lives. I lift up to You the lives of these two very special men."

Glen Davis pauses, he then says, "Go ahead Carlos, this is what you came down here for."

With tears already streaming down his brown-skinned face and with his voice breaking up, Carlos Diaz takes a deep breath and begins, "Oh God, oh God, I know I have never come to You before, except maybe that time in Iraq when I called on Your name and said I wasn't ready to die. I know You heard me then, and I know You are going to hear me now. I just ask You to forgive me of all the things I have done wrong in my life, and You know how many things that is. I ask You, Lord, that You let Jesus be my Savior. I do not know if I was a Christian when I was a Catholic, but God, I want to be a Christian like Sheldon Mitchal is. I want to be saved from all the wrong I have done. Please make Yourself real in my life, Jesus."

The young twenty-six year old man with Mexican blood running all through his veins begins to cry. His face is covered in tears of relief. His friend and confidant Sergeant Glen Davis grips his hands even tighter and says, "That's good Carlos, very good. Your turn, Major. Just say what is on your heart."

Sergeant Glen Davis then grips Scott McQueen's hands a little tighter and says again, "Just say what is on your heart, Scott."

U.S. Air Force Major Scott McQueen, with his head bowed and his eyes tightly closed, prays to his Maker. "God, I know I have never come to You before. I know I have never even been in one of Your churches. I do not know very much about You, but I believe that You did come to this earth two thousand years ago and walked among us as a man named Jesus. Heaven knows I am not perfect, that I am a sinner. Only You God know about some of my sins. You know I've cheated on my wife. You also know how much that really bothers me. God, I ask You to make me a better person, whatever it takes. Bring Jesus into my life to be my Savior please, and set me on a faithful path with my wife and my wonderful children You have given me."

As Major Scott McQueen ends his prayer for salvation, small tears come out of his eyes as he opens them. He says, "I was unfaithful to my wife once a few years ago, and no one else knows that."

A very relieved and completely exhausted Carlos Juan Diaz opens his eyes and says, "I've never felt so free in all of my life."

"You guys did great," Davis states. "This will turn out to be the most important night in your lives. I want to end this evening with a prayer of thanks if both of you will bow your heads with me again."

Sergeant Glen Davis then pulls the two men's hands he has been holding separately into the middle of the little round metal table.

In the country of Kuwait, in the middle of the Middle East, at the darkest hours of night, all three Christian men bow their heads. With his big powerful hands clasped around the hands of Specialist Diaz and Major McQueen, Sergeant Davis begins to pray. They sit undisturbed only a couple hundred feet from the edge of the Persian Gulf where a very large crew of men, some Americans, some from Kuwait, some from Europe, and others, subcontractors from countries like India, Pakistan, Bangladesh, Nepal, the Philippines, and the world, are unloading the massive gray Navy ship the Mendonca.

Glen Davis prays a prayer of thanks and protection over his two new Christian brothers and their extended families. The constant activities, the sounds and smells of diesel engines revving up and roaring past, have no affect on the three U.S. Military men, Diaz,

Davis and McQueen as they sit under the open-sided smoking pavilion.

With heads bowed and eyes closed, as tanks and trucks and soldiers pass by, Sergeant Glen Davis prays deeply and from the heart. He includes in his prayer portions of Scripture he has in memory. When he is finished praying, there is not a dry eye on any of the three tough, seasoned American soldiers.

As Sergeant Davis concludes his prayer of thanks and blessings, Diaz thinks to himself, *I have never heard anyone pray as long, or as deep and heartfelt as Sergeant Davis just did. I have heard people pray before, my mother and my grandmother. I have heard priests, bishops and deacons in the Catholic Church pray, but I have never heard anyone pray like Davis just has. His prayer came straight from his heart. It did not sound like it had been written centuries ago by someone else, or printed in a prayer book thousands of miles away and then sent here. He prayed from deep down inside of himself with real meaning and feeling. This is the most real thing I have ever experienced.*

"Guys, this is only the beginning. A great beginning, but only the beginning of your Christian walk," Sergeant Davis says. "This does not mean life will be on easy street from here on out. You will both still have challenges and failures. You will face many trials and tribulations. We are all in a fallen and sinful world and we still live in our fleshly bodies that still have sinful desires."

Davis picks up his bottle of water and takes a big drink. Diaz and McQueen sit and listen as he continues, "It's just that now you can call on the name of the Lord, the name Jesus for help and assistance in your daily battles because you are both His. You will find that many times in the years to come you will have to yield your own will and your own desires over to His will. You will have to do this over and over again. Sometimes, that may not be easy. Just remember, it is always best to yield to His will."

"We have just begun this. How do we know His will, and how do we know if we get off track?" Specialist Diaz asks.

"Carlos, this is where reading the Bible comes in," Sergeant Davis answers. "God's will for your life and what He wants you to do, will always line up with what is written in His Word, the Bible.

And that small, quiet, still voice you may hear in your heart that speaks to you, the one I made mention of will always line up with what is written in the words of the Bible when it is from God. It will all become much more clear to you as you grow as a Christian. You do not have to understand everything right now."

"Kind of like when I first went to boot camp and I had to learn to yield my will," Diaz says. "I know I didn't understand all of that then, but I do now."

Having never thought of it that way, Sergeant Davis laughs and then replies, "Yeah, that is sort of what it is like. Only with God you can be sure He is right all the time."

"I've never wanted to read the Bible before," Diaz says. "Now I really want to. I'm curious to find out what is in it."

"Can we lose what we have just done by getting off track?" Major McQueen asks with a very serious look on his face. "If we continue to sin and can't change our ways, will we have to do this again someday?"

"This is a very important question you have asked," Davis states. "I believe with all my heart that once you have made the decision that you two have both made tonight, to ask Jesus into your hearts, to be your Savior, that He will do just that. He will be faithful to us even when we are not faithful to Him. I believe completely that once you have been saved you will always be saved. The book of Romans says very clearly that nothing can separate us from the love of Christ. The Word of God also says in the great little book of Philippians, Chapter one, verse six that 'He who began a good work in you will carry it on to completion until the day of Christ Jesus.' This tells me that our eternal destiny depends now on Jesus and what He did. Not on us."

"I hope this is true," McQueen says. "I know I still have a lot of things to clean up in my life to be as good a person as I know I should be."

"Believe me, Major McQueen, God will help you clean those things up more than you think He will," Davis tells the thirty-eight-year-old father and husband.

Diaz smiles and exclaims, "God's got His work cut out for Him if He's going to clean up my life!"

"He can and He will, Carlos," states the Sergeant. "You will have to do your part, and a good place to start is to read Philippians. It's a little book in the middle of the New Testament. It is a very good place for both of you to start reading the Bible. I can get a couple copies of those little camouflage Bibles we have over here from one of the Military Chaplains tomorrow for you guys."

"That would be great," McQueen replies.

"If you can't, I can get a Bible from Mitchal anytime," states Diaz. "I think he has two of 'em. A camouflage one and a big black one he keeps in his foot locker."

Sergeant Glen Davis has a sudden thought come into his mind about Specialist Diaz. *Wow! If this guy, with the chip he has had on his shoulder, can come to Christ, anyone can.*

CHAPTER TWENTY-NINE

If He Wins, You Win. If He Loses, You Lose

While temperatures in the northeastern half of the country are steadily dropping, the wind is really beginning to pick up in the nation's capital. It is almost three P.M. on the East Coast. The U.S. Presidential Candidate who had a very comfortable six to nine point lead in nearly every major poll taken over the past two weeks leading up to this weekend, has now seen his lead completely vanish in less than twenty-four hours. The California man is now scrambling to try and regain the upper hand on an election to the highest political office in the land, if not the entire world. Senator Walter Franson has rerouted his trip from Pennsylvania to Florida and is scheduled to make a short stop at Dulles International Airport on the outskirts of Washington D.C.

A scheduled stop in Atlanta has been canceled after Rigger Watson strongly advised Franson that it would be in the Senator's best interest to skip his Georgia commitments. It was a stop that had been planned to help two Democratic candidates who both looked like they may have realistic chances to win the tight races they are facing, one a Congressional seat south of Atlanta and the other a U.S. Senate seat. Walter Franson is stopping in D.C. for a one-on-one, face-to-face meeting with Watson, the man pulling the strings behind the scenes in this venture to win the White House.

CCN Network News President and programming boss, Rigger Watson sits in a big black limo inside the gates of the Washington D.C. airport waiting to receive his friend and political crony. Watson has just talked with Franson on the phone and knows the Senator's plane should be landing in less than ten minutes.

Watson has something he needs to share with the Democratic

Party's candidate for the U.S. Presidency that is extremely confidential. Something he needs to say face-to-face with no chance of anyone else listening in. Watson will not take much of the California Senator's very valuable time on this Saturday afternoon three days before the people of the United States go to the polls to determine who will lead the world's foremost superpower for the next four years. But the time he does take will be very valuable time to both Watson and Franson.

As he sits in his limo waiting for Franson, he makes a quick phone call to one of his news investigators, Bill Brandt. Earlier in the day Watson had tasked Brandt with finding out everything he could on the two Boston cops who had pulled over Senator Franson's campaign manager Mike Swenson and arrested him. Swenson had been stopped for running a red light and arrested for driving while intoxicated. In his car, Swenson had with him two young teenage boys, also drunk and barely clothed.

Watson learns from his phone call to Brandt that there is absolutely nothing CCN can use against either of the two Massachusetts Police Officers to make this embarrassing situation look to have been politically motivated. Both police officers are family men with squeaky clean records themselves.

One of the arresting officers is an African American man who has been on the Metro Boston Police force for over twenty years. He has also been a very active member of his union and even donated large portions of his time to help campaign for many different Democrats in Massachusetts over the last couple of decades.

The other arresting officer in the Mike Swenson ordeal is a man of Latin American background whose wife works for the Kennedy family as a housekeeper. This officer and his wife both moved to Massachusetts from the Dominican Republic in the late 1980's when the officer's younger brother played baseball for the Boston Red Sox. After just three seasons his brother blew out his arm throwing a ball into home plate from center field during a spring season game. It was this officer's ethnicity and his brother's baseball connections that had helped get him onto the Boston Police Squad.

Watson now knows there is not a direct angle to tie the arresting officers and the Republican Party together to spin this political disaster from the point of view that the Republicans were behind the arrest of Mike Swenson. Rigger Watson pulls a generic black cell phone out of his coat pocket. It is the same untraceable cell phone that the CCN President keeps hidden in the lower left hand drawer of his desk. He places a call to the last number that had been called from this phone, a cell phone that only Watson himself knows about. As he sits at the Dulles International Airport in his stretch Mercedes-Benz S-Class limousine with very darkly tinted windows and waits for the arrival of the man expected to be the next President of the United States, Watson listens as the phone he is calling rings three times and then is answered.

"Hello," says the man's voice on the other end of the line.

"Yes, let's proceed with the plan just as we talked about earlier," Watson says. "Same price as the other job?"

"No," the man says. "This will be three times what you are paying for in Colorado. I've had a month to plan that. This thing in Boston is stretching the limits of my resources." The man pauses, and then says, "But don't worry. I can handle both orders."

"I have no problem with that," Watson replies. "You have never let me down in the past."

"Boston will be done before morning, just as you have requested. And your other order is already in the process."

"Same bank and account number in the Cayman Islands?" the CCN Network News President asks.

"No," the man answers. "The account at the bank in Dubai. You should already have that information."

"Yes. Yes, I do. OK, the one in Dubai," Watson replies. "The money will be there within the hour."

"Good," the man says. "I'll check with Dubai, and then your Boston order will be carried out."

"The money will be there."

"Good. We will not talk again. Ever. I am closing down my operation after this. Goodbye."

The untraceable generic black cell phone Watson is holding to his ear goes dead. The man is gone. Watson sits in the back of his black limo all alone wondering what the guy looks like he has just finished talking to, a man he has done business with for over ten years and has never once met in person. Watson knows that the man knows what he looks like. Everyone who owns a computer can Google Rigger Watson and come up with hundreds of pictures of the person who runs the nation's largest television news network. The CEO of CCN wonders if he will ever hear the man's voice again. Part of Watson hopes he doesn't.

With the identity of the man he has just talked to still on his mind, Rigger shuts off the phone and puts it back into the inside pocket of his gray overcoat. There is no end to what Watson will do to have his man, Senator Walter Franson, living at 1600 Pennsylvania Avenue in Washington D.C.

As Watson thinks about the series of events, he has just put into action, one of his other cell phones rings. He normally carries three different phones with him. Today with the small generic black one, he has four. Looking at the caller ID on his personal cell phone, Watson sees it is his daughter in Los Angeles.

"Hello my darling, how are you?" Rigger answers the call from his spoiled daughter. "I see you made it up before noon today."

"Daddy, I get up before noon a lot of days. Plus, we're in a different time zone out here," his daughter laughs. "Anyway, I don't have to run the whole damn country like you do."

"I don't run the country, Honey," Watson says, "Just CCN."

"Whatever, Dad, I know better than that," in an excited voice she continues, "Oh, daddy! I'm going to be on stage with Flash tonight at his concert. He's flying in this afternoon from Toronto. We're going to go to the Ocean and hang for a while first."

Trying not to go into one of his rants, Watson fires a question at his daughter about the lead singer of a British pop band she has been dating for the last few months, "If Flash Freeman is seeing you, what's this crap on the covers of all the tabloids about him and that damn Christian country music singer?"

Watson's daughter, Marcia McNally, is a part time actress and full time fame hunter. She hopes someday to attain more than just the fifteen minutes of fame she now has because of who her father is. Marcia McNally Watson goes by just Marcia McNally most of the time because of how it sounds, and to separate her a bit from her famous father. Rigger's first wife's maiden name was McNally. He was only married to her for a little over four years. Marcia is Watson's only child, and the two of them do have a close relationship. As hard and as coarse as he is, Rigger Watson has stood by his daughter through all the things she has experienced as a result of her reckless lifestyle.

Marcia hopes that someday she can achieve a real level of fame apart from her father so she can feel like she is his equal. She has been on the covers of a variety of supermarket tabloids, normally because of the romances she always seems to find herself falling in and out of, but she has never graced the cover of anything her father feels is respectable. She knows her father doesn't approve of any of the guys she dates. She hopes that her career will someday evolve to the point where she will land on the covers of magazines like *People* and *Vogue*.

After she hears what her father asks about the world famous British rock star possibly dating the country music superstar Angie West, Marcia McNally scolds her father, "Now Daddy, you know as well as anyone, that stuff they put on the covers of those magazines is B.S. There's no way Flash is going to be seeing anyone as square as Angie West. They were just at the same restaurant in London at the same time. The paparazzi took their pictures when some music producer introduced them. There's no truth to what was written in *The Globe*."

Watson's daughter continues in a fashion somewhat reminiscent of one of his rants, proving she definitely is his daughter. "Hell Dad, Angie West's own freakin' people are probably behind it to try to spice up her image. You know how those people are, you're one of 'em."

"Watch it."

"Well, you are. But Dad, I'm not stupid. I know Flash would do her if he could. He's a man, and any man would. You know you would too. Am I right?"

She pauses briefly and Watson stays silent. Feeling a little jealous after thinking about what she just said, she goes on, "I know there's no damn way that Jesus-loving wench would let someone as wild and crazy as Flash Freeman touch her. Besides, she doesn't have what it takes to be with someone like him. That's why he loves me so much. I can hang with him, Daddy. Flash and I were made for each other."

"At least you're back to guys again," Watson says knowing his daughter is always borderline out of control.

"We are not even going there again! I'm over that!"

"Good!" Watson replies. "I'm glad to hear it." Even though he is a liberal democrat and is happy to have the vote of the homosexual community, the people closest to Watson know he despises anyone who is gay. He just never shows it in public.

"Rigger Watson! I told you that was just a phase. I'm done dating girls, so you get over it!" McNally fires back at her father who sends her about six thousand dollars a month for spending money on top of the eighty-five hundred dollars a month she receives as a monthly paycheck from the CCN News Network. Watson has his daughter listed as an employee in the books of CCN.

"What do you need, Darling?" Watson asks. "I'm at Dulles and Walter's plane is about to land. I have a couple more calls to make before I speak to him."

"Oh, nothing Daddy. I just wanted to tell you I'm going to be on stage with Flash and his band Ax-Handle tonight at the Staples Center. He wants me to walk slowly out onto the stage like I own it during the start of one of his new songs. He is going to walk around me and sing while I just stand there and look real sexy and disinterested."

With her long bleached-blonde hair and color enhancing contact lenses giving her dark green eyes, Marcia McNally is a very attractive girl. She is only about five foot five, but with the four inch heels she always wears she will be almost as tall as the rock star she will be sharing the stage with tonight.

"I can do that, Dad," McNally says as she giggles. "Flash thinks it will maybe help me get the movie part I just tried out for this week."

"That would be good," replies Watson.

"Oh, I hope you can see it. We're going to be live on MTV tonight. The whole nation will see us. I'll text you before he has me come up on stage. His new song, "Torn Between Terrorists" is number one all over the world. The song I'm going on stage for is a new one he just wrote called "Terminal Temptation"."

"Why can't you date a doctor, or a lawyer, somebody

respectable?" Watson asks.

"Oh Daddy, quit it. Flash is great, you'll love him." she replies. "Give Uncle Walter my love, and tell him good luck. Oh, and Flash would love to play at his inaugural ceremonies with his band Ax-Handle. They love everything Senator Franson stands for."

"That's good."

"And tell him I'm going to vote for him twice, once here in L.A. and once in Florida. I already sent my ballot in back there. It's a system my friend Jamie worked out. So I better get to stay in the Lincoln bedroom twice."

"I love you, Honey, and I'll see if I can get to a TV when you text me that you will be on," Watson says. "Have fun. I love you, and be careful out there."

"Bye, Daddy. Love you too."

Watson's limo is parked inside Dulles International Airport where his former fraternity brother Senator Walter Franson's plane is scheduled to land. As he reaches into the inside pocket of his gray overcoat to get the black cell phone, he sees the Boeing 747 he has been waiting for come into view in the distance as it slowly drops out of the sky and makes its way towards earth to land on the runway.

After he powers the untraceable cell phone back on, Watson places a call to an international number. An automated answering system in Switzerland receives the call. In heavily accented English, Rigger Watson hears these options, "Press one for an account balance. Press two for a transaction. Press three to speak to a representative of World Funds Brokerage and Banking. And press four to hear these options again."

After listening to all four options, Watson presses the number two on the small keypad of the generic black phone.

From Zurich, Switzerland the automated banking system gives these options, "Press one for a transfer of funds into an existing World Funds Brokerage and Banking account to make a deposit. Press two for a transfer of funds from one World Funds Brokerage and Banking account to another World Funds Brokerage and Banking account within the World Funds Brokerage and Banking system. Press three to transfer funds out of a World Funds Brokerage and Banking account and into another participating international monetary associate in this automated system."

After hearing the second set of options, the President of CCN pushes the number three to transfer funds out of the bank in Zurich, Switzerland. He knows he has only one chance to get the account numbers correct. Watson follows the prompts to enter the correct numbers of the WFBB account he is withdrawing funds out of today. When prompted to enter the international bank number where the money is being sent, Rigger is very careful to enter the correct number of a United Arab Emirates owned bank in Dubai. He is even more cautious as he enters the individual's account number for the final destination of the funds being transferred, reading the numbers out of a little black book.

While he awaits confirmation that the transaction has gone through, Watson looks up from his phone. He sees the 747 has landed and is turning at the end of the runway. Watson looks down at his watch to see what time it is. Once the six million dollars in American currency has been wired from one bank account to the other, there is no way of reversing the transaction. The money will be in the hands of the recipient. If an account number has been missed by only one digit, it could bring everything Watson is trying to accomplish to a stop.

"Your transaction has been successful," Watson hears an automated voice say. "Thank you for your business. May I help you make another transaction? If so please press one. If you would like a confirmation number of the monetary transfer just completed, please press two. If not, please push nine to end this call."

Very carefully as his hand shakes slightly, Watson presses two to receive a WFBB confirmation number to confirm the transfer of the six million dollars to the bank in Dubai. After he writes down the number on a small slip of yellow sticky note paper he has in his coat pocket, Watson pushes the number nine button on the phone to end the call. He sticks the yellow sticky note to the inside cover of the little black book.

Watson waits to receive a text message from the man the funds have been wired to. He expects this text will come within a few seconds. The generic black phone makes a single loud beep. Watson looks down and sees he has received the text from the man in New

York City. It reads, 'Wire transfer received. Job paid for in full. Nice doing business with you. Have a good day.'

There is no going backwards now. The plan that is in place cannot be stopped. What has been paid for will be done. This is not the first time Rigger Watson has used this system. He already had all the necessary numbers to the banks and the accounts at his fingertips in his little black book, an old fashioned little black book with little tiny lines inside to be filled in with people's telephone numbers and addresses. He keeps the book on himself at all times and only he knows about it. The only time it is not in arm's reach is when he sleeps at night. He has a small safe hidden in the floor of his house where he puts the secret little black book when he sleeps. When he is not home, he puts it in a specially made locked cigarette case and slides it between the mattresses of whatever bed he might be sleeping in away from his own house.

Little black books have had a history of being filled with the numbers of different people an individual might want to go have fun with. Rigger Watson's little black book has the telephone numbers and contact information of people a person would hope never to meet, not ever. Along with the contact information and telephone numbers, Watson's book also contains a vague record of the different services Watson has bought and paid for over the years with funds that were not directly tied to him. Everything is in code, a secret code devised by Watson when he was the president of his college fraternity. The entry in the black book for the man Rigger is doing business with today contains the account information for five different international banks from five different countries abroad.

Six million dollars is the most Watson has ever paid for these kinds of services. If Watson's plan works, he will consider it a bargain for what is at stake.

Looking up from the text message he has just read, Watson can see that Senator Franson's plane has made its turn at the end of the runway and is taxiing towards where Watson's black limo is parked on the tarmac. Painted in great big blue letters all across the side of the Boeing 747 is, *Vote The People — Vote Franson For President!*

After receiving the text message from the man now on his way to Boston, Watson clears all the text messages off the black phone. He punches into this phone one more number to call before he meets with Senator Walter Franson. Watson knows this conversation will not be very long. The enormous 747 carrying the Democrat from California who is the leading candidate for the U.S. Presidency is about to arrive alongside of the CCN owned Mercedes-Benz S-Class Limousine.

From the private confines of his personal limo, Watson waits as the phone rings in his ear. The voice that answers has been muffled to disguise the identity of the person on the other end of the call.

"Hello, is this you, Charley?" the muffled voice asks.

"Yes, this is Charley," answers Watson.

"Are we on go?"

"Yes, we are."

"Tonight?"

"Yes," answers Rigger Watson.

"OK," answers the voice. "I will do my part."

"I will talk to you tomorrow."

"Yes, you will."

The call ends and Watson deletes the history of all the calls he has made on the phone. He then shuts it off and puts it in the inside pocket of his suit jacket beside the little black book. The 747 carrying Senator Franson to this private meeting is now within a few hundred feet of where Watson waits in the black limo.

As the plane comes to a stop out in the middle of the tarmac, a small crew of airport personnel quickly rolls an airplane ramp up to the rear exit on the left side of the plane. Watson's chauffer slowly pulls the black Mercedes limousine up close to where the ramp comes down to meet the ground. The plane and the car both sit for a moment as everything comes to a standstill except the brisk breeze that is whipping across the cold, hard surface of the tarmac in the nation's capital. The outer door in the rear of the 747 above the stairs opens and slides out of the way allowing Senator Walter Franson to exit the plane. He walks out on the top of the ramp by himself and begins to walk down the stairs. Rigger Watson, the most powerful Democrat in America, stays sitting in his big black foreign-built car and waits.

As the Senator reaches the last couple of steps at the bottom of the stairs on the airplane ramp, Watson leans forward inside the black Mercedes-Benz and tells his chauffeur, "Don't get out of the car. Let him open his own door."

With no one else having exited the Boeing 747, the man hoping to become the next President of the United States of America walks directly over to the back end of Watson's limousine and opens the door on the left side of the car. He ducks his head down and asks sarcastically, "You want me to get in, or just stand out here on the tarmac?"

"Get in," Watson replies.

Following the orders he has just recieved, Franson gets in the car with the most powerful media man in the United States. The Senator knows very well the man he is about to have a private meeting with has no scruples.

———

"Guys, there are two very important things I want both of you to remember from this night," Sergeant Glen Davis says. "The first is when it comes to being a Christian there is no gray area. A person is a Christian or a person is not a Christian. It is black or white. You are either in or out. And you guys are both in forever. You are both Christians, never to be lost again. And that is the greatest thing that can ever happen to you."

Both Diaz and McQueen nod their heads at Davis and then look at each other for a moment before returning their attention to the Sergeant.

"Also, as you grow as men and as Christians remember this. When you battle the Holy Spirit, either He will win or you will lose. If He wins, you win. If He loses, you lose. The Holy Spirit is God down here on earth with us today as we continue to live out the rest of our lives as mortal men."

As he sets down his nearly full bottle of water, Specialist Diaz asks, "That is how God speaks to us here on earth, right?"

"Yes," answers the black man who grew up in Miami, Florida on the wrong side of the law. Davis then finishes what he hopes his two new friends will remember forever. "It is the Holy Spirit you must yield to in the internal struggles we all face on a daily basis as Christians and as men."

"I think I see what you are saying. God always knows what is best for us," says U.S. Air Force Major Scott McQueen. "When you battle the Holy Spirit, either He will win or you will lose. If He wins, you win. If He loses, you lose. That's kind of catchy."

"Yes Major, it is," Sergeant Davis replies. "And trust me, guys, because of our selfish nature we naturally have as human beings, you will both have internal struggles and battles with the Holy Spirit between what you want to do and what you should do."

After drinking the last bit of his water, Sergeant Glen Davis scrunches up the plastic bottle and puts the cap back on it. He then tosses it out of the smoking pavilion and into a metal trash barrel about twenty feet away.

"Good shot, Sarge," Specialist Diaz says as he laughs.

"Yeah, when I was a kid I thought I would grow up to be a professional basketball player. That was before I got into all that trouble in Miami," Davis replies. "What God has shown me over the years is that His purpose for my life was to be available to help young men like you get your lives on the right track. A purpose I now understand is far more important and rewarding than being an NBA point guard would have been. In time, He will show you both what His purpose is for each of your lives as well. The secret is to try and keep your ear tuned to Him so He can show you that purpose."

CHAPTER THIRTY

L'Ambroisie dans la Place des Vosges

It is seven past eleven as FBI agent Wikett turns back into the old California produce warehouse an hour to the east of the sandy beaches of the Pacific Ocean. He is mourning the loss of his friend and fellow federal agent Antonio Ramirez Garcia. With the car radio in the Cadillac Escalade shut off and no phone calls, the silent drive by himself from the warehouse to the Home Depot and back has allowed today's events to really sink in.

Chace Wikett cannot help but ask himself, *Why couldn't I have hit Eddison somehow when I shot at him?* He knows that would have prevented the crazy Cajun from killing Agent Garcia. Any number of things could have changed the outcome of the early morning's events. Wikett wonders how he is ever going to be able to tell Tony's wife and family what has happened. Over and over in his mind he has wished they would have just detained Eddison and the two Muslim terrorists in El Paso like he wanted to.

These thoughts continue to circulate through the mind of the man who feels partially responsible for his friend's death. Chace Wikett and Antonio Garcia were as close of friends as two people could be. The two men had known each other for over twenty years. Wikett thinks back to the first time they met in college when he and Garcia were both drunk and nearly got into a fight in a bar over a girl. It was not too long after that incident that Chace completely quit drinking. A month later, the young and cocky Tony Garcia also quit drinking to get serious about his education and improve his physical fitness.

FBI agent Garcia was one of the most physically fit people Wikett had ever known. Tony was also one of the most serious family men he has ever known. As he drives the blue Cadillac Escalade around to the rear of the abandoned brick building, the complete silence he is experiencing makes Wikett think about something he is constantly telling his kids at home in Dallas when they leave the TV on nonstop or have loud music playing all through the house. Chace will tell them, "When you've got all that crap blaring into your heads non stop, you never have a chance to think your own thoughts." Right now, in complete silence, he can definitely hear his own thoughts.

As he thinks about the peace that can be brought on by silence, Wikett realizes the quiet time he has just had all to himself has been hard on his emotions but good for his mind. He pulls up to the door at the back of the warehouse and brings the vehicle to a stop. After he shuts off the dark blue Escalade, FBI agent Chace Wikett stays sitting behind the wheel and bows his head forward. With his eyes closed, he prays, "Oh dear Heavenly Father, I do not understand Your ways sometimes. I do not understand why this friend of mine, a good man, had to die and a bad man is allowed to live. I know that You did not cause Tony's death. I also know that You can and will bring some sort of good from all this bad that has happened."

Wikett pauses and wipes a tear from his face, "Oh Lord God Almighty, I pray that You will pour out Your grace and Your mercy out on Tony's family. That You will give his children and his wife peace. That You will comfort them in the coming days. That You will draw them closer to You and to Your Son, Jesus Christ. I thank You in the holy, sweet, precious name of Jesus."

Wikett pauses as he fights back his emotions, "Lord God Almighty, I ask You to give me the strength, the courage, and the know-how and wisdom to carry out the rest of this day. I also pray to You God for the salvation of this man Roddy Dale Eddison, I pray Lord Jesus that You will in some way bring him to know You so that possibly Agent Garcia's death will not have been in vain. Thank you Lord God Almighty. I ask these things of You in the blood of Jesus."

Agent Wikett opens his eyes and wipes more tears off of his cheeks. He grabs the three plastic sacks with the items he bought at the local Home Depot and gets out of the seventy-five thousand dollar vehicle. He unlocks the back door of the building where the Texas FBI agents are holding Eddison. Before he enters the warehouse, he sets the three plastic sacks down along the outside edge of the foundation behind a large wooden pole.

Quietly Wikett walks up to the Ford Excursion parked inside the large abandoned warehouse. He carefully wakes Agents Swanson and Gasperson who were both catching some badly needed sleep. He then motions for them to follow him. With Eddison locked securely in the twelve by twelve room and still taped to a wooden chair, Swanson and Gasperson follow Wikett back out the door he just came through.

Standing outside of the warehouse, Wikett reaches down and grabs the plastic sacks he set behind an electrical pole. He then hands the two other Dallas based FBI agents each a couple cans of the black spraypaint he just purchased at the Home Depot. When he does, he says, "We're going to paint all the windows black on this building."

"Good thing there aren't many windows," comments Swanson. There are only seven windows on the old building, three along one side and two on each end, and none of them very large.

"After that we will turn the clock up about seven or eight hours and try and make Eddison think he's slept all day," says Wikett.

"Sounds good to me," states Gasperson as he turns to walk to the farthest windows.

"You think it'll work, Chace?" Swanson asks.

"It's worth a try," claims Wikett. "I'll get these windows here if you'll get those over there around the corner."

"I'm headed that way," says Swanson.

Trying to convince Eddison he has slept about seven times longer than he really has is a shot in the manufactured dark. If it works, *great*, if not there will still be time for other methods of psychological trickery that may work. Worst case scenario, Wikett can always resort to the type of torture he has seen work overseas. Something inside of the Texas FBI man tells him that from the way Eddison popped off and said what he did earlier, the time trick may very well work. Eddison's pride seems to indicate he would like to try and make fools out of the men interrogating him. In a matter of minutes, Wikett will know if the deception is successful or not.

As the three men meet back at the rear door of the warehouse, Wikett tells them, "We need to stay quiet when we roll the Excursion away from the door of the room. I then want you, Billy Joe, to sneak in there and turn that clock on the wall forward to about seven-thirty."

Of the three Texas FBI agents, Gasperson is the man best suited for this job. It is in his blood to be able to sneak into an area and accomplish a task most could not, and then sneak out with no one ever knowing he had been there. Gasperson has Native American blood running deep through his veins on both sides of his family tree.

Billy Joe Gasperson's grandmother on his mother's side is three quarters Comanche Indian and two of his great grandfathers on the Gasperson side of Billy Joe's ancestry were descendents of the great Apache Tribal Chief Mangas Coloradas, also known as Red Sleeves. Gasperson's Native American heritage helped get him into the FBI, but his skills and superior intelligence is what will keep him in federal law enforcement for many years to come if that is what he chooses to do. There is a part of Gasperson that would like to someday get into politics, but he has not told any of his fellow FBI agents this.

Without the crazy Cajun ever knowing the door to the interrogation room has been opened, Gasperson successfully slips in and turns the clock forward to 7:23. Luckily for the FBI agents, the glass cover that had originally set over the face of the old clock was missing. All Gasperson had to do was move the small arm counter-clockwise to seven. While Gasperson was setting the clock, Agent Wikett stepped out of the warehouse and made a quick phone call.

When Wikett came back in, he walked straight towards Big John Swanson and Billy Joe Gasperson, who were standing outside the interrogation room waiting for his lead. Without breaking stride as he approached the door to the room, Wikett says, "Guys, we're going to do it now. This should be simple. Just follow my lead. If it works, it will work right off the bat."

Both Gasperson and Swanson turn and walk with Agent Wikett towards the room. They are about a half a stride behind him. Neither say anything. They have both worked with Chace Wikett for years, and they both know the man they are following has a plan that will work if anyone does.

When FBI agent Wikett gets to the little square room right in the middle of the warehouse, he kicks in the door with his foot, busting the latch right out of the old, dry wooden door. Sitting there duct taped into an old wooden chair, with his head hanging down and off to one side and his chin against his chest, eyes completely shut, is Roddy Dale Eddison. He is asleep. Wikett reaches over and flips on the lights to the room as he walks past the switch. When Wikett flipped on the lights, Eddison reluctantly started to open his eyes and wake up out of the deep sleep he had fallen into. As he steps across the room towards Eddison, Wikett says in a loud voice, "You sorry S.O.B.!"

The former Texas A&M field goal kicker then kicks off two of the four legs from one side of the chair the crazy Cajun is taped to. Eddison, who had been so soundly asleep just seconds prior to this, crashes to the hard concrete floor with a thud. His shoulder and arm take the brunt of the three-foot fall. Eddison lays there still taped tightly to the broken chair. He is trying to come awake and get his bearings, but he is very surprised with the sudden events and the immediate threat of physical punishment it looks like he will be faced with. FBI agent Wikett has given Eddison the impression that he is mad enough to kill someone.

After kicking the legs out from under the chair that has been supporting the out-of-shape Leesburg, Louisiana man, Wikett grabs the table sitting in the middle of the room and throws it up against the wall. With only the 60-watt light bulb hanging directly above where the table had just been, and nothing but darkness coming through the opened door leading out into the warehouse, it appears to be night. Everyone's shadows are very long inside the room. Wikett makes sure to stand out of Eddison's view of the clock hanging on the wall.

After causing such a ruckus and surprising not only Eddison, but also the two agents working with him, FBI agent Chace Wikett yells at Eddison, "How the hell could you just sleep in here like a little baby all day when you knew those damn Arabs were going to blow up a bunch of hard-core bikers at a Harley Davidson rally in Riverside this afternoon? You are one sorry S.O.B.!"

"What?" a slightly dazed and dumbfounded Eddison asks as he looks up at Wikett. "What did you say?"

"You heard me, you sorry piece of trash," Wikett tells Eddison. He then drops down to one knee and grabs Eddison by the head with both hands and points Eddison's face and eyes towards the clock hanging high on the west wall of the little room. "You see that clock?"

"What?" says Eddison as he looks directly up at Wikett after seeing the clock, "But—what did you say?"

Wikett tightens his grip on Eddison's head and then says very abrasively, "It's well past seven o'clock, you idiot. You've slept all afternoon while you knew those two Muslim terrorists you hauled out here from El Paso were going to blow themselves up at a biker rally in Riverside. They killed over ten thousand people at that motorcycle rally. The blood of all those bikers is on your hands, Eddison!"

"A motorcycle rally?" Eddison asks in a daze.

"Yeah, one of the biggest biker rallies in California," replies Swanson from the opposite side of the room.

The surprised and disorientated Cajun then blurts out, "They were... They're supposed to blow up a rock concert at the Staples Center tonight. A concert with that British freak Flash Freeman. That's what was supposed to happen."

"Really?" Swanson asks sarcastically.

"I never would have helped them if I had known they were goin' to blow up a bunch of bikers," says the man guilty of the murder of Antonio Ramirez Garcia.

Agent Wikett stands up. He leaves Eddison on the floor.

Now confused, Eddison pauses before turning his head up towards Wikett and asking him, "Are you lying to me?"

"You let all those Americans die... bikers to boot," Wikett acts like he didn't hear the question as he stands directly over Eddison. "If you really didn't know it was going to be bikers, you damn well better prove it. Tell these two men exactly what those Muslims told you was going to happen."

Wikett walks to the door and stops. When he turns around, he tells Eddison, "You convince 'em that those Muslims lied to you or you'll never see the light of day again. I'll kill you before morning. That's the only way you live today."

Turning his head towards Gasperson and Swanson, the Texas FBI lead says, "Get everything out of him by any means possible."

Wikett leaves the room. As he does, Eddison yells back at him, "I thought it was going to be a rock concert in L.A." He turns to Gasperson and Swanson as they approach him and says, "I really thought it was going to be a rock concert in L.A. tonight. I never would have helped them if..."

Wikett heads to the exit door on the back side of the building where the Cadillac Escalade is parked. As he walks across the large dark warehouse, he runs a number of scenarios through his head pertaining to the information he was able to trick the Cajun truck driver into giving him. Outside the old abandoned produce warehouse, FBI agent Chace Wikett opens his cell phone and places a call to a man named MacKuenn in Washington D.C.

———

Tomorrow will definitely be a day Alexia Klien will never forget. For the first time in over three years, she will see the only man who has ever held the combination to the lock on the deepest parts of her heart. Alexia can feel goose bumps on the back of her neck as she thinks about it. Today has been a day like no day she has ever lived before as she watched the confusing events at the busy Paris airport. Meeting Amaya Blazi, the young American girl who is spending a year of her life as a Christian missionary in Africa has caused Alexia to experience things deep down inside herself she did not know existed. Everything combined with hearing Severo Baptiste's voice this afternoon have let her mind and her heart go places she never knew they could.

Today is not over though. It is late in Paris, at least by U.S. standards. Americans generally eat dinner between six and eight P.M., but it is not uncommon for the French to wait to sit down for the evening meal until well after ten. With so much going on inside of her mind, CCN's number one broadcast journalist is having a tough time keeping focused. Alexia is in the middle of some impromptu on-the-street interviews in a very fashionable and historic part of downtown Paris. The interviews will be followed by a late night dinner filled with wine and laughter at a fine French restaurant. All those working with her tonight from the CCN Paris Bureau will be invited. It will be a time of fun and joy for most in attendance. Alexia will put a happy carefree face on for the occasion, but she knows it will only be a game she will be playing, a game she is very good at and far too familiar with in her life.

A few hours ago when she had completed some real interviews with known people, Alexia wished she could just go back to her luxurious five-star hotel room. Finish the hot soothing shower she cut short this afternoon to get to work on time, crawl into her big comfortable king-size bed and sleep like a child for twenty-four hours until Severo knocks at her door. This is what she still wishes she could do.

Performing these impromptu interviews on the street with whoever just happens to walk by is something Alexia has not done for nearly ten years. On her way up in her career when she worked for station WGAT out of Atlanta, they would send her out to do this same kind of on-the-street reporting. Usually it was not about anything really important, or at least anything that she felt was important.

On this very lovely night in one of the most scenic places in the famous French city, la Place des Vosges, the oldest and one of the most beautiful and intimate squares in all of Paris, Alexia chuckles to herself. She remembers a time when she had been sent out on an assignment by WGAT to ask the citizens of Georgia what they thought of the dilapidation of certain interstate overpasses in and around the city of Atlanta.

Less than a year out of college, Alexia was twenty-three at the time. She was sent out with a driver and a camera man to one of the largest Post Offices in Atlanta during the middle of the day to ask people a scripted question. The question the young reporter was instructed to ask people as they exited the U.S. Postal building was, "Would it bother you to know that there are holes in some of the roadways on the overpass bridges here in Atlanta, especially some that are on Interstate 20 that are big enough that an orange could fall through them?"

What makes Alexia laugh to herself this night in Paris, France well over a decade later, is when she thinks of one of the last people she interviewed that day and his response to her. She asked the scripted question of a man in a black cowboy hat, a very attractive rough and rugged-looking man, who was only in Atlanta on business from Odessa, Texas. His answer to her question was, "Well darling, I guess it might bother me if I dropped an orange on one of those I-20 overpasses, but I'll try not to do that."

It was not only what he said that she found so funny that day in front of the busy Atlanta Post Office, but also the way he said it in his deep, slow, half-serious West Texas drawl. The tall, rugged Texan's response was good enough to get him a date later that evening with the young, up-and-coming news reporter. In fact, Alexia and the rich Texas oilman J.D. Whattley saw each other off and on for over two years after that.

She was still in occasional contact with the tough Texas rancher right up until the time when she met Severo Baptiste in Salt Lake City at the Winter Olympics in 2002. Alexia really liked Whattley, but she knew he would never move off his 100,000 acre ranch about forty-five miles Northwest of Odessa, Texas. And there was no way she was going to live that far away from civilization.

Whattley was also the kind of old-fashioned guy that would have expected his wife to be right next to him in everything he did, whether roping and doctoring a sick cow, or pulling up the pipe on an old oil well. A long-term relationship with the romantic Texan was not something Alexia felt she could yield to in her twenties. When she first met Severo Baptiste, there were things about Severo that kind of reminded her of an international version of J.D. Whattley from West Texas. The exception was that there was something very mysterious about Baptiste. With Whattley there was no mystery anywhere, you got exactly what you saw each and every time.

A couple of years after she quit seeing him, Alexia received a short letter from the Texan. She was beginning to be seen on the CCN news network on a national level all across the U.S. The letter from the rough and rugged Texan wished her the best of luck in her broadcast career. Whattley also told her that he had met the woman of his dreams. He met a feisty brunette in June of 2002 on a Friday night at a rodeo in Big Spring, Texas. He proposed to her on the following Tuesday and the two of them were married the next Saturday night in San Antonio on the River Walk. In his letter, Whattley said it was a whirlwind, eight day romance. The Texan said it was like nothing he had ever experienced before and the best thing that had ever happened to him.

Alexia remembered when she first read the Texan's letter she knew just exactly what he was talking about with the whirlwind romance. She felt the very same thing when she first met Baptiste, only she was not as quick to act on her emotions as her Texas counterpart was to act on his.

On this night in the French capital, she is doing something she only dreamed she might get conned into again by David Letterman on his show. Alexia is out in the middle of complete strangers on a sidewalk to do short interviews with some of them that she and CCN are able to stop as they pass by. It is comical to her as she thinks about it. Tonight she may end up talking to just about anyone from anywhere who might walk by in a very public forum, and tomorrow in a very secret setting she will sit down across from Prince Charles in complete privacy.

As the clock on her cell phone turns to ten P.M., the black sky that has been visible above the lights of the city is disappearing behind a cloud cover slowly making its way across Paris. For some reason, Alexia feels a little vulnerable to the crowd as she continues her work. On top of everything, she feels that what she is doing is not really all that earth-shattering. In her opinion, it is a waste of her time and CCN's resources.

After finishing a short interview where she got opinions on the upcoming Presidential election in the United States from a married couple, an American man and his French wife who now live in a small town just north of Paris, Alexia turns to the Frenchman in charge of the evening's activities for CCN France. She says to him, "I'm really getting hungry, and I'm definitely ready to be done with this crap."

Wanting to let her know he is in control, he tells Alexia, "Just a couple more interviews. I am looking for a certain response to the question about America's role in fighting global warming."

Alexia knows different. It's just a little power struggle waged by a Frenchman that wants much more than just a couple of extra interviews from the beautiful American journalist. She is tired of playing the games she has been playing with this man in charge of a large portion of CCN Europe. Alexia tells him, "One more and we're done. Then everyone goes to dinner or I'll just catch a cab to my hotel."

"You're the boss," the Frenchman sarcastically says. "But you better make it a good one."

Alexia turns and looks down the street. She sees a man in his mid-thirties walking towards them at a decided pace. He is alone and dressed in a very sharp-looking black Armani suit with a rich burgundy colored tie that has small designs of silver and gold scattered across it. He glances directly at Alexia and she knows this is someone she can get to stop for an interview. She approaches him with the CCN microphone in her hand and smiles at him. He smiles back and slows the pace he is walking at until he stops in front of Alexia and the CCN cameraman.

With the crowd of CCN employees staying back except the camera man and a couple of guys holding lights, Alexia tells the man, "Hi, I'm Alexia Klien with CCN Network News and we are on the streets of Paris tonight looking for people's reactions to the upcoming U.S Presidential election."

The man smiles, but doesn't say anything.

"Would it be alright to ask you a few questions about the upcoming election in the United States?" Alexia asks.

"That would be fine by me," the man says.

Alexia can tell by his accent he is not French, but most likely Italian. Before she begins the interview, she asks, "Off the record of course, just for my own curiosity, do you mind telling me where you are from and what it is that brings you to Paris on this beautiful night in November?" Alexia pauses for just a second and before the man can respond, she says, "My guess is you're from Italy." The seasoned broadcast journalist knows that by asking him these questions in a slightly flirtatious way it will open him up to be more truthful and forthcoming when she asks him the important questions regarding international politics.

"You are right. I am from Italy. Rome in fact," the man says as he smiles at Alexia. "I am a lawyer and I'm in Paris for business. I represent the Vatican in matters relating to property people bequeath to the church. Tomorrow we are having a special ceremony at the Basilica du Sacré-Coeur de Montmartre for a woman who has given the church two priceless Vincent van Gogh paintings and a large vineyard in the Bordeaux region of France."

"Really?" Alexia asks somewhat surprised. "Two Vincent van Gogh paintings just given to the Catholic Church?"

"Yes," the Italian attorney says as he looks Alexia squarely in her eyes. "You should come and see the paintings. They will be there all day tomorrow."

"Oh, I'm afraid I am going to be busy with work," Alexia says as she finds she may have gotten this man to open up a little too much.

"Are you Catholic?" the man asks.

"No, I'm not really anything," Alexia replies. She realizes this answer may actually cause the Italian man to close up and not be as willing to respond to her interview questions as openly as she wishes, so she tells him, "If I didn't have so many things already scheduled tomorrow I would love to visit the church. I've seen it from the outside when I've been in Paris before, and I've heard its very beautiful inside."

"Oh it is," answers the Roman lawyer about the Catholic Basilica that sets on the highest point in all of Paris. "You should really come and see it before you leave. You will feel closer to God there than any other place in the city."

Hearing this, Alexia thinks back to her trip this afternoon with Amaya and Jeff Blazi and Matthew James. She thinks to herself that she felt closer to God riding with the three American Christians in a little green Citroen than she ever has in any church building she has ever been in. Knowing she needs to put a stop to the chit chat and get on with the interview, she says, "I will try and go see it before I leave Paris. But now I'd better get back to work and ask you about world politics. Do you still have time for a few questions?"

"Yes, I do. Fire away," replies the Italian. "Oh, I'm sorry. In the world we live in today I shouldn't say, 'Fire away', should I?"

Alexia laughs as she realizes he is making a humorous reference to the American media's attempt in the past to eliminate all gun comments from their dialogs. She smiles and says, "I'm not touching that one... Oh, but maybe I will. How is it that someone from Italy is so up to speed on what was primarily an issue with gun related phrases in the States a good while back?"

The Italian lawyer laughs and then says, "Oh, I have a client who is from the U.S., actually Minnesota. He is a good friend of mine, Scott Kuelmann. We hunt together. He and his wife have a villa and an olive orchard outside of Prato—an hour north of Rome where they live part of the year. He is in the clothing business. I remember him telling about how the American media made such a big deal about gun related phrases after a female congresswoman was shot by some crazy nut in Arizona, like it was the gun phrases themselves that were responsible for the shooting."

"Yes, I do remember that," the CCN reporter solemnly replies.

"Kuelmann has a clothing line, you may have heard of its brand name—*Scott James*? He has some really nice shirts."

"Yes, I have. They are nice shirts, I like the colors." Alexia then asks him, "Are you ready for some real questions?"

"*Cara sicuro*," he replies in Italian with a smile on his face,

"Sure, darling."

"Good, let's start," Alexia says. She looks at her cameraman and asks, "Are we ready?"

"Anytime," the cameraman replies.

Alexia turns her attention back to the Catholic lawyer and asks, "What effects do you think the projected outcome of Senator Walter Franson winning the U.S. Presidential election will have on the relationship between the European Union and the United States?"

As he begins to answer her question, Alexia's attention in suddenly stolen when, out of the corner of her eye, she sees a woman in the distance. The woman looks like the same tall, mysterious redhead she had seen earlier in the day in the fashion boutique. Alexia completely loses her focus on the man from Italy she is interviewing. This never happens to her.

As her eye contact shifts away from the Italian man in the middle of his reply, she turns her head and stares at the woman she has seen with very long, red hair who is approaching a small crowd of people. The people are about a hundred feet away from where Alexia stands. Still looking in the direction of the small crowd waiting outside a very expensive and fashionable restaurant, l'Ambroisie in downtown Paris, Alexia knows the woman she has in her sights has to be the same woman she watched board a plane to Moscow, Russia only about eight hours earlier. For a brief moment Alexia stands perplexed.

The Italian man she is interviewing stops in the middle of his response to the question about the United States and the European Union. He turns and looks back over his shoulder in the same direction Alexia is looking. She realizes she must try and recompose herself and finish the task at hand. With the woman still in her peripheral vision, Alexia redirects her focus back to the Italian man. She says, "I'm sorry, I thought I saw someone I knew."

"That's alright. My opinion on world politics is not really very important."

"Oh, yes it is," Alexia responds quickly. "Everyone's opinion is important."

"That is where you and I will disagree," the Italian man states. "Who was it you thought you saw? A man or a woman?"

"It doesn't matter," Alexia replies. "A girl I went to school with."

"A girl? Are you sure?" the man asks. "It wasn't a man named

Severo Baptiste that you thought you saw, was it?"

Alexia's eyes open wide. She is stunned to hear what the Italian man says. At the same second the Roman lawyer asked Alexia about Baptiste, the woman she was watching walked into l'Ambroisie. The restaurant is located in a very exclusive hotel in the Marais district of downtown Paris. Reservations at l'Ambroisie normally have to be made a month or more in advance. The woman walked straight through the crowd of people and into the restaurant. She was only in Alexia's view for a few seconds.

Alexia stands with her mouth agape and stares at the Italian man. She asks him, "How do you know Severo Baptiste? And how do you know that I know him?"

The man laughs. "I thought that was you in the photo. But I wasn't sure. My brother and Baptiste are good friends. I recognized you from a picture Severo has in his house in Rome."

"Really?" Alexia says as she glances quickly towards the entrance of the restaurant where the woman just disappeared and then back to the Italian man. *Severo has a house in Rome?* Alexia wonders. For a moment there is silence with her mind jumping back and forth between this man's knowledge of Baptiste and wondering if that really was the woman who just walked in the front door of the l'Ambroisie. *What should I say next?* She wonders. After the moment of silence, Alexia asks, "Severo has a picture of me in a house he owns in Rome? I didn't know he had house in Rome."

"Yes, I've been there a couple of times. The last time was in August. He was having a party for a few of his close friends and I went with my brother and his wife."

Alexia can't believe what she is hearing. She turns to her cameraman and says, "You aren't taping this, are you?"

"No, I'm not. You are off subject here."

"Thanks," Alexia says. She looks back to the Italian man and asks, "So can you tell me, did Severo have a date at the party you attended?"

"No," the man says as he laughs lightly. "My brother says Baptiste hasn't seen anyone since the girl in the picture," he pauses and smiles, "Which is you, right?"

"You are the one who has seen the picture. I haven't," Alexia replies. "I didn't even know Severo had a home in Rome."

"It is you in the picture," the lawyer assures her as he laughs again. "There is no doubt."

"Klien, I think it's time we get on with this interview," asserts the Frenchman in charge of the evening's schedule. "You still have some questions I would like you to ask this gentleman." The Frenchman is a little put off by all the talk about Severo Baptiste.

Trapped between running into someone who knows Severo and wondering if that really was the mysterious woman she just saw again from two years earlier in Washington D.C. with U.S. Senator Walter Franson, Alexia tries to return her focus to work. She asks the Italian man, "Are you ready for more questions?"

"Shoot," he says as he smiles. "Oh, there I go again."

Alexia forces a smile and continues. "If you do not think your opinion on world politics is really very important, what is your view on what the United States is doing worldwide to help curb the emissions of carbon dioxide gases and slow the rate of global warming?"

"You have got to be kidding," says the Italian. "I think they are doing just like all the other countries worried about global warming. They are blowing smoke up people's... Well, you know what I mean. Global warming is a joke if you ask me. Now, I think you have a good idea of my opinion on that."

Alexia turns to the Frenchman in charge and asks, "Is that the response you've been looking for?"

The Frenchman stays expressionless.

As Alexia returns her focus back to the man she is interviewing, she quickly glances in the direction of the French restaurant in the distance. When she does, she sees there is no longer a small crowd of people in front of l'Ambroisie. Though it is dark and a cloud cover is moving across Paris making it even darker, the view of the door to restaurant is clear for a moment as there are lights in the area that are shining brightly.

"I don't even know where to go with the rest of this interview," Alexia tells the man from Rome. "You don't think your opinion on world politics is important, and you laugh at the notion of global warming. There is not much we are going to get from you, is there?"

"I am not one of the people pulling the strings on what happens in this world we live in," the man says. "You really need to find one of those guys." He pauses and then continues, "But when you do, they probably won't tell you much more than I will."

As the man finishes his statement, Alexia can see the door to the famous French restaurant open. From over the shoulder of the Italian man she is interviewing, Alexia sees the redheaded woman step out of the glass door set in the tiny walkway leading into l'Ambroisie. The woman is then followed out by two other people, a man and a woman, all three of them laughing as they walk in a direction away from where Alexia stands with a CCN microphone in her hand. Alexia gets a good look at the face of the redhead. *It has to be the same woman. It has to be,* she thinks.

"Yeah, I understand what you're saying," replies Alexia to the Italian man as she tries again to refocus all of her mind back on her job. Inside she knows the real story is walking away from her in the form of a tall, sexy woman with long, red hair hanging down the middle of her back. But Alexia knows that anything, any story uncovered in Europe that would hurt Senator Franson's chances of winning the White House, would go against her own personal political views and most likely cost her everything she has worked so hard to attain.

Frustrated with how the on-the-street interview with the man from Rome is going, the Frenchman in charge of CCN Paris steps in and declares, "Sir, thank you for your time. But I think we are done here."

"That's good with me," Alexia says as she again looks in the direction the woman and two other people went. She sees them as they round a corner of a large building in the distance and disappear in the growing darkness of the European night.

The American broadcast journalist knows deep down inside it is her responsibility as a reporter to follow the mysterious woman through the streets of Paris tonight, but she doesn't. Alexia can't help but think, *Did I really see who I think I did?*

CHAPTER THIRTY-ONE

Cape Buffalo on the Congo

Most of America is preparing to brace itself for the first large snow storm of winter. It's a storm that is poised to make its entrance the night before the entire country will go to the polls to decide who will be its next leader.

Temperatures have dropped nearly fifteen degrees in the last hour while the wind in the nation's capital has increased from a mild ten miles per hour to thirty, with occasional gusts up to forty. But, it is a comfortable seventy-two degrees inside Rigger Watson's Mercedes-Benz parked on the tarmac at Dulles International Airport as Senator Franson closes the door behind him after getting in the back of the black limo.

It is three P.M. on the East Coast and the leading U.S. Presidential candidate has seen his comfortable lead in the polls completely disappear. It has vanished in less than twenty-four hours. Senator Franson's advantage in the race for the White House disappeared faster than any candidate in recent history after it became public knowledge that Mike Swenson, his campaign manager and a known homosexual, was picked up by police in Boston with two drunken teenage boys.

Swenson was booked on Friday night. At last report, further charges are still pending. Swenson has been released on one hundred thousand dollars bail. It is estimated by political pundits from both parties that the Democratic candidate for the Presidency has lost ten percent of the popular vote in the eight hours since the details of the Swenson story broke all across the nation on FX News shortly after seven A.M. Eastern Standard Time this morning.

Inside the black CCN-owned limousine, the Senator sits in the very back seat directly across from Watson, who faces the rear window of the expensive vehicle. There is a small table-like platform between the two men. They both sit in plush leather seats.

With the doors shut and the window closed between them and the chauffeur, Franson braces himself for one of Watson's filth-laden rants. Franson is to the point where he is getting tired of Watson's temperament and behavior, but he still has to put up with it for a little while longer. The funny thing is, it was this very same temperament and behavior that had won Watson so much friendship and favor over forty years ago when the two men were boys in college. Most of the guys in the fraternity that Watson and Franson belonged to really thought Rigger Watson's rants would take him to the very top of the political ladder. His antics were seen as admirable in their college fraternity setting.

In later years, it was Watson's personality and temperament that kept him from being elected to public office. Since he couldn't win his way into politics, Rigger proceeded to marry his way into enough money, power and prestige to buy his way to the top of the American political system. Senator Walter Franson knows this too well. He is totally aware that without the money that CCN Network News boss Rigger Watson sends his way, the opportunity to become the President of the United States would not even be a possibility. Hundreds of millions of dollars are affected by Watson's influence.

"Hello, Rigger," Senator Franson greets his comrade.

"How was the flight?" the President of CCN asks.

"The flight's been OK. So far we are just ahead of the bad weather."

"Don't get me started on the damn weather, Walter. It seriously irritates me that we can't do anything about that."

"What do you have for me, Rigger? And I don't need one of your lectures."

"Yeah, you're right! A lecture won't help," Watson fires back quickly, "If it would have, we wouldn't be here right now. I gave you plenty of lectures about that queer and you never listened to one of 'em. So another one today after the fact isn't going to work. But I've got something that will."

"What's that?"

"You aren't going like it!"

The Democratic presidential candidate takes a deep breath and asks, "Why's that?"

"There's only one way I can see for this to turn around in as short a time as we have," Watson states in a stern voice.

"And how's that?"

"Someone has to take one for the team."

"What exactly does that mean?"

"You really want to know?" the most powerful media man in America asks.

"No," the Senator replies. "Something tells me I don't really want to know."

"Well, you're going to know so you don't get caught off guard by this when it happens," Watson asserts. "You can't get caught with your pants down like we did this morning with what took place in Boston."

Senator Franson pauses, a little taken aback by how calm, cool and collected Watson is in this exchange which he thought would be much more heated and explosive. The Senator then nods his head and says, "OK. But just what the hell do you mean by someone's going to have to take one for the team?"

CCN Chief Rigger Watson raises his hand up behind his own head and grabs the back of his neck and squeezes it. He then slowly lowers his hand back down. In a slow, low, deliberate voice he tells Franson, "Swenson must walk the plank."

"What?" the surprised California Senator asks. "Kill him?"

"Somebody has to pay the price for this. And it's not going to be me. I've got too much invested to lose the White House because of Mike Swenson."

Franson says nothing. Watson continues, "He's the one that got us into this damn mess—and he's the one that will get us the hell out of it."

"This is ludicrous, man! This is crazy! It's impossible, Rigger! Have you gone mad? How the hell are you going to pull it off?" Franson pauses, "And just how in Christ's name will this help us?"

"I'll tell you what's ludicrous, Walter. It's you letting that fag be in charge of your campaign in the first place. What's up with that? Did Swenson know something the rest of us didn't about one of those high-dollar Russian whores you were always hooking up with when you went on all those trips to the Middle East a few years ago?"

Taken aback by the question about the numerous taxpayer-funded trips to the Middle East, nineteen of them in total over a seven year timespan, the most powerful U.S. Senator on the Democratic side of the aisle in Washington D.C. again asks, "How is Swenson's death supposed to help us?"

"It is the only way we can turn this thing around with Swenson and those two naked teenage boys and get a sense of sympathy coming back our way in only two days," Watson states. "It's what I call the Michael Jackson effect. When Swenson is dead, half the people's anger will turn to sorrow."

The very calculating and callous news man pauses to let his last comment sink in, he then continues, "And believe me, Walter, the only way we can win this damn election is if we stop the direction this thing is headed immediately, and then turn some of those votes back our way. And we will only do it by appealing to the feelings and emotions of the voters in the middle. Hell, you know the voters in the middle don't care one damn bit about polices or politics. All they care about is their feelings. Right now, they're mad as hell at Swenson for what happened in Boston. And believe me, Walter, all of that anger is flowing right back at you."

Watson stops talking. The Senator from the West Coast sits in the back of the black Mercedes-Benz limousine dumbfounded at what he is hearing. He reaches up and runs his right hand over his forehead and through his gray hair. What scares him is that he knows Watson is serious, and he also knows that what Watson is saying might be the only way to turn the tide on the negative situation he has found himself in only three days before the election. For the first time in his political career, Walter Franson feels like he is in way over his head.

"You getting this?" Watson asks.

"I'm still in the car," Franson replies sarcastically.

"If Mike Swenson commits suicide it will give us forty-eight hours of news time to turn this thing around. I'll make it seem like the excessive pressure brought on by the Christian conservatives against homosexuality made Michael kill himself. Those same voters that are mad as hell at you and him today, in two days will be feeling sorry for the dead queer and they will be feeling sorry for you too. Many of them will then vote for you. It is as simple as clockwork. If I know anything, I know what will flip the swing voters, and this will top anything I have ever seen. We won't get all of 'em. But we will get enough of them to stop the bleeding and survive this damn thing." Watson pauses as Franson sits stunned and silent. Watson continues, "Anyhow, it's a done deal. It's already in play with no way to stop it."

"Well hell, that's just great to know!" Senator Franson says, annoyed at everything he has heard. "You've already got this whole damn plan in motion."

"Yes, I do."

"So I can't stop this?" asks Franson. "And I don't have any say in it?"

"No, you don't have a say in this," Rigger replies as he stays completely calm. "And no, you can't stop it, either." Watson pauses and then continues, "Especially if you know what is good for you."

"What's that supposed to mean?" Franson asks. "Is that a threat? Did you just threaten me?"

"It's just what I said. A lot of very important people have a lot riding on you winning this election, me included. You take that however you think it should be taken. But believe me, you damn well better take my advice here, Walter."

Angry, Senator Franson stares at Watson for a moment before he says, "You know Mike Swenson is my friend?"

"I don't want to know anything about the kind of friendship you had with him," Watson replies.

"That's not what I meant!"

"I remember seeing how jealous Swenson was of all your girlfriends, especially the redhead," remarks Watson.

"There wasn't anything like that between me and Mike!"

"Hell, Walter, how would I know? Politics changes a lot of people. And you're the one who kept him on your payroll."

Senator Franson is irritated and offended by Watson accusing him of being gay. Knowing just exactly who he is dealing with, and just how dangerous Watson can be, the Senator from California tries to keep his cool. He asks Watson, "So, how's this going to be done, and where?"

"You don't need to know how. Just leave it to me," Watson tells his former fraternity brother. "All you need to know is that it's going to happen. And Walter, don't even think of trying to stop it."

"I can't be a part of this, Rigger," the U.S. Senator and the leading candidate in the United States Presidential race tells Watson. "There's no way I can be any part of this."

"You already are," Watson informs him.

"I don't like this," states Franson.

"You don't have to," Watson says. "We haven't come this far to turn back now and you are in it as deep as anyone."

The Senator sits and shakes his head in disbelief. "I don't have a taste for it like you do, Rigger."

A surprisingly calm and cool-tempered Rigger Watson laughs. He then tells his long-time political cohort, "Walter, I know what you do have a taste for. So, if you want to keep yourself where you are, you damned well better play this game by my rules and let me make all the tough decisions. And remember whose car you are sitting in, Walter. It's mine."

"That's great!" Franson says as he realizes something. "You got all this on tape, don't you?"

"You damn right I do," replies Watson. "And you aren't any smarter than when I first met you."

Senator Franson shakes his head back and forth in disgust and then says, "I guess it could give us a boost in the polls, kind of like the sympathy boost John Edwards got when his wife was diagnosed with cancer."

"What! John Edwards?" Watson fires back as his eyes pop open in total disbelief when he hears the comparison Franson makes between himself and Edwards. "Oh, that's great, Walter. There's a role model for you. You stupid or what?"

"You know what I mean."

"Let's just hope your affection for beautiful European women doesn't take us down the same deadend road Edwards went. If you remember, his run for the Presidency didn't exactly turn out too well."

"I was only referring to the cancer thing with his wife."

"All I know, Walter, is you better hope like hell that fling you had with the tall, sexy redhead from Russia doesn't come out in the next two or three days," exclaims Watson. "Or you'll end up just like Swenson."

"I've taken care of that," Senator Franson claims. "I can guarantee it won't come out."

"For your sake, it damn well better not," Watson fires back at Franson.

"I took care of it."

"How?" Watson asks.

————

The news crew hurries to get their cameras and gear put into the two small CCN vans parked well over a block away as a light mist can be felt in the air on this beautiful November night in Paris. With the impromptu interviews over, Alexia turns back to the Italian lawyer who knows Severo Baptiste. She reaches her hand out to shake his and says, "Thank you for your time tonight."

"You're welcome," he replies. "It was actually quite fun."

Alexia laughs and with a smile remarks, "It wasn't fair that you knew who I was before I started the interview."

"Oh, but I didn't," the man says. "It wasn't until you looked away when you thought you saw someone you knew that I realized you were the same woman I saw in the picture at Baptiste's house. The woman my brother told me holds Severo Baptiste's heart in the palm of her hand."

Alexia blushes, "Didn't you recognize my name?"

"No, I never knew your name. I don't know if my brother even knows your name. But it is you in the picture in Severo's house in Rome." He laughs and then says, "But I do know your name now. It's Alexia Klien."

"Yeah, but I don't know your name, do I?"

"I am Martino Angioletta."

Alexia nods her head and smiles, "That sounds like a good Italian name."

The lawyer for the Catholic Church laughs. "When I see Baptiste I will tell him I met you." He then looks down at his watch.

"I'll probably see him before you do," Alexia replies. "He's coming to see me while I'm here."

"That would be good for him from what my brother says," returns Angioletta. "It has been great meeting you Alexia Klien. I had better run now. Or I will be, as you Americans say, fashionably late for a date."

"I will tell Severo hello from you, Martino," Alexia says.

"He will like that. But tell him my brother is Santino Angioletta. Severo may not remember my name."

"I will," Alexia replies as she nods her head to the man as he looks down at his watch again and starts to walk off. What Alexia knows about Baptiste that the Italian man does not know is that Severo remembers the names of every person he has ever met. It is something that has always amazed her. In fact, Baptiste remembers everything about everything he ever encounters, right down to the very last detail without ever writing anything down.

Alexia has watched Severo sit down in front of his laptop and type out a story in a matter of minutes that would take most people hours or even days to complete. He would do it without any notes, pulling up information out of his brain that is weeks, months, or even many years old. And he would never miss a single detail. Alexia has often wondered if the freelance journalist didn't miss his true calling in life. That maybe he should be running some large corporation, or even be the leader of his country, or maybe even the European Union. Alexia has been around a lot of very smart people in her life and none of them have ever compared to Baptiste. She is still baffled to hear that Severo owns a home in Rome. The Severo she knows never seemed to be interested in owning anything bigger than his suitcase.

With the Italian man gone, Alexia turns to the Frenchman in charge of CCN Paris and says, "Time to eat. I'm starving."

The man who has had his mind set on spending the entire night with Alexia frowns at her. He knows his chances of bedding the American beauty tonight are gone with all the Severo Baptiste talk that he has just heard. He shakes his head and tells her, "That was not a good interview. There wasn't anything in it we can use."

"I didn't think we would find anything out here tonight to use," Alexia fires back. When she does, she hears a little voice inside of her say, *You just watched the biggest story in France, maybe the world walk away from you. You know that woman has been intimately involved with Senator Franson.*

Alexia is surprised. Normally her conscious never bothers her when she looks past something that might damage someone in her own political party. Alexia wonders where the voice came from. She knows it had to be her conscious telling her she should do what is right, but it seemed more like a voice to her. *Was it a voice, or just my conscious on an empty stomach?* She wonders.

"I've got to go to the van," the Frenchman tells Alexia and two other CCN employees who are still standing where they just finished the last interview. "I'll bring the crew back and we will all go catch dinner somewhere."

After the French Bureau boss is gone, one of the CCN employees that Alexia has known for years hands the American broadcast journalist her purse and a black CCN rain jacket. She tells Alexia, "If you want to get out of here before we all go to eat, here's your chance. I'll cover for you."

"What will you say?" Alexia asks.

"I will lie," the woman says. "I'll say you spotted someone you knew from the States and left with them."

"I may take you up on that," Alexia says as she slips on the rain jacket because the mist in the night air is getting heavier. "I was thinking about coming up with a lie of my own to get out of this dinner and go to my room and get some rest."

"I'll do whatever I need for you, just go girl, go."

"You may not have to lie after all," Alexia proclaims as she sees someone she recognizes exiting the l'Ambroisie restaurant. She quickly turns to the woman she has been working with and tells her, "Thank you very much. I just saw a guy I know. I'll see you tomorrow."

"You take care, girl. See you in the morning," the CCN employee says as Alexia spins back towards the restaurant and takes off in a jog to catch the person she just saw.

After jogging nearly fifty feet, she closes the distance between the man she just saw leave the fancy French restaurant and herself. Alexia slows to a fast walk and yells, "Matt James!"

He doesn't hear her. She continues to walk faster than the man whose attention she is trying to get as she yells his name again. He does not notice that he has been yelled at twice as he continues to walk and talk with the three men who are with him. Now only about thirty feet behind, Alexia again yells out, "Matt James!"

In mid-sentence of a hunting story he is telling, Matthew James stops and turns around. The three older gentlemen with him all stop and look back at the tall, beautiful black-haired woman that has just summoned their friend. One of the men, a tall gray haired man in his seventies allows, "Matt, this looks a lot more interesting than the story you've been tellin' us about hunting Cape buffalo on the Congo River."

Matt laughs as Alexia catches up to where he and his friends are now standing. She says, "Wow, am I glad to see you, Matt."

In total amazement to see Alexia, Matt throws his arms up and jokingly replies, "Why, Alexia Klien, I haven't seen you in forever."

"Wow, Matt, I feel like I've been saved by the grace of God," Alexia tells Matt James who she had just met earlier in the day.

"That's the only way anyone is ever saved, Miss Klien—by the grace of God," the Christian missionary replies.

As Matt makes his comment about salvation, Alexia glances back over her shoulder and sees the CCN news crew and the Frenchman in charge are returning to where she just left. Some of the members of the news crew are still wearing their dark blue networks news coats that have the letters CCN in very large red print across the back of them. The Frenchman is asking the woman who had handed Alexia the black rain jacket a question. Alexia then sees the woman point off in a different direction than she is headed with Matt and his friends. The Frenchman then shakes his head in disgust as a group of Japanese tourists, all with cameras around their necks, suddenly walk up to the CCN news crew and start asking questions of the members who are wearing the dark blue CCN coats.

Thinking about what she just put on to ward off a late evening Paris rain shower and knowing it has a small CCN logo on the front, Alexia quickly turns her attention back to Matt James and asks, "Matt, look at this coat I'm wearing." She spins around to show him her back, "Does it say *CCN* in real large letters on the back of it?"

"No, it doesn't," he says as he laughs.

Alexia sighs in relief and says, "Oh, thank you. That's a good thing."

"What it says in great big white letters is *FX News*."

"Oh, aren't you the funny one," Alexia replies. "I'll bet that's what you wish it said."

"You know I do. That would almost make you perfect if you worked for FX. You know you are pretty enough to work for them."

Alexia smiles back at him, "I guess I should take that as a compliment. But on the other hand that was kind of sexist, wasn't it?"

"No, it was the truth," Matt replies. "You know FX has a whole host of pretty girls. But even though you work for CCN, you're still the prettiest, Alexia."

One of the men with Matt James, a short, stocky man in his late sixties with very little hair, says in a very deep and slow voice with a serious southern drawl, "Missy, he's right, you are better lookin' than all those pretty girls on FX. But I still like their views on things better than on your network. FX News gives both sides of the story and they don't hide anything."

Instantly, Alexia feels guilt rush over her for doing the very thing this southern gentleman is accusing the network she works for of doing. With her responsibility as a reporter thrust back into her thoughts, to keep from having to make eye contact with the man in his sixties, Alexia casually glances back to where the CCN crew had been standing the last time she looked. She sees them beginning to walk off in the opposite direction. Alexia then asks, "Am I holding y'all up here?"

"No, not at all," Matt replies. "We've got all night to talk to you, Miss Klien." He turns to the three men with him and asks, "Don't we, guys?"

The three men, all of them over sixty years of age, smile and agree. Something inside of Alexia nearly causes her to tell Matt James not to call her Miss Klien anymore. Before she does though, something else in her stops her, and she says, "You are all too kind. Don't let me hold you up anymore. Which way are you going?"

Matt points in the opposite direction from where the CCN crew just went.

"Good," Alexia states. "I'll walk with you for a while, if that's OK."

"Of course that's OK, Alexia," Matt says, "Oh, please excuse my manners. Let me introduce you to my friends. They are all from the States and supporters of the mission work we do in Africa. Alexia Klien, this is Glen Nutter from Wyoming, George W. Haythorn from Texas, and John Berry from your home state of Georgia. The four of us are sort of having a mini-missionary meeting tonight. These gentlemen all brought their wives over to Paris on vacation, so Amaya and I decided to plan our trip around theirs."

"It's very nice to meet all of you," the CCN broadcast journalist replies.

The three wealthy American Christian men return their greetings and Alexia and the four men take off walking at a moderate pace in one of the most scenic parts of Paris. There are people scattered about everywhere talking and walking and taking in the sights of the romantic city. The slight mist that had been in the air has let up as a cool and gentle breeze picks up out of the southwest. Half of a very bright moon is shining just above the rooftops of the historic buildings to the east.

"Are you out here tonight all by yourself?" Matt asks.

"No, I just finished doing some on-the-street impromptu interviews with a news crew from here in Paris," Alexia replies. "I was supposed to go to dinner with the crew, but I didn't really want to. When I saw you leaving that restaurant, I took it as a chance to escape from one of those long, drawn-out, late-night French dinners with too much wine and flirtation, if you know what I mean."

"Yes, I know what you mean on the long dinners and too much wine," Matt says. "But I'll have to use my imagination on the too much flirtation. Knowing men though, I think I know what you mean."

"Yeah, the guy that runs CCN over here has had his sights set on me for years. He set tonight up to try and... well, you know what I mean."

Matt laughs and asks her, "Have you encouraged him any?"

Walking along a cobblestone sidewalk with small cafés and bistros on each side of them, Alexia turns to him and says with a smile on her face, "What would make you think that, Matt?"

He laughs. "You're right. I never should have thought it."

As Matt finishes his reply, Alexia is stunned to see who is sitting at a small table out in front of a little bistro that she and the men are walking towards. It is the tall, slender redhead she watched board a flight for Moscow earlier in the day, the same woman she saw less than half an hour ago walk out of the restaurant Matt James and his friends just left.

Alexia reaches over and grabs Matt by the arm and stops him. As the two of them stand less than fifty feet from the little bistro, she asks him, "Matt, do you see that woman up there sitting with that couple? The woman with the long red hair."

"Yes, she came in the restaurant before we left. She wasn't there very long. Only long enough to maybe take a couple of sips out of a glass of wine the people she met with had waiting for her. I remember it well. George and I commented on how quickly she left the restaurant."

"This is crazy, Matt, but I need you to come with me when I walk up to her. I think I may know her. Or at least I know I've seen her before. I've got something I want to ask her. She may be part of a story."

"Sure, whatever you need. I can even pretend to be your date."

"That'll work. Just don't say anything. Just stay by my side if you would. I don't know how this will go."

As Alexia turns to start walking towards the bistro, Matt tells her, "Your wish is my command." His suspicions are definitely raised.

The three older gentlemen have continued to walk while Matt and Alexia stopped. They are now at least fifty feet ahead of them. One of them looks back over his shoulder and says, "Do you two think Mr. Matthew James has found his Mrs. James tonight?"

"Don't know, but she sure has some long legs to go with that long hair," the softspoken Glen Nutter allows. "Other than her politics, he could sure do worse if you ask me."

"If she's from Georgia, she's got to have some good ol' Christian roots somewhere in her family tree," John Berry declares. "Maybe with a little watering from the Word of God those roots will sprout. You never know."

The three men continue to walk on ahead and past the bistro.

Sitting at a small table in front of a classic French building is the woman Alexia had seen earlier in the day at the Boutique de la Renommée. The woman is sitting with a man and a woman who both look to be in their mid to late forties. The three of them are talking and enjoying a bottle of fine French wine. The table they are at is right next to the sidewalk and has a white umbrella above it just big enough to keep the weather off the people at the table. It is a table for four. One chair sits empty.

With her heart beginning to beat as hard as it did earlier in the day at the airport when she first tried to call Severo Baptiste, Alexia looks at Matt and says, "Here goes nothing. Don't leave me."

Not really knowing what to think of Alexia's sudden insecurity,

Matt James reaches over and grabs her hand and squeezes it. He then tells her, "I'll be right here."

"Thanks," replies Alexia as she turns her head towards Matt and says, "Let's go."

"Wait! Wait just a minute, Miss Klien," Alexia stops and looks back at him with a look of curiosity.

"What?" she asks.

"The rain coat you're wearing. You know, the one that doesn't say FX News on the back? Well, it does say CCN in small red letters right here above you heart," Matt James says as he points to where the letters are on the black rain jacket.

With her heart about to jump out of her chest, Alexia quickly unzips the jacket and slips it off. She then scrunches it up in as small a ball as she can as fast as she can and stuffs it into her purse as she comments, "That was a close one. I didn't even remember I had that on."

"I thought you might not want to be wearing that to do whatever it is you are going to do."

"Thanks Matt," Alexia says as she turns to walk the last forty feet to the bistro. "Let's go do it."

"Sounds good to me," Matt remarks as he smiles.

The two of them approach the table where the woman is sitting.

CHAPTER THIRTY-TWO

Napoleon Bonaparte

Texas FBI agent Chace Wikett finishes his phone call to Martin MacKuenn in Washington D.C. MacKuenn is a man Wikett has known for over two decades. They worked covert ops together in parts of Eastern Africa. MacKuenn is now part of DHS, the Department of Homeland Security. Wikett knows that MacKuenn will do the right thing with the information he has given him. Chace would trust MacKuenn with his life. There were times twenty years ago when Wikett did just that.

Wikett makes one more quick call to the man in the FBI that he reports to, a man Chace is not sure he can trust to do the right thing. Chace tells him the bare basics of what he has been able to get out of Eddison. The man instructs Agent Wikett to pass everything he knows on to the FBI on the West Coast and then be of any assistance they need him to be. This man has only been Chace Wikett's boss for a little over a year. The woman who had previously been above Wikett in the Federal Bureau of Investigation was axed by someone in the current Democratic President's administration whose toes she had stepped on. The rumor was that with her anti-abortion beliefs she did not fit the mold that the liberal democrats in charge felt a powerful woman in Washington D.C. should.

Before getting off the phone call with his new boss, Wikett informs him that he has already talked with Martin MacKuenn at DHS and that MacKuenn had assured Wikett they would be heavily involved in any operations from this point forward in California. This news stumps the man Wikett now reports to for just a moment. He then comments on the possibility of that being a good thing. The one thing Wikett has been able to figure out about the man above him in the Bureau's chain of command is that he is a true politician. He is someone who always tries to keep everyone thinking he is on their side, whether he is or not. This is what makes Wikett not sure if he can trust the man.

Returning to the interior of the old abandoned warehouse where Agents Gasperson and Swanson are still interrogating the Leesburg, Louisiana man, Wikett knows he needs to call California FBI agent Bart Kennedy. Before he does, Chace wants to find out if his men have been able to learn anything new from Roddy Dale Eddison.

Wikett sticks his head into the small, square room in the middle of the warehouse that is still dark because the exterior windows have all been painted black. Agent Wikett motions for Big John Swanson to step outside the room for a moment.

"How's it going?" Wikett asks as the two men walk back behind the tan Ford Excursion parked inside the warehouse.

"Eddison still thinks he has slept much longer than he really did. He has no idea yet that we tricked him into telling us everything he knows," Swanson replies.

"Have you learned anything new?"

"He's told us some things, but nothing really any different than what you heard. Mostly stuff about his motives for helping the Muslims. It would be quite comical if it wasn't so deadly. The guy is definitely clinical."

"Has he let on to anything more that I need to know before I call Kennedy?"

"No," answers Swanson. "The meat of what he's said has to do with a planned attack on the rock concert at the Staples Center tonight."

"You guys keep at it. I'll be back in here after I call Kennedy," Wikett tells Swanson.

The two men both turn to walk away from the back of the FBI vehicle when Wikett stops and says, "Hey John, I called Martin MacKuenn in D.C. and told him what we are dealing with out here. He said he'd make some calls and be back in touch with me. He said he'd put everything into action to cover all the bases out here tonight at the rock concert to keep this from being a Kennedy-run show."

"That's good to know," Big John Swanson allows, "Considering how flaky Bart Kennedy is."

"That's what I thought," Wikett agrees. "I didn't think we wanted to go on from here blind with Kennedy leading the way."

"That's for sure."

"Not knowing what a liberal is going to do in something like this scares the hell out of me. Martin assured me he'd have people in place before Kennedy even knows it."

"That is good to know," Swanson adds as he nods his head in agreement. "I'm with you, Chace. I don't trust anyone like Kennedy who is more concerned about their own career and headlines than they are the people they're supposed to be protecting."

"I'm going to go call Kennedy and let him think for a moment he can be the hero of the day," Wikett pauses and laughs very lightly. "But I don't think he'll be real happy about the call I made to MacKuenn."

Outside the warehouse the winds from the northwest are picking up as the heavy dark clouds that brought some early morning November rain showers to Southern California are long gone. The wind is quickly drying out the area around the old brick building. Wikett's phone rings three times before the man from Boston answers it. "Hello, this is Agent Kennedy."

"Yeah Bart, this is Chace Wikett. We got something out of Eddison."

"That's good to hear. What is it?"

"He's told us that he thinks the planned target is some kind of an attack on a rock concert tonight at the Staples Center. He even knew the name Flash Freeman, who is playing there tonight."

"Do you believe him?"

"Oh, yeah. We tricked him into thinking it was already nightfall," Wikett says. "We told him that the two terrorists he hauled out here bombed a biker rally in Riverside this afternoon and killed over a thousand hardcore bikers. Eddison went off about how it was supposed to be an attack on a rock concert with the British freak Flash Freeman tonight at the Staples Center. I'm sure that is what he believes."

"Really?" Kennedy replies. "Wow. I was thinking about going to that concert. I really like Flash Freeman's music."

That doesn't surprise me, Wikett thinks. "Well Bart, I've already made some calls up the line and informed them about what we've learned."

"Who have you called?"

"Our boss in D.C. and Martin MacKuenn."

"Why the hell did you call MacKuenn? We can handle things out here without his help," Kennedy fires back.

"This being a national security crisis," Wikett replies. "He should know."

"I think the FBI is well enough equipped to handle this."

"You don't have enough experience to carry all the eggs in this basket, Bart." Wikett replies. "Your ego may say you do, but you don't."

There is silence on the phone as Wikett waits for Kennedy's reply. When he doesn't get one, Wikett continues, "Oh, and Bart, you be a team player on this and what you and me know about you will stay secret."

Wikett waits again as there is just silence on the phone.

"Are you still there?" Wikett asks.

"Yes, I'm still here," the Massachusetts native replies as he realizes the dreams he has of entering politics on a national level may have vanished with the ill-advised affair he had with a male philosophy professor in college. "I think this phone conversation is about over though."

"Just make sure you work with MacKuenn, if you know what I mean."

"Yeah," Kennedy says with a tone of disgust in his voice, "I will." He ends the call.

FBI agent Chace Wikett returns to the interrogation room.

"Why in the world would you help Islamic terrorists kill Americans? I thought you good ol' boys from the south were patriots through and through?" Wikett asks Roddy Dale Eddison, who is still duct taped to a wooden chair.

———

With the late evening clouds drifting off to the east and a bright half moon hanging under them, the night is as romantic as any night in Paris has ever been. The smell of a gentle fall shower still lingers in the air. The city is alive and happy.

Laughing at something she has just heard, the tall, slender woman with long, flowing, dark red hair reaches for her glass that is nearly half full of a burgundy Merlot. A half empty bottle of 1997 Château Mouton Rothschild sits on the table in front of her. As she picks up her glass to take a sip of the expensive French wine, she sees Alexia approach her table from the side. The woman gracefully sets down her wine glass and turns her head towards Alexia. A man with a well-trimmed beard and a blonde woman are sitting with the redhead. They too turn their attention to Alexia Klien and Matt James, who are now only a few steps from the little round table that sets out in front of the bistro.

The man sitting at the table leans towards the woman and whispers in Russian, "I think I have seen her somewhere. Maybe on TV."

Just reaching the table and stopping to stand behind the empty chair that is closest to the sidewalk, Alexia looks at the woman and then addresses those there with her with a polite glance and a nod. Her eyes back on the woman, Alexia asks in French, "Have we met before?"

In French, the woman responds, "No, I don't believe so."

Not wanting to divulge her name, Alexia doesn't introduce herself to the woman, but in French she continues, "Would I have seen you in Washington D.C. a couple of years ago? Maybe at a Christmas party?"

For a very brief moment Alexia sees something in the woman's deep dark green eyes that tells her she is definitely the same woman she had seen with Senator Walter Franson on the 18th floor of the Renaissance Park Hotel in Washington D.C. The cutting glare that flashed in those green eyes that Alexia has never been close enough to see into before was a look that scared her. What Alexia saw for a brief second in the woman's eyes was a sudden appearance of evil. Real evil. Instantly the text message warning that Severo had sent just eleven hours earlier registered with her. What he said may be true. Alexia can feel her legs tremble as she stands there for what seems like an eternity waiting for the woman's response to her question.

What seems like minutes to Alexia is only a few seconds before the woman speaks, this time in English with a strong Russian accent. "No, I am afraid I have never been to Washington D.C." The tone of the woman's voice is still pleasant and peaceful, but it has a seriousness to it that cuts like a knife. Without saying it, the woman lets the American broadcast journalist know their conversation is over.

Alexia can feel her arms trembling as she just wants to turn and run. She smiles and returns in English, "I am so sorry to have troubled you."

Matt James could not understand anything that was said in French. But from what he saw with his own eyes and heard in English, he can tell that something about all of this is very suspicious. He cannot wait for Alexia to turn around and walk away so he can ask her what this is really about. The encounter he just witnessed was not like anything he thought he would see when he first agreed to be Alexia Klien's tag-along friend.

Matt witnessed the same evil look in the woman's eyes that Alexia did, but it had not scared him as it did her. He has seen this look before. In the deepest and darkest parts of Africa, Matt James is accustomed to looking into the eyes of witch doctors and shamans, people who are still caught up in the ancient practices of their cultures. They quite often have the same look of evil in their eyes.

As Matt and Alexia turn and walk off from the table, the man who is sitting between the mysterious redheaded woman and the shorter blonde states, "I know where I have seen her. She is a news reporter for an American news network."

Alexia cannot believe what she has just done. She felt safe having Matt with her, but she would have felt a lot safer if she had had Severo Baptiste with her tonight. There is something very unsettling inside of her as she thinks about the look of evil she saw for an instant in the redheaded woman's deep, dark green eyes. It was a look that said, "Don't you dare come any closer to me or I will..." Alexia can't think about it anymore. Now far enough away from the table they just left to talk, Alexia turns to Matt and says, "Thanks, I couldn't have done that without you."

"Who was she? Or should I not ask?"

"Matt, I really don't know. It's just that I know I've seen her before. I know I have."

"There is no doubt in my mind that you have seen her before. And Alexia, she knows you have seen her before. I don't know the story behind any of this, but if you would like me to see you to your room, I will." Matt James pauses and then says, "And this is not a romantic come-on. I saw a look in her eyes I didn't like."

"Yes Matt, I saw the same look. For an instant it scared me. But I think I'll be alright. I really should be finding a taxi though," Alexia says. "Where are your friends, Matt?"

"Are you sure you'll be alright? That look was dangerous."

"Oh, there they are," Alexia replies to her own question as she sees the three older gentlemen who had dined with Matt at the famous French restaurant. They are waiting about a hundred feet in front of where Alexia and Matt are walking. The three men seem to be just watching people pass by them as they stand patiently beside a large statue of Napoleon Bonaparte on a horse.

When Matt and Alexia catch up to the three men, the gentleman from Wyoming, Glen Nutter turns and looks at the statue. He says, "Miss Klien, I think I might have sold that man that horse."

"No Glen—you sold me that horse," states George Waldo Haythorn as he laughs. "And then I gave the horse to that there Frenchman when he was just a young boy."

Everyone laughs except Nutter.

"No wonder I don't remember things so well anymore," Nutter replies with a slight stutter. "Waldo, we sure are gettin' old if you knew Napoleon when he was just a boy."

As she continues to laugh, Alexia turns to Matt and asks, "Were they like this at dinner?"

"They are like this all the time," Matt James says as he smiles and shakes his head.

Who is that woman? Alexia wonders as she walks off with Matt James and the three wealthy American businessmen.

———

"I took care of it," Senator Franson says again for the third time.

"Walter, I have a hell of a lot wrapped up in this. Time, energy, and money. Lots of money," CCN Network News President Rigger Watson states as he raises his voice. The two men sit in the rear of Watson's black Mercedes-Benz limousine on the tarmac of Dulles International Airport in Washington D.C.

"Don't you trust me?" Franson asks as he looks down at his watch. His Boeing 747 sits right beside the limo. The Senator knows he needs to be getting back on the plane to continue the final campaign push towards the Presidency.

"Do I trust you? Do you really want me to answer that?"

Franson gives Watson a dirty look.

"Tell me Walter, just how did you take care of the affair you had with that Russian whore you were so in love with?"

"That is uncalled for even by you, Rigger. The places you have been and the things you have done. She wasn't a..."

"Are you going to answer the question? You know if I demand it, which I am..."

"Yeah, I'll answer your damn question. You going to shut off that recording device you have in this car?"

"No," says Watson. "Answer the question."

"Whatever, after what you already have on me this isn't going to make any difference," the Senator replies.

"You're figuring this out, Walter."

The Senator takes a deep breath while he shakes his head in disgust. He then grudgingly says, "I've made a deal with a group of men from the Middle East and they have paid her a very large sum of money."

"What countries?" Watson asks as he cuts in on his political pawn.

"The group represents most of the countries in the Middle East, all the major players. I've agreed to stand with them on a number of issues they have with Israel. You'll like it, Rig. It'll strengthen our presence in the Middle East in a way like no President in history ever has. Even more than the guy in office now."

Watson sits shaking his head. "I don't quite understand why you brought Muslims in the Middle East into something that has to do with your love life. I know you think you love the woman, but there are better ways to keep her quiet without making it an international incident."

"It's a lot more complicated than that," Franson replies. "And yes, I do love her. Killing her is not an option because someday, when I am done doing the things you want me to do, I plan on spending the rest of my life with her."

"Oh, don't bullshit me with the long walks on the beach and the laying in the sand crap, Walter," Watson cuts in, "I mean, you can do that someday. I don't care. But if you think that woman will still be there in eight years—or four if you're a one-term flop—if you think she will be waiting for you..." Watson stops and shakes his head. "I'll tell you this, Walter, the best way to eliminate a problem like that is to bury it. You just remember I told you that someday when you're facing the same damn questions Bill Clinton did."

"What I am telling you is, it's a lot more complicated than even you know. She is not a whore. This thing is very complex, and there are a lot more people involved in this than even you know about."

"Like who?" Watson asks.

"Like people with more power than you and I have."

Watson's eyes get big. "What are you saying? You been set up?"

"I'm saying I have this under control," Franson states. "My people in the Middle East have our backs covered on this. I wasn't just screwing around on all those trips I took over there."

With a bit of a surprised look on his face, Watson tilts his head to one side and asks, "What do you mean?"

"What I mean is, you are not the only one who has a lot of money invested in me," Franson says with a newfound confidence.

"Maybe you're smarter than I've given you credit for, Walter."

"Most people are smarter than you give them credit for," Franson states.

"With all your newfound international playmates, just remember it was me that personally drug down the two top Republican candidates in this election for you," Watson reminds Franson. "It wasn't someone from overseas that pushed that Governor from the Southwest or that conservative Congresswoman out of the race."

"You had plenty of help from the rest of the media on the left."

"Yeah, but I led the charge," fires back Watson. "And don't you forget it."

"Don't worry Rig, I won't."

"You didn't have a chance against that conservative Governor, especially if he would have picked the Congresswoman for his running mate."

"Rigger, I've got a plane to get on."

"Then go get on the plane."

"I'll talk to you when I need to," Franson allows as he reaches for the door to get out of the black Mercedes-Benz. He stops before he opens the door and says, "But next time Rigger, show some respect and have your chauffeur open the door for me."

"Good luck! You go get 'em, kid," Watson says as Franson closes the door to the Mercedes-Benz.

Senator Walter Franson gets out of Watson's limo and walks through the cold wind up the steps of the airplane ramp to his Boeing 747. His thoughts are on a woman from Russia that he met over ten years ago at the Winter Olympics in Salt Lake City, Utah.

As his limo pulls away from where the big plane is parked, Watson gets out his personal cell phone and calls Shirley Hienz.

"Hello, Rig."

"I'm going to have Ed drop me off at Bernie's," Watson says. "I want you to be there when he does. Get that table in the back. I need a drink. Maybe we will go do something after that."

"OK, Honey, I'll be there. You going to want a double on the rocks?"

"Yeah, at least one to start with. Hell, order me two, as thirsty as I am, the first one won't last long."

"I'll be waiting," Shirley Hienz tells the man she loves.

CHAPTER THIRTY-THREE

Turn Water into Wine

"You really want to know why I did it? You get me some water and I'll tell you," Eddison replies to Wikett's question.

Wikett turns to Swanson and says, "Get a bottle out of the back of the Escalade."

"You're drivin' a Cadillac? How 'bout you in an expensive car on taxpayer money? You ain't any better than all the rest of 'em."

"You want some water? You better start telling me why you were helping those terrorists from Yemen." Wikett knows from what agent Swanson has told him that they already have some of this information. He wants to hear it for himself though. Also, by making a suspect repeat the same thing over and over, sometimes they will slip up and say something they have been holding back.

"Get me the water first."

"Why would someone faithful to the KKK help Muslims kill Americans?" Wikett asks. "Working with dark-skinned people against whites? That goes against the Klan, doesn't it?"

Swanson comes into the room with the water. Wikett holds his hand up to stop Swanson. "There's your water. You answer my questions and you can have a drink."

The beady-eyed man from Louisiana sits staring at the 16 ounce bottle of cold Dasani water. He licks his dry lips and says, "It's kinda like huntin' gators out in the swamp. Sometimes you have to do things that just don't make sense to most people. You got to take risks. Sacrifice a goat or a pig or something to get you a big gator."

"What's hunting alligators got to do with helping Islamic terrorists kill Americans?" Wikett asks as he shakes his head in disgust.

"You goin' to give me a drink of water?"

"Give him a drink," Wikett says. "A small one."

Before Swanson gets to him, Eddison asks, "You goin' to untape my arm so I can grab the bottle?"

"Not a chance," Swanson fires back. Big John gives the Cajun a small drink of water and then tells him, "You want more, talk more."

With no doors or windows open to let the air flow through, it is starting to get rather warm in the small room inside the abandoned warehouse. Even though Eddison thinks it is past eight P.M. and dark, the sun is still high in the sky over the West Coast of the United States. The temperatures today in this part of California are supposed to push the low eighties.

"Why the reference to gator huntin'?" Wikett asks again.

"It's like this," Eddison says. "This country's forgotten what happened on 9/11. All I was doin' was primin' the pump a little. You know sometimes you got to pour some water away to get more water."

Wikett looks over at Swanson and Gasperson.

Roddy Dale Eddison stops when he sees Wikett look away. He then grins and says, "Anybody killed today just before a big election will be like a pig or a goat used to bait gators. What I was doing was for the good of this country. Good for all of us." He stops again and then looks at Swanson and says, "Hey you, I need another drink."

Without saying anything, Big John Swanson gives Eddison another drink of water.

"I still don't understand why you would help terrorists blow up a biker rally in Riverside." Wikett says, just to see if the crazy man's story stays the same.

"I told you I thought they were going to blow up a rock concert," Eddison fires back at Wikett. "They were supposed to kill a bunch of long-haired California druggies wearing earrings, kids with their noses and eyebrows pierced. You know, West Coast city kids and liberal hippies—California types. Not a bunch of bikers."

Eddison stops and looks around at the three FBI agents sitting in the room with him. They don't say anything. Eddison then asks, "Why is it so hot in here if it's dark outside? Shouldn't it be gettin' colder?"

"So how's it going to help your cause that they've killed a bunch of good ol' boy bikers like yourself?" Wikett asks.

"It'll still wake up the people of this stupid-assed country we live in," Eddison replies. "I would have rather it been them spoiled, rich kids, and the gay-loving Hollywood types, and damned sure that English fag Flash Freeman."

Gasperson laughs. "Freeman's a fag? You seen the hot chicks that guy dates. You'd trade places with him in a heartbeat, you ignorant redneck."

"You just wait and see, you Mexican," Eddison says to the man with Native American blood running through his veins. "A hundred years from now I'll be the one seen as a hero if this gets rid of the Muslim-lovers we have runnin' this damn country. I'll be seen as the hero, not you, you wetback."

"I'm an Indian, you idiot. A Native American," Gasperson tells him. "My ancestors were here long before yours were."

Agent Wikett cuts in. "How does it make you feel that you killed a real hero today like FBI agent Tony Garcia?"

Eddison looks directly at Wikett, "Your friend I killed was named Garcia? He was a Mexican," Eddison pauses, "Right?"

Shifting his attention from Wikett to Gasperson, Roddy Dale Eddison smiles and unashamedly says, "Yeah, I killed me a Mexican today. You guys could kill me right now and I'd die happy. The only way I could die happier is..." Eddison stops and looks around at all three FBI agents in the room. He then finishes his statement, "The only way I could die any happier is to kill me a nigger, an Indian and a Jew today, too."

FBI agent Swanson prepares to reach out and grab his fellow agent Billy Joe Gasperson who Big John is afraid may attack Eddison after that comment. Gasperson does not. He stays cool and calm and says nothing.

Wikett does not stay so cool and calm. In a loud voice he tells Eddison, "You might die happy on this side of death, Roddy Dale. But I'll guarantee you the moment your last breath leaves your lungs, and you reach the other side of dead, you will be as far from happy as anyone can be!"

Gasperson chuckles a nervous laugh and shakes his head slowly. He then says, "You're as sorry as a humn being can get. I'd really like to see just how happy you'll be when you go straight to Hell, Roddy

Dale Eddison."

"We're done with him," Wikett says as he leaves the room. Agents Gasperson and Swanson follow.

"Can I have the rest of the water?" Eddison asks.

Swanson stops at the door after Wikett and Gasperson leave the room. He stares back at Eddison and says, "No. Where you're going this ain't enough water to help you."

After he steps out of the room, Wikett feels his phone vibrating. He looks down and sees it is Martin MacKeunn calling from Washington D.C. "This is Agent Wikett."

"Yeah Chace, this is MacKuenn. I wanted to let you know I've got everything handled. I've got people already in place. We will have the Staples Center covered like it never has been before."

"Good," says Wikett.

"We're getting on a plane in a few minutes. It'll be five hours before I get there, though. My guy on the West Coast is Sam Davidson, you can trust him. You may have met him the last time you were in D.C., I think he was still here then."

"Was he a tall blackman who used to coach Jr. College basketball in Alabama before 9/11?" Wikett asks.

"Yeah, he did. I'll text his number to you. Oh, and he won't take any shit off Kennedy either."

"Good!" Wikett replies, "That's why I called you. I knew you'd do what they wouldn't, considering their history in these matters."

"That's for sure," MacKuenn acknowledges. "I've got to go get on that plane. Call Sam, I'll text his number to you now."

————

As Alexia and Matt walk through the Marais district of Paris, she thinks about what tomorrow will bring. Knowing she has to interview Prince Charles and hopefully French President Nicolas Sarkozy and his wife Carla Bruni, Alexia knows she needs her rest. The three older gentlemen who are all supporters of Matt James' missionary work in Africa are walking about ten steps ahead of Matt and Alexia when she hears her phone make a sudden beep. She has a text message.

Almost afraid to look at the text after thinking about the mysterious red haired woman who she just confronted out in front of the French bistro, Alexia fears that the text may be from her. Alexia knows her fear is irrational. The woman doesn't even have her phone number. Alexia opens the text message just sent to her from the Paris CCN employee she is good friends with who held her purse tonight while she did the interviews. The woman's text message reads, "He is NOT very happy that you left before dinner. I think it's funny. I told him you saw someone you grew up with. See you tomorrow."

Thinking about the Frenchman who runs CCN Network News in Paris, Alexia reflects about how men with power and position have been trying to seduce her ever since she was a teenager. She can remember at the age of seventeen entering a Miss Teen Georgia pageant in Atlanta. One of the men who sponsored and helped run the competition became infatuated with her. So much so that she withdrew from the competition because of him and had her father, a lawyer, send the man a letter pinpointing exactly why his daughter dropped out of the contest. She never entered another beauty pageant again.

It was at about this time in her life when she decided she wanted to be in broadcast journalism instead of pursuing a career in modeling or the movies. Reminiscing about the Miss Teen Georgia pageant, the name of the girl who eventually won the competition nearly twenty years ago pops into Alexia's head. It was Stephanie Jo James. Everyone called her Stephanie Jo because there were three other girls named Stephanie in the contest that week in Atlanta.

Walking under the bright street lights of Paris with Matthew James from Savannah, Georgia, Alexia remembers that the very beautiful blonde Stephanie Jo James was also from Savannah, Georgia. She turns and asks, "Matt, do you know a girl from Savannah named Stephanie Jo James? She wouldn't happen to be your little sister, would she?"

Matt laughs. "No, she's not my sister, or even one of my many cousins. Funny thing is, I do know her though. My mother and her mother tried to set us up on a blind date once."

"Really?"

"Yeah, I was home from Africa for a couple of weeks and my mom thought my social life needed a boost. It was after my first full year over there as a missionary."

"Did it work?" Alexia asks.

"Not really. We both got wind of it through one of my buddies and his girlfriend. We met for soda, but that was it. She was in grad school and neither of us was looking for any kind of relationship at the time."

"Stephanie Jo was very pretty if I remember right," Alexia says.

"I guess she is now married and has a couple kids, but not a very happy marriage from what my mom says."

"That's too bad. I really liked her."

"How do you know her?" Matt asks.

"We were both in a beauty pageant together in our teens."

"Stephanie is beautiful, but I think you are more beautiful," Matt says as he and Alexia walk down a very romantic street in Paris.

"Thank you, Matt."

"I'd guess a smart and beautiful woman like you always has a special man waiting in the background to take you off to paradise from time to time," Matt pauses as they continue to walk. "Am I right?"

As though her thoughts and emotions had not been racing around in her head and her heart enough already, Alexia has to answer a question about Severo Baptiste. She says, "Yes... I guess I do in some kind of a lost and hopeless romantic way. I will see him for the first time in three years tomorrow night here in Paris."

"Really... three years?" Matt comments. "Wow! That's a long time."

"If I think about it too much," Alexia says. "It is all I can think about. I don't really know how I feel about it either," she pauses. "But to answer your question, Matt, yes I do at this moment."

After walking a short distance beside her and not saying anything, Matt responds to what Alexia has just told him. "Sounds somewhat complicated, but intriguing."

"It is that, complicated and intriguing," Alexia allows.

"Well, Miss Klien, I'm not looking for any kind of a relationship, not with what I have on my plate in Africa. But I would have made an exception for you."

Alexia laughs and says, "Oh, you would have?"

"Yes, I would have," Matt smiles and then laughs a little at himself. He looks at Alexia as they walk and then tells her, "If you are ever at a time in time when you don't have such a man in your life, I would consider it a great honor to take you to dinner and share a bottle of fine wine with you. It wouldn't even have to be here in Paris."

She laughs again, "Oh, you would, would you? And where, then? In Zimbabwe?"

He laughs and says, "I don't plan on being a missionary in Africa for the rest of my life. I know someday soon I will be moving back to the States to reenter the business world."

"I'll tell you quite honestly, Matt, if it were not for the man I am going to see tomorrow night, I would be asking you out."

"Oh, really?" Matt smiles. "You would?"

"You are probably the best offer I have received in quite a while. I don't meet very many men with the sweet substance that you have."

"Thank you," Matt says as he walks stride for stride with her.

"What's this with the bottle of wine?" Alexia asks in humor. "I thought you were a Christian, and here you are trying to get me drunk."

"Maybe I was going to get myself drunk."

"I thought serious Christians didn't get drunk."

"I am not being serious."

Alexia turns her head towards him as they walk and in a very inquisitive way she asks, "Seriously though, you do drink wine? I didn't think Christians were supposed to drink."

"The first miracle Jesus performed was to turn water into wine," Matthew James answers her question with confidence in what he is saying. "What the scriptures tell us is not to be a drunkard, not to overindulge in the spirits of alcohol."

"Matt, do you know that since meeting you and Amaya Blazi today I have had more thoughts about things relating to Christianity than maybe in any other day I have ever had?" She pauses and then asks, "Isn't that strange? I mean, all in one day."

"No, that's not strange. It just means the Holy Spirit is working on you." Matt wonders if he should go any further with the conversation. The Holy Spirit inside of him tells him he has said enough.

When she hears Matt mention the Holy Spirit, something inside of Alexia makes her feel a little uneasy. She is not sure what it is. She knows it is not Matt James. She has been completely comfortable walking and talking with him this evening. Something else inside of

Alexia tells her it's her own stubborn unwillingness to yield to what she knows deep down inside to be right.

As the two of them have now reached an area where there are some taxis, Alexia looks at the time on her cell phone and says, "I really should be catching a cab."

Hearing this, Matt turns to head towards the taxi stand where a line of empty cabs awaits passengers. Matt yells to his three friends walking in front of him and Alexia, "Hey guys, wait up, she's catchin' a cab here."

The three men stop. Glen Nutter says in his quiet, gentle voice, "If he kisses her, I say he has found his Mrs. Matthew James."

"I'll bet a dollar he doesn't," says John Berry of Summerville, Georgia.

"I'll take that wager, John," George W. Haythorn replies.

"I hope that doesn't cause you to have a relapse, Waldo," Glen Nutter says to his longtime friend who he knows used to have a terribly bad gambling problem.

The three older men all laugh.

As they reach the waiting taxi, Matt and Alexia give each other a brief hug. Matt says, "I don't know who this lucky guy is, but the best of luck to the two of you. May the love and grace of Jesus Christ find you both."

"Thank you very much for everything, Matt," Alexia replies. As she is getting into the taxi she continues, "Maybe someday we will have that dinner and a bottle of fine wine. No promises. But we may."

Her Saturday in Paris is almost over—only a short cab ride back to her hotel is left. Today has been the most incomprehensible day Alexia Klien has ever lived in her thirty-six years of life on this earth.

She cannot help but think that in just twenty-four hours she will be with Severo Baptiste. Most likely she will even be in his arms. As much as she wants this, maybe more than anything else in the world, it also scares her, maybe more than anything else in the world.

When Alexia gets to her room on the eleventh floor of the Hotel Gabriel Issy les Moulineax, she is completely wiped out. She has nothing else left mentally, physically, or emotionally. Alexia barely gets herself undressed before she falls into bed, sound asleep. It is just after midnight.

CHAPTER THIRTY-FOUR

Two Bites out of a Five-Bite Candy Bar

With the temperature hovering around eighty degrees, a slight breeze blowing in off the Pacific Ocean, and the mid-afternoon sun shining brightly in a cloudless sky, for the people in southern California the first Saturday in November has turned out to be nearly perfect. The day has not been so perfect for FBI agent Chace Wikett and the men he works with from Texas.

Wikett, Swanson, and Gasperson have just left a hospital on the east edge of Los Angeles and are en route to a restaurant to eat their first meal of the day. The three Texas FBI agents stopped to check on the wellbeing of fellow agents Rance Patton and Daniel Craddick. Both men were injured in this morning's action involving Roddy Dale Eddison and the two Islamic terrorists from the Middle Eastern country of Yemen. Patton and Craddick are both doing well. They are in pain, but very happy to still be alive.

Eddison has been fingerprinted and booked. He is now in the custody of federal law enforcement officers at an unnamed Los Angeles area hospital. He is facing first degree murder charges for the killing of FBI agent Antonio Ramirez Garcia. There is a long list of other charges still pending. At some point today, Wikett will have to call Garcia's wife and tell her of Tony's death. He wishes he could do this in person.

En route to an Outback Steakhouse—Gasperson and Swanson's choice—Wikett is traveling alone in the Cadillac Escalade. He makes a call to his wife. He has yet to tell her of Tony's death, and he knows it will seriously upset her. Even though she is a woman of strong faith, she constantly worries about her husband and what he does for a living. Many times over the years she has wished he would leave the

FBI and do something not as dangerous.

Only a year ago, Jerry Jones offered Wikett a position in charge of security over the new Cowboys' Stadium. It was a position that would have paid nearly twice what he makes with the Bureau. Chace turned it down because he felt his skills were still needed in the defense of his country, a country he loves and honors, a country he sees going in the wrong direction in so many ways. As the call he has placed to his wife rings in his ear, Wikett thinks that maybe the time has come that he should call the owner of the Dallas Cowboys and offer his services to the man who told him, "Anytime, Chace. Anytime you change your mind I will have a position for you with America's team, even if I have to make one."

Wikett chuckles to himself as he thinks of what Jerry Jones told him. For twenty years now Chace feels he has already been on America's team. Only the America's team he has been on is the one that plays its games in secret, in the dark, instead of on national television in front of millions of people. As he waits for his wife to answer the phone, he thinks about the life that Tony Garcia has given today for the team that plays its games in the dark. It reminds Wikett of a man named Pat Tillman. A man who gave up the game played in front of the bright lights in billion dollar stadiums on national television to play a game played in the dark, a game played in some of the darkest places on planet earth. *Now there is a true hero, regardless of the circumstances surrounding his death,* Wikett thinks. *It's a shame he had to die.* Just the fact that Pat Tillman would give up the life of an NFL football player to fight in the War on Terrorism is almost unthinkable by today's standards.

"Hello, Honey. I wish you were here," Wikett's wife says as she answers the phone.

"I do too, Darling. I have some really bad news to tell you, so brace yourself."

"What is it? Do I need to be sitting down for this?"

"Yes, that would be best," Chace tells his wife.

As Sharon Wikett pulls out a chair from the kitchen table she says, "OK, I'm sitting down. What is it?"

The Texas FBI agent pauses and then takes a deep breath, not wanting to have to do what he is about to do. "Tony has been killed in a shootout."

"Oh, no! Oh, my God, Chace," Wikett's wife begins to tremble as so many thoughts begin to race through her head. Her hands instantly shake uncontrollably. She cannot seem to get a breath as visions that she has seen of her own husband losing his life in a shootout run through her mind.

"Are you OK, Sharon?" Chace asks.

Wikett's wife takes a deep breath and replies, "I am in shock. Does Cindy know?"

"No, I have not called her yet."

"Chace, I have to be there when you do. Let me pull myself together and get over there before you call her. That is the least we can do." Wikett's wife is still trembling as tears begin to fall out of her eyes and on to her cheeks.

"Yes, Honey. I will wait."

Immediately Sharon Wikett stops everything she is doing this afternoon—including overseeing her daughter's sixteenth birthday party—and goes straight over to the Garcia residence, which is only about a ten minute drive away from where the Wikett's live. She will be there when Chace calls to tell Tony's wife of his death. Chace knew this would be her reaction.

While Wikett talks to his wife in the Escalade, Gasperson and Swanson get out of the Ford Excursion and head into the restaurant.

"How many will be in your party?" the hostess at the Outback Steakhouse asks.

"Three, there's one more coming," Big John Swanson answers as he and Gasperson stand in the entrance of the restaurant.

Wikett is still finishing the conversation with his wife. He knows that as soon as he is off the phone with her, he will have about twenty to thirty minutes before his wife is able to throw on some non-party clothes and drive over to the Garcia residence. Once Sharon gets there, she will call Chace and let him know he can make the call he so dreads. This will be the toughest call FBI agent Chace Wikett has ever made in his life. As he thinks about it, he feels so fortunate to be blessed with such an incredible wife to help him in times like this. He also feels fortunate to have been blessed with such a great friend as Tony Garcia over the last twenty some years.

"Do you want to wait here for your friend?" the hostess asks, "Or would you like me to seat you now?"

"You can seat us now," Gasperson replies.

"Follow me," she says.

"Man, am I ever hungry," states Swanson. "All I've had to eat today is two bites out of a five-bite candy bar."

"Why only two bites?" Gasperson asks as he and Big John follow the young woman in her late twenties to their table.

"Cause I dropped the darn thing in the mud this morning when I opened it. I ate the part that didn't get dirty."

Gasperson laughs and says, "Knowing you, John, I can't believe you didn't eat all of it anyway."

"I'll tell you, about noon when my stomach was growling like a grizzly bear, I wish I would have."

As Wikett walks towards the restaurant after finishing the phone call to his wife, in his mind he thinks about how much our country has changed in the last fifty years. Something he heard a long time ago pops into his head. *A nation usually gets the leadership it deserves.* As he walks the thought continues, *But what can a person expect from a country where the wishes of a small minority who want the Bible and the Ten Commandments banned from public places are actually granted those desires against the wishes of the majority?* He shakes his head to himself. *Sophistry, pure sophistry.*

Reaching for the front door of the steakhouse, *Fifty years ago,* he recalls, *The sixties.* That is when prayer was taken out of schools. Wikett remembers recently seeing a chart showing the decline of American values tied directly to the early 1960's. A Sunday school class Chace and his wife regularly attend just recently watched a video series produced by David Barton. The video series had a graph of statistical data showing the decline of SAT scores in the United States after the court ruling banning prayer in American schools. Barton also showed graphs of the increase in such things as unwed teenage pregnancies, sexually transmitted diseases, single-parent homes, divorce rates, crime and drug use all across the nation, these increases all beginning at the same time. Wikett wonders if he isn't fighting a losing battle as an FBI agent in today's society.

"I'll bet you're with the two guys I just showed to their table," says the unwed mother of three who works two jobs to try to keep food on the table for her children.

"If it was two big ugly guys from Texas, then probably so," Wikett replies.

"I kind of thought they were cute. Especially the dark headed one," the hostess says as she laughs and turns to lead Wikett to the table where the two other FBI agents are seated.

As she seats Wikett, Gasperson gets up to go use the restroom. When Chace sits down in his chair across from Big John Swanson who he helped lead to Christ today, he realizes he is not fighting a losing battle as an FBI agent. In fact, as he looks at his friend across the table from him, he is reminded that the war is already won even though there are many battles yet to come.

"Have you called Tony's wife yet?" Big John asks.

"No, I haven't. But I will have to within the next hour, as soon as Sharon gets there."

"It's good that your wife will be there, Chace," Swanson says. "You guys all went to the same church, didn't you?"

"Yes," Wikett replies. "Which brings me to something I want to share with you, John."

"Sure. Let's have it, I'm all ears."

"What I'm telling you right now is that God wants all of you," Wikett pauses and then continues, "All of you, everything. If He can't have all of you, He will take what you can give Him. But He wants all of you, Big John. Do you know what I am saying?"

With his eyes focused directly into Chace's, Swanson nods his head and replies, "Yes, Chace, I think so. I believe I am at a place in my life where I want to give Him all of me. I really do."

"That's good, John. Real good," Wikett says. Wikett knows everyone has to come to that place on their own. He wishes it didn't take things like a friend's death to bring some people to this point, but he knows it does.

FBI agent Gasperson returns to the table just as the waiter brings a small loaf of bread and some cinnamon flavored butter Swanson had specifically requested. Normally the Outback serves just regular butter with their bread, but Big John, being addicted to the cinnamon butter that is served with the bread at all the Texas Roadhouses, asked to have some cinnamon mixed into their butter. When the young man waiting on them sets down the loaf of bread and the butter in front of the three hungry federal agents, Swanson asks, "Didn't you bring any bread for these guys?"

The waiter stands there not sure if he should laugh or return to the kitchen for more bread. Wikett tells him, "Don't pay any attention to him. But I am sure we will go through more than one loaf."

Thirty minutes later, just as Chace finishes off a delicious medium-rare, sixteen-ounce ribeye, he feels his cell phone vibrate in his pocket. He pulls it out and looks at the caller ID. It is his wife. FBI agent Chace Wikett answers her call.

———

In the nation's capital with the thermostat turned up to a cozy seventy-two degrees in a second story apartment three and a half blocks from the CCN Network News headquarters, Rigger Watson is just waking up in a queen-sized bed. It is a little past eight P.M. on the East Coast. The weather outside on this Saturday night in November is much cooler than normal as the slow-moving Arctic cold front pushes its way south and east out of Canada. The wind has been blowing steadily all afternoon ahead of a cold front the nation's capital knows is coming.

Shirley Hienz has already been awake for almost an hour. She has taken a shower, fixed her hair and redone her makeup. This has been her life for more years than she would like to admit. The apartment is nothing special. It has a couple of bedrooms, a small bathroom and a kitchen that has not been used in years.

Watson's chauffeur, Ed Brokerman will bring the car around to the back of the apartment building after Rigger calls him. Watson is very hands-on when it comes to running his news network, except for the few hours three or four times a week when he is hands-on with Shirley Hienz. Everyone knows where he is when he disappears during that time, even his wife, but none of them care.

Normally on a night like this Watson will check up on anything new that may have happened in the world while he was busy with his mistress before he decides whether to go out to dinner, back to work, or go home to his wife. He usually chooses work or dinner. He generally doesn't get home until after midnight.

Recently an article about Rigger Watson was posted on an obscure right wing website. One of the things it claimed was, "It is said that in retailing and in real estate the three most important things are location, location, location. With the man who runs CCN Network News, Rigger Watson, the three most important things are power, power, and power." The article was the source of numerous punch lines with the late night comedians on the other networks. Had the piece not been picked up and used as the lead for a slow news day on the Drudge Report, hardly anyone would have known about it, and very few would have read it. The author of the piece, a conservative writer from central Nebraska named Mick Staggmeyer, did not paint CCN's Watson in a very favorable light.

In a meeting a couple mornings after the article was on the Drudge Report, Watson himself quoted it in a rant he went into about how the government needs to crack down on the internet and begin to regulate the opinions spread over it. It was quite comical to all who heard his rant. Watson didn't mean it to be. Rigger was also very adamant that conservative talk radio needed to be completely shut down. One thing the people who work for Rigger Watson have learned over the years is to never bring up the names of Rush Limbaugh, Sean Hannity, Glen Beck or Bill O'Reilly. To Watson these men are as evil as the four horsemen of the Apocalypse.

In the apartment before he even turns the flat screen TV on to watch CCN News and see what has happened in the time he has been busy indulging in carnal pleasures, Watson knows the option he will choose tonight is dinner. He is going straight to dinner at one of Washington D.C.'s finest restaurants located just down the street from the Renaissance Park Hotel.

The man who owns the very trendy and fashionable French restaurant Watson and Hienz are going to dine at tonight is a business associate of Watson's. If someone were to look into each man's books there would be no trace of actual business between Watson and the man who owns the French restaurant, but the two men are business associates nonetheless. Tonight Watson needs to discuss a couple of matters with this man before the earth-shattering news of a U.S. Presidential candidate's campaign manager committing suicide hits television screens all over the country in the coming morning.

When Watson and Shirley arrive at the French restaurant, they enter through the rear entrance and are taken to a private dining room near the kitchen. Halfway through the meal Watson is joined by the man who owns the restaurant. When he arrives, Shirley excuses herself from their company and heads to the ladies' room.

The meeting between Watson and the owner of the restaurant lasts only about twenty minutes, but everything they need to cover is covered. Watson and Hienz finish their meals and exit the rear of the building just as they had entered.

The weather in Washington D.C. is starting to show the signs of an early winter storm. The cold front pushing its way across the U.S. is beginning to make itself known to the common people on the streets of the city. In the short time Watson and his mistress have been in the French restaurant, the temperature has dropped ten more degrees. As he walks to his black Mercedes-Benz limousine, Watson hopes that the storm will move across the nation faster than predicted.

A winter snowstorm of the magnitude that has been forecasted hitting the northeastern two-thirds of the United States on the night before a very pivotal U.S. Presidential election will severely depress the turnout at the polls in three or four states that are crucial to the race for the White House. Watson knows that if the Democrat Party is not able to bus the people from the lower-rent districts to the polls in communities like Cleveland, Columbus and Cincinnati, Ohio, and places like Philadelphia and Pittsburgh, Pennsylvania, or cities like Detroit and Chicago, the chances of Senator Walter Franson winning the Presidency are slim to none.

Politicians have had this storm on their minds for days now, and there have been very heated battles on Capitol Hill about what to do in case the winter weather disrupts Tuesday's election. The Democrats are all pushing for the nation to either extend the election for an extra day or two, or even postpone it for one full week until the second Tuesday in November. Those on the right are demanding the election go forward on the day it is scheduled to be held as the country has been doing for over two hundred years.

Since this winter storm has raised its ugly head, numerous negative comments have been made on CCN by its anchors in the past days about how damaging it was to lose control of the House of Representatives in the last midterm election. Watson has been behind this network theme. He has vowed to do everything he can to keep the Senate and the Presidency from falling to the Republicans in this election. Normally the approaching winter snow storm would be something Rigger Watson would be dwelling on and stewing over, but tonight his mind is preoccupied with news that will be bigger than any kind of winter snow storm.

With dinner over and his very important meeting concluded, it is time for Watson's next decision. Tonight, instead of heading home to his wife and his multi-million dollar mansion in McLean, Virginia just Northwest of D.C., Watson will stay in his townhouse apartment. Not the one he and Shirley Hienz use periodically over the lunch hour during the work week that is just down the street from Bernie's Bar and Grill, but the one CCN foots the bill for that is located just across the Potomac River from the CCN headquarters. The townhouse apartment is equipped with all the necessary equipment and technology Watson needs to run the network. Very seldom does Hienz ever stay at the CCN apartment, but tonight is an exception.

The upcoming election is the excuse Watson gave his wife for staying the night in D.C. The truth is, he wants to be able to watch his daughter at the rock concert in L.A. without any interruptions from his wife who doesn't get along with Watson's daughter from his first marriage.

Watson also wants to be on top of the story he knows is going to break sometime in the middle of the night about Mike Swenson. It is not uncommon for Rigger Watson to stay at the CCN townhouse apartment when he is manufacturing the news.

CHAPTER THIRTY-FIVE

Indecision Will Kill You

The bright sunrise broke over the wide-open horizon to the east at only a few minutes past six A.M. this morning on the sands of the Arabian Desert. That was nearly two hours ago. With a perfectly clear sky in all directions, and a sun that is already heating everything it sees to temperatures way warmer than normal for this time of year in the land of oil and of wars, it is definitely going to be another very hot day. Word has gotten out that the famous female country music singer who performed last night at Camp Arifjan is going to make a quick visit to three of the brave Americans who risked their lives for the safety of all others the day before at the U.S. Air Force Base Ali Al Salem.

There must be over a hundred soldiers gathered around the canvas tent of U.S. Army Privates Will Tillord and Sheldon Mitchal, and it's not quite eight A.M. yet here in Kuwait. Specialist Diaz is on his way from his tent. He still doesn't truly believe that Sergeant Spicer Davis really knows Angie West. Either way though, he is not going to miss out just in case Sarge really does know her and she shows up at Tillord and Mitchal's tent.

This is a very special morning for Carlos Diaz as he makes his way through the vast number of American men and boys who have shown up for a chance to get a glance at a real American beauty. Diaz cannot wait to tell his friend Sheldon Mitchal that he accepted Jesus as his Savior the night before down on the pier at the edge of the Persian Gulf. Diaz is actually more excited about becoming a Christian than he is about having a chance to see the very beautiful country music singer. One day ago Carlos wouldn't even have believed it himself had someone told him he could change as much as he has in one night.

Making it through the crowd of onlookers, Diaz arrives at the tent of his two injured friends and fellow soldiers. Diaz sticks his head into their tent and says, "Hey, you guys got quite a following of fans out here."

"I don't think they are here for us," Mitchal responds.

"It's been a little tough to sleep in with all the noise out there," Private Tillord allows.

"Can I come in?"

"Of course, Diaz," Mitchal replies.

Diaz steps into the green canvas tent. He sits down on the end of a black, hard plastic footlocker at the end of Mitchal's bed. When he does, he clasps his hands together and squeezes them. He then says, "Hey Mitch, I've got something I want to share with you."

"What's that, Dee?"

"I accepted Jesus Christ as my Savior last night down on the pier. It was the coolest thing I've ever done. I have never experienced anything like it, man," Diaz tells the one person he wants to share his new faith with the most.

"That is great, Diaz, that's great!" Mitchal says as he smiles. "I am happy for you, man. Best decision you will ever make."

"Yeah, Sergeant Glen Davis led me through everything just like God had set the whole thing up. The Air Force Major who drove me to the SPOD last night even accepted Jesus too. His name is Scott McQueen. It was incredible, man. I wish you could have been there, Mitch."

With tears instantly beginning to form in his eyes, Private Mitchal sets a book he was reading down and says, "Diaz, I was praying last night that you would. I am so happy for you. You can't imagine how happy I am for you."

The young man from Glenrock, Wyoming in the same tent with Mitchal and Diaz knows that the conversation he is listening to between the two tough American soldiers is something serious and special, but he is not completely sure what to make of it himself. At nineteen years old there are still things the young Will Tillord doesn't want to let go of that he thinks he would have to give up to become a Christian.

There is something inside of Tillord that wants to do exactly the same thing he has just heard Diaz did last night, yet there is also something inside of him telling him he should wait. Having already experienced what it is to be with a woman, Tillord doesn't want to have to give that part of his young life up until he finds the girl he wants to marry. He wants to be free to play the field for a few more years. Tillord just sits and listens to Diaz and Mitchal talk about Diaz's experience the night before.

"Thanks for being such a good example, Mitch. You are a big part of why I finally decided to turn to Christ with my life," states the U.S. Army Specialist.

"I don't really think I am that good of an example," the humble Private from Queens, New York replies. "I mean, I am far from perfect."

"I know. None of us are, I know that," says Diaz. "But Sheldon, you have a peace about you that most people over here don't have. I know I didn't have it before last night. But I do now. I feel like the world has been lifted off my shoulders."

"It has been, Diaz. A world of sin has been lifted off of you."

"Man, I know what you mean there. I've done stuff that you two couldn't even think of doing," Diaz allows as he speaks to his friends. "And now I am forgiven for all of it."

"I'm glad for you, Dee," Mitchal returns.

"It's funny though, Mitch," Diaz says. "Something a Sergeant I had in basic training used to say popped into my mind right when Sergeant Glen Davis asked me if I wanted to pray to become a Christian."

Hanging on every word he is listening to, Tillord can't help but get into the conversation. "What was that?"

"Indecision will kill you," answers Diaz. "Indecision will kill you."

"Wow!" Mitchal voices as he sits up in bed and repositions a pillow behind his back. "That's cool."

Knowing that indecision is just exactly where he is with this Christian stuff, Private Will Tillord stays quiet and doesn't say anything more. Mitchal and Diaz continue talking.

About twenty minutes later, the three soldiers hear the crowd outside the green army tent start chanting, "Angie! Angie! Angie!"

Diaz jumps up off of the footlocker and sticks his head outside. When he does, he sees the crowd of soldiers split in the same fashion the Red Sea must have split for Moses in the Old Testament. In the middle of the two walls of soldiers still chanting, he sees Sergeant Spicer Brent Davis walking with country music superstar Angie West holding on to his good arm—the one that wasn't injured the day before.

Diaz cannot believe his eyes.

———

Sitting in the large and extravagant office of his CCN townhouse apartment, Rigger Watson is eagerly anticipating a text message on his personal cell phone from his daughter in Los Angeles. He is busy receiving phone calls as he patiently waits for news that only he knows is coming from Boston, Massachusetts. The calls he is taking are the typical ones he will get only two and a half days before a pivotal U.S. Presidential election. Political strategists, congressional candidates, state governors, senators, and representatives of all the above are calling Watson in hopes that his CCN media influence will swing an election somewhere in their favor. This is a never-ending process for Watson. He loves it. The power he is wielding at this time is what he thrives on.

Only Shirley Hienz is with Watson in the townhouse apartment. She is helping him by sorting through the emails he has received, thousands of them from the very same people who have been calling constantly now for weeks. He picks and chooses which calls to take and which ones to make. Hienz goes through the emails and narrows them down so he can do the same with them. She knows how Watson will answer most things, so many of the emails get her response as though it was his.

In the middle of a conversation with a governor from a state in the Northwest that wants CCN's help in a tightly contested U.S. Senate race, Watson's personal cell phone rings. Because of what is on his mind, his first reaction is that it is someone calling him about the Michael Swenson issue that should be transpiring any moment now. It is not. It is his daughter Marcia McNally in Southern

California.

It is a little before eight P.M. on the West Coast. She is calling on her cell phone from inside the Staples Center, home of the Los Angeles Lakers. Tonight the entertainment on center court will be the British rock band Ax-Handle, led by Liverpool's own Flash Freeman. The world famous English rock star Flash Freeman is Watson's daughter's current celebrity squeeze.

"Daddy, Daddy, Flash is going nuts out here!" she says with the tone of fear in her voice. "The Feds are arresting every single person coming into the concert tonight that looks like they are Arabic. I don't know what to do. He's going crazy."

"What?" Watson asks as he gets up to walk to the door of the office. "What's going on, why are they doing that?"

"I don't know. I guess someone told them there was going to be a terrorist attack here or something."

"I have not heard anything like that, Honey," the most powerful news man in America replies. "If that was so, I would have heard about it by now."

"All I know is, Flash is mad as hell! He thinks this whole damn thing is because he's been talking about converting to Islam."

"I wouldn't put it past the FBI to do something like that right before an election," Watson states.

"He's in a rage! There's no telling what he might do when he gets on stage," Marcia McNally says with panic and fear in her voice. "I'm scared, Daddy. I'm scared. What if Flash starts a riot? You know how much his fans love him."

While still going through Rigger's emails, Hienz gets a text message on her own phone. She immediately says, "Oh, my God, Rigger! Mike Swenson has committed suicide." She pauses with her mouth wide open and then again says, "Oh, my God. Why would he do that? Did you hear me, Rig?"

Still in the middle of the phone conversation with his daughter, Watson acts like he didn't hear Shirley Hienz. But he did.

————

Curled up under the soft, silky blankets of her comfortable and cozy king-sized bed, Alexia Klien is sound asleep. She has her head lying on one pillow with her long legs wrapped around another as she tightly squeezes a third close to her chest with her arms. The room is without a hint of sound. Alexia is dreaming of being a little girl and growing up as a princess in a king's court in France nearly five hundred years ago. In her dream she is the most beautiful princess in all the land and the princes of all the neighboring countries want to journey to her castle and make her their bride. This is a dream Alexia has never had before.

In the midst of her wonderful dream where she is about to tell her father the king which prince she wants to marry, she hears the ringing of a phone. It does not completely awaken her. With her arms wrapped firmly around the big pillow she has been holding tightly next to her almost naked body, she rolls over hoping the sound of the cell phone stops. In the complete darkness of her plush Paris hotel room her phone continues to ring. Alexia is still deep into her dream as she thinks it might be the prince she has just picked calling her.

She reaches out with one arm, the other still holding onto the pillow, and fumbles around trying to get a feel for the phone. By now she has awakened a little more and she can tell by the sound of the ringtone that it is her very best friend Angie West who is calling. Alexia is able to get her little blue cell phone found and opened just before it switches over to her voice mail.

"Hi, Ange," Alexia says in a slow sleepy voice as she rolls back over and curls up in a ball under blankets, pillows, sheets and a big soft comforter.

Realizing Alexia is still asleep, Angie West laughs and asks, "Hey, girl, did I wake you?"

"Oh... Yes, you did."

"I suppose you were having a really good dream too, huh?"

"Yes... I was," Alexia says with a yawn.

Angie laughs as Alexia wakes up a little more.

"Yes, Ange... I was. It was incredible. I wish I could go back to sleep and finish it."

"Really?" laughing even more than before, Angie asks, "So do I get to hear all about it?"

"Oh, it was silly," Alexia replies as she laughs. "But it was really fun."

"Really fun. That's always good in a dream."

"Yeah," she laughs. "I was a princess in a fancy French castle and my dad was the king. It was really silly."

"Then what?" Angie asks.

Giggling like a little school girl, Alexia rolls over in her bed. "Let's see if I can remember it all. I was just at the part where I was picking which of the handsome princes I wanted to marry. And there were a lot of them to pick from." Alexia starts laughing.

"Go on, I want to know which one you picked."

"OK. Then, when you called," Alexia giggles again, "I thought it was the prince I picked calling me, but they didn't even have phones back then."

They both laugh.

"Hey, it might just come true," Angie says with a bit of seriousness. "You never know when you will find the right one... 'Cause I just did!"

"What?" Alexia asks as she suddenly sits up in bed. "What did you just say, Ange?"

"What do you think you heard me say?"

"You know what I heard you say, girl!" Alexia fires back. "Now come out with it."

"OK, if I must."

"Yes, you must, and now."

Angie laughs, and then says, "I found Mr. Right."

"You found Mr. Right? Where? Who is he?"

Angie doesn't say anything.

"Are you still in the Middle East, Angie?"

"Yes, I'm in the Middle East. I'm still in Kuwait," Angie says with a smile on her face. "Remember when we were joking about me finding the man of my dreams on the sands of the Arabian Desert in U.S. Army fatigues?"

"Yes!"

"Well, it happened. I found him. Right here in Kuwait. A soldier."

"You've got to be kiddin' me, girl. You know you'll never be happy with someone who's not a cowboy," Alexia tells the country music singer and professional barrel racer from just outside of Oklahoma City.

"He is a cowboy. A real one, from Abilene, Texas. My brother even knows him and says he's a really good guy."

"Get out of here! No way! You're making all this up because of the silly dream I just told you about."

"No, I'm not!" Angie returns. "I guess I've even met him before. My brother said he stayed at our place and roped for a couple of days when I was about twelve. But I don't remember it. There were always different guys coming to rope with Trevor."

"What's his name?"

"Spicer Davis," Angie says quickly without hesitation.

"Spicer? What kind of name is that?"

"Actually, it's Sergeant Spicer Brent Davis over here in the war zone."

"As soon as I get off the phone with you, I'm calling your brother," Alexia responds suspiciously. "Trevor will tell me the truth."

"Hey girl, I am telling you the truth," Angie proclaims. "I found my man here in the Middle East in camouflage and I can't wait to see him in Wranglers and a black 20X felt hat riding a good-looking bay horse." She pauses. "First though, I have to find out if he likes me."

"What?" Alexia asks as her mouth drops open. "You don't even know if he likes you?"

"No, not really. Not yet."

"Is he blind? How could he not like you?"

"I don't know. I'm not perfect." says the country girl from central Oklahoma.

"You don't know if he likes you?" Alexia asks again, confused. "Really now, Ange, get real."

"I don't know. I'm sure he likes me as a friend. But I just met him."

"Oh, Angie darling, you are pretty close to perfect. As close as I know. And perfectly naïve if you are not making all this up."

"Well it isn't like we had a date or anything," Angie says sheepishly. "I just know he is the one. I don't know how, I just know it."

"Does he know he is the one?"

"I don't know... Trevor's going to find out if he is interested for me," she answers back with less confidence than you would think someone of Angie West's stature would have.

"Gonna find out if he's interested? You got to be kidding me, girl," Alexia says shaking her head in total disbelief in her pitch dark hotel room. She then asks her friend, "Angie, did you let him know that you were interested? That you are attracted to him?"

"No, not really. We are on an Army base," Angie replies with some hesitance. "I didn't think I should be flirting with anyone over here."

"That's what they sent you over there for!" Alexia Klien proclaims.

"I don't think so! At least that's not how I see it."

"Whatever! But you flew all the way to the Middle East, you meet Mr. Right, and you don't even tell him you like him? What is the matter with you, girl? This ain't a time to be playing hard to get," Alexia laughs and shakes her head back and forth.

"Well, it's true."

"Oh, Ange, I know now you're not making all this up. Only you would be this innocent."

"What should I do?" Angie West asks.

CHAPTER THIRTY-SIX

Kabul, Afghanistan

It has been over five hours since FBI agent Chace Wikett made the short five minute phone call to Tony Garcia's wife. Chace cannot get over the deep empty feeling he has inside because of the loss of his good friend. He knows Tony is in a better place. But he also knows there is a wife and three wonderful children in Dallas, Texas who are going to miss their father and husband in ways Wikett cannot even imagine. Chace has been on his phone off and on this afternoon with his own wife who was quick to attend to her friend Cindy Garcia. From what Wikett's wife has told him, Tony's wife has held up fairly well throughout the day. Sharon Wikett is most concerned with how her good friend will handle the coming nights that will be so lonely and empty. It is a nightmare every woman and mother married to a law enforcement officer lives with on a daily basis. As he continues his work at the Staples Center in Los Angeles, Chace feels for his own wife in Texas.

This night in California things are going well for the various law enforcement organizations who were all called in to protect the safety of the people attending the sold-out rock concert. Agent Wikett is helping his long-time friend and former covert CIA spy, Martin MacKuenn, oversee the coordination of the evening's operation. So far, the different federal, state and local law enforcement officials have detained nearly five hundred individuals who were either of Arab descent or known to be radical Muslims.

There have been minor protests outside the security border that was set up four hours before the concert was scheduled to start. The protesters are of the normal variety—young people with piercings and tattoos all over their bodies, green, purple and orange hair and clothes that are way too baggy. They are kids who do not have anything better to do, and have most likely never had the guidance they needed. There are also a few old hippie holdovers from the sixties and seventies who just love to come out and protest anytime they get the chance so they can relive their anti-Vietnam days. As Wikett watches the small number of protesters, he feels sorry for the misguided youth of America. He has vowed to himself to do all he can to help fill the shoes of his friend Tony Garcia in the raising of the three children that were left behind today.

Texas FBI agents Gasperson and Swanson are helping with the interrogation of those of Arab descent who have been detained. It is not yet known if the two escaped Islamic terrorist from Yemen are in the four hundred and eighty-some people who have been held back from attending the Flash Freeman rock concert. With the speed at which information travels in this age, it is very possible that the real terrorists could have easily gotten wind of the increased security surrounding the Staples Center tonight and completely avoided attempting to attend or attack the concert.

In an extensive search of the building prior to the opening of its doors to the public, the FBI, aided by the L.A. bomb squad did find four of five necessary components that could be used to mix a homemade explosive device in a very quick and crude fashion, a device that nevertheless would do extensive damage. The components they found were all items that can be bought on the open market most anywhere. The volume of the components and the location where they were found clearly showed that someone definitely had some sort of deadly and destructive action planned for the evening. The key to discovering who had planned this will be in finding the individual or individuals who brought the bomb-making elements into the Staples Center and then uncovering who it is that has funded the purchasing of the materials. Surveillance video of the hours and days leading up to the rock concert are already being gone over by federal officials. The break the authorities are hoping for is to arrest someone attempting to bring the fifth and final explosive element into the facilities.

In retrospect, Wikett knows that if Agent Tony Garcia could do it all over again, he would still give up his life to save the lives of the twenty thousand crazed and screaming fans of Flash Freemon who will pack the Staples Center tonight to hear someone sing and play music that goes against everything Antonio Ramirez Garcia stood for. Wikett knows this because he knows that his friend and fellow FBI agent, Tony Garcia, was closely acquainted with a Man who two thousand years ago gave up His life for the lives of many, many more than will be in the Staples Center tonight. This thought puts a smile on Chace Wikett's sad face.

————

In complete shock, Shirley Hienz sits in an office chair behind a computer. She hasn't heard a response back from her boss and lover Rigger Watson yet, but she hasn't looked away from the cell phone she is staring at either. For a brief moment after she told Watson that Mike Swenson had committed suicide and Rigger did not respond to her, a thought about the man who runs CCN came into her head. She cannot believe she had this thought. She sits for a few seconds in a trance as fear grips at her very core.

"Honey, I will call you right back," Watson tells his daughter in L.A. as he stands motionless behind Hienz. "Something really big has just come up."

"Rigger, did you hear me?" Shirley says as she turns to look at him, "I just got a text that said Mike Swenson killed himself."

"That can't be so, that would ruin us. There's no way Walter can win if that damn queer went and killed himself."

When Hienz hears Watson's response, some of the fear she felt a moment ago seems to leave her.

Watson goes on to ask, "Who sent you the text?"

"That same young girl, the intern that's sleeping with a guy at FX News," answers Hienz.

"What? Who the hell is this girl anyway?" Watson barks back in a loud voice. "If this is true too, we need to make her an investigative reporter instead of a coffee girl."

"I can show you the text."

"Who's she sleeping with at FX anyway?"

"I don't know," Hienz replies.

"Well, we need to find out and try to keep this thing going

between her and whoever it is," Watson tells his mistress.

"Do you really mean that?" Hienz asks puzzled.

Watson laughs and then answers, "Hell yes, I mean it. We pay millions of dollars a year to people to try to get the story first, and then along comes some little girl making what, ten dollars an hour? Hell yes, we need to try and keep her doing whoever it is that's stupid enough to tell her everything at FX."

"I think she makes $9.25 an hour."

"OK, whatever... that's ten dollars an hour to me," Watson says sarcastically. "About Swenson... how'd it happen and where? How'd he kill himself?"

"I don't know."

"Find out what you can," Watson orders. "I've got to get back to Marcia, she has something in L.A. that may be as big as the Swenson thing. And if he is dead, we may need the California thing to offset it."

While making this last statement to his longtime assistant and bedmate, Watson formulates just exactly what he is going to do with the information his daughter has just called him with. Information that the FBI is arresting numerous people who look to be of Arab descent outside the Staples Center in Los Angeles, this is something that CCN Network News President Rigger Watson cannot believe has just fallen into his lap.

Whether it is true or not that conservative-slanted federal law enforcement officials have possibly over-stepped their boundaries, the story that CCN will run with on the Sunday morning news just forty-eight hours before an election is that unnamed sources within the Bureau say the FBI concocted the entire Los Angeles area terrorist threat to try to scare people to the polls to vote Republican. Watson knows that in news time, it will take at least three or four days for the truth to come out, if it ever does. By that time, the Presidency of the United States will be firmly in the hands of the Democrats, and two weeks later the story will be lost. No one will care about it.

Watson heads out of the office in the CCN-owned townhouse and to the kitchen to pour himself a cup of coffee. As he walks, he pulls out his personal cell phone and calls his daughter in Southern California back, "Hey sweetheart, sorry about that, but some scumbag just killed himself and it's going to be all over the news in a few minutes. How's Flash now?"

"I don't know, Daddy, he went back into his dressing room. I think to pray to Allah or something. He's still really mad," Marcia tells her father.

"OK, Honey, you go and tell him you have talked to me and I'm going to do something about it. Tell him to do his show and we will have cameras out in front of the Staples Center in ten minutes. If Flash wants to call me, he can."

"OK, Daddy," Watson's only daughter replies. "I'll text you when I am going on stage with Flash. Love you."

"Love you, too, Honey. I've got to go. I have some important phone calls to make."

———

"Email him or something, let the poor boy know you think he's hot, I guess. I don't know, I've never had this kind of problem before," Alexia tells her friend.

"What if he already has a girlfriend back in Texas?" Angie asks.

Alexia laughs at the utterly ridiculous question she has just heard from her friend. The CCN broadcast journalist then says, "He will get rid of any girlfriend he has once he finds out you think he is the one."

"I hope so."

"Is he hot?" Alexia asks.

"Well, yeah... what do you think? It's almost a hundred degrees over here right now," Angie replies, being a little facetious.

"That's not what I meant," Alexia replies as she laughs and shakes her head. "You know what I mean. Is he easy on the eyes?"

"He's rugged and rough. Built really nice, and very buff," Angie West says of Sergeant Spicer Davis.

"Oh, that's even better," Alexia says. "I can't wait to see him. Sounds like your version of my Severo Baptiste."

"Whoa! Wait a minute, Klien" Angie interrupts. "What did you just say?"

"Ah, I said, *my* Severo Baptiste?" Alexia replies sheepishly as she thinks.

"Yes, you did," Angie says as she laughs.

"I did. Oh my God, I did. And I meant it," Alexia responds, surprised with what she just heard herself say.

Angie laughs at her high society friend, who with only a little work could be a country girl just like herself. She jokingly asks, "Are we now back to your dream about you marrying a prince in France?"

"Maybe."

"Is Severo the one you picked?"

"I don't know," Alexia replies as she giggles. "Somebody woke me up from my dream."

"I'm sorry."

"You couldn't help it, Ange. You had to tell me about your spicy prince from Abilene, Texas."

Both of them laugh.

Angie glances at a clock on the wall where she waits to board a flight to Kabul, Afghanistan. She is at U.S. Air Force Base Ali Al Salem. She sees she has a little over an hour before the U.S. Military transport plane she is leaving on will be departing from Kuwait. "I'm flying out of here for Afghanistan in about an hour."

"How many days will you be there?" Alexia asks.

"I think just a couple. I can't remember."

"So, just how are you going to make contact with this Spicy Davis guy? Or should I ask, how is your brother Trevor going to make contact with him if Spicy is in Kuwait?"

"My brother already has Spicer's email," Angie says. "That's how he got a hold of me over here. Spicer emailed Trevor yesterday to get my cell phone number."

"He's interested, very interested if he was getting a hold of Trevor for your number. You just need to let him know you're interested," Alexia tells Angie.

Angie laughs, and then says, "Yes, I know and yes, I will. But isn't that kind of like the pot calling the kettle black? When are you going to tell Severo that he's the one?"

"I'm waiting for him to tell me."

"I thought he already did?"

"Kind of," Alexia says. "But that was a long time ago."

"Talk about a time not to be playing hard to get," Angie fires back. "You better not play hard to get too well, or you'll be the one left out of the game, Alexia darling."

"I know. But it is so damn complicated," Alexia replies in a very serious voice. "Love shouldn't be that complicated."

"Life shouldn't be that complicated, but it is," Angie says. "You're the one who has control of your future. No one else does."

"I know," Alexia allows.

"So? Are you going to tell Severo he's the one?"

"Hey, Ange, I haven't even told you about my day yesterday."

"No, you haven't, you said it was real crazy or something," Angie replies.

"Yes, it was."

"Are we officially changing the subject? Away from Severo Baptiste?"

"Yes, we are. Anyway… It was the wildest day I have ever had in my life. I mean, it all started out normal. I went shopping on the Champs-Élysées. I didn't even plan on buying anything."

Angie laughs. "I've heard that before."

"Then, in the very first boutique I am in, I see this woman I had seen before in Washington, a mysterious woman every bit as beautiful as you."

Thinking over just exactly how much she really wants to share with her conservative friend, Alexia pauses and then continues, "Anyhow, I can't tell you all of it, but when she left the boutique, I followed the woman to a café and then all the way out to the airport where she got on a plane headed to Moscow."

Angie interrupts her and asks, "What? Why did you follow her all over Paris? And Moscow? Why Moscow? This sounds like spy stuff you were doing. Did you think of that? What if she is a spy—and now they think you're a spy?"

Alexia is taken back by what she hears her best friend say. "I never thought of that. I just know it was all very crazy. Someday I will tell you more about it."

"I hope so."

"Hey, in the Paris news studio last night I saw the info about the attack on the airbase in Kuwait. CCN didn't think it was news-worthy enough to have me ask any questions about it in my interviews."

"Oh, Klien! I didn't tell you! The guy I met was in the guard tower that almost got blown up yesterday in the attack. He broke his arm when he was thrown..." Angie stops talking for a moment after losing her train of thought. She then continues, "Alexia! He's here! The guy, Spicer Davis from Texas is here right now and walking right towards me."

"You get off the phone, girl, and let Spicy know you are interested in him," Alexia tells her closest friend in the whole world. "Now, do it! Love you, Ange. Call me when you get to Kabul."

"I will, I'll call you. Thanks. But what do I say? Pray for me so I know what to say. Bye."

World famous country music superstar Angie West ends the call on her iPhone, severing the international cellular connection between her and the most popular CCN Network News broadcast journalist in America. Alexia Klien and Angie West are two women, two girls just trying to find their way through life.

In Paris, France, in a completely dark hotel room, Alexia thinks about the last thing her friend Angie said to her. "Pray for me." Alexia Klien wonders to herself if she even knows how to pray.

CHAPTER THIRTY-SEVEN

Fresh Raw Cuts of Media Meat

After he finishes a quick call to his daughter in L.A., Rigger Watson returns to his townhouse office where he sits down in a very expensive brown leather office chair, a chair that when his daughter first saw it, she had a fit because it was made out of cowhide. When this happened, Watson just laughed at her. He then asked his daughter what she thought that expensive Givenchy purse she was carrying was made of, she looked at it and said, "My purse is black, Dad. Everyone knows cowhide is brown like your chair." He laughed and thought about asking her what color she thought leather from black cows was, but he decided not to.

Sitting comfortably in his chair of pure cowhide, Watson makes two short phone calls to the West Coast. He dispatches some of CCN's top people in Southern California to the Staples Center immediately to cover the developing story he thinks is of the utmost importance. Normally, this is not something Watson would handle himself. But given the time issue, this being late on a Saturday night right before an important election, and the possible political ramifications he can produce by airing a news story about people having their civil rights violated because of their ethnicity, Watson handles the dirty work himself.

"What have you been able to find out about Swenson?" Watson asks Shirley Hienz when he gets off the phone.

"I guess it's true. Everyone is fixing to run with it. It seems he hung himself in his father's garage," she says as her voice breaks up a little.

"He what?" asks Watson. "Was the dead queer trying to blame his father for him being gay or something?"

"I don't know!" Hienz fires back. "But it seems to me you don't have much respect for him. I liked Michael."

"Yeah, everyone liked Michael Swenson. He was a very loving guy, wasn't he?" Watson sarcastically says. "He loved the boys and the girls. It's just that he loved the boys a little too much. He damn sure wasn't the person Walter should have had running his campaign for the Presidency."

"It almost sounds like you're happy he's dead," states Hienz. "If I didn't know better, I would think you had something to do with it."

"And just what would I have to gain by Swenson killing himself? If I was going to kill him, I would have done it six months ago when it wouldn't have cost us the White House," proclaims the President of CCN.

"Well, I feel sorry for him."

When he hears this, Watson knows his plan to pull on the heartstrings of the American voters in the middle will work. At least he knows it will work with a big enough percentage of them to help offset the negative effects of the leading Presidential candidate's campaign manager being caught with two naked teenage boys in Boston. *That was all Mike Swenson's fault in the first place,* Watson thinks as he chuckles to himself about his well thought out plan.

"You go ahead and feel sorry for the little fag," Watson tells his mistress and personal assistant. "I'm going to continue to try and win an election regardless of what I have to do."

"You can be so cold sometimes," Hienz says to the man she thinks she loves. "Don't people mean anything to you?"

"They do if they vote straight down the line Democrat," CCN Chief Rigger Watson replies.

"Well, I'm sure Mike did," Hienz fires back sarcastically.

"That, I'll bet he did," Watson replies with a smirk on his face.

Shirley Hienz doesn't say anything.

"Hey, we're about out of coffee," Watson states. "Why don't you get your ass up and go make some more and quit feeling sorry for little Mikey."

In the larger than normal work-at-home office where he and Hienz are both working, Watson grabs the remote and turns up the volume to the flat screen TV he has turned to CCN as Hienz heads to the kitchen. He stands up to stretch his legs and listens to one of his own anchors giving a special report on the findings of the Massachusetts State Police who are currently in charge of the investigation into the apparent suicide of one Michael Fitzgerald Swenson. Standing there in deep thought, Watson deliberates about what he should do next in spinning the Swenson story.

Returning from the kitchen, Hienz continues about the task of going through Watson's emails. She sits and thinks about how unimportant what she is doing really is in this world. She wonders if she were to just delete all of Watson's incoming messages instead of attempting to reply to some of them if it would have any effect on things. She also wonders how Watson really feels about her.

She tries to fight back tears that are forming in her eyes as she remembers the sweet and fun times she had dining with Mike Swenson. She and Swenson would quite often be left alone together for long periods of time when she would accompany Watson to meet with Senator Walter Franson over the years. She wonders if it was the pressures of the political race that brought Mike to the point of doing what he did, or if it was the shame he felt deep down inside over the choices he made in his personal life. He had told her once that there were things in his life he wasn't proud of, but just couldn't stop doing. Shirley Hienz reaches up and wipes a tear off of her cheek with a Kleenex.

Hearing how his own CCN Network News anchor is reporting the Swenson story, Watson is convinced he will not have to do anything more with the story he has created. Just as he suspected, with no coaching from above, the nameless Saturday night news anchor on CCN is presenting the story just as Watson would have him do, very sympathetically.

Watson knows full well that by the middle of tomorrow morning every single liberal news commentator on all the Sunday morning news talk shows will be portraying Mike Swenson as the victum. They will be painting the big mean heartless Republicans as the evil haters of homosexuals. The tides of public opinion will be turned back in the favor of Senator Walter Franson. Mike Swenson is a martyr for the cause.

With a smile on his face, Watson thinks that the six million dollars he wired to that secret bank account in Dubai might very well be the best use of campaign funds by anyone in history. The money

Watson wired overseas has been filtered out of the campaign slush funds of numerous Democrats at every level of politics from all across the United States a few hundred dollars at a time. He chuckles to himself about how stupid so many of the people in America are. *They will devour whatever dish I serve on their TV screens as long as it pulls at their hearts and not their minds. It gives a whole new meaning to a TV dinner,* Watson thinks as he laughs to himself.

Late on this Saturday night, Watson is confident to the point that he no longer feels he needs to dirty his hands anymore orchestrating the desired outcome to the tragic story he caused. An outcome of sympathy towards Swenson, subconsciously transferred to Senator Franson, has automatically materialized on its own. Watson focuses his efforts on two more morsels of media meat that are sitting right in front of him on a great big silver platter.

Two fresh raw pieces of Grade A, prime, very newsworthy cuts of raw media meat just waiting to be seasoned, sliced and cooked to the desired temperature and texture of the master chef, Rigger Watson. Fresh media meat then fed to the consumers—anyone with a TV tuned to CCN—how, when, where, and in the way Chef Watson wants.

Anyone on a steady diet of Chef Rigger Watson's buffet, dining daily on the deadly and dangerously distorted donuts, drinks and desserts of the CCN cafeteria, and partaking of the morsels of medium-rare to well-done news media meat, will surely see the death of the moral absolutes that individual grew up with. Any person who feasts solely on food from the kitchen of the left-leaning liberal information buffet, CCN News, will run the risk of having their future torn right out of their soul. Torn out never to return.

With a cup of steaming hot coffee in his hand, Watson walks over and sits back down at his desk. Setting the coffee down, he pulls a large yellow note pad out from under some papers that are stacked on one side of the desk. With the yellow note pad in hand, he leans back in his brown leather office chair and spins around where he can see the TV. He starts to formulate a list of the news stories he wants CCN to devote the most time to in the hours leading up to the election.

Most importantly, he is setting the media menu for the entire nation for Sunday and Monday. The two days before the election will be crucial leading up to Tuesday morning when the polls open.

Sunday will be more crucial than Monday because the eyes of the whole nation will be home and tuned to their television sets all across America. "Give me a person's eyes and ears for thirty minutes a day, and I will get you their votes," is a quote Rigger Watson has been famous for stating within the circles he travels.

Watson knows he won't get everyone's eyes and ears, but he knows he only needs fifty-one percent of the public to accomplish what he wants. Although CCN won't get fifty-one percent of the television viewership of the United States all on its own, Rigger knows he has very willing accomplices in the three big major television networks who have been in existence for decades, and who have all been very liberal for most of those decades. The only foe he has to worry about is FX News. It is Watson's longtime philosophy that if his people will take off and run in a direction with a news story, everyone else will follow except FX. Then, in their attempt to be fair and balanced, they will even have to follow to some degree to keep from looking as though they are completely off the page on a story.

It is a formula that has worked to precision over the last twenty years. In a recent election for the U.S. Presidency, the head man at CCN was even able to sway those on the right to nominate their weakest candidate to be the representative for the Republican Party, an old, retired, bald man who had a history of straddling the fence on many issues. The Republican nominee was a bad campaigner with a reputation of being a little hotheaded. The nominee from the left, a man with a questionable background, very little experience, and an absolute joke for a running mate had no problem defeating the old war hero Watson personally handpicked to be the Republican Presidential candidate in that election.

Without the help of the liberal left media led by Watson in the primaries, this old war horse from the right wouldn't even have made it to the Republican Convention as a potential Presidential candidate, let alone won the nomination of his party. The likeable old bald guy was such a bad candidate that he even had a difficult time getting reelected to the U.S. Senate in his home state in the last mid-term election. Why the right falls for Watson's tricks is anyone's guess. Rigger Watson lacks in a lot of areas, but one thing he is very good at is making out the media menu for the whole nation on his large yellow note pad. He is so good at it that it has made him one of the most powerful men in America.

Tonight, as he begins to list the news stories he feels are vitally crucial to putting Senator Franson in the White House, Watson stops and takes another look at the TV screen in his office. He grins as he sees a fullscreen picture of Mike Swenson being shown on CCN. As the picture is on the screen, one of Watson's anchormen is reading a list of all the good and charitable things that Michael Fitzgerald Swenson had done in his fifty-two years of life—a graduate of Harvard with a Ph.D. in Philosophy, a clerk to a U.S. Supreme Court Justice, an avid supporter of youth soccer all across America, and last but not least, the longtime campaign manager for U.S. Senator and Presidential candidate Walter Franson.

Watching this, Watson smiles inside as he knows the sympathy he will create with Swenson's apparent suicide will be worth at the minimum three to five percentage points at the polls all by itself. He thinks about setting down the yellow note pad and not even making out his media menu, as Watson himself even calls it. But knowing one can never win by too much, he puts pen to paper and begins his list from top to bottom of what he wants CCN to focus on for the next two days.

The first thing is obviously the Swenson story. Secondly, he writes down how he wants to see the story he has just been informed about by his daughter on the West Coast. The FBI/Flash Freeman story is how Watson writes it down on his list of media menu meals ready to feed the ignorant public. In this story, Rigger wants to see the FBI painted as the bad guys for the profiling of free people as terrorists just because they look like Arabs. Watson wants to see this story spun to make it look like a conservative faction of the FBI concocted the entire terror alert at the Staples Center for the sole purpose of creating enough fear in the citizens of California to cause the state to possibly fall Republican for the first time in recent history in the race for the White House.

The third and forth news stories he lists on his yellow note pad are relatively smaller stories that just need to be twisted and turned a little to be able to be used for his cause. Watson knows that these stories alone will not sway large amounts of people to the left, but when served with the main dishes, they will make very tasty side plates. The first of these two smaller stories Rigger writes down is the one from Baton Rouge, Louisiana where Watson wants attention put on how proficiently the current Democratic-led administration handled a potential terrorist threat to an NFL football game in the Louisiana Superdome. The top man at CCN wants special emphasis put on how the current resident in the White House, who most view as being weak on terrorism, was able to do something George W. Bush could not do, and that is protect the historic city of New Orleans.

The next news story, the forth one on the list behind the Superdome story as he calls it, is one Watson will use to rile the anti-war crowd. CCN will put emphasis on the ever-increasing dangers of being in the Middle East too long by spinning the story of the first attack on a Military base in Kuwait. In large capital letters he writes to stress the fact that seven American soldiers were killed needlessly in Kuwait today. He will also make sure the take from the story is that America must get out of the lands surrounding the Arabian Desert and leave those poor down-trodden and oppressed people to straighten out their own messes without us making them worse. Watson knows this story won't do a lot, but it will raise the emotions and tempers of some on the left who still hate the fact that we as a nation were in Vietnam too long and have been in Iraq and Afghanistan too long. Some of them may not have the gumption to get out and vote on Tuesday until the passion they had in their hippie days of the late sixties and early seventies is woken again by Watson's version of the Kuwait story. "Every vote counts," Watson says audibly as he nears the bottom of his list.

If only I had the power to stop that damned snow storm, Watson thinks as he looks back up at the flat screen television on the wall in his CCN owned townhouse. The network has just broken to a commercial, but before it did, it aired a weather teaser to stay tuned to hear the latest on the winter weather forecast. As he mulls the coming storm around in his mind, he puts his pen to the yellow paper in front of him and prints in very large capital letters at the bottom of the note pad: STRESS THAT THE REPUBLICANS DON'T WANT THE POOR TO VOTE! After he writes these words down, he frowns as he thinks about all the military votes that have already been cast by absentee ballot. *Damn, I wish this early season arctic cold front could stop the overseas mail from arriving.* He shakes his head in disgust as he thinks about the ramifications of more military votes making it to the ballot box than the Democratic Party can get from the unemployed poor people it busses into the precincts. *At least this country doesn't have a damned voter ID card yet,* is Rigger Watson's last thought as he finishes the menu of media information he wants CCN to feed the American people in the forty-eight hours leading up to the election. Watson sets down his large yellow note pad and picks up his half-empty cup of coffee.

Watson takes one sip of his coffee. It's a touch cooler than he likes it so he decides to go to the kitchen and top the cup off with fresh brew. As he gets out of his leather chair he feels a vibration in his shirt pocket followed by one single, loud, high-pitched beep. With his coffee cup that has the words, "If You Aren't Dead—You Still Have a Chance," written on it in his left hand, he reaches in his pocket and pulls out his personal cell phone with his right hand. He has a new text message from his daughter Marcia McNally in Los Angeles. The text message reads: "I am about to go onstage with Flash. Wish me luck. I hope you get to see it Daddy."

In what is Rigger Watson's night of making history the way he wants it made and creating the news in America, he walks out of his office into the living room and turns on the large screen TV that he watches the Washington Redskins play football on when they are not playing at FedEx Field in Landover, Maryland. When the team is playing at home, Watson watches the games from the CCN luxury box suite at the stadium where he always entertains a number of important people, from politicians and celebrities, to Wall Street executives. He switches the channel to MTV and sees that the rock concert in the Staples Center is underway. He stands there for a moment and sees that the warm-up band is just closing. Flash Freeman's band Ax-Handle has yet to make its appearance. *Marcia must have sent me the text a little early,* Watson thinks as he walks on into the kitchen to warm up his coffee with the fresh pot Shirley Hienz just brewed.

After filling his coffee cup, he grabs a half eaten sack of Lays sour cream and onion potato chips off the counter and opens them and eats a handful of chips. His personal cell phone begins to vibrate again, but this time it rings, signaling he has an incoming call. Watson looks down and sees that the number of the person calling him is blocked. The screen just says "Private."

With a good idea of who it is, Watson leaves the kitchen and makes his way to the nearest restroom. He answers the call. "Hello, this is Rigger Watson." He closes the door to the restroom.

"Yes, this is me, but I never got any pictures," a man whose voice Watson recognizes says. "I watched the house just as you instructed, all day long. We never saw the man come or go. Never saw anyone come or go from the front or the back. Not until... you know who's parents got home and opened their garage door and discovered what had happened."

"What?" Watson asks.

"Yeah, I have no idea how the guy did it. It's like Swen... the fag really did hang himself."

"Damn it!" Watson fires back. "No names, you idiot."

"Yeah, I know," the man says, "But..."

Watson cuts in. "The man had to get in there somehow."

"We don't know how. And we watched the house all day."

"Who is *we*?"

"Don't worry, they have no idea I am working for you."

"Damn it, this was our only chance to find out who he is."

"Well, whoever he is, he's good. I don't want him coming after me. Hell, he could kill you and you wouldn't even know he did it."

"I think that is how killing someone is supposed to happen at this level," Watson says sarcastically.

"Yeah, I suppose so. That's why I am only a private eye, I guess."

"Shit! I don't like this."

"Well, it is what it is. That's all I can tell you. I have no idea how he did it. But I was there when the garage door opened. It wasn't pretty either."

"That's enough. I'll talk to you later. Don't call again until I call you," Watson says. He pushes the red button on his phone ending the call. With a worried look on his face, Rigger's appetite for the bag of salty sour cream and onion potato chips he still has in his hand is gone.

Returning to the kitchen, Watson picks up his coffee and puts the chips back on the counter. When he walks back into the living room, Rigger sees Flash Freeman's band is on stage and playing some kind of music he cannot stand. As he stands there listening to the heavy metal band Ax-Handle and sipping his coffee, Watson wonders how the man he hired and paid six million dollars to for the murder of Mike Swenson was able to get in and out of Swenson's parents' house without anyone seeing him. Rigger really wanted to know who the man was, or at least what he looked like. Watson has been doing business with him for nearly two decades.

In a trance, thinking about the mysterious hitman a friend and business associate of Watson's had hooked him up with in 1993 shortly after the death of Deputy White House Counsel Vince Foster, Rigger again wonders if his friend and the hitman were responsible for Foster's apparent suicide. This has always been a question in Watson's mind. Rigger never got a chance to ask his friend about Vince Foster before his friend also died a somewhat mysterious death in 1996 in an airplane crash in the Florida Everglades. In the three years between Foster's death and his friend's death, Watson could never muster up the courage to ask his friend, a man who had made a large fortune trading international currencies, if he had had a hand in Foster's suicide. One of the things that made Watson suspicious was the secret association his friend had with the Clintons.

Feeling a vibration again and then a beep, Watson looks down and sees his daughter has sent him another text, "I'm going on as soon as they finish this song Dad."

To this day, Watson believes his friend was not really on flight 592, the ValuJet that crashed into the Everglades on May 11, 1996, killing all 110 passengers aboard it. Rigger believes someone who looked like his friend was put on the plane in his place, sort of a Manchurian Candidate kind of thing. Everything in Watson believes his old business associate and fellow Democrat is living abroad somewhere on the billions of dollars he made before his supposed death. The idea of doing this same thing has some appeal to Watson, especially in the last few years as FX has gained more of the market share in the news industry. Rigger thinks it would be easy to do. Not as easy for him as his friend, because of the public face the head man at CCN has, but it would still be easy given the international connections a person acquires running the largest news network in the world.

"Hey Shirley, she's coming on now. Get out here!" Watson smiles as he sees his daughter walking out onto the stage of a rock concert that is being broadcast into millions of homes on MTV for millions of people, young and old to see.

"Wow, Rigger, she does look sexy," Shirley comments.

"Yeah, she does," Watson says with a smile. "She looks just like her mother looked when I first met her."

Hienz frowns and shakes her head, knowing if there is any woman other than his daughter that Watson has ever truly loved, it is his first wife. Rigger left his first wife to marry the very wealthy and politically connected woman he is now married to, whom he seldom spends any time with.

"This can't hurt her career getting all this publicity tonight," Shirley says as she is quick to forgive Watson of the comment he didn't even realize had hurt her feelings.

"Yeah, it won't hurt. But I still can't stand that guy's music," Watson replies. "And why does he have to have all those rings in his nose and his ears? He needs a damn haircut too."

Shirley Hienz laughs and then says, "You sound just like someone on the Religious Right, Rigger."

"Religious Right or not, he looks like a little thug, if you ask me."

"Well, Marcia looks great," Hienz remarks, "Sexy, but not too sleazy."

"Yep. Well, I hope this helps her," Watson says. "I've got to get back to work. We've got an election to win."

As soon as he turns away from the TV and returns to his expensive brown leather office chair, a disturbing thought enters into Watson's head. *A Manchurian Candidate? Is that how the man from New York was able to kill Swenson? Did he somehow program Mike to commit suicide?* Rigger Watson's whole body goes numb as he starts to think of what a large can of worms it could be if the hitman from New York is somehow able to gain control of someone's mind without even being present in person. The man Watson hired to watch Swenson's parent's house swore no one came or left all day long, yet Michael Swenson did hang himself in his father's garage. This Pandora's box even scares Rigger Watson.

CHAPTER THIRTY-EIGHT

A Small Flock of Birds

Awake and smiling, but still hidden under the covers of her comfortable king-sized bed, Alexia lays curled up in a ball with her arms wrapped around a big, soft pillow. She is happy for her friend Angie West. In the complete darkness of her business suite on the eleventh floor of the Hotel Gabriel Issy les Moulineax in Paris, Alexia giggles to herself as she tries to return to the dream she was having when Angie called her just a short time ago. It is not working. She is too excited to fall back asleep.

After rolling around some and even attempting to count sheep, Alexia sticks her arm out from under the covers and reaches over in the darkness to the bedside table and finds the remote control for the TV. She turns it on and begins flipping through the channels. There is not much that interests her on the various French and European stations she surfs through. She could watch a news channel, but she is not really ready to wake up and be serious about life yet. A news channel is the one thing that is sure to bring her out of the French fairytale she is still fantasizing that she lives in and back to the real world where she does live.

After switching through over a dozen channels, none of them in English, she lands on a channel that is showing a movie in black and white. Immediately Alexia recognizes the old movie and giggles to herself. It is *Casablanca,* the love story of all love stories, which was set partially in Paris, France. What is so funny to Alexia is that this movie reminds her of the relationship she has with Severo Baptiste; a real, true love that will never die, and yet, may never get to live to its fullest.

As she giggles to herself about the movie *Casablanca,* something makes her sad at the same time she wants to laugh. After watching the part where Humphrey Bogart and Ingrid Bergman are in Paris and in love and all is well, Alexia rolls over and wraps her arms back around the soft pillow she had held close to her all night. With one eye open and the other closed, Alexia tries to watch some more of the movie. She also wants to go back to the dream she was dreaming when Angie West woke her with a phone call. With the TV in the room still on, and both arms wrapped tightly around her silky, soft French pillow, squeezing it as though it was Severo Armand Casimiro Baptiste, Alexia falls back to sleep.

An hour or so later on this morning just two days before a major Presidential election in the United States, Alexia loosens her grip on the pillow and rolls over in bed. She yawns and slowly starts to wake up a second time. The TV is still on and the movie channel that was playing *Casablanca* is now playing another old black and white American classic.

As she rolls around and gets comfortable with a couple of her pillows shoved behind her back next to the headboard so she can sit up and see the TV, Alexia smiles to herself. It has been forever since she has seen the movie that is playing, and it is one of her favorites. It is *Mr. Smith Goes to Washington,* a movie she loved the very first time her father made her watch it when she was just fifteen years old. She was taking a civics class in high school and was asking her father a lot of questions about how the government really works. John Klien, Alexia's father, went out and found a video of the old Jimmy Stewart classic for his daughter, who was a freshman in high school, to watch.

John Klien suggested to Alexia, one of the most popular girls in school, that she invite a number of her friends over to watch the movie as a group, like a class project. This was something his young and prideful daughter would not even think of doing. Inviting a bunch of her hip, top-of-the-social-ladder friends over to watch some old black and white movie made in 1939 was something a fifteen year old Alexia Klien could not bring herself to do.

Finally, after a great deal of coercion from her father, Alexia gave in to his persistence and watched the famous old flick. When she did, she was completely amazed at just how much she liked the movie. She watched it two more times before it had to be returned to

Blockbuster. The third time she even did as her father asked and invited some of her closest friends over and they watched it while laughing and eating popcorn.

Mr. Smith Goes to Washington became one of Alexia's favorite movies of all time. Watching it caused her to want to watch more black and white movies in the years to come. Just a few weeks ago, the busy broadcast journalist missed a luncheon date on a Saturday afternoon with a guy who had asked her out because she got glued to her television watching an old 1931 classic called *Private Lives.* It was actually quite humorous to Alexia—the movie and forgetting the date with someone she didn't really want to go out with anyway. It wasn't very humorous to the guy though.

As she leans back against her pillows in her king-sized bed all alone in the exquisite comfort of a Paris hotel room, Alexia Klien, one of the most recognized faces in the world, now realizes that the old black and white Jimmy Stewart classic she almost never watched, had a great deal of influence in shaping who she became. More precisely, it helped shape what she became. She had not only watched it those three times when her father rented it, but also a number times all by herself while she was in college at the University of Georgia studying broadcast journalism and political science. One of her friends who had watched the old black and white classic with her when they were freshmen gave her a VHS video tape of the movie as a gag gift for a high school graduation present. Funny as that was, it turned out to be one of Alexia's favorite graduation presents.

Jimmy Stewart, who is possibly the greatest American actor of all time and played the lead in *Mr. Smith Goes to Washington,* was absolutely fascinating to a young and idealistic Alexia Klien.

Now, as she watches this great American movie for the first time in well over ten years and for the first time since she has reached the pinnacle of her chosen profession, Alexia realizes the unbelievable truths that this Frank Capra classic tells are still very much a real and scary part of American politics today. Alexia also realizes just how much she has changed since the first time she saw the movie.

Alexia is awake now and not very happy with the ways in which she realizes she has changed. A part of her wishes she could go back to being the innocent child she was when her father first made her sit for two hours and watch *Mr. Smith Goes to Washington.* She sees how she has compromised herself and sold her innocence for success and fame. This is the very thing that Jimmy Stewart's character Jefferson Smith did not do when faced with the same types of choices in the movie. Jefferson Smith does not heed to the pressures of success over substance in the 1939 classic, and that was what made this movie so special to Alexia when she was just a fifteen year old freshman in high school.

Early on this Sunday morning as she sits upright in her big, comfortable bed in the plush Paris hotel room watching the incredible old black and white movie that helped shape her life, Alexia goes over in her mind the things she experienced in the past twenty-four hours. She reflects on running into the mysterious redhead at the fashion boutique, the very same woman she had seen before with Senator Franson in Washington D.C., seeing the Middle Eastern man with the little black attaché case that turned out to be some kind of a small laptop computer with who knows what on it, meeting the sweet and wonderful Amaya Blazi, her brother and Matthew James, and the inspiring ride she shared with the three of them into the historic French city from the airport, and most definitely, the text messages and the phone conversation she had with Severo Baptiste as she got to hear his voice for the first time in over a year, then finally, as night fell, seeing again and speaking with the mysterious woman in front of a French bistro as the woman denied that she had ever been to Washington D.C.

Now wide awake, Alexia realizes that this old movie, which is funny in so many parts, but also very serious just under the surface of the humor, has caused her to lose the fun loving and happy feeling she woke up with. Alexia sees she is living right in the middle of a modern day *Mr. Smith Goes to Washington.* Only her life is not a movie. *Are you going to do what is right?* A voice inside her head asks.

Laying there in the near darkness of her hotel room under a pile of covers, Alexia watches the movie all the way to the end. She then points the remote control towards the television and switches the channel to what she knows will be a BBC news channel. When she does, Alexia cannot believe the news story that she sees the BBC is reporting on. She knows it is true, but she just can't believe it.

Mike Swenson has committed suicide.

———

The day is still dark as the sun has yet to peek up from the horizon to the east that is the two great deserts of Southern California. The seats are very comfortable in the Gulfstream V jet that the two Texas FBI men are strapping themselves into as they prepare to fly back to Dallas early on this Sunday morning. Agents Wikett and Swanson ready themselves for takeoff as Bureau man Billy Joe Gasperson is still sound asleep in his room at the Hilton in Los Angeles. He is waiting to fly back to the Lone Star State later in the week, when he will accompany fellow FBI agents Danny Trey Craddick and Rance Patton, who are both injured. More than likely the body of the deceased federal lawman Antonio Ramirez Garcia will be sent back home on that same flight.

Looking out the small round window of the slender sleek jet into the early morning darkness and thinking about everything that took place the day before in California, and also what took place in his own personal life spiritually, Big John Swanson looks over to his friend and fellow FBI agent Chace Wikett and asks, "Isn't it amazing over the centuries how so many men have thought they were smarter than God?"

"It sure is, John."

"I know I did," states Swanson. "For a long time."

"There are still a lot of people who think they are smarter than God," Wikett replies as his cell phone begins to vibrate and then ring in his shirt pocket.

"That's for sure," Swanson says as he looks back out the window of the plane. "The world is full of 'em."

As the government-owned Gulfstream V begins to taxi towards an open runway at the Los Angeles International Airport about an hour before the sun rises above the great Mojave Desert to the east of L.A., Wikett quickly pulls his phone from his pocket and answers it. It is Martin MacKuenn in Washington D.C. "How are you doing this morning, Chace?"

"I'm barely awake. I'm a little short on sleep, if you know what I mean."

"It was a long night," comments MacKuenn.

"Did you sleep at all last night?"

MacKuenn laughs. "I live in a state of short-on-sleep."

"Yeah, I guess you do," Wikett replies. "Your plane couldn't have left L.A. until after midnight."

"I slept on the plane."

"That's what I'm fixing to do. I've got tickets to the Cowboys game today, so as soon as I get home, my sons and I are headed to the stadium."

"I'll be watching that game here at home and pulling for the Redskins all the way."

"You're from Wisconsin, I would've thought you'd be a Packers fan," Wikett replies.

"Oh, I am. And next week, I'll be hoping they beat your Cowboys."

"Well Marty, you could still cheer for the Cowboys this week."

"Living in D.C., I've got to pull for the home team."

"You want to wager a couple of steak dinners on the two games?" Wikett asks, "This week's and next?"

"Sure, why not," MacKuenn replies.

"With his first real smile in twenty-four hours, Chace turns to Swanson and says, "Marty's going to take us both to the Ruth's Chris Steakhouse next time we're back east, Big John"

"Hey, I'm not that confidant of the Redskins and the Packers," MacKuenn fires back as he hears what Wikett told Swanson. "I might be able to splurge for the Sirloin Stockade if I lose both games."

"Do they even have a Sirloin Stockade in D.C.?" Wikett asks.

"I don't know. But if the Cowboys beat the Redskins and the Packers, I'll find one."

Both men laugh.

"So Chace, speaking of the Cowboys, are you going to take that job Jerry Jones has offered you? This is all off the record of course." Martin MacKuenn is one of the few people in Washington D.C. that Wikett would even consider discussing his other opportunities with. Wikett and MacKuenn had been through hell together on more than one occasion in the time they both spent with the CIA in East Africa.

"After what I have experienced out here, and being around more of the Bart Kennedy types we have these days in the Bureau, it is very tempting," Wikett answers as the twelve passenger aircraft he is aboard waits on the runway for clearance to take off.

"I'm not trying to run you out of the business, but boy I think you ought to think real hard on it. It would be a great opportunity for you," MacKuenn replies. "I know if Daniel Snyder offered me a position like that, I'd jump all over it."

"I thought you liked the Packers better than the Redskins. Wouldn't you want a position like that in Green Bay instead?"

"Are you kidding? That is a great place to visit in the spring and the summer and early fall, but you aren't going to get me to live there in the winter," MacKuenn says. "That has to be the coldest place on God's green earth."

Wikett laughs.

"Chace, it's below feezing in Green Bay over a hundred days a year usually," replies the man from the Badger state. "I'm not moving up there any time soon."

"Back to business, were those the two guys from Yemen that we caught with the detonators last night?" Wikett asks.

"From what we can tell they were," MacKuenn answers. "We've got people flying into L.A. from Mexico City today who had a better look at them than you guys did."

"Man, I think it was crazy to let those two Muslims cross the border like we did. It's like playing Russian roulette, if you ask me."

"Yes it is, Chace. That's why I'd be taking that deal Jerry Jones offered you, if it was me. If Franson wins this election, which it looks like he will, things aren't going to get any better in either one of our agencies."

"Well, Marty, if I see Jerry today at the game I'll tell him I will take the job on one condition," Wikett says. "That you move to Dallas and be my right-hand man. I won't tell him you bet on the Packers and Redskins against America's team though."

MacKuenn laughs and allows, "If you get that done, I'll be right there with you cheering for the team with the blue stars on their helmets."

"I'll see what I can do," Wikett says as he laughs. "Hey I think we're about to take off. I better get off the phone."

"Yeah, I need to get on my way to church too. Take care, Chace. Oh, and if the Cowboys win, ribeyes at Ruth's Chris Steakhouse it'll be for you and Big John."

"I'll hold you to it, Marty."

"Adios, Amigo."

"Later, Marty," Wikett says as he laughs to himself about the way his Washington D.C. friend and Wisconsin native mispronounced the words 'adios' and 'amigo'. Chace thought Martin sounded almost as bad as Matt Damon did in the recent remake of the great John Wayne western, *True Grit.*

———

As Shirley Hienz takes her coat off to hang it up in her office at CCN, her cell phone begins to ring. She looks down at the caller ID. It is Jim Edwards calling from Boston, Massachusetts. Shirley answers the call. "Hello, Jim. How's your cheerleader?"

"Fine," he says. Hienz can sense a tone of seriousness in Jim's voice that is not usually there.

"What's up, Jim?"

"Are you alone?"

"Yeah, I'm in my office."

"Well, there are some real unusual rumors going around up here in Boston."

"Like what?"

"The things surrounding the death of Swenson," Edwards says.

"That's normal. Isn't it?"

"Some of what people are saying is normal, but then there's something about a mysterious phone call that Swenson got from a private number. It was the last number on the caller ID of his cell phone that he talked to before his death. An inside source I have in the Boston Police Department told me he has heard that the private number of the last person to call Swenson had originated from an international cellular number traced back to China."

"To China?"

"Yeah, and it even gets wilder than that. There is no record of Swenson ever calling that number in the past or ever receiving a call from that number before," Edwards pauses. "And the call lasted over twenty minutes. After the call Swenson never made or received any more calls, even though numerous people had tried to call him. And the authorities say that according to their records, Swenson's phone is the only number the phone from China has ever called in the United States."

"What?" asks Shirley Hienz as she tries to process everything she is hearing.

"Oh, and China denies that the call came from there," adds Edwards. "They deny the number even exists."

"Have you told Rigger all this?"

"Yeah, but when I talked to him this morning, he said it all sounded like a mix-up to him and not very viable." Edwards pauses, "Well, he also said he wasn't real concerned about rumors. Then he told me to have a good time and asked me if I had seen the polls this morning. It was just a strange phone call. It was like Rigger was totally disinterested in the actual suicide."

Shirley Hienz sits down behind her desk and her legs and arms begin to tremble. She remembers the feeling she had the night before when Rigger Watson showed no remorse for what had happened with Senator Franson's campaign manager. At the moment, she can't bring herself to say anything to Edwards. She sits in her CCN office chair in fear as she continues to protect the man she thinks she loves.

"I don't know, Shirley. I know Rig never liked Swenson, but..." Edwards says. "It gave me some real bad vibes, if you know what I mean."

"He has a lot on his plate today, Jim. You were probably just out too late last night," Hienz replies, not letting on that she feels the same bad vibes.

"I suppose you're right. I mean it ain't like Rigger really cares that much for anyone. Sorry, Shirley. You know what I mean."

"I'm afraid I do Jim, only too well. Hey, you have fun up there, and don't do anything I wouldn't do."

Jim laughs and says, "I'll bet I already have."

"See you when you get back," Hienz replies as she turns on her computer.

"Yeah. Thanks for your ear, Shirley."

"Any time, Jim," Hienz says as she ends the call with her hands shaking and her heart in her throat. She knows what she is thinking is true. She is startled when her phone immediately rings again. It is Watson. "Hello," she says.

"Are you here yet?" Watson asks. He left the townhouse to come into CCN headquarters at six A.M., a full hour before Shirley Hienz even got up.

Today and tomorrow, the Sunday and Monday before a U.S. Presidential election, are what Rigger Watson lives for. There are so many stories and leads coming into the studio via email, cell phone, faxes, and text messages. It is almost impossible to keep up with all that can possibly affect the outcome of so many different crucial political races across America.

Watson's ability to keep tabs on just how to spin all of them to create the desired outcome for the Democratic Party is a set of skills unequaled by anyone else in the business. He is an absolute genius at this. It has been said by his friends and his foes that he is the master manipulator. Today and tomorrow are two days that he will be at the cutting edge of every story that leaves CCN and lands on the television sets of the American public. It is a game at which he is both experienced and gifted. Where Watson acquired these special skills is questionable at best. The manner in which he uses them should give some indication as to their origin.

"Yeah, I just got to my office," Hienz tells her boss as she opens an email from her sister.

"Come down here and take a look at some poll numbers we are just getting. It's awesome. I don't think I've ever seen something turn around so quickly," Watson pauses. He then goes on to say, "We don't have the full eight point lead back so it's not like we've got it won yet, but we've got the momentum turned around and a couple of points back."

"Really," Shirley comments to sound interested even though her mind is somewhere else.

"Yeah, and half the nation isn't even awake yet."

"I'll be right down as soon as I get a donut and some coffee," Hienz replies as she reads the email from her sister.

"Hey, grab me a cup of coffee and a donut too, one of those

chocolate ones with nuts," Watson says.

"I will."

"I'm telling you, Honey, I really think Walter is headed to the oval office. I was a little worried yesterday."

"I hope you're right."

"Now if this damn snow storm will just speed up a little more and hit tonight instead of Tuesday, I know he'll win," Watson asserts with a bit of a laugh.

Shirley Hienz stays silent.

"If the weather doesn't stop us, you and I may be the first ones to sleep in the Lincoln bedroom under Walter's reign," the CEO of CCN states.

"I know it's sure colder out there than it was yesterday," Hienz replies as she thinks about how when it comes right down to it, Watson's wife will probably be the one with him in the Lincoln bedroom.

"They say it's moving faster than they thought it was going to," Watson replies. "They think the bad part will be past Ohio and Pennsylvania for sure by Monday night."

"That's good."

"Hurry up with the coffee and donuts, Honey," Watson commands. "I'm hungry. In fact, bring me two of those chocolate ones with nuts. See you in a minute, I've got to get off the phone."

"I'll be right down there, Rig," Hienz says as the call ends. She feels a little queasy knowing what she knows she knows about Watson. She also realizes she can't tell anyone about it, even if she wanted to.

Still looking at the email from her sister asking her what her plans are for Thanksgiving, Hienz sits and stares at the computer screen for nearly a minute with questions about Watson's innocence and guilt running all through her head. She shakes off the thoughts about Watson's guilt and sends her sister a reply stating that she would love to fly to Chicago to spend the holiday with family. In all the years Hienz has been involved with Watson, she has never spent a holiday with him unless you count Halloween, but never a real holiday.

After putting her computer in hibernate mode, she gets up and walks over to the window where she stares out at the wind blowing through the trees that are just outside her office. After watching a small flock of birds fly from one tree to another and then back to the first tree, Shirley Hienz turns around and walks to the door of her office. She opens it and steps out into the hall. She stops for a moment and thinks about how Rigger Watson is able to make the people of America do the same thing she just watched those tiny little birds do in the face of an approaching winter storm. They flew from one tree to another, and then back to the original tree they were in, all in a matter of seconds. She shakes her head in disgust with her own life and then heads down the hall to get her boss and herself coffee and donuts.

CHAPTER THIRTY-NINE

The Tea Party Candidate

For the second day in a row the weather is again nearly perfect in Paris, France. It is just a few minutes past noon this Sunday, and slightly warmer than normal, with temperatures hovering right around sixty. The sky is mostly clear, with a soft, gentle breeze barely blowing out of the southwest. The streets are full of tourists and travelers. As she gets out of a taxi in the center of the city, Alexia Klien thinks that a more fascinating and romantic place on earth could not be found.

Yesterday, when she had some time all to herself, she chose to do a little shopping on the Avenue des Champs-Élysées. Today, all she wants to do is take a slow stroll along the banks of the Seine River. Her two o'clock interview with Prince Charles has been pushed back to three, giving Alexia a short window of time to kill. Against the wishes of those in charge at the CCN Paris Bureau, she grabbed a cab to take a short ride from the location of the interview to the waters of the romantic river.

As she walks alone along one of the most beautiful rivers in the world, she can see the Eiffel Tower to the south and west of her. A large riverboat has just passed by and is slowly floating under one of the many scenic bridges. The boat is full of tourists laughing and talking and taking pictures of everything. Alexia knows it would be so easy to lose herself in this atmosphere, to say the heck with the world and her career and just live life one day at a time in this city. Her mind is filled with thoughts of the man she will see tonight for the first time in over three years.

She has so many questions she wants to ask him. Twice this morning she has tried to call him, and both times she got his answering service. She never left a message. He has sent her one text message which she received while she was in the shower. It said, "Alexia darling, I love you. I can't wait to see you." She texted him back two times and never got a response. He had said he was in the Alps skiing. Even as beautiful as it is in Paris this afternoon, she wishes she was on a ski lift with him. Alexia wonders why it is that the closer the time comes to seeing him again, the more she misses him and the more she wants to see him. As much as she wants to ask Severo about the mysterious woman from yesterday with the long, red hair, the woman he told her could be very dangerous, what she really wants to ask him about is what he thinks the future holds for him and her. As Alexia walks and dreams of what might be, her cell phone rings. It is time to catch a cab back to do the interview Rigger Watson sent her to Europe to do.

———

In Dallas, Texas, it is fifty-three degrees and mostly cloudy, with a stiff breeze coming out of the north as FBI agents Wikett and Swanson walk to their vehicle in a parking garage at DFW Dallas/Fort Worth International Airport. The airport is moderately busy this morning with people coming and going from the Metroplex, as the Dallas/Ft. Worth area is called. The Metroplex is the fastest growing metropolitan area in the United States.

A number of the people arriving on flights this morning at DFW are wearing the burgundy and gold colors of the Washington Redskins. Each time Wikett sees someone in their Redskins garb his desire to see his family increases. He can't wait to wrap his arms around his sixteen year old daughter, wish her happy birthday from yesterday, hug and kiss his wife, and grab his two sons and head back out the door to go watch the Cowboys hopefully defeat the Washington Redskins.

"Chace, I talked to my wife back there while we were waiting at baggage claim, and she is going to come by your house and pick me up so you don't have to drop me off," Big John Swanson tells Wikett.

"That's great. It'll give me a little more time at home before the boys and I need to leave for the game."

"I thought you would like that. Plus, after talking with her, my wife decided we might try and make the late service at the church your family goes to."

"You'll like it, John," Wikett replies. "But I'd better warn you, it is going to be quite a bit livelier than those old Lutheran churches that you said you grew up in."

"I figured that. Actually, my wife has been to your church a few times," Swanson says. "I never knew it until this morning. I guess she has been going some when I've been gone."

"That's good, John," Wikett allows with previous knowledge of what he's just heard. Chace even knows that Swanson's wife had asked his wife to pray for John's salvation a few months back.

As they reach Wikett's personal vehicle, a three-quarter-ton dark gray Dodge Mega Cab pickup, his cell phone begins to ring. When he looks at the caller I.D. he sees it is Martin MacKuenn in Washington D.C. calling back. Chace throws the keys to Swanson and tells him, "You drive, this might be important."

Wikett sets his suitcase and computer bag in the big back seat of the truck and answers his phone, "Yeah Marty, you wantin' to back out on that bet?"

"No, the bet's still on," MacKuenn replies. "What I called about is, when I got out of church about ten minutes ago, I found out that over two weeks ago the FBI on the West Coast had a tip that they needed to look into the activities of a wealthy Muslim in Los Angeles. A movie producer. But Bart Kennedy stopped the investigation because the wealthy Hollywood celebrity has been a big contributor to the Democratic Party over the last ten years."

"That figures," Wikett responds as he shakes his head and pulls the passenger side door to his pickup shut.

Able to overhear what MacKuenn just said, Swanson looks over at Wikett and frowns. John then turns the key and fires up the 6.7 liter Cummins turbo diesel engine and begins to back out of the parking spot. As he backs up, Swanson reaches down and shuts off the radio so Wikett can still hear the man from the Department of Homeland Security.

"It gets worse than that," MacKuenn says. "We traced the purchase of the bomb-making materials that were found inside the Staples Center yesterday to two employees of the very same movie producer. Two employees of his that he has been paying about ten times what they would normally get paid in Hollywood for what they do. All three of those men are of Arab descent and they all have ties to the Muslim Brotherhood. The whole thing stinks, if you ask me."

"It's sad to say, Marty, but none of this surprises me."

"It seems like Bart Kennedy felt it was in the best interests of the Democratic Party to not disrupt the money flow from the Middle East coming through the movie producer. Millions of dollars, from what we have been able to piece together. It's all a bunch a liberal bullshit I tell you." The tone in MacKuenn's voice is one of anger.

"I'll agree with that. Politically correct B.S. is what it is," Wikett states. "We got any proof that will hold up against Kennedy?"

"Nothing with teeth... at least not yet. Right now they just say its insubstantial evidence and pass the blame on down the line to someone not as important as a Kennedy," MacKuenn says. "By the time we have something on him, they might actually move him somewhere else. Promote him. Shoot, Chace, if Franson wins this election, Bart Kennedy may end up being your boss or my boss."

"No, that won't happen. I'll go work for Jerry Jones first," Wikett states. "I might anyway, if Franson wins."

MacKuenn laughs and then jokingly asks, "Chace, you know we work for the people not for the President, don't you?"

"What do you think has kept me where I've been the last few years with this left-wing communist liberal we have in office right now? It's been the people, and only the people."

"Me too," MacKuenn says. "It's been damn tough though. A couple of times I thought they were going to run me out of Washington because I didn't line up with the way they do things."

"I'm glad they didn't, Marty," Wikett states. "I don't know who else could have run that show like you did yesterday in L. A."

"Thanks, Chace," MacKuenn replies. "Well, we're pulling in our driveway. Have fun at the game."

"I will. Take care. And thanks, Marty."

"You too, Chace. Tell John adios."

"Will do. But when you take me out for steaks at Ruth's Chris in D.C., remind me to teach you how to pronounce adios correctly. You sound like a Yankee."

"I am a Yankee."

"Sorry Marty, I can't help you with that."

Both men laugh.

"I'll let you go now," Wikett says.

"Adios, Chace," MacKuenn says with a very distinct *'Wisconsin'* accent this time as he gets off the call.

———

The man across from Alexia politely gets up and reaches his hand out and offers it to her to shake. She cannot believe the time is up and she is done speaking with him. The sixty minutes that were agreed upon seemed to fly by, and there were so many more subjects to discuss. But people of his stature normally have very rigid schedules to keep, and then must be on their way. She shakes his hand and thanks him and says goodbye.

Alexia tells those working with her that she needs some time to herself to compose her thoughts. The CCN Paris News crew who are at the secret location where the interview just concluded back off of their star and give her what she has asked for. She feels she has just finished what has been the most important assignment she has ever been given as a broadcast journalist. Before doing the interview, Alexia did not feel this way. She has just sat across from a man some believe may become very powerful in the near future. For an hour the very attractive and lively American reporter sat and questioned a man she really wasn't all that interested in even meeting before today, let alone interviewing.

Now, after the time she has spent sitting across from him with the CCN cameras rolling and bright lights shining on both him and her, Alexia realizes she has been mesmerized by the soft, gentle, and seemingly thoughtful responses of Prince Charles of Wales. She cannot help but think to herself how she had so seriously underestimated this man's persona.

Never before has she interviewed someone who seemed to have the right answer for every single question she asked. In the past, Alexia had conducted interviews of people who always seemed to give the correct answer to every question. But she could always tell when those types of individuals were being phony and just saying what they felt the public wanted to hear, pure politicians. There was something distinctly different in this interview this afternoon. When Prince Charles gave answers to difficult questions that Alexia might normally disagree with, there was something about him that made her believe what he was saying. Also, he seemed to know the questions she would ask before she ever asked them, yet none of the interview was scripted. This was an interview set up by CCN to have no boundaries. CCN Network News broadcast journalist Alexia Klien was free to ask whatever she wished, which is what she did.

What stunned her the most was the way in which he answered her questions about the thousands of years of turmoil in the Middle East. The solutions Prince Charles had on how to solve these long-standing issues between the Arabs and the Jews nearly convinced Alexia that peace really could be attained in an area of the world she thought would never see true peace. Now leaving the room where the interview took place, she realizes she felt a type of hope she had never really felt before for the world she lives in while listening to the man she just interviewed. Yet there is something about that hope that did not seem right to her as she thinks back on it. She cannot quite put her finger on it.

Yesterday, when she rode with the three American Christians from the Charles de Gaulle International Airport to her hotel, she had felt a peace and a hope also, a peace and hope that was different than what she felt right after her interview with the Prince of Wales. She realizes the peace and hope she felt with Amaya and Jeff Blazi and Matthew James was a more real and genuine peace and hope than what she felt while interviewing Prince Charles. Alexia wonders just what it was she felt that was so overwhelming while sitting across from a man she previously had very little respect or admiration for.

Walking down a hall to leave the building, Alexia knows she must redirect her focus to prepare herself for her next interview with French President Nicolas Sarkozy and his wife Carla Bruni. This is what she has been looking forward to ever since the plan was put together ten days ago for her to fly to Paris to do the various European interviews. She will be traveling by herself to the Presidential Palace for her next assignment in the back of a CCN limousine. Because of the time constraints between the two Sunday afternoon interviews, the network sent different crews to work each location.

As she leaves the plain red brick building where the interview with Prince Charles took place and walks out into the open air, an imaginary weight seems to lift itself off of her shoulders. Her head is much clearer and her thoughts are not as heavy. Alexia suddenly feels as though there were forces at work within that structure foreign to any forces she has ever experienced before. With chills now running up and down her spine, she climbs into the limo that will transport her to her next assignment. For some reason, Alexia feels that the interview she just finished with the man from England may have more far-reaching implications than any interview she has ever done. She does not know why; there is something about it she cannot understand or comprehend. She thinks it must have something to do with Prince Charles's ideas for peace in the Middle East. She has never experienced anything in an interview even close to what she experienced this afternoon.

As the French limousine slowly makes its way through the heavy Paris traffic, Alexia hopes the next interview will leave her a little less internally intense and emotionally drained. That maybe it will be more playful and spontaneous. As she thinks about it, the interview with Prince Charles itself was not really that stressful, it was actually quite relaxing. But then after she left the interview, she realized that she had not been the one who had steered the direction the conversation went. He did. Alexia Klien cannot remember ever being the one who was led in an interview that she performed. It just simply never has happened before.

Now, all alone in the back of the limo on her way to meet with the President of France and his beautiful wife, Alexia is still unable to shake her last assignment out of her mind. She closes her eyes and says, "OK, God. Help me make sense of this."

Immediately she opens her eyes, surprised with what she has just done. Alexia tries to think of the last time she ever asked God for anything. The only thing she can come up with is when she was twelve years old and the family dog, a Basset hound named Sparkles that she grew up with, was run over out in front of their house. She prayed to God that He would bring Sparkles back to life. When it did not happen, she can remember getting very mad at God. This tragic event was not made any easier as it happened at a time in Alexia's young life when her parents were having troubles in their marriage.

Riding down a busy street in the historic city of Paris, Alexia asks herself if it has really been over twenty years since she has called out to God for help. As she sits captivated by this thought, her cell phone vibrates. She looks down to see she has just received a text message from Severo Baptiste. She opens it. It reads, "Darling Alexia, I hope to make it in to Paris in time for dinner tonight. Maybe as early as eight depending on my flight. See you then."

Her thoughts are now on him.

———

With five inches of fresh, powdery snow blowing about because of a harsh twenty-mile-an-hour wind out of the northwest cutting through everything in its path, the conditions on the flat, wide-open plains an hour east of Denver, Colorado are not pleasant. With two hundred head of hungry broken-mouth cows still to feed, Kris Glover and his son Kole are in a hurry. But the weather conditions have made it tough to be in a hurry. If they can get the rest of their morning chores finished in the next forty-five minutes, Kris and Kole will still be able to get cleaned up and make it into church with the rest of the family.

These two hundred head of old Black Angus cows that are nearing the end of their usefulness are all that remains on the list of unfed animals on a Colorado ranch that has been in the Glover family for five generations. That is, if you count Kole's newly born son Gene, named after his grandfather who passed away a year and a half ago from cancer. Little Gene David Glover is only three weeks old. Kole and his wife have been married for two years. They met in college, and as soon as both of them graduated they tied the knot. When they got married it was their hope and that of everyone else in the family that Kole's grandfather Gene would live long enough to see a grandchild born. Unfortunately, he did not.

Gene Allen Glover had battled lung cancer for three years, in and out of remission while flying from one specialist to the next. About three months before he passed away, while standing in the walkway of the big wooden barn that his grandfather had built back in 1927, Gene threw his hands up and said, "No more. I'm tired of all these doctors and drugs. If God wants me to come home, why should I fight it?" It wasn't more than ninety days until his son Kris dug a hole in the ground out east of the home place, and the family laid the man they all loved to rest. The Glover ranch has a family cemetery on it, down in a low valley along a pond and a creek. It is surrounded by cottonwood trees that have been on the place longer than the Glovers have.

The little cemetery is the resting place for all the Glovers, except two. Gene's uncle Charlie was lost at sea in 1942 when the aircraft carrier he was aboard, the U.S.S. Yorktown, was sunk after being hit by two Japanese aerial torpedoes during the Battle of Midway. Twenty-four years later in 1966, the Glover family lost another member to the defense of the great nation in which they live when Gene's younger brother, also named Charlie after the uncle he never knew, was shot out of the sky in a helicopter he was piloting over the jungles of Vietnam. The bodies of these two fallen American war heroes were never found. The Glover's all feel their land has been paid for twice, once with hard work and money, and a second time with blood.

This morning, Kris is driving a large four-wheel-drive John Deere tractor with a fifteen hundred pound round bale of alfalfa hay on the front loader and another bale on the three-point hitch on the back of the tractor. Kole, Kris's only son, is all bundled up to brave the harsh winter winds and a temperature that is not supposed to get out of the single digits today. Kole is riding ahead of his dad to open and close the gates they have to go through to feed this last set of black cows. He is also checking the older cows from just above ground level on the young horse he is riding. The two men are doing their morning duties as American ranchers, producers of beef for men and women and children all across the United States and the world.

After he opens a large green metal gate for his father to drive through, Kole chases some cows out of the way of the tractor on the little gray gelding they call Barney. One of Kris's good friends, Tim Tillord from Glenrock, Wyoming, gave Kole the horse as a college graduation present. Inside the warm tractor, Kris reaches up to switch the radio from FM to AM. Kole had fed the livestock the day before when Kris and his wife attended a Tea Party rally in Colorado Springs for a good friend of theirs who is running for the open U.S. Senate seat. The station Kole had been listening to was not to the liking of his fifty-two year old father. *Rock-n-roll is nothing like it was in the 70's and 80's,* Kris thinks, as he searches for 850 KOA on the AM dial. The 50,000-watt talk radio station out of Denver is what the older Glover wants to listen to this morning.

Less than a minute after Kris switches the radio to the powerful voice of the Rocky Mountains, a special report comes across KOA. All other broadcasting is suspended as some very tragic news is reported from a location about four hours west of where the Glover family lives and ranches. When Kris hears the special news bulletin come through the expensive Pioneer speakers his son had mounted in the tractor, he pushes in on the clutch and sits there in shock with the big green tractor just idling. The old wily cows quickly dart around Kole and the young horse he is mounted on to steal some hay off the front and the rear of the tractor.

Outside the tractor in the cold, a puzzled Kole Glover sits on the gray gelding and stares at his dad. He cannot understand why his father has just stopped the tractor and does not seem to be moving forward to the area south of a grove of evergreen trees where they normally roll out the round bales to feed the cows when the weather is bad.

KOA is reporting that Kathy Whittenburg, the wife of a close friend of Kris Glover's, has been killed in a plane crash on this very cold and brisk morning. Just last night in Colorado Springs after the political rally sponsored by the Tea Party, Kris and his wife Christine had gone out to dinner with Craig and Kathy Whittenburg. Kris Glover and fellow Colorado rancher Craig Whittenburg had been college roommates almost thirty-five years ago at the Lamar Colorado Community Junior College. For two solid years the pair of reckless young men ran around and did everything together. They drank more beer, got in more fights, and chased more girls than any other pair of ranch kids at the two year learning institution in the small town of Lamar in Southeastern Colorado. When his father Gene handed him the bill for the pickups and horse trailers he tore up while raising hell when he was supposed to be studying in those two years, Kris decided he would maybe just come home and work on the ranch rather than put his father through two more years of expenditures at a four-year school. Gene Allen Glover thought that was a wise decision, given the cost of the education that he himself was getting raising his son Kris.

Tired of the wind and the snow blowing directly into his face, Kole has turned and trotted his colt on down the pickup trail that leads to the grove of evergreens about a quarter of a mile from where his father and the tractor sit with the hay. He is in need of some relief from the weather himself. All two hundred black cows have now encircled the large green tractor loaded with their ton and a half of breakfast. Kris sits stunned to hear that the woman who he knows very well, a woman who had come out of practically nowhere to take a sizeable lead in the race for Colorado's open U.S. Senate seat, has been killed.

The report that has come across the "Blow Torch of the Rockies" as 850 KOA is called, says that Mrs. Kathy Whittenburg of Rocky Ford, Colorado and eleven other people in the private twelve-passenger aircraft they were flying in has gone down in a very remote part of the Rocky Mountains. The plane was lost off of radar early in the morning and the wreckage has just been spotted by satellite imaging on the side of some very steep cliffs on a tall mountain southwest of Buena Vista, Colorado. The report says that with the weather, it may be a week or more before authorizes can reach the site.

Kris Glover sits in shock in his sixty thousand dollar John Deere tractor as he feels tears begin to well up in his eyes for the loss of his good friend's wife. He left his cell phone in the house this morning on its charger, and he can't even call Craig to console him. He wishes he could, even though something tells him it might be too early for that. Sitting there in a trance looking out at the hungry cows all around him, Kris hears more details about the people who had been on the flight with Kathy Whittenburg during a last weekend charge to win a very coveted U.S. Senate seat back into Republican hands. The special report states that it is rumored that there were two very famous Colorado athletes who were also flying on the small jet this morning en route to Grand Junction. They were all planning to attend a midmorning prayer breakfast with a large group of Christian conservatives that had gathered from all across the western slope to show their support for Mrs. Whittenburg.

The names of the pilots and the others have not been released yet. But word was that one of the athletes was a former professional football player who had become very active in conservative politics in Colorado after retiring from a long and successful career with the Denver Broncos. If this is the case, it will be a big blow to the entire state of Colorado on many different fronts.

Speculation on who the other athlete was points in the direction of a gold medal Olympic skier who recently switched from being a Democrat and lifelong pro-choice activist to becoming a conservative Republican, and standing firmly against the idea that a woman has the right to have an abortion. She made this major change in her attitude towards abortion after she lost a second straight child to a miscarriage in less than a year. If the rumors are true, the pro-life movement nationwide will mourn the loss of this young woman who had also just recently committed her life to Christ.

Kathy Whittenburg was without a doubt one of the strongest Tea Party candidates to emerge in this year's election cycle. She was a superb speaker with a Yale Law degree, an attractive woman in her late forties and a mother of three sons and a daughter. She had never run for public office before this, but she had been very active in politics on the local and state levels in Colorado. Recently, she just represented a large group of ranches and farmers pro bono in a legal battle against the federal government in a case where a large portion of privately held land in Southeastern Colorado faced annexation. The case gained national attention because of the efforts of Mrs. Whittenburg in defeating the U.S. Government. Today, the Tea Party, Republicans, and conservatives everywhere have suffered a severe blow. Many thought that with her Yale Law degree and her personality, the sky was the limit for Kathy Whittenburg's political aspirations. Rush Limbaugh had tagged her as the second coming of Margaret Thatcher.

Wiping a tear off of his cheek with his red neckerchief, Kris Glover gets a hold of his composure. He looks around to see where his son Kole is. When he doesn't see him, he slowly lets out on the clutch of the tractor to continue on to the spot up by the evergreens. As he gets closer to the grove of trees, he sees Kole is working his young horse in some tiny circles attempting to teach the colt something and stay warm himself. With the snow blowing sideways everywhere except on the south side of the four long rows of evergreens that were planted by Kris's father Gene in the 1970's, trees that are now all twenty feet tall or taller, Kris Glover rolls out the two bales of second cutting alfalfa to feed the cows that feed his family.

CHAPTER FORTY

Birds of a Feather Flock Together

"I thank both of you so much for allowing me into your home to do this. It was such a pleasure. And it was an even greater pleasure meeting the two of you," Alexia tells French President Nicolas Sarkozy and his beautiful wife Carla Bruni as the three of them sit in the room inside the French Presidential Palace where Alexia's forty-minute interview of them has just concluded.

"Oh, it has been our pleasure," Carla Bruni replies. "Hasn't it, Dear?" she asks her husband.

"It definitely has been," Sarkozy states, "Very enjoyable."

As the members of the CCN Network News crew hurry to put up their cameras, lights, and other filming gear, to prepare to leave the Presidential Palace as quickly as they can out of courtesy for their hosts, Alexia says, "I feel like I could talk to both of you all evening. But I suppose I need to be letting you go. I'm sure you have plans."

"Yes, we do have plans," Bruni responds as she looks over to her husband, "And you are invited to stay and join us in those plans."

Nicolas Sarkozy follows his wife's wishes up with, "Yes, you must stay for dinner tonight. We are having a few people over. Not a big party, just a small group of our closest friends."

Knowing it would be incredibly foolish and impolite to turn down an offer like this, Alexia smiles as thoughts of Severo Baptiste, the man she is supposed to meet later tonight for dinner, come into her mind for the first time in an hour. Caught between two things she really desires to do and knowing it will be nearly impossible to gracefully turn down the French President's invitation to dinner, Alexia hesitates before she answers.

Recognizing the look of indecision on her face, President Sarkozy looks over to his wife and says, "Something tells me she may already have plans for the evening." He then looks back over to Alexia and asks, "Am I right? Have we interrupted something you already had planned?"

"Well, yes I was... I am supposed to meet an old friend for drinks," Alexia replies not telling them it is for dinner she is to meet with Baptiste. "It is someone I have not seen for quite some time. Someone very special to me." Alexia still wonders if Severo may somehow know Carla Bruni or her sister the Italian actress because of how he defended their honor once in a conversation she and he were in with another couple while playing punto banco at a casino in Monte Carlo. She has yet to ask Carla Bruni if she knows Baptiste. Alexia did not think it appropriate to bring up during the interview.

"Who is it that you are to meet, may I ask? If you do not mind, I could possibly invite them to come join us," President Sarkozy tells Alexia. She is a little puzzled that the President of France would offer to invite someone whose name he hasn't even heard yet to the Presidential Palace for a dinner party with some of his closest friends.

Now feeling a little uneasy about how to get out of this situation she has gotten into, Alexia smiles to Sarkozy and says, "Oh, it is someone I used to date a few years ago. He is a journalist. I don't know if he would even fit in here."

"Does he have a name? Or is that a secret?" Carla Bruni asks in a humorous manner with a smile on her face. She then laughs and looks to her husband. She looks back to Alexia and says, "I am so sorry. I didn't mean to put you on the spot."

Alexia laughs to break any tension there might be. She then smiles and replies, "His name is Baptiste. Severo Baptiste."

"Severo Baptiste? I would love to have him here for dinner," French President Sarkozy comments. "I have asked him here on a number of occasions and he always tells me he would love to, but he just doesn't know when."

Alexia sits stunned. Her eyes feel like they must be the size of silver dollars as surprised as she fears she looks.

"That settles it. You are staying for dinner. You are our hostage," Sarkozy says. "I will call Baptiste myself and tell him the ransom for you is his attendance at one small dinner party tonight at the

Presidential Palace."

Alexia cannot believe the sudden turn of events.

Carla Bruni tells her, "Alexia, if you would like, I know I have something you could wear tonight. If you would like?"

Still stunned and amazed, Alexia shifts her attention to the President's wife and replies, "Yes... yes that would be fine. You are too gracious."

Nicolas Sarkozy pulls out his cell phone and brings up a number. He calls it. After what could have only been a few rings, Alexia hears the French President say in French, "Severo, this is Nicolas, Nicolas Sarkozy. I have someone held hostage here who would like to see you tonight, but the only way that I will let that happen is if you let me send a car to come pick you up at the airport and then you must return to my house for dinner."

Stunned, Alexia wonders how French President Nicolas Sarkozy knew Severo Baptiste was flying in to Charles de Gaulle International Airport tonight. She had not said anything about Baptiste arriving in Paris tonight via plane. As though she didn't already have enough questions for Severo—and now she has more.

On the other end of Sarkozy's phone call, Severo laughs as he listens to the French President. He then replies jokingly in French to Sarkozy, "Hello Nick, this would not be some kind of a scheme to lure me into a trap and capture me, would it?"

"Baptiste, I would not know what to do with you if I did capture you," Sarkozy responds in humor. "And I know I do not have the resources to keep you captured if I did."

Both men laugh. Then Baptiste says, "I shall come to your home in your car under one condition."

"What is that, Severo?" asks the French President.

"That when you send your car to get me, the bait must be in the car waiting for me." Baptiste pauses. "That is the only way I will play your game."

"What will keep you from stealing our guest and taking her somewhere private where you have her all to yourself?" Nicolas Sarkozy asks the man whom he knows well.

Baptiste smiles to himself on the other end of the phone. "I give you my word, Nick. We will return to your palace for dinner and drinks. After that, I cannot promise anything. These are my terms, take it or leave it."

Sarkozy grins and replies, "If you give me your word, that is good enough for me."

"I thought it would be."

Nicolas Sarkozy laughs at his friend and says, "I will ask our hostage what she thinks of coming to the airport to meet you."

"Only Alexia and your chauffeur," Severo demands. "I do not want to see you or Carla until I get to your lair."

"How long before you will be at CDG?"

"Two hours."

Sarkozy looks down at his watch, "Right at eight o'clock then?"

"*Oui,*" answers Baptiste.

The French President looks over to his guest and in English asks her, "How do you feel about accompanying my driver to the airport to pick up your friend? It is the only way Severo says he will come join us for dinner."

Alexia is shocked at what has just transpired. After almost stopping, her heart begins to race rapidly, almost to the point of pounding so loud the others in the room can hear it. With an unlimited number of thoughts and questions racing through her mind, she smiles and says, "That would be fine I suppose, if that is what he wants." Alexia pauses and then asks, "What time did he think he would be in? At eight? Is that what I heard you say?"

"Yes," Sarkozy tells Alexia. He then turns his attention back to Baptiste, "My car will be at the airport at eight o'clock, and your friend will be there waiting for you."

"*Merci,* Nick. Tell her I look forward to seeing her. I will talk to you later, Nicolas." Severo ends the call.

Before the French President can tell Baptiste goodbye he realizes the call is over. He goes ahead and says, "*Au revoir*" out of habit.

———

The traffic on the Tom Landry Freeway, a portion of I-30 between Dallas and Fort Worth, Texas, is traveling at a snail's pace. One car moves forward a few feet as another car beside it inches ahead, and then everyone stops and sits and waits for the next phase of incremental movements. Chace Wikett and his sons are trapped in the standstill traffic. They are on their way to the game and hoping to watch a Cowboys victory. The two boys sit in the backseat of the Wikett family's dark blue Chevy Tahoe.

Less than a mile from the exit he needs to take to the football game, Wikett overhears his youngest son read the words off of a large billboard that sets just to the north of I-30. Chace looks to the billboard to see if his ten year old has read the sign correctly. He has. The large sign reads, "Only God Knows How Many Apples Are In A Seed." Wikett wonders if his son understands the meaning behind the sign. He then hears his twelve year old start to explain the meaning to the younger boy. Chace smiles and returns his focus to a political talk show on the radio as he reaches down and turns the volume up a couple of notches.

The radio is tuned to WBAP 820 on the AM dial. Wikett is listening to a special weekend election show as other fans of America's team around him slowly make their way with Wikett and his sons to one of the most phenomenal sports stadiums in the world.

What Chace hears coming through the speakers of his family's vehicle is a report about what had happened the day before in Los Angeles, California at the Staples Center. The local weekend radio talk show host is playing a segment of what a CCN Network News television anchor said earlier in the morning on a national TV newscast. The news anchor for the leading news network had stated that the FBI acted outside of its bounds in the arrests and searches of hundreds of Arab Americans the day before in California. The CCN anchorman went on to infer that unknown sources within the Bureau had hinted that the entire terrorist threat on the West Coast of America was concocted, that a conservative faction of the FBI had fabricated it in an attempt to scare the voters in California to vote Republican. Texas FBI agent Wikett cannot believe what he is hearing.

With the traffic moving no faster than a turtle, Agent Wikett picks up his cell phone and calls Martin MacKuenn. He then asks his boys to be quiet as he turns down the radio. His two sons do just as their father asks. With his cell phone routed through the radio, he hears it ring three times before it is answered. "Hello, this is Martin MacKuenn."

"Yeah Marty, this is Chace again."

"Are you trying to back out on our bet now?"

"No, this call is not about football," Wikett states. "Have you been paying any attention to the news?"

"No, I've been taking a nap," MacKuenn replies. "Trying to catch up on some of that sleep I've been missing out on."

"Well, I just heard on the radio that CCN is trying to say we orchestrated the whole ordeal yesterday out in L.A."

"Oh, I did hear something to that affect this morning. I guess I didn't pay much attention to it. It was some left-wing nut on a morning show I heard on the way to church. After my wife and I got home I fell sound asleep in the recliner watching NFL Today."

"I can't believe the nerve of CCN to politicize a terrorist threat in Los Angeles," Wikett states with anger in his voice. "Why can't they report the truth? That the Muslim Brotherhood is who was behind the threat."

"What CCN is doing doesn't surprise me when you consider who runs that network," MacKuenn says.

"Oh, yeah. Rigger Watson," Wikett replies. "He's a real piece of work."

"I'd love to catch him with his hand in the cookie jar just one time," MacKuenn comments.

"It just flat makes me mad."

"What do you expect from those people?" MacKuenn asks. "They'll do whatever it takes to win. And they don't care who it hurts."

"Yeah," Wikett replies. "And by the time the truth comes out, most of the people in this country won't care anyhow. That is... if the truth ever does come out."

"Kind of a sad state this nation is in," comments MacKuenn. "People don't care. They are too busy watching *The Bachelor* and *Dancing with the Stars* and crap like that or waiting for the next James Cameron film to be shoved down their throats."

"I take it you weren't a fan of *Avatar* then?" Wikett asks.

"Hell no, I wasn't. That was a bunch of new age communist crap the public ate up like caviar." MacKuenn declares.

"I agree," comments Wikett.

"Hey, I thought you and your boys would be at the game by now."

"We're in traffic right now. We'll get there before kickoff, but not by much. Speaking of Hollywood and the left Marty, I've got something for you to think about. I was in a conversation with a guy the other day that we both know. We worked overseas with him some. He's a big supporter of our current President."

"OK, I'm with you so far. I think I know who you mean."

"I asked him this. Whose work does he think Hollywood is doing these days? God's or Satan's?" Wikett pauses. "The guy answered me back and said, 'Oh, there's no question, the majority of Hollywood is doing Satan's work.' Then, I asked him who the majority of Hollywood is supporting these days politically? The left or the right?"

"That's good, Chace." MacKuenn comments, "I like it."

"I then asked him where the majority of Christianity is lined up, especially evangelical Christianity, with the left or the right?"

"How did he like that?" MacKuenn asks. "I'll bet he didn't."

"No, he didn't like that at all," Wikett replies as the traffic starts to move a little quicker.

"As my old grandpa in Wisconsin always used to say, 'Birds of a feather flock together,'" MacKuenn states. "I see it every day here in the nation's capital."

"That's just what I told the guy," Wikett says as he laughs.

"Speaking of birds," MacKuenn replies. "Like grandpa also used to say, 'If it walks like a duck, talks like a duck, looks like a duck, and quacks like a duck, it must be a duck.'"

Both men laugh.

"Putting all humor aside, did those questions you asked that guy make him think a little?"

"I don't really know. He just sort of bulled up and got mad. He didn't want to discuss the issue anymore. He acted just like a donkey," Wikett says as MacKuenn gets a kick out of the comparison the Texan made between the liberal and the animal symbol for the Democratic Party.

After he quits laughing, MacKuenn states, "Yeah, people hate to be proven wrong—it's their pride."

"I hoped he would think about how God sees things," Wikett says. "Make him think about God and politics in a serious way."

"It's quite obvious which side of the issues Hollywood and the mainstream media are on. I don't understand why people can't see it."

"It is crystal clear to me that Hollywood is working for Satan most of the time," Wikett states.

"With the unrest in the Islamic world, I think we will start to see more people from the left start coming over the fence to get on the right side of things."

"I am afraid Martin, that we will only see that when they successfully attack us again here in the U.S." Wikett asserts.

"Then the tolerance the left preaches, but doesn't abide by, will be thrown out the window like it was after 9/11," says MacKuenn.

"Don't even get me started on tolerance. The left has hijacked that word," replies Wikett. "Tolerance is what made people like Charlie Sheen and Lindsay Lohan who they are. Not enough discipline as kids."

"There's two Hollywood types who need to turn their lives to God instead of the fame the world offers them."

"Yeah, Marty, it is sad... But who knows, maybe someday they will find Jesus. He is the only One who can heal all their hurts."

"Chace, I almost forgot, speaking of Hollywood, have you heard about the new Michael Moore documentary he is coming out with?"

"No, I don't guess I have had the pleasure yet. Enlighten me."

"Oh yeah, Michael Moore has got a documentary in the works that blames the Jews for the entire Holocaust."

"You've got to be kiddin' me?" replies Wikett.

"Yeah, I am... but that proves the point. You believed me that he could and would do something like that," MacKuenn says as he laughs. "There's nothing too off the wall for Hollywood to try."

"Marty, that is all too true to even be funny today."

"It is... yesterday we saved their lives in Hollywoodland and today they are blaming us for it."

"Well, I just know it makes me mad like nothing else to hear CCN is doing what they are with what we did yesterday in California to protect them. They are flat assed lying to the American people."

"I'll get on the horn back here in Washington and see if I can't ruffle a few feathers this afternoon," MacKuenn tells Wikett. "It might cost me my job, but I'll do it anyway."

"If you need any help Marty, call. I'm ready to let my voice be known," FBI agent Wikett asserts. "I don't really care if I keep my job or not. I may have a new one by the time this game is over."

"You did right out there yesterday, Wikett. You know it and I know it regardless of how they paint it." MacKuenn tells his friend.

"Thanks, Marty."

"Chace, let me leave you with a thought from our sermon this morning at church—Never shy away from doing right… And you will never be blessed for doing wrong."

"I agree with that," states Wikett.

MacKuenn continues, "The way I see it, CCN's Rigger Watson, even if he is able to make part of the American people believe that we were in the wrong out there in L.A., God still knows the truth. And in the end, you and I both know who will truly be blessed."

"That's for sure. I'd better be getting off the phone, we're about to turn off the interstate to the stadium."

"Go Redskins," MacKuenn says. "And God bless you and your family, Chace."

Wikett laughs. "He has, Marty. He has," Chace replies as he looks in the mirror at his two sons. "God bless you too Martin."

When he gets off of the phone, Chace Wikett's oldest son asks, "Dad, why don't we think about God anymore than we do? I know I don't think about Him except on Sundays when we go to church."

Realizing his son has just listened to every word he has said in his conversation with MacKuenn, Wikett replies, "Well Kelly, it has a lot to do with our selfish nature. A selfish nature we are all born with. Do you understand what I am saying?"

Chace Wikett's twelve year old son nods his head up and down and says, "Yes."

"Hows come they don't teach us about God in school, Dad," asks Chace's ten year old son.

"They should Kasey, they really should," replies Wikett as he realizes he and his wife need to get back to spending some time with their kids in family Bible study.

"I can't wait to see Tony Romo and DeMarcus Ware!" shouts Kasey Wikett as they near Cowboys Stadium.

"I want to see the cheerleaders," says Kelly Wikett.

CHAPTER FORTY-ONE

A Driving Rainstorm

With the night lights of Paris shining radiantly through the rear window of the five hundred and fifty thousand dollar Rolls Royce Phantom Limousine, as fine and elegant a vehicle as Alexia Klien has ever been in, the American broadcast journalist sits alone in the backseat of the car specially built for the country of France. The world seems to be at her fingertips as she travels north at 130 kilometers an hour on the A1 Autoroute. It is the same road she was on just yesterday in a small French sports car with three people she had just met from America. Alexia knows the airport and Severo Baptiste are only a few minutes away.

Wearing one of the most elegant dresses she has ever had on, something the French President's wife has loaned her for the evening, a bright blue Roland Mouret that gently covers each of her shoulders with a deep V down the middle of her back. The dress is tight and sleek as it holds firmly to every curve on her long lean body. It stops just below her knees, letting her legs extend to the stunningly sexy Martinez Valero black high heeled shoes Alexia was able to find in Carla Bruni's private wardrobe. Not only do the two women, who are so much alike in so many ways, possess the same dress size, they are also able to wear the same shoes. With Alexia's feet being only a touch narrower, the Martinez Valeros feel like a godsend after getting out of her own shoes, a pair of Emilio Puccis she had bought in New York a bit too small because she just loved them and could not find a pair a half-size larger.

Tonight as she awaits seeing the only man she has ever truly loved, Alexia is very comfortable in the way she is dressed. *If looks can kill, Severo Baptiste does not stand a chance,* she thinks to herself as the Rolls Royce slows down to exit the freeway and make the turn into Charles de Gaulle International Airport. Her heart is beating fast with the anticipation of seeing a man she has not seen for nearly a third of a decade. Her mind is outracing her heart with so many questions. Questions about the redheaded woman, the man the redhead was with, Severo's home in Rome she never knew anything about, and now this friendship he seems to have with the French President.

Where do I start? Alexia thinks to herself. *Or do I simply not ask any questions? Do I just let him talk... listen to his voice and enjoy being with him?* In a matter of a few minutes she will know what she will do. But right now, only a mile away from seeing the man she last saw over five thousand miles south of here in Johannesburg, South Africa, Alexia is scared, nervous, and not sure what she will say when she sees him. *The questions can wait,* she concludes as the silver and gold Rolls Royce slows down to stop in front of the area for passenger pickup.

———

When Watson holds up his hand and points to the news broadcast, everyone stops talking and looks up to the television set hanging high in a corner of the long narrow room. The screen is covered with a map of the state of Colorado with black dots representing the major communities and blue and green lines running between the towns to represent the roadways. A large yellow-shaded area in the center of the map shows the metropolitan Denver area. A solid bold red line originating in Colorado Springs and stopping in the middle of the Rocky Mountains represents the path of a flight that never reached its destination. As the anchorman's voice can be heard, the four people in the conference room all listen intensely.

"We have breaking news for everyone in the nation this afternoon. Tragic information coming out of Denver, Colorado as the names have been released of the twelve people who lost their lives early this morning in the crash of the Cessna Citation X carrying U.S. Senate candidate Kathy Whittenburg. The plane was en route to Grand Junction, Colorado from Colorado Springs when it unexpectedly lost altitude and crashed into a rough section of the

Rocky Mountains. The FAA has not released any further details that would point to the cause of the crash, other than the pilots did report a sudden loss of engine power about ten minutes into the scheduled flight. After that, the plane simply plummeted into the side of a mountain," Markus Daniels, a Sunday afternoon anchor, reports on CCN.

After the network switches back to him from the map of Colorado, Daniels turns and looks into the camera, "It is with sincere grief that we report that the two suspected Colorado sports celebrities who were assumed to also be aboard the flight were indeed among the names of those who lost their lives in the crash." As the CCN News anchor continues, the network shows a split screen with the pictures of the athletes on each side of the split. Daniels states, "Jeremy Jacobs, the former All-Pro tight end for the Denver Broncos, and Christie Smith, a gold medal Olympic downhill skier from Golden, Colorado, sadly were aboard the flight to accompany Senate candidate Kathy Whittenburg to a campaign rally on the western slope."

"Damn it, I wish they wouldn't have been on that plane," Rigger Watson voices in the CCN conference room as he and three network executives strategize on how to report all the stories coming into the network in the hours leading up to an election now less than two days away. "It's one thing to have some radical right-winged mother of four go down in flames in the mountains, but to have two beloved athletes of that same state with her is not going to help us win Colorado for Franson."

With a surprised look on her face, the one female executive shakes her head in disbelief at her boss. She asks Watson, "Do you not have a heart?" He gives her a quick stare. She then says, "Doesn't any part of you feel sorry for the families of the people who died in that tragic plane crash?"

Watson continues to look at her and holds his hands up with his palms facing the ceiling. He asks her in a very sarcastic tone, "What am I going to do? Hell, I didn't cause the crash." He pauses as thoughts of what did cause the crash go through his head. Watson knows he has just lied to her. He then says, "Anyway, it serves 'em right... a black man and a Colorado ski bum abandoning their own people to support someone like that damn pro-life Tea Party protégé Kathy Whittenburg."

In an unusual show of rebellion against Rigger Watson inside the CCN Network News headquarters, the female executive who has only been with CCN for about six months gets up out of her chair and heads to the door to leave the conference room. As she approaches the door, she looks to Watson and says, "You are one sorry, heartless jerk. I don't have any desire to be around you. I've met Christie Smith. And she was a really good person." She leaves the room as she slams the conference room door behind her loudly enough that everyone outside of the room looks to see what is happening.

With a smile on his face, Watson looks at the two remaining executives in the room and says, "I guess I made her mad."

The three men return their focus to the CCN News special report. "... wreckage of the plane has been located by rescuers. But, with the winds as strong as they are today in the Rocky Mountains, officials with the Colorado Search and Rescue Authority have stated it may be three or four days before anyone can be dropped into the area where the aircraft carrying U.S. Senate candidate Mrs. Kathy Whittenburg has gone down. And that is only if the winds and the snow let up."

Daniels is interrupted by anchorman Adam Brown, "The terrain the Cessna Citation has gone down in is some of the most treacherous in all the lower forty-eight states. The chances that someone could survive a wreck of this magnitude is zero. This will certainly put a damper on the Republicans' hopes of winning back control of the U.S. Senate. They were certainly counting on the strong showing by Mrs. Whittenburg to win back the Colorado Senate seat."

Daniels then cuts in on Brown, "And Adam, with the death of Kathy Whittenburg hanging over Colorado and the Colorado Republican Party it is very unlikely they will now be able to carry the state for the Presidency, something the Republicans were going to have to do to win back the Oval Office."

"Yes Markus, it has been a very tragic and unexpected turn of events all across the nation this weekend."

"Sadly it has, Adam. And we are only two days from the election."

"I've never seen a pre-election weekend like this either," states

CCN anchorman Adam Brown. It all started with the needless death of Mike Swenson, and now the untimely accident in the West to a woman who really did have a good chance of making it to Washington D.C. to represent the people of her state. What else could happen is what I ask."

"Yes Adam, that question has crossed my mind too," anchorman Markus Daniels replies, "And all of this, combined with the expectations of the first major winter storm to sweep across America this week and blanket the entire Northeastern two thirds of the nation with snow. It is surely going to make the next few days very interesting and intense for everyone concerned with the direction the United States of America is heading."

———

A mild cold front has moved into Paris in the last hour. A slight breeze out of the northwest has picked up a bit, and a scattering of gray clouds seem to be gathering to the north of the city with Charles de Gaulle International Airport sitting in the middle of their path. The potential for a minor thunderstorm hangs in the cool fall air.

Alexia thinks to herself how romantic it would be to ride back to the Presidential Palace in the back of a Rolls Royce limousine during a driving rainstorm with the arms of the man she loves wrapped around her. As she thinks this, she sees a flash of lightning off in the distance to the northwest, and within a few seconds she can hear the faded sound of thunder. With her thoughts captivated with visions of seeing Severo Baptiste, her heart skips a beat with fear and hope. They are at the airport.

Just as the chauffeur asks if she knows where to stop, Alexia pushes send on her cell phone and a text message is sent. She can feel her hands tremble after she finishes the simple procedure. Raising her eyes from her phone to look out the side widows of the silver Rolls Royce limousine with gold trim, she replies in French to the driver, "I don't know yet. Just wait here, I guess."

No sooner did she get the words out of her mouth than her phone begins to vibrate. It then makes a sharp beep. Alexia looks down and sees she has a text message from Severo. Quickly she opens it. It says, "I am at the third entrance from the end."

Alexia is filled with so much anticipation and excitement. She is almost unable to inform the driver which door he needs to pull up to. After a moment of hesitation, she takes a deep breath and says, "It's the third entrance..." She stops herself in mid-sentence and repeats in French, "It is the third entrance from the end."

"Thank you," the chauffeur replies in English with a smile on his face. After driving the short distance, he begins to slow down to stop. He then says as he looks in the mirror, "Do not worry, Mademoiselle, you look gorgeous tonight."

"Thank you very much. You are too gracious," Alexia returns.

As the car comes to a complete stop, Alexia can see through the large windows of the French airport the man she last saw in an airport in South Africa three years ago. He is on his way out of the building carrying one small brown leather handbag in his left hand with a computer case draped over his right shoulder. He looks just like she remembered him. Brown hair with a touch of gray, hair that looks like it was in bad need of a haircut a week ago. It is very thick, almost to the point where it hangs over his ears, but not long enough to be considered long, just unkept. He looks like he needed to shave three days ago, which is about how often he usually does. He also looks like he doesn't care about any of this. He is who he is, and that is that. Just a shade under six feet tall, without an ounce of fat on him anywhere and built like a Roman-Greco wrestler—which he did quite a bit of growing up—Baptiste has the presence of a man who owns the very ground he walks on. His dark brown eyes have an intensity that can be seen from far away, and his jaw often looks to be clenched. He is still everything her mind has painted him to be in her memories.

Alexia cannot stand it. She cannot stay in the car even though a light rain is beginning to fall. After telling the chauffeur not to get out, she opens the car door and steps out over the curb onto the wet sidewalk in front of the airport. She does not have a coat. She had no idea it was going to rain. She didn't care about the weather when she walked out of the Presidential Palace and climbed into the most expensive vehicle she had ever been in. All that was on her mind was the man she is about to embrace.

With the scattered raindrops falling on her beautiful blue dress, she makes her way to the door Severo is just coming through. When he sees her in the very sexy, sleek dress, her long flowing black hair hanging over her shoulders and down her back, he instantly stops and stares. The rain itself has not really hit yet, but anyone would know it is not far away. As fast as she can move in the black four-inch Martinez Valero heels, Alexia runs to Severo Baptiste as he stretches his arms out to wrap them around her. A moment or so after they meet and embrace, a bolt of lightning strikes only a few kilometers away. It hits the ground and is followed by booming thunder that startles Alexia. The rain starts to pick up immediately.

Severo takes a step backwards and looks at her and then at the car. He then looks back at Alexia and says in a slow, deep voice as rain gently lands on and around them, "Darling, I do not know which looks richer, you or the Rolls. On second thought, it is definitely you."

Alexia laughs and gives him another hug. She then backs up a little and suggests, "Don't you think we should get in the car?"

Baptiste laughs at her and replies, "I never thought you should have gotten out of the car." He pauses, and then says, "But I'm glad you did."

The two of them then quickly make their way to the silver Rolls Royce parked along the curb in front of the French airport. Severo opens the door for Alexia and climbs into the rear of the car behind her. As Baptiste closes the door, the bottom falls out of the sky and rain begins to pour from the heavens.

About halfway to being soaking wet in the tightly fitting French designer dress she is wearing only for the evening, Alexia says, "I suppose we should turn up the heater and try to dry off."

"You are right," Severo replies with a slight grin on his face and a sparkle in his dark brown eyes. He then playfully asks, "Is there anything we can use as a clothesline back here?"

Alexia laughs. She then tells the chauffeur, "We are ready to go back to the Sarkozys."

"Thank you, Mademoiselle," he replies.

"No, thank you for driving me out here," she says.

"The pleasure was all mine," returns the driver of the expensive car as he pulls out into traffic to return to the French Presidential

Palace.

Alexia looks at Severo. He returns the look as he stares deeply into her dark blue eyes. She smiles and he says, "You are so lovely. So lovely. I cannot believe it has been so long since I have seen your face in person." He pauses and then continues, "I see your face everyday. It's all that is ever in my mind."

Alexia cannot stand it. She leans over to him and places her lips on his. The two kiss for what seems like minutes. The two kiss for what *is* minutes. Alexia can feel goosebumps all over her body. She never wants to let go of the man she has a hold of. She pulls him closer into her as he draws her closer to him. She then says, "I have missed you so much."

With the rain beating down on the top of the half a million dollar car, the two of them hold each other tightly as they fall gently back into the rear seat of the silver and gold Rolls Royce limousine. They relax with their arms around each other and say nothing more as they sit and watch the lights of Paris draw closer and closer through the darkness. The raindrops that are falling from heaven are pelting the windshield in front of the chauffeur. Every few kilometers, the flash of lighting can be seen out the back and the side windows as the storm is passing Paris to the north. Alexia feels completely comfortable with the silence she and Severo are sharing.

She wishes she could just tell the chauffeur to drive them somewhere quiet, to a small café, somewhere that just the two of them could dine alone. Share a bottle of wine, a few laughs, some conversation, a smile or two. A place where she didn't have to share him with anyone, and he didn't have to share her with anyone. This was not the deal they have made though. As tough as it is going to be, she and Severo are headed back to dine with French President Nicolas Sarkozy and his wife in the nearly three hundred year-old Élysée Palace. But, Alexia and Severo both know the time will come tonight when they will be finished with their obligation to the Sarkozys and will be able to finally be alone with each other.

For now though she can relax in his arms and enjoy the sound of the life-giving rain as it pounds down on the vehicle she and Severo Armand Casimiro Baptiste are riding in. As she does, Alexia closes her eyes and her mind returns to the dream she experienced this morning. She smiles inside as she lays there against her prince, envisioning that she is the princess of France and it is her father's car that she and her lover are being taken in to the king's castle to be wed in front of all the people of the land. Alexia giggles inside at her own silliness. She closes her eyes even tighter and pulls Severo closer.

As the breathtakingly immaculate vehicle nears the exit it must take to get off of the French freeway and continue on its course to the palace and the private dinner party, the questions Alexia has had in her head all day start to resurface. The rain outside the Rolls Royce has nearly stopped. Severo can sense that the silence he and she are enjoying is coming to an end. He decides to talk first.

"So how have your interviews gone? Everyone cooperative?"

Surprised to hear him speak, she turns her head slightly, and from only a few inches away from his cheek she says, "Oh, they have gone well." Puzzled, she then asks, "What makes you ask?"

"I don't know. Just curious."

"Yes... yes they have gone very well. The interview with Prince Charles was unlike anything I have ever experienced, but it still went very well."

"Yes, I have heard that before about him," Baptiste says.

"Really?" Alexia asks, "From who?"

"Oh, just people."

Alexia then pushes herself away from him just a little so she can look at him. With her piercing blue eyes looking directly into his dark brown ones, she asks, "Do you know him like you know Sarkozy?"

"No, not like I know Nicolas," Severo replies. "I have met the Prince, but I do not know him well."

She turns her head slightly sideways and with a funny look on her face she asks, "Is there a lot I don't know about you?"

Severo just grins at her as his eyes light up and stare into hers. He says nothing.

"I mean, like I never knew you had a house in Rome," she replies to his smile. "I met... it was during an interview with a lawyer from Italy last night on the street. I met a guy... Well, he said he had seen a picture of me in your home in Rome. How long have you had a house in Rome?"

Severo smiles again and says, "I have had some good fortune financially in the years since we last saw each other. I have tried to invest it wisely in real estate. That is all." He pauses and then answers her first question, "But Darling, you know you know all the important things about me."

She smiles back at him as she wonders to herself how she was able to stay away from this man for so long. The soothing sound of his voice makes her heart melt. She wants to crawl into his arms and fall asleep forever. Well, part of her wants that, but another part of her wants to do more. Alexia decides the rest of her questions can wait until later. After dinner, or maybe even until tomorrow.

CHAPTER FORTY-TWO

Christie's in London

The dinner party at the French Presidential Palace is over and everyone but she and Baptiste have left. Before the dinner party, Severo did shave and run a comb through his hair, but he still looked like he just came from some battlefield in North Africa during World War II. It is a look he cannot escape. The questions she has in her mind for him have only increased.

Alexia is astonished at how the evening with the small group of Nicolas and Carla Sarkozy's friends has gone. Everyone at the party seemed to have more respect and reverence for Severo Baptiste than they did their host, the French President. For the three and a half hours they were in the Élysée Palace, it was like Severo was the man who ran France, not Sarkozy. Alexia had been everywhere with Baptiste in the past and has always sensed this presence about him, but never in a place this grand—a palace where men like Charles de Gaulle and Napoleon Bonaparte had once lived. She has the feeling that not everyone at the party knew Severo, but they all knew about him.

There was one moment in the night that Alexia will never forget. Someone in the party brought up the U.S. Presidential election and the death of the leading candidate's campaign manager that has happened right before the election. The whole room of people seemed to be interested in putting their two cents worth into the discussion about Swenson's death and his lifestyle. Some thought it was only a suicide committed by a sad and hopeless homosexual not wanting to face his shame. Others knew there had to be some foul play involved somewhere. One guy even said he had heard from a friend in the

United States that there was a rumor that maybe Swenson was programmed to hang himself because of a suspicious phone call from China he had received less than an hour before his death. Kind of like in the movie *The Manchurian Candidate,* the guy said. Baptiste had stayed completely out of the conversation until somebody asked him what he thought. Severo's words brought the whole place down in laughter and ended the conversation on that topic. What Severo said even went against the views of many, if not most in the room. But none of them challenged him on his point. They just laughed right along with everyone else in the crowd.

When asked what he thought on the subject of Mike Swenson's apparent suicide, Baptiste simply said, "Man was not made to sleep with man. Man was made to sleep with woman." When he spoke these words he never cracked a smile. Baptiste was dead serious, and when everyone in the room busted out in laughter at his wisdom and logic, Severo never even grinned. He just sat there and watched everyone's reaction to his statement. It was a calculated response. Alexia could tell that it was his way of ending the foolish talk about something he was done listening to. No one in the room brought anything else up about Swenson, homosexuality or the U.S. Presidential election for the rest of the night. Severo Baptiste owned the crowd, and everyone in the room knew it.

Having said their good byes to the Sarkozys, Alexia and Severo return to the same vehicle that brought them both here from the airport. Carla Bruni was so wowed by Alexia and her radiant personality that she gave Alexia the blue Roland Mouret dress and the Martinez Valero shoes as a gift. Bruni stated that she would never be able to wear them now anyway, because she did not feel she could do them the justice that Alexia had. Alexia graciously accepted the gift from the woman she now feels she has a connection with.

As he gets in the silver and gold Rolls Royce, Baptiste reaches to pull the car door shut. When he does, the chauffeur gently closes the door to the vehicle. Baptiste, who is not accustomed to being driven anywhere by a chauffeur or anyone else for that matter, brings his hand back to himself and chuckles inside about having someone close a door for him tonight. The chauffeur walks around and gets in behind the steering wheel of the Rolls so he can escort them to Alexia's hotel room. She wonders what it is about Severo Baptiste that she does not know. As the time nears midnight, the weather over Paris is beginning to feel like it did when Alexia picked Baptiste up from the airport. There is a heavy cloud cover and a stiff breeze out of the northwest as cooler temperatures and moisture fills the air. The only thing that is lacking from earlier in the evening is the thunder and lightning.

"Mademoiselle," the chauffeur asks as he drives the large car away from the Presidential Palace. "Where would you like me to take you?"

"The Hotel Gabriel Issy les Moulineax," answers Alexia. "Thank you."

"You are welcome," he returns in English.

Alexia turns and looks at Severo. "You amaze me. How did I stay away from you so long?"

Severo smiles and says nothing.

"What is it about you that all those people in there tonight were so taken with you?"

Baptiste grins. Then, with a smile he says, "I don't know. Maybe the same thing that has you so taken with me."

"You fascinate me, Severo Baptiste."

"No, Alexia Klien. It is you who fascinates me. I am the one who does not know how I stayed away from you for so long." He pauses, "It was not easy."

"I am so sorry. I really am," Alexia expresses.

"You are forgiven." Severo says as he looks into her eyes. "This night would never have been, had we not been apart for so long. You do know that?"

"Yes, this night has been very special," Alexia declares as she fights back joyful tears she can feel starting to form. "It has been like a dream."

With his dark brown eyes sparkling as the lights of Paris shine through the windows of the expensive vehicle, he stares at her with a smile and says, "Darling, your dream is not over yet. There is still part of this night left... a part I hope will be even more memorable than the French Palace and the Rolls Royce."

Alexia knows what he is talking about. She smiles to tell him she agrees with him. He reaches over and takes her hand and squeezes it softly. He then looks deeply into her beautiful blue eyes and says, "Alexia, I love you. I love you with all my heart. You are the only woman I have ever loved, and the only one I ever will love. I am so pleased to be with you here tonight."

Alexia is speechless as her heart melts. She cannot believe she told him no that night on the bank of the Nile River in Cairo, Egypt five years ago when he asked her to marry him. She knows if he ever asks her again, she will not hesitate to say yes.

"I am yours Severo... all yours. You may do with me as you wish."

"I wish to do with you only what you wish, my darling. I am your servant for tonight..." He pauses, "And for as long as you want me."

Alexia giggles inside as she thinks about how she has had just the right amount of wine to really enjoy herself. As she thinks about the fine and expensive wine that was served tonight at the Élysée Palace, her mind recalls that Severo didn't hardly touch his. He only took a few sips from his glass which stayed mostly full all night. She asks him, "Darling, did you not like the wine they served this evening? I noticed you barely drank any of it."

"It was superb," says Baptiste.

"Why didn't you drink more of it, then?"

"In that group of people tonight, I wanted to keep my wits about me. I will explain later," Severo replies. "But I do have a surprise for you in my bag."

As they travel in the rear of the custom-built Rolls Royce with the lights of Paris passing by them, Baptiste reaches in his brown leather bag and pulls out a 1971 bottle of Romanee Conti La Tache and hands it to Alexia. She smiles. He then asks her, "Do we open it here or wait till we get to the room?"

The bottle of wine is older than she is.

"As much as I would like to have it here, I think we should wait until we get to the room," Alexia replies with a grin on her face.

"We are talking about the wine, right?" Severo asks.

"That can also wait until we get to the room," she says.

He then pulls out another item from his clothes bag, a black velvet-covered case. It is about five inches wide and twelve to fourteen inches long and about an inch tall. He asks her, "Alexia darling, do you wish to wait until we get to the room to open this also?"

Her bright blue eyes open wide, Alexia smiles and looks at him, "Can I open it here, or do you want me to wait?"

Severo holds out the black case. "I would love to see you open it right now."

With her hands trembling oh so slightly, Alexia reaches up and takes the jewelry case from Baptiste. Her heart begins to beat harder with anticipation. Before she opens it, she looks up into Severo's brown eyes and without saying a word she tells him she appreciates his gift. She then slowly looks down to the black case and gently opens it. Alexia cannot believe what she sees, as the item in the case sparkles with every ray of light that comes into the car from the passing street lamps. *This had to have cost him a year's worth of income,* she thinks. There are more diamonds strung together to form a necklace in the black case than she has ever held in her hands before.

Severo reaches into the case and lifts the custom-designed diamond necklace out and has Alexia turn so he can place it around her neck. He then says, "Let me see how it looks."

She turns to face him.

He smiles, "You make the necklace look so much more beautiful than it does in the case."

Alexia does not know what to say. She can feel the diamonds touch the bare skin on her neck. She looks into his eyes and says, "I am speechless."

"Do you like it?"

"How could I not like it?" Alexia replies. "Did you have to sell some house like the one in Rome to buy this for me?" This is the thought that was in her head. She wishes she hadn't said it, but she did.

Severo laughs. He then tells her, "I told you I have had a certain amount of financial success recently. And I have sold a number of stories for some good money."

Alexia knows that Severo seldom ever uses his real name on the articles he writes. She also knows how fast he can turn out a story when he wants to, so in her mind what he is telling her would be possible even though she hasn't seen anything he has written in a newspaper or magazine for years. Normally something inside of her can recognize his style. One of the things she doesn't know about him is that some of the stories he sells are never read by the public. Baptiste deals more in information than he does in news and entertainment. He has found that there are people out there who are willing to pay a lot more money for some types of information than there are people willing to pay for newspaper or magazine articles.

"So, you have been writing?" she asks as she runs her fingertips over the diamonds around her neck.

"Some, but if you must know, I have personally brought each and every one of these stones out of Africa myself in the past ten years. I even had some of these diamonds on me when I last saw you in South Africa. This necklace is something I have had in my mind for you for a long time." Severo pauses, "It was made just for you, Darling."

Alexia is stunned at what she has just heard. The questions she has for him start to resurface in her thoughts. She knows she needs to ask one or two that are pressing before they get to the hotel and to the room. She reaches up to feel the necklace on her neck to make sure it is really there. The stones feel so smooth and so rich to her touch. She can see their reflection in the window. She has never felt worth as much as she does right now. Her mind races back to the questions.

She is about to ask Severo something, when he says, "I suppose you want to know more about the woman with the red hair and the tall older gentleman with her in the pictures you sent me, right?"

Alexia smiles and shakes her head in disbelief. "Yes I do, I was just about to bring that up. How did you know?"

"I could see it in your eyes."

She knows he is telling the truth. Baptiste could always see everything she was thinking in her eyes. Alexia then asks, "So, what is it that makes the woman with the red hair so dangerous?"

"She used to be a Russian spy," Severo says without hesitation. He pauses and then continues at a slower pace, "Or, that is what I have been told. I don't know if she still is for sure. But she keeps very dangerous company at times."

The American broadcast journalist freezes as she hears what Severo says. She has had this same thought go through her mind in the past thirty-six hours, but every time it did, Alexia dismissed it as only part of her own wild imagination. Now her fears for the country she grew up in, the country she loves, are realized. Alexia wonders what she should do with what she now knows about the woman she saw with U.S. Presidential candidate Senator Walter Franson. She knows that if she does anything it will cost her the career she has worked so hard to achieve.

Severo pauses as he sees he has lost her attention for a moment. He asks, "Are you OK?"

"Yes... yes, I am OK," she replies. "What about the man? Who is he, do you know?"

"My sources tell me he is an arms dealer," Severo says. "Not the biggest one out there, but a player in that racket."

This surprises Alexia even more than hearing that the woman was a Russian spy.

Alexia does not know she is sitting with one of the biggest arms dealers in the world. Nobody knows Baptiste is one of the biggest arms dealers in the world, except for Severo himself. His commercial enterprise of trading weapons of war is only one of the multifaceted endeavors that are in his private business portfolio. When Baptiste told Alexia he had personally carried the diamonds he gave her out of Africa himself, he did not tell her that those were only a mere fraction of the expensive stones his hands have touched and carried out of that continent over the last twenty years.

"An arms dealer?" Alexia comments about the tall gray haired gentleman she had seen with the mysterious woman. "And she is a Russian spy?" She says as she continues her thoughts out loud.

Baptiste has full knowledge of the relationship the Russian redhead has been involved in now for over a decade with the Senator from California, a relationship that Baptiste himself had a hand in setting up. He had hired the woman from the land of Dr. Zhivago to fly to the Winter Olympics in 2002 for the express purpose of seducing Senator Walter Franson. Out of curiosity, Severo asks Alexia, "Darling, why was it that you were so intrigued with the redheaded woman to follow her like a spy yourself yesterday?" He knows with Alexia being a reporter she won't give him all her reasons. He is just playing a little game with himself for his own enjoyment.

Not wanting to lie to Baptiste, but not desiring to tell him everything she knows about the Russian woman, Alexia pauses before she answers the man she still thinks is just a freelance journalist. She then says, "I just had a feeling she might be a story... I am sure I saw her in Washington D.C. a few years ago."

Just like a cat will play with a mouse before he eats it, Severo smiles and asks, "What was she doing when you saw her in Washington D.C.?"

"Ah... she was with some guy I knew. He's a guy that is in the government sort of," she stops and then tries to redirect the conversation away from the redhead. "When you say the man that was with her was an arms dealer, what kind do you mean?"

"Military," Severo replies about the gray haired gentleman that he himself has sometimes used in the past to front certain transactions between countries or people in turmoil.

Feeling that maybe Severo knows more about the two people than he is letting on, Alexia attempts to dig a little deeper. "The Muslim man in the airport had a small black attaché case that turned out to be a little laptop computer. Why would he have passed that to the gray haired man who then sat down and typed in it for a while and then gave it back to the Muslim?"

"I'm sure it had to do with some transaction they were involved in, mostly just for money I'd say," Baptiste replies, telling Alexia all he is going to tell her about a deal he not only knows about, but is behind. It was the very deal he had on his mind over a decade ago when he flew to the Salt Lake City Olympics to put his plan of blackmail and espionage into action. The thing he did not count on back then in 2002 was meeting the woman who would steal his heart at those Games—the young CCN broadcast journalist Alexia Klien, who is now wearing the necklace he has had specially made for her. The cat is done playing with the mouse. He will now change subjects.

"You are so incredibly beautiful tonight, my Darling," Baptiste says. Alexia responds with a smile.

Curiously, Severo wonders if the woman he is looking at has any idea that the necklace she has around her neck would easily fetch a price as high as five or six million dollars if it were to be auctioned at Christie's in London. The stones the necklace is crafted out of are the very best of all the diamonds he has had come through his possession.

Severo lets his eyes soak this moment into his memory as the two of them ride in the back of the French President's Rolls Royce. A light rain has started to fall on the roof of the vehicle and the chauffeur has had to turn on the windshield wipers. The moment could not be more romantic when Severo says, "You look so incredibly radiant and refreshing in that necklace. The only way you would look any better, is if the diamonds were all you were wearing."

Alexia blushes as what he says as it sends chills up her spine. She then replies in a very sexy voice, "I will see what I can do about that in a few minutes."

Severo smiles. He does not say anything. But his eyes speak volumes.

Alexia decides that any more serious questions she has can wait until breakfast. There are more important things to think about now. She leans over to him, and the two of them embrace in a very passionate and prolonged kiss as the chauffeur slows the Rolls Royce down to turn onto the street where Alexia's hotel is.

"We are at your hotel, Mademoiselle," the driver of the car says as he interrupts the romantic embrace of the two people in the back of the limo.

Alexia and Severo then get out of the silver and gold Rolls Royce limousine and enter the front doors of the Hotel Gabriel Issy les Moulineax. A light rain that started falling on the limo in the middle of the trip from the Élysée Palace to the hotel slowly increases as the night wears on.

———

"With the worst of the season's first winter snow storm making its way out over the Atlantic Ocean at this hour tonight, the country as a whole can rest assured that everyone who needs to get to the polls to vote tomorrow morning will be able to do so," reports CCN Network

News anchor Karl Darwin at 10:07 E.S.T. on Monday night from Washington D.C.

"Yes, the American people sure dodged a bullet when mother nature decided to push the big storm out to sea a day sooner than what was originally forecast, Karl," adds anchor woman Donna Carter.

Darwin then cuts in on his CCN co-anchor, "Officials in most of the major cities that were hit by the early season Arctic cold front report they already have city snow removal crews scheduled to work late into the night to get their municipalities ready for tomorrow's historic election. The progress of the nation will not be held hostage by mother nature as you put it, Donna."

As he turns down the volume on the flat screen television he has been watching in his office, CCN President and CEO Rigger Watson grins and tells his former fraternity brother, "Walter, in twenty-four hours we'll know for sure if we've been able to pull this thing off. I think we have."

"I hope you're right," Franson replies as he speaks into his cell phone from three thousand miles west of Watson and the Nations Capital, Washington D.C.

"The polls we have look a hell of a lot better than they did forty-eight hours ago." Watson laughs. He then continues, "Thanks to myself, I might add."

U.S. Presidential candidate Senator Walter Franson from California smiles at what he hears on this, the eve of the election. He then says, "I've got to give it to you, Rigger. You did turn this thing around a lot faster than I thought it could be done."

"Thanks, Walter. I'll take that as a compliment from you. I haven't gotten very many of them from you in the last two decades since I made you a Senator."

"You know I appreciate what you've done for me, Rigger."

"You damn well ought to. I put you where you're at," Watson states. "And I'm the one who has put you in the White House too, Walter."

"We're not out of the woods yet, Rigger," Franson allows. "I'm not going to feel safe until tomorrow night when the polls close and this election is over and I am announced the winner."

"Well, unless your secret European love life finds its way to FX News in the next few hours, I don't see anything that can change the outcome of this now."

"That is not going to come out," Franson asserts. "As I've told you Rigger, I have that covered."

"I damn well hope you do. But..." Watson pauses, "If it did come out at this late an hour on the night before an election we could easily deny it. We could maybe even turn it around and hurt your challenger with it for playing such dirty politics so late in the game."

As Watson concludes his own personal news-spinning brainstorm, Senator Franson's mind is filled with the image of the Russian woman he hasn't seen in almost a year. As much as he wants the White House and the power that goes along with it, he wishes he could have her also. He knows there is no way right now to have both—one has to come before the other. *Everything has a natural order of things,* Franson thinks, while he hopes the woman with long, dark, red hair still wants to be with him as bad as he wants to be with her. *Time... Time is all that stands between me and her,* Franson tells himself.

When the Senator doesn't say anything back, the head man at CCN News goes on to say, "If something does come out about the redhead, it'll take a week or two for anyone to prove it, and by then nobody will care except the right-wing fanatics. It'll be too late. It'll be old news, back page stuff, internet fodder." Watson pauses. "You still there, Walter?"

Finally broken from the overseas fantasy he let himself escape to for a moment, Senator Franson nods his head to himself and says, "Yes, I'm here. But we're not going to have to worry about that, Rigger." In his room in a fancy Hotel in San Francisco, Franson looks at his watch. "Hey, I've got to get off the phone. I've got an interview out here with Katie Couric in about twenty minutes."

"Talk to you later, Walter. Tell Katie hello from me. And tell her I've got an anchor position for her at CCN whenever she wants it," Rigger Watson says before he hangs up.

"Sure, Rigger," Franson returns with no intentions of mentioning Rigger Watson's name to anyone.

CHAPTER FORTY-THREE

T7 Vertebrae

It is a little after nine P.M. in France and the first Tuesday in November is nearly over. Four thousand miles to the west of Paris the people of the United States are still filing in and out of precincts and voting booths by the millions. This will go on for many more hours across the land of the free and the home of the brave before the winners of the thousands of different political races on the local, state, and national levels will be known. A majority of the people in Europe could care less about what is taking place on the other side of the Atlantic Ocean.

Without a cloud in the darkness, the lights of the romantic city shine brightly in the perfectly clear sky as Alexia Klien leaves the Paris news studio, she sees Severo Baptiste waiting for her outside the CCN building. This will be the last night they spend together on her trip to France. Alexia flies back to the States in three days, but Severo has to be on a plane before the sun comes up to fly off to somewhere in Northern Africa. This is what he has told her. A hot new story he wants get on the front end of before his competition beats him there is how he explained it. There is a story, and there is competition for business where he is headed, so everything he said does have an element of truth to it. It is just that he did not tell Alexia the whole story. A CCN Network News broadcast journalist would be the last person Severo would share the whole story with of what he is doing and where he is going. Actually, he will be the only one who will know the whole story of the business he is not really competing for, but already has.

Baptiste sits on a bench about fifty feet away from the front door to the building she has just left. Alexia knows he is there to meet her because of a phone call they just had a few minutes ago. As she turns and walks down the city sidewalk towards him, she looks up into the sky and thinks about how beautiful the night is. She also realizes that just as her feelings for him have not changed in the five years since they were officially an item—their way of parting has not changed either. She has work obligations and oceans to fly over, and there is always another war zone somewhere for him to go report on. Nothing has really changed in the years that she has not seen him, except that now she knows she cannot live without him. That is the one thing that has changed. She knows she loves him more than anything else in life, and in a few hours he is going to be out of her life again. Alexia would love to ask him to skip his trip to North Africa and stay with her for the next three days in Paris, but she knows he won't. One of many things that Severo is very serious about is his work. This, among many other things, is something the two of them have in common.

He stands up as she approaches the bench. "Where in my city do you desire to dine tonight, my Darling?"

"Is this your city, my Prince?" Alexia asks jokingly. "I thought you were from way south of here," she laughs, "Somewhere closer to the Mediterranean?"

"All of France is mine, Darling. And tonight I give you Paris," Severo says playfully. "It is yours, all of it."

She knows he is feeling the tension of the two of them about to say goodbye once again. With him and her, he generally always tries to make light of what is a heavy situation. Alexia wonders if this is because he knows he is going into very dangerous territories and it brings out the playful and light-hearted man she loves, or if he is only acting this way to keep her from getting down about their inevitable farewell. She has always assumed it was a little of both.

With a smile on her face, Alexia laughs at him and replies, "If all of Paris is mine... then all I want is a light dinner, some fine wine and you."

Severo returns the smile and takes Alexia by the arm. "I know just the place where your wish will come true. Walk with me. It is not far from here."

They walk.

This is the third night the two lovers will spend in the same exquisite and luxurious French hotel room. The passion that once defined their relationship, a passion that began at the Winter Olympics over a decade ago in Salt Lake City, Utah, has not weakened or decreased with time and absence. It has grown stronger. Two nights ago after the dinner party at the French Presidential Palace, their first time being together in five years, left Alexia at a loss for words to explain the physical pleasures she had forgotten she once knew. Any doubts she may have ever had about who she was to end up with in her life were answered that first night. And yet, there was something she felt that she could not put her finger on, something that said what they did was not right. *Was it guilt?* She asked herself the next morning.

The second night together, last night, they had a quiet dinner for two at a very exclusive and elegant French restaurant that sat in one of the most scenic parts of Paris. It was a place where they could look out over the Seine River as it made its way towards the Eiffel Tower in the distance. A place where the lights of the city shone brightly through the large windows of the open-sided restaurant where only the wealthiest people can afford the prices that are not listed on the menu. Severo told Alexia that it was an old friend of his family that ran this restaurant, and that was the reason they were able to get a table on such short notice, a table that sat by itself in front of a large window looking out over the river. What Severo did not tell her that night, was that the old family friend who manages the restaurant, one of the most prestigious eating establishments in Paris, manages it for him. Severo Baptiste is the proprietor of the place where they dined, which is really why they enjoyed the best table in the house. Other than Baptiste and the manager, no one else in the establishment, including the vast number of its employees, know who the true owner is.

The view from the restaurant they ate at last night was seductive to say the least. That is also how Alexia would describe the second night she and Severo spent together in the room at the Hotel Gabriel Issy les Moulineax—seductive. It was much more reserved and romantic, slower and more gentle than the night before. Where the first night they were together was full of raw passion and physical pleasure, the second night was pure lovemaking until they fell asleep in each others' arms and awoke in each others' arms. As great as both nights were, the funny, unfamiliar feeling she had after the first night was still there in the morning after the second night.

"Dinner tonight was exquisite," Alexia tells Severo as they exit the elevator on the eleventh floor of her hotel.

He laughs.

"Who would have known that we would find a paper sack with crackers and cheese and another bottle of 1971 Romanee Conti La Tache laying at the foot of a tree behind a park bench along the river tonight?" Alexia says as the two of them walk to her room.

Severo smiles as he lets her open the door to her business suite.

They enter her room.

There is something she notices inside of herself with Baptiste that is different this time when compared to five years ago. Something she can not quite figure out. There is a smidgen of guilt she has never before experienced, at least not for a really long time. Alexia has wondered all day where it has suddenly come from. She thought she had gotten over all that in college. *Why is it back now?* Alexia wonders. *I am thirty-six years old and very experienced in life. Does Severo feel it too?* She asks herself.

On this third night together with Severo, as she ponders where this tiny amount of conscious she has acquired has come from, suddenly the name of her new friend pops into her head. Amaya Blazi, the young and innocent nineteen year old Alexia Klien look-a-like from Roswell, New Mexico, the girl giving a year of her life up because of her faith. *Could it be that God Himself is trying to tell me something?* Alexia wonders.

As she and Severo both prepare for bed on this third night together, Alexia looks over to him as he stands on the other side of the large bed wearing only an unbuttoned white long-sleeved shirt. She asks, "Sweetheart, would it be alright if we just hold each other tonight?" She pauses and then continues, "I mean, if we don't make love? I just want you to hold me."

The man she knows so much about, even though there is so much she doesn't know about him, walks over to her side of the bed. He takes hold of each of her hands with his and looks deeply into her beautiful blue eyes and says, "I could not think of a more sweet way to spend a night with you, my Darling." He pauses and squeezes her hands more tightly before he confesses, "Holding you is the sweetest part of being with you. That is what I have missed the most in all these years since Cairo." They both know what is meant by, "Since Cairo."

Alexia's heart sinks as she hears him speak about the city in Egypt. "I am so sorry I did not respond like you wanted me to then. I was scared, really scared..."

"It's OK, Alexia. I now know how much I do truly love you. You are the only woman I have ever known that I want to give my life for. As much as I loved you five years ago on that night as we stood at the edge of the Nile, I did not know then what I know now." He stops and looks even deeper into her eyes. When she doesn't say anything, Severo continues, "Only because of our separation do I know that I would die for you if I had to."

Alexia stands holding onto his hands. She is wearing only a large burgundy colored silk shirt. It is the look she knows he likes best. Tears begin to fall out of her eyes. She cannot believe that in only a few hours this man who is holding her hands, who holds her heart, will again walk out of her life. The first time it happened, she caused it and convinced herself it was for the best. She has never gotten over that first time and has been mad at herself ever since. Now, as she stands holding his hands before they lay down together for the third time in three nights, the last time in who knows how many nights, she does not know how she will cope with him being gone in the morning. *What will I do? How will I get through it?* She asks herself.

As Alexia has tears running down both cheeks, Severo smiles softly, then gently he says, "Let's go to bed. Sometimes it is good to cry yourself to sleep. I will hold you, Darling."

He takes her and carefully lays her down on the bed. She pulls the covers up over them. The two of them cuddle up together and wrap their arms around one another. Her tears slowly cease. Right now she would give up everything to be able to get on the airplane and fly to Africa with him. With that thought in her mind, she begins to run her fingers across his back where he has a scar that starts just below the T7 vertebrae and runs for nearly three inches along his spine.

"I think your scar is smaller than it used to be. It's not as rough as I remember it being," Alexia comments as she gingerly runs her fingertips back and forth over the old injury.

Severo says nothing.

"Didn't you get this in Africa?" she asks, thinking of where he is off to early in the morning.

"Yes."

"How long ago was that?" She pauses as she lies beside him and continues to slowly run her fingers up and down the scar. When Severo does not answer, Alexia asks, "You never have told me how you got this injury."

"It was nineteen years ago. The scar was made by an American CIA operative," Baptiste says, as he recalls something that seems like it happened just yesterday. "He used a knife to dig a bullet out from between two vertebrae in my back. We were in a small grass hut in the jungle somewhere along the border of the Sudan and Uganda." He pauses, and then asks, "Do you really want to hear this?"

"Yes, I want to hear it. I want to know everything about you."

Why Severo Baptiste is still alive is anyone's guess. He has dodged death more times in his life than nine cats have nine lives.

"The bullet was lodged between the bones in my back. It was stuck in the soft tissue of a disc, the man with the CIA said. I had no feeling in one leg is all I remember. With his knife, he cut into my back and removed the bullet. I don't think a surgeon at John's Hopkins could have done what he did."

Baptiste pauses and kisses Alexia on her neck.

"The amazing part was, we were under heavy assault by a small group of radical Muslims when he did it. His partner, another CIA man, held off the enemy while he carved on me. They wouldn't move me until they removed the bullet."

Alexia kisses him on his neck and gives him a small peck on his cheek as she runs her hand through his hair. She then says, "I'm glad you are here."

"I would not be, except for those two Americans."

"What were their names?" Alexia asks as she returns her hand to the scar in the middle of his back. "If I ever meet them I want to be able to thank them for saving your life for me."

Knowing he should not do what he is about to do, Severo breaks one of his own rules and whispers the names of people who know a different side of him than she does. "The guy who cut the bullet out of me was a man named Chace Wikett. And the one that held off the Muslims was Antonio Garcia. Maybe the toughest person I have ever known."

Severo lays there and cannot believe he just told an American broadcast journalist the real names of the two CIA men who saved his life. They hadn't even told Baptiste their real names. Years after he was trapped in a heated battle beside those two men in the jungles of East Africa, he had someone dig up their information for him at Langley. He did this so he could set up a secret and anonymous college fund for the children of the two men to whom he owed his life.

"But Darling, if you ever meet them, you can't say anything about what I just told you. Thank them, but don't tell them why you are thanking them. They are CIA, remember." Baptiste knows that the two men are now FBI, but he is not going to tell Alexia that.

She kisses him on the neck and then on the lips. She then tells him, "Don't worry, Honey. Your secret is safe with me."

That is one secret of a thousand, Severo thinks to himself. He gently kisses her on the neck and works his way towards her ear. When he reaches her ear, he whispers, "I love only you. I may be gone in the morning, but I will ask you to marry me again when the time is right. That I promise. Good night, Love."

Alexia closes her eyes. As she is about to drift off into dreamland, she feels Severo gently kiss her on the forehead. He then says very quietly, "Alexia Klien, you are the only woman I have ever known that I would give my life for."

In the darkness of her French hotel room, Alexia falls asleep in his arms without the slightest thought about the election that is taking place halfway around the world from her.

————————

"With what we have been able to tell looking at the exit polls, Senator Franson looks like he should win this election in a squeaker," Elliot Anderson, an executive producer for one of the three major television networks says as he speaks into his iPhone.

"The way I've got it counted, we have 265 electoral votes right now, and that is giving them Ohio," returns CCN President Rigger Watson, "But, giving us Pennsylvania."

"Yeah Rigger, I don't think we're going to win the Buckeye State, not with them having their Vice Presidential candidate from Ohio," replies the executive producer. "Pennsylvania is in the bag though. It wouldn't have been if that snow storm had hit like they thought it would."

"I know that," Watson replies. "It just about drove me nuts three days ago. And there was nothing I could do about it."

"We sure dodged a bullet there," Anderson states as he looks at the results of some updated returns coming in from New Mexico that show Franson pulling ahead in that pivotal toss-up state.

"We will win this thing for sure if Colorado falls our way." Watson states, "Which, it sure looks like it should from what I've seen."

"That's what we're thinking up here in New York too," comments Anderson, the man who Watson occasionally strategizes with over how the major political events that take place in the United States will be covered. "Speaking of dodging bullets, Rigger, I hate to say this because it sounds kind of callous, but that plane crash in the Rocky Mountains Sunday morning might actually be the difference. It might be the very thing that wins us the White House and saves the Senate for us."

"Yeah, it looks like we're going to keep the Senate for at least two more years," replies Watson, as he sees the same results Anderson just saw come across a computer screen in his office at the CCN Network News headquarters in Washington D.C.

"The Swenson thing still confounds me," says Anderson. "I would never have guessed the public opinion on him being arrested like that would have hurt Walter like it did on Saturday. I thought the American people would have been more tolerant than they were. And then to see it turn around and come back in our favor when Mike did what he did. The whole thing still has me scratching my head in disbelief. And on top of that, to hear the rumors coming out of Boston about the phone call he received from China... None of it makes sense."

"I know what you mean, Elliot. I still can't make heads or tails out of that one either. Swenson was a good guy if you ask me," Watson returns. "I sure can't see what would have made Michael do what he did when we were so close to winning the Presidency. It was real tough on me. I know it had to be tough on the Senator too to lose such a valued friend as Mike."

"It's funny how the fate of a nation can hang in the balance of something like an accidental plane crash in the Rockies or the lifestyle and the actions of someone's campaign manager who isn't even running for office."

"It sure is," states Watson, as he wonders who the man is that he wired nearly ten million dollars to in the past two weeks.

"Don't quote me on this, Rigger," Anderson says, "But I sure am glad it looks like we are going to come out on the winning side of these tragedies. I hate seeing people get killed or killing themselves, but it sure worked out for the best this time."

"If you are in our business, Elliot, you should know that people die every day," Watson says.

"Yeah, they do."

"Hey, I've got to be getting off the phone," Watson claims as he thinks about something he needs to do. "I'd better let you go."

Elliot Anderson tells Watson goodbye and hangs up.

As he sets his cell phone down on his desk, Watson sees that the state of New Mexico is now being called for Senator Franson. Before his face can even form a smile, the phone he just set down begins to ring. It startles Watson. It is Franson. The CEO of CCN answers the phone.

"Can you believe it, Rigger? I think we are really going to win this thing!" an ecstatic Senator Walter Robert Franson shouts into the phone as the people in the background from where the Senator is calling are celebrating over the call of another swing state to go their way. "Rig, I know we haven't got it in the bag yet, but with New Mexico it makes it almost impossible to lose."

"We still need Colorado or Nevada, Walter."

"We'll get 'em. Both of 'em. Those states are full of people from the coasts," Franson says. "From the numbers I've seen, I predict we will win Colorado and Nevada before the night is over, and that will clinch the deal."

"When it does happen, Walter, just remember who put you up there," Watson remarks, "And what I did to do it."

"Oh, I will, Rigger," states the Senator. Then in a humorous tone he asks, "How could I ever forget with you always reminding me?"

"I'll talk to you later, Walter. You had better tend to your party guests," replies Watson who is barely able to hear his longtime friend and cohort because of the festivities in the background of the phone call. Watson ends the call before Franson can even say goodbye.

In his CCN office all alone with thoughts of the hitman he has never seen still in his head, Watson wonders what would happen if someone were to hire the mysterious man to come after him. The thought troubles Rigger Watson. He knows what the man would do.

———————

When am I going to start doing what is right? Alexia asks herself as she runs out of the house and jumps in her 1988 red Pontiac Fiero GT. As she gets behind the wheel and speeds off to her friend Susan's house, she knows it is not now. In an argument she has just had with her parents, seventeen year old Alexia Klien knows she is in the wrong. But her selfish pride won't let her admit it. Susan, who is also a junior in high school, will understand. She just went through this same battle with her parents two weeks ago, when her college-age boyfriend wanted to take her with him on spring break. Alexia knows Susan did not win her battle with her parents either, but she will be someone who understands and cares. As the mad and unhappy seventeen year old girl approaches the intersection where she had her first wreck that day and totaled her sporty little Pontiac, she starts to scream.

Suddenly with her eyes wide open, Alexia is shocked. It has been forever since she has thought about her first car, or that fight with her parents, or the wreck she caused at the intersection of Cherrywood and Vine on that day. She lays there in bed in the French hotel room and wonders where the dream she just had came from. She can still feel the arm of Severo Baptiste underneath her neck, he has not left yet. *How long have I been asleep?* Alexia wonders. She slowly turns her head so she doesn't wake up the man beside her who she knows needs his rest. The small alarm clock setting on the bedside table beside her says it is 2:06 A.M. She has hardly been asleep for two hours. In two more hours Baptiste will be waking up to leave.

As she lays there and tries not to wake the man beside her, the dream she just had comes back into her mind. Now, nearly twenty years later, Alexia wonders, *Why did I fight with my parents like I did over wanting to go with that guy to Fort Lauderdale? I knew then it wasn't right, but I still wanted to go.* In her Paris hotel room lying beside the man she really does love, Alexia is so glad her parents didn't let her go to spring break in Florida with the college football player she was dating back then. They knew what was best for her.

With her teenage years on her mind, the thought of the time when her father wanted her to watch the old black and white classic, *Mr. Smith Goes to Washington* comes back into her mind for the second time in the few days she has been in Paris. She fought her father's wishes then too when he wanted her to watch the movie that he thought would teach her something about politics, things that she would not learn in school. He was right then also.

Lying beside Severo, Alexia closes her eyes and tries to go back to sleep. The thoughts of everything she now knows about the Russian woman she had seen with Senator Walter Franson are racing through her head. She has seen the exit polls that came out just before she left the CCN Paris studio tonight and knows he is most likely going to win the White House and be the next President of the United States. Thinking about what she covered up by staying silent, she is overwhelmed by guilt. She opens her eyes and stares at the face of the man sleeping next to her. In the near darkness of her Paris hotel room, she wonders what it is that makes people fight against doing what they know is right. After taking a mental picture of the man she does not know when she will see again, Alexia closes her eyes. Without knowing when, she falls back to sleep.

Before the small alarm clock goes off, Severo wakes and gently slides his arm out from underneath of the head and the pillow of the woman he is cuddled up to. He carefully makes his way out from under the covers so he doesn't wake his sleeping beauty. After reaching down and unplugging the cord that runs to the alarm clock, he quickly and quietly gets dressed. Without turning a light on, he puts tooth paste on his tooth brush and runs it across his teeth a few times. He then throws the tooth brush in his shaving bag that is already packed in his leather clothes bag. From the top of the mahogany desk he takes a pen and a piece of scratch paper off of a note pad and writes out a short message by the light of his cell phone. He leaves the note underneath Alexia's little blue phone so he knows she will see it. After he sets his bag and computer case by the door, Severo walks back over to the bed. He slowly and carefully bends down and gives Alexia a kiss on her forehead and then whispers very quietly, "I love you."

She moves her head oh so slightly and without opening her eyes, she says, "I love you, too." She never wakes up.

Severo Baptiste gently stands back up. He pauses for a moment to watch her lay there wrapped up in satin sheets and a big, silky, soft comforter with her long, black hair flowing all over her pillow, Severo smiles. He then slowly backs up, turns around, and carefully makes his way to the door. Baptiste leaves her room and very gingerly closes the door to her business suite behind him so he doesn't wake her. He then catches a cab to the airport to get on his own personal Learjet 60XR to fly deep into the continent of Africa. Much deeper than he told Alexia he was headed. Severo is on his way to Zimbabwe.

CHAPTER FORTY-FOUR

An Email

In the deep and sound sleep she has fallen into, the world has become a very black and white place to her. Very vividly, she sees herself sitting all alone in the witness chair of an old wooden courtroom. Alexia sits all by herself between the judge's bench and the jury. The jury box with an oak railing around it is just off to her left. It is full. All twelve old, hard, wooden chairs that sit in the long, narrow rectangle have people in them, six jurors in the front row and six jurors in the back row. All twelve citizens who sit in judgment of her have faces that are sour and unhappy. They look as though they have already made their minds up that she is guilty as charged.

After she has scanned the jury on her left, she looks over to her right and sees that the judge has not come out of his chambers yet. A court reporter and a court clerk both wait patiently at their appointed places in the room. Two men in gray suits sit at the prosecution table. When she looks out across the courtroom behind where the prosecution and the defense are assigned to sit, she sees the most disturbing thing of all. Half of the spectator section is completely full. Not one more person could be squeezed into the numerous long, wooden, church-style pews that stretch all the way back to the entrance doors of the spectator section that is directly behind the prosecutors.

On the opposite side of the walkway that splits the audience in two there is not one single person sitting in the area behind the defense. The long, wooden, church pews on this side of the courtroom are all empty. Not one individual has come to support her. But even more disturbing than that, there is no one sitting at the defense table. The accused who sits in the witness stand at this moment in her dream, Alexia herself, has no one to defend her of the charges that have been brought against her.

In this very vivid and real dream she is having at this early hour of the morning, Alexia knows that she is guilty, and she has no chance of being found innocent and set free. On this first Wednesday morning in November, four thousand miles east of where the old, wooden courtroom in her dream sits, the accused knows she will have to pay the price for what she has done wrong. The American broadcast journalist tosses and turns in the posh Paris hotel room. She is not able to wake up in the king-sized bed that she now occupies all by herself. A tired and restless Alexia Klien twists and thrashes at the pillows and the sheets in her bed as she struggles to escape the coming judgment. As hard as she tries to wake up, she cannot. The trial must go on.

Locked in the witness stand, with half a courtroom staring silently at her, all of them wanting blood for the wrongs she has done them, Alexia sits and trembles in fear in her seat. The door to the judges's chambers opens and into the room walks the judge himself, a stern and strict looking man with white hair and very steely gray eyes. He approaches the bench and all present in the room stand to show him honor. He takes his place behind his bench and reaches out and grabs his gavel. He raises it to strike judgment on the accused. When he has the gavel at its highest point before bringing it down to strike the sounding block, he stops. As he holds the gavel up in judgment, the Judge asks in a very loud and deep voice, "Is there not one person who will come to this young woman's defense for the wrongs that she has done society?"

The crowd of people that all sit on the left half of the courtroom begins to chant, "Guilty, guilty, guilty..."

Full of fear in her empty, dark hotel room, Alexia fights to wake herself from this nightmare she is having. Her heart is pounding rapidly and she has even broken into a sweat, but sleep will not let her out of where it has taken her. In the witness chair, the thirty-six year old woman from Atlanta, Georgia sits in fear that she will soon be no more.

As the Judge raises the gavel even higher, he says, "I ask one more time, will anyone come to the defense of this woman?"

The accused, Alexia Klien, closes her eyes as tightly as she can in her dream and in her sleep in the king-sized bed. She grimaces as she prepares to have her verdict known to all. As the solemn and sober Judge begins to drop the gavel to the block and announce her sentence, the doors of the courtroom open. To the total and complete surprise of Alexia, a man enters into the old, wooden courtroom. As He walks up between the two audience sections, the one side completely empty and the other side completely full, the people in the room all go deathly silent.

The man enters into the area between the prosecution and the defense tables. Without stopping, He approaches the bench and the Judge. He stops directly in front of the white haired Judge and looks up to him. He then looks over at the accused. Alexia looks into this man's eyes. Never in her life, has Alexia ever seen eyes as kind and gentle as His.

Without any hesitation or regret in His voice, the man who just entered the courtroom looks back over to the Judge. He says, "Sir, I will defend this woman of all her charges. And if she is found guilty, I will take her sentence upon Myself. I will trade My life for hers."

"What is your name, Son?" the Judge asks seriously.

"My name is Jesus. Jesus Christ. I am from Nazareth. I was born in the town of Bethlehem. I will stand in her place, if that is what she wants."

Suddenly it is pitch dark as Alexia looks around her hotel room. She is shaking profusely and her hands and arms are trembling in fear. Now she is wide awake, and she wants to go back into her sleep and into her dream. She wants to tell the man who came to her rescue that yes, she wants Him to defend her of all the charges that were brought against her. She cannot though, her eyes are wide open and she is wide awake. The dream is gone, and all that remains is reality.

She lays there with her heart beating harder than it has ever beaten. She has just experienced the most vivid and realistic dream she has ever had. The thoughts of the things happening in this world she lives in suddenly seem so small and insignificant. Alexia Klien does not feel that she has ever been more awake and aware and alert in all of her life as she is at this moment. The trembling and the shaking have stopped and her heart-rate is slowly returning to normal. The sheets she is lying in are damp, but the room is very warm, so the moisture from her perspiration does not really bother her right now.

Her mind feels as sharp as it ever has. A Bible verse she once had to memorize as a small girl comes into her mind. *John 3:3 I tell you the truth, no one can see the kingdom of God unless he is born again.* Alexia repeats it to herself under her breath to make sure she remembers it correctly. It was over twenty-five years ago that she was in an Easter pageant in a theater in downtown Atlanta. John 3:3 was the only line she had in the play. As she remembers it, she was either eight or nine at the time. *That is a long time for a seed to set dormant,* Alexia thinks as she ponders the meaning of the verse.

A calmness and peace starts to come over her when suddenly she is frightfully startled by the ringing of the hotel telephone. Snapped back into fear because of the shock of the sudden noise in the otherwise totally silent and dark room, Alexia has no idea who would be calling her on that number this early in the morning. She has the ringer to her cell phone shut off, it is on vibrate. That land line phone has not rung in the five days she has been in this room. She decides not to answer it. If it is someone she knows, they will call her cell phone.

With no idea what time it is except that it has to be after four because Severo is gone, Alexia slips out from under the covers of her soft bed to retrieve her cell phone from the desk on the other side of the dark room. It is laying where she left it, with the screen facing down to hide the light that says it is being charged. She is able to find it with very little trouble in the darkness. When she picks it up she feels there is a single piece of folded paper that her phone was laying on. As she unplugs the charger, the light on the screen brightens up and she can see Severo has left her a note. Quickly, she glances at her phone to see what time it is. Her phone says she has five missed calls. All of them are from her boss, Rigger Watson, with the last call coming only a couple of minutes ago. *That had to be him on the hotel phone. Rigger can wait. I'm going to read Severo's note,* Alexia thinks as she looks at the time on her phone. It is only a couple minutes past five A.M. Paris time. In her mind she does the math. *It is eleven P.M. in America. Franson must have won the election if Rigger has called five times in the last thirty minutes,* she thinks.

Using the light of her cell phone, she unfolds the piece of scratch paper that has the hotel's name and emblem in the upper left-hand corner. The note Severo left for her reads, "Alexia, these three days and nights we have spent together will be the start of a new life for both of us. Let us leave our old lives behind and begin anew. Love, SACB." As she reads the note a second time she realizes she doesn't even remember kissing him goodbye when he left. Yet, something tells her that she did. Tears of sadness and of joy start to fall out of her eyes as she stands with barely anything on in the middle of her dark Paris hotel room and reads the little note a third and a fourth time.

She wipes the tears off of her cheek with a towel that has been left on the chair in front of the desk. It was the one Severo used when he got out of the shower before they went to bed. Alexia makes a mental note to be sure and stick the towel in her bag later. It still has his scent. She then decides that instead of calling Watson back, she will listen to the messages he left her. She hasn't had to talk to him yet in the five days since she left the U.S., so why break that streak now.

When she listens to the messages, they say exactly what she thought they would say. Senator Walter Franson has won the Presidency. CCN was the first network to call the election for Franson at just shortly after ten P.M. on the east coast. Watson left her four messages out of his five phone calls. He was ecstatic in the first two and a half messages about the victory for his candidate. Two and a half messages were all that Alexia could stand to listen to. The sound of Rigger Watson's voice ranting and raving over the Senator's victory was more than she could stomach. The guilt Alexia feels over hiding a real news story that could have made a difference in the world and in the history of the great country she grew up in and loves is too much for her to handle. Especially while listening to her boss boast about winning the White House. When she is done with the messages, she erases them—all four of them. She wishes she could erase the guilt she is now feeling.

With the note from Severo in her fingertips, Alexia makes her way back to her big, comfortable bed and crawls back under the covers. She hopes she can return to the dream she was having so she will be able to answer the Judge about the man she wants to defend her of all the things she has done wrong. If not, she giggles to herself as she thinks, I would settle for returning to the dream where I am the Princess of France. With the note from Baptiste gripped firmly in her right hand, she wraps her arms around a big, soft pillow and pulls it in close to her body, pretending it is Severo. She wishes that she was his wife. With her eyes closed and a small smile on her face, Alexia's mind settles back to her courtroom dream. She drifts gently back to sleep.

———

As Matt James holds the door to one of the many entrances to Charles de Gaulle International Airport open for Amaya Blazi to walk through, another man approaches the doorway, one who looks to be in quite a hurry. Matt and Amaya have arrived at the airport a full two hours before their commercial flight to Johannesburg, South Africa is scheduled to depart. They are in no hurry themselves. The man with a brown leather bag in one hand and a carrying case for a laptop computer draped over his shoulder stops and reaches for the open door Matt is holding open. The man's intent is to allow Matt to go ahead and accompany the young woman he is obviously with into the airport building. Matt does not let go of the door. Instead he tells the man, "Go ahead, sir. I can tell you're in a hurry. We have all the time in the world."

The man graciously nods his head and says in English with a French accent, "Thank you so much. We need more people like you in this world." The man smiles kindly towards Amaya and begins to proceed into the Paris airport. When he gets a good look at the nineteen year old American girl, he stops. He tells Amaya Blazi, "You look amazingly like someone I have seen." He then goes on his way.

After the man is gone and Matt has stepped into the building himself, he looks to Amaya and says, "Something tells me we need to pray for that man. I don't know why, but Amaya, I do think the Holy Spirit has laid it on my heart that you and I need to lift him up in prayer."

"OK," Amaya replies as she thinks about what Matt has just told her. She then says, "He definitely seemed to be someone on a mission of some sort."

"Yes, he did," Matt replies.

"I don't know what it was," Amaya comments. "But when he looked at me and spoke to me, I could feel the presence of incredible human power in that man. It was in his eyes. I don't know if it was evil or it was good... but it was very powerful."

"I got the same feeling when I held the door for him," Matt says. "Let's go over by that empty counter and say a short prayer for that man's life and his journey."

"Sure, Matt, that's a good idea," Amaya replies. "It can't hurt."

Only fifty feet inside the entrance of the Charles de Gaulle International Airport, Christian missionaries Amaya Blazi and Matthew James take a hold of each other's hands and bow their heads. Matt says a short, but powerful prayer for Severo Baptiste. Before it is even daylight, the face of the man they have just prayed for is burnt permanently into the memories of the two American Christians on this day in the entrance of the airport just outside of Paris, France.

———

After she yawns, Alexia slowly begins to open her beautiful blue eyes. She reaches up and moves her long, flowing black hair away from her face and her mouth. Even though she hasn't, the American broadcast journalist feels like she has just experienced a full night's sleep without any interruptions. But it is still dark on the other side of the long, thick burgundy colored curtains that hang in the window of her hotel room. Because of this, Alexia knows it was not that long ago that she was awoken by the horrific dream of the old, wooden courtroom and the judge with the gavel. A few hours before that, she was startled awake after dreaming that she was wrecking her very first car after a terrible fight with her parents. *What has caused all this?* She wonders. *There was also a goodbye kiss from Severo in there somewhere,* she thinks. She hopes. *It must be around six,* Alexia guesses.

Considering everything that disturbed her sleep during the night, she feels surprisingly refreshed. *Love will do that for you, I suppose,* Alexia thinks as she lays there with her legs tangled up in the sheets and her arms holding a big, soft pillow tightly against her body and tucked under her chin. For the last hour, she has pretended the pillow she is hugging is Severo Baptiste.

With her eyes half-closed again, Alexia tries to fall back to sleep, but her mind won't let her. The thoughts of everything she has experienced in the past few days are running through her head, from the redheaded woman who turned out to be a rouge Russian spy, to the latest dream about the old courtroom. *If I get anything out of this trip to Paris and my stay in this room, it will be some of the most memorable dreams I have ever had,* she thinks. *I really should get up and write them down,* she tells herself. With that thought on her mind, Alexia gets out of bed.

Still wearing only the burgundy colored button-up shirt, an extra-large, she slips on a pair of silky black shorts she has laying on one of her clothes bags. Unlike her friend Angie West, Alexia is not a light traveler on a trip like this. It takes a small army to transport her luggage to and from the airport when the time comes. Angie can throw a handful of outfits into a bag, a couple pairs of shoes, and some makeup, put a pair of boots on her feet, and take off to travel the world and never look back.

This morning as she gets up, Alexia turns on a lamp and walks over to check her cell phone still lying on the desk. She sees she has a new text message from her friend Angie, the country music singer who is supposed to fly home to the states sometime today from Afghanistan. Alexia opens the text message and it says, "Boo hoo boo hoo boo hoo. Your man won the Presidency and America was the BIG LOSER because of it. I ain't talkin to you today. I'm mad. Love you. Hope you and Severo are doing GOOD." Alexia smiles at her friend's text. She also knows deep down inside that her friend is right.

Alexia is about to set her phone down as she receives another text message, this one from Rigger Watson. She opens it only because she has her phone in her hand, otherwise she really doesn't want to know what Rigger has to say. As she reads it, Alexia can tell it is the type of text message Watson sometimes sends out to numerous people all at once. It was not meant for her personally. The generic mass text message that the CCN Network News CEO and President sent out late on Tuesday night to probably over a hundred or more CCN employees says, "Guys, I was worried Saturday, but I guess the world didn't change that much in three days. Good work crew."

When Alexia reads the part of Watson's text message that says, "the world didn't change that much in three days", her mind is instantly taken back in time two thousand years. She recalls that it was three days that the man Jesus was in the grave before the stone was rolled away by angels sent from Heaven by God—and Jesus was resurrected from the dead. With just the lamp on in the dark hotel room, she does *not* feel like she is alone. Alexia feels like there is another presence in the room, a presence much bigger than herself. She completely forgets about the Presidential election and everything else. For a brief moment she thinks about trying to pray, but she doesn't know what for. She hasn't really tried to pray since she was a little kid. She decides not to.

Knowing she can't go back to sleep because she tried, and not wanting to watch anything on TV, Alexia decides to check her emails. She hasn't looked at them for a couple of days. After getting her computer out of its bag, she sets it on the mahogany desk and opens it. After pushing the power button on the thin, sleek, Dell laptop, Alexia walks back across the room and shuts off the lamp she had turned on. After returning to the desk and her computer, she quickly plugs in her cell phone and lays it beside her open laptop.

First, Alexia checks her CCN account and sees that she has received over a hundred emails in the last two days. Most of them are the stupid variety she would never waste her time even opening. She downloads the important emails from her CCN account to her silver laptop so she can go through them on the flight back to the States.

For a moment, Alexia thinks about shutting her computer off and trying to go back to sleep. But then she decides to check her two personal email accounts that she uses only for her closest and best friends, her Hotmail and Yahoo accounts. While Severo has been in Paris, her emails have been the last thing on her mind. She pulls up her Hotmail account and types in her password. The inbox appears and shows that she has twelve new emails. After quickly scanning them to see who they are from, she decides not to open any of them. As Alexia is about to sign out of her Hotmail account, the third email from the top catches her eye. It's the subject that she notices. It is an email from a woman she knows who lives in Manhattan and is a Broadway playwright. The woman is married to a very wealthy man. The subject of the email from the woman says, "Yea for the Supreme Court!!! Franson Wins... Women will STILL have the Right to Choose!!!"

Without opening this email, the American broadcast journalist knows exactly what it will be about. Rumors have been floating throughout Washington D.C. that one or possibly even two of the conservative Justices on the Supreme Court are likely to retire soon.

Speculation is that they have both been waiting for the upcoming election in hopes that a pro-life Republican would win the White House. The word on the street in the nation's capital is that the two conservative men, one a white man and the other an African American are tired of fighting the left, and, given the one man's age and the other man's health, there is no way they both will be able to make it four more years. This, combined with the very ill health of one of the liberal justices on the court, means that the judicial balance in America rested solely on the outcome of Tuesday's election. A newly-elected President Walter Franson will more than likely have the opportunity to name as many as three new justices to the U.S. Supreme Court in the coming years, if not the coming months.

The email from the woman who lives in New York is a celebratory message over the fact that a woman's right to have an abortion will stay safely in the hands of the Democrats. Alexia opens it out of curiosity to see if she was the only person the Broadway playwright sent this email to, but she was not. The list of women who received the short celebratory email that originated from a mansion the woman and her husband own in the Hamptons, reads like a who's who of female celebrities. Something about the email bothers the American broadcast journalist.

As she sits in a chair in front of the large mahogany desk in the mostly dark Paris hotel room looking at the woman's email and thinking about the real implications of the hotly contested abortion issue, Alexia suddenly hears a voice. It says, "You know it's not right to kill a baby before it ever has the chance to see the light of day." Alexia freezes in total fear when she hears these words. She asks herself if she really heard what she just thought she heard. *Where did it come from?* She knows she heard it, but where did it come from? As she sits and thinks about it, she realizes it was a voice she heard in her heart and not in her head. *How is that even possible?* She wonders. Without closing the email from the woman in New York, Alexia signs out of her Hotmail account.

Staring at her computer and thinking about the words she just heard, Alexia again thinks about pulling the lid down on her Dell and returning to her pillows and sheets for a couple more hours of rest. Reaching up to grab the lid, she stops when she hears something inside of her say it will only take a minute or two to check your yahoo. Alexia pulls up Yahoo mail and types in the email address she uses only with her very best of friends.

Not expecting anything special to pop up in this account since the most special person in her life just left her room only a little more than two hours ago, Alexia continues on in habit as she enters her password. As Yahoo opens, she immediately sees she has seven new emails in her inbox. The latest email she has received is only a matter of minutes old. It is an email from her newest best friend. Alexia's life is such that she always has three or four best friends at the same time. Sometimes five or six, just depending on how busy her life is and how many different circles she is traveling in.

The newest of the seven unread emails in the inbox of her yahoo email account is only twenty-six minutes old. The email is from Alexia Klien's nineteen year old exact look-a-like Amaya Blazi, the tall and extremely beautiful girl from Roswell, New Mexico.

This email is from a young girl less than a year out of high school, who is spending her first full year away from her family and her friends in the dangerous and deadly continent of Africa. The young girl from New Mexico is giving this part of her life as a Christian missionary to some of the poorest people on earth. Amaya's email reads:

For my new best friend Alexia Klien-----This is Amaya.

We are flying out of Paris early this morning to go back to Zimbabwe.
Matt James and I will fly into Johannesburg, South Africa today, and then we will get into Matt's own plane and he will fly us to Zimbabwe. I am at the Paris airport right now waiting for our flight... If you can, please pray for us.
Actually, Alexia, I do not know where you are with God... I do not even know if you are a Christian. I hope you know God and His Son Jesus. But if you don't, think about this:
When you were a small child and you could not hear your father when he would say something because he was too far away, you could say to him, "Daddy, Daddy, I can't hear you, would you

please come closer? Please come closer to me so I can hear you, Daddy."

Well, Alexia, my new best friend, God will do the very same thing. Just ask Him, and He will come closer to you. Just ask Jesus to come closer to you if you want to know Him. He will do it.

Call on His Name. Call on the Name of Jesus.

In the Love of Jesus,
Amaya Dawn Blazi

After she reads the email sent to her from her new friend, Alexia has a question come into her thoughts. As she runs it through her mind a second time, she even speaks it out loud to herself. "What is life really all about?"

After hearing herself speak these words in the darkness of her French hotel room, Alexia gets up out of the chair she has been sitting in and takes a couple steps across the soft rich carpet towards her bed. She stops as she feels tears start to form in her eyes. With the thick curtains pulled completely shut, the only light in the room is from the 13-inch screen of her open laptop computer and the charger to her cell phone.

The American broadcast journalist is now in the middle of her hotel room all alone. She stands between the dark mahogany desk where her computer sits and the king-sized bed as the tears swelling up in her eyes begin to fall to her cheeks. In the lonely Paris hotel room with the email she just received from Amaya Blazi still fresh on her mind and in her heart, Alexia Klien drops to her knees at the foot of her bed.